IF MY HEART COULD SEE YOU

Sherry Ewing

Kingsburg Press
SAN FRANCISCO, CALIFORNIA

Kingsburg Press
P.O. Box 475146
San Francisco, California 94147
www.kingsburgpress.com

If My Heart Could See You is a work of fiction. Names, characters, places, and incidents are a product of the author's imagination. Locales and public names are sometimes used for atmospheric purposes. Any resemblance to actual people, living or dead, or to businesses, companies, events, institutions, or locales is completely coincidental.

Cover Photo: Lamia by John William Waterhouse (1849-1917). This media is in the public domain in the United States. This applies to U.S. works where the copyright has expired, often because its first publication occurred prior to January 1, 1923. {{PD-US}} This work is in the public domain in the European Union and non-EU countries with a copyright term of life of the author plus 70 years. {{PD-old-70}}

Cover Design: Mari Christie at www.MariChristie.info
Editor: Barbara Millman Cole

Book Layout ©2013 BookDesignTemplates.com

If My Heart Could See You/Sherry Ewing -- 1st ed.
ISBN 13: 978-0-9905462-0-7
eBook ISBN: 978-0-9905-462-1-4

For my son Sean

*The warrior and hero in our family
who has made this mother so very proud.
His courage was the inspiration behind this novel.
I love you, son!*

Acknowledgements

Although this is my debut novel, I feel the need to express my thanks to the multitude of people who have supported me along the way. I couldn't have done this without their support.

I would like to first thank my mother for her encouragement to write faster as I sent her chapter after chapter of this story. It wouldn't be a NASCAR Sunday without me sitting at your house writing with my laptop. To my daughters, Jessica and Robyn, I'd like to say that Mom loves you both very much, especially when you remind me I'm not listening. I couldn't have done this without your patience for allowing me to get lost in my writing. A special word of thanks to Jessica for her insight into what I needed to fix with my initial story. For someone who never critiqued a manuscript, you did a great job.

To Evangeline Gaff and Mimi Madison of our Hopeless Romantic's Unite ~ Carpe Diem Club: My very first beta readers who have become true sisters of my heart. I sincerely thank you ladies for your kind words, encouragement, and most importantly your friendship.

Tricia Linden has my heartfelt gratitude. Your enthusiasm to remind me that I really am an author is what keeps me motivated to write another page. I am humbly indebted to you for sharing your knowledge with me, along with having you as my critique partner and friend. You help make my stories better. Thank you just doesn't seem like it's enough.

I also must give my thanks to Monica McCarty, a truly gracious lady, who took time out of her busy schedule to initially answer questions from an aspiring author. She pointed me in the direction of Romance Writers of America by suggesting I join this wonderful organization. It's been the best thing I've done for my writing career. Thank you Monica...you didn't steer me wrong.

Thanks to my editor, Barbara Millman Cole, who took my story and made it shine. I am fortunate to have you on my team.

Last, but certainly not least, I would also like to offer a special word of thanks to Carissa Weintraub and all my fellow authors at the San Francisco Area chapter of Romance Writers of America. Your friendship, along with your willingness to share your insight about this business, has been invaluable to me. I am truly lucky to be associated with such a wonderful group of people.

If My Heart Could See You

ONE

The Year of Our Lord's Grace 1174
Scotland's Border

YOUNG KNIGHT MACLAREN STOOD with steady feet upon the narrow parapet and looked down into the inner bailey, surveying the destruction and devastation below. Ian, the guardsman ever by the youth's side, had the same grim expression as his charge.

The constant thunder of a battering ram slamming upon the solid oak door echoed harshly throughout the keep. Afore long, the wooden portal would give way, and with its demolition, all hope would surely depart from the occupants who had fled inside to find safe haven. Too soon, the enemy would be within, causing more lives to be lost in the castle's defense. The siege had been bloody, lasting more than two fortnights, and, in truth, 'twas surprising the battle endured as long as it had, given the small number of knights available to defend the castle walls.

For nigh unto sixty years, Berwyck Castle had known peace over its land while governed by the last remaining descendants of the Scottish clan MacLaren. The castle and its people, however, had grown accustomed to constant upheaval, being between two kings struggling for power and control over the region. Situated on a cliff high above the raging sea, the castle towered over a prime port for transporting goods into the interior of the country, both north and south. Its location, bordering Scotland and England, had been the cause of many a battle over the centuries, and the fortress had changed liege lords more often than most could remember. With the arrival of the enemy, and the breaching of the curtain wall, 'twas but a matter of time afore England would once again call this castle its own in the name of their king.

Although young in years and slight of frame, the fledgling knight had fought valiantly and bravely, never giving quarter, even whilst the enemy relentlessly pressed forward in determination to win the day. Only at the command of the castle's laird and chieftain of the clan did the knight order the garrison to fall back into the keep to protect the family within. Moments earlier, all had watched in horror as a sword laid low their liege and his eldest son, though they continued to pray that perchance the leaders had been spared and yet lived.

Blood, of those whom the young MacLaren's loyal garrison had slain, covered their armor, and the stench assaulted their senses. The cries of the wounded and dying were but a soft whisper on the wind and had all but quieted. MacLaren knew all of Berwyck's inhabitants were now focused on the newest threat to come, as the castle's last defense was about to fall. The distinct sound of splintering wood rang out into the chilled air. The warriors atop the battlement grimaced at the forecast of what their future held.

"Ach, 'twill not last much longer now," Ian predicted.

"Aye Ian, our fate it seems has been sealed," the young knight said, retrieving the sword that had been carefully laid up against the stone wall. "We shall soon be held accountable for those lives we have taken this day."

"I do not relish swearing fealty to some English pig," Ian cursed loudly, "especially as our laird and the dead of our fellow clansmen lay scattered on these cold grounds, awaiting a decent burial."

The young knight flinched at the mention of their lord.

Ian mumbled his apologies for his loose tongue.

"My sire and brother died in battle...in truth they would have had it no other way," was all young MacLaren said.

"We know not if they have as yet perished," Ian said gravely. "They could still be out there and in need of our healer."

"Let us pray 'tis so," the knight whispered with a slight catch to the words spoken. "I must also offer my thanks, whilst I am able, for guarding my back. I do not know if I would be standing afore you now without your unwavering aid."

Ian gave the knight a short bow of respect afore answering. "'Twas my honor, duty, and oath to your father that I should always do so, as you very well know. I, and the rest of your garrison, will endure to guard you 'til our last breaths leave our bodies."

"You have served me well these past years, not only as captain of my guard, but also as my friend."

"I pray I will be allowed to continue to do so. But, perchance, 'twould be best if you changed your garments," Ian suggested.

A heavy sigh came from his young charge.

"Nay...I see not how 'twill serve my purpose, but might only worsen my plight given what I see entering the bailey." The knight nodded with a shiver of fear in the direction of the barbican gate with its ruined portcullis.

"Mayhap, 'tis still to our best interest. 'Twould be wise to change A—" Ian began, but clamped his mouth shut as the knight held up a gloved hand.

"Spare me your council, Ian. Have you ever known me to follow meekly along like some pampered fool?"

"Ach. 'Tis a first time for everything."

The young knight shrugged. "Not today nor any time in the near future. Besides, 'twill hardly be time, as I believe such an opportunity has now left us."

The two leaned over the battlement wall to get a closer look at the procession entering their home. The first horse among many clipped clopped its way into the inner bailey. The rider held high a blood red standard stamped with the blackest of dragons, giving evidence to its owner's identity.

The reputation of the one following his colors preceded him. He was well known throughout the kingdom as the scourge of both England and France. Legend held, he had made a pact with the underworld, allowing him to forever remain invincible in battle. 'Twas said no person or thing ever survived at his clutches, and all who encountered him trembled in his wake.

The youthful knight was no different. 'Twas clear to the young MacLaren as he watched his realms impending doom that all he feared had come to pass. Berwyck Castle and his lands were lost to the Devil's Dragon who arrived to claim his new lair.

Dristan of Blackmore surveyed the carnage around him with disgust 'til his eyes at last leveled on the soul his gaze had sought, Hugh of Harlow. With the briefest of nods to his guardsmen, they dismounted from their steeds as one.

The twelve men who rode with him had been at his side for years and were loyal beyond what he could have dared hope. They trained and fought together 'til each knew how the other moved without question. Their unity went even to their garments. Dristan along with his men were all dressed in black armor, their mounts and their trappings the same, every shield embossed with the fire breathing dragon bearing his coat of arms. The only bit of color to be seen was from their dark red capes, draped from their shoulders and billowing in the wind like the running of blood, seeping into the ground from the dying.

Dristan's career had been of one campaign after another for his king, and tournaments throughout the years. The sight of death was one to which he had become accustomed. 'Twas the cost of waging war. But this...this...

At the raising of his arm, the men who were about to breach the keep's door with the battering ram stopped their movement, awaiting their lord's instructions. He motioned to the one he had left in charge, realizing in this moment the mistake he had made by doing so. Hugh of Harlow could be ruthless in nature when he felt superior to others, but generally he followed orders without question. Apparently, in this battle, he had given no thought to the directives given him, and instead, had done as he saw fit in bringing down the barbican gate and portcullis.

"My lord," Hugh said with a slight bow.

Dristan glared in silence at the man afore him, who began to sweat under his commander's close scrutiny. In the blink of an eye, Dristan's fist slammed forward and sent Hugh flying through the air to land upon his back on the ground.

SHERRY EWING

The peasants who had fled to the castle for shelter fell to their knees in terror and crossed themselves in alarm. Dristan's rage showed more than any words he might utter, and those who knew him not feared for their very lives, as they watched him stalk to the man now beneath his feet.

"You worthless pile of dung!" Dristan bellowed. "Did you give no thought to who will till my fields and tend my castle whilst you carelessly slaughtered all in your path?"

"I did as you commanded my lord and took the grounds in the only way I knew," Hugh said defiantly, as he gained courage with his words. "What is the price of the lives of a few peasants, as long as I have won this victory in your honor?"

"Fool that you are! What triumph have you scored me? Have you not heard my words, or do you plan to attend the soil yourself?" Dristan yelled at his vassal. "What of their lord, his knights, his family? Did you not think perchance they might not still serve me as well, or did you plan to slay them too? You annihilate all in your path with no thought and leave but angry, wounded men, who would just as soon put a knife in my back now than aid me with defending my lands!"

Hugh picked himself up, dusting the dirt from his backside, and stood afore Dristan with a look of contempt on his features. "If you need someone to work the ground, mayhap you could use that one," he said, gesturing towards the knight looking down from the battlements. "He slew enough of our men that time in the fields would serve as just penance."

Dristan looked above to the young lad in question and noticed the tattered remnants of a ribbon that boasted the MacLaren clan's tartan, waving in the air from his arm. "You forget yourself Hugh, if you think to instruct me on how to deal with those who would serve me," he said with disdain and, raising his arm, pointed towards the boy. "I have witnessed what that boy has done this day and from what I have seen, he has fought with more honor in his young life and inexperience than I could ever say about the years you have served me. Now get thee from my sight, and take my horse. Mayhap time spent in the stables will improve your ability to follow orders and help you remember, I am your liege lord!"

Hugh grudgingly took the reins of Dristan's destrier. Thor seemed to have no desire to go anywhere with the man, as he pulled and tugged to no avail. Thor stood his ground with only a shake of his luxurious black mane and a snort directed towards Dristan to voice his displeasure.

Dristan chuckled and patted the stallion's neck. "Go Thor. All will be well."

As the horse was finally led to the stables, and several serfs were ordered to do the same with his guardsmen's mounts, Dristan turned his attention to the pressing matters at hand.

"Riorden," he called to his captain.

"Aye, my lord?"

"Take a half dozen men inside, lest those within are still prepared to battle. Somehow I think these Scots, too, are weary of watching their kinsmen felled and would like this blood bath to be over."

"'Twill be done, my liege."

"And Riorden," Dristan continued as his captain paused in his stride. "Bring me the young knight. I assume he is their lord's son, and 'twill be fitting that he should plead his fealty to me afore all others."

Dristan watched as Riorden and his men breached the last remains of the door. It took but a few choice words spoken to those knights of the old lord left to defend the Great Hall 'til they sheathed their swords in defeat.

Satisfied no further blood would be shed this day, Dristan went about securing his new lands in the name of his king. As was always the case wherever he appeared, adults and children scampered out of his way in fear. Their cries of terror now filled the hall as he entered his new domain. He gave a weary sigh. Sometimes having a fierce reputation could be bothersome indeed, but unfortunately for his peace of mind, 'twas one necessary to maintain.

Two

DRISTAN HEARD THE HEAVY FOOTSTEPS of tired men, clanking down the stairs in their cumbersome armor. The one he had summoned was at last approaching. He turned from the blazing hearth to watch the lad stride into the Great Hall flanked by several battle weary soldiers. 'Twas clear they stood afore him most reluctantly.

Silence filled the air, and Dristan took his time assessing the well-seasoned warriors. The only exception to the group was the young boy, who stood with a look that would have alone felled the most ferocious of enemies. Dristan was used to seeing such a glare of loathing. Only time would tell if the boy could learn to get past the hatred he was feeling.

The remains of the hall door slammed closed with a loud crash, and the sound of someone fast striding had all heads turning to see who approached.

"You insolent whelp! Who gives you the right to glare at your new lord in such an ill manner?" Hugh yelled as he came abreast of the group. Afore anyone could stop his act, Hugh raised his hand and struck the boy in the face, bringing him to his knees from the force of the blow. His gauntlet left blood, trickling down from the knight's right cheek.

The distinctive sound of swords, coming free of their scabbards, echoed in the hall as the boy's guardsmen advanced to protect their charge.

Hugh raised his fist in threat. "Get thee back and let me finish my work so he never again questions who is lord here!"

"Cease your madness!" Dristan roared. His angry voice shook the rafters.

The Devil's Dragon of Blackmore buried his fist in Hugh's face yet again and sent him to the floor. Dristan reached down and grabbed the man, bringing him face to face that he might see the rage in his lord's eyes.

"You have erred again by presuming to act on my behalf," he hissed, "but I'll be damned if you shall continue to do so further today or any other day henceforth!"

Two of Dristan's garrison knights stepped forward at his command and bowed. He flung a stumbling, humiliated Hugh towards them.

"Find the dungeon and take this worthless fool there 'til I decide his fate. Mayhap, I'll let him rot there for a spell, 'til my temper cools!"

Dristan turned back towards his personal guard and each man knew, by the look on their lord's face, he struggled not to finish Hugh off immediately. He motioned with his hand again to the Scotsmen guarding the young knight.

Although hesitant, one by one, they put their blades back into their sheaths and returned to stand behind their charge, who remained kneeling on the floor, slightly swaying.

Dristan moved to assist the young knight and the boy's guardsmen raised their hands 'til they hovered over the hilts of their swords. Dristan dismissed them, more concerned with helping the youth stand and regain some dignity.

"What is your name, boy?" he demanded.

The knight stubbornly remained quiet, glaring at his new lord with all the hatred a body could muster. Young MacLaren wiped the blood from his swollen cheek.

"Your name boy," he repeated. "I assume you have one."

"Aye," the youth muttered with defiance.

"And yet you cease to tell me."

"His name is Aiden. Aiden of clan MacLaren, my liege," Ian said.

Dristan judged the man with a single glance. "And who are you that you speak on his behalf?"

"He is Ian, captain of my garrison."

"The boy speaks." Dristan stated. "And I assume these are your remaining knights?"

"They are the rest of my personal guardsmen, who yet live."

Dristan scowled whilst allowing himself a moment to consider the young man afore him. *Mon dieu* but the lad could not be more than ten and six if that. His face was not truly determinable since 'twas covered with the dirt and grime of battle, but it looked as if 'twould not grow even a small bit of fuzz to cover his cheeks any time soon. A lock of fiery red hair escaped his chainmail helm, which did not surprise Dristan in the least, given the lad's Scottish heritage. His eyes could be blue, but that, too, was hard to tell in the dim light of the hall. 'Twas also difficult to conclude the lad's form as he was still wearing his armor. Somehow Dristan felt he would not have much meat on his bones given his small stature. 'Twas then he noticed a strange oddity with the young knight.

"You have not won your spurs, I see," Dristan commented dryly. "Did not your sire squire you out?"

"He saw to my training himself."

"'Tis most unusual."

Aiden only shrugged as if no further answer was necessary.

Dristan saw the look of satisfaction on the boy's face when his two men returned after finding new lodgings for Hugh. He could only imagine what was going through the lad's head. Surely he felt a sense of vindication that a wrong had been righted.

A slight smile began to alight on Aiden's face.

The smile did not go unnoticed by the Devil's Dragon.

"I understand you have a twin sister. Is she above in the solar with the rest of your family?" he questioned sharply.

The boy's grin quickly vanished with his start of surprise.

"My sis-sister?"

"Aye. Your twin, or so I have been told," Dristan replied, trying to find some patience with the youth.

"Your k-king knows of us?" Aiden stammered in shock.

"'Tis King Henry's business to know those he plans to conquer and lands he will claim as his own," Dristan stated simply. "You have not answered my question...is she above?"

The boy's mouth opened, but afore any words could be spewed forth, his captain again spoke out.

"She was asked to travel with her Aunt to Edinburgh prior to the siege, my lord," Ian provided as an explanation.

Dristan's brow furrowed in irritation and saw how Aiden's chin raised up a notch. Perchance there was yet hope for the youth.

"We shall deal with her when the time comes. But tell me now...will you pledge fealty to me as your new liege lord, young Aiden?"

"Do I have a choice?" the youth asked obstinately.

"We all make choices, boy. 'Tis a heavy burden we must bear. You are now the clan leader, and as such, 'tis your responsibility to think of the well-being of your family and clansmen afore yourself."

"You would allow me to remain head of my clan...to care for my family?" the youth's look was filled with skepticism. He had not expected these words from the terror of England.

"This castle is but one of many I have claimed in the name of King Henry." Dristan put his hand upon the boy's shoulder, amazed he even had the strength to lift the heavy sword for the past several days. "Perchance one day I may leave it unto your keeping 'til such time as I return. Give me your oath of fealty, Aiden, and your men, as well. 'Til I know you have been trained properly and can hold up against the fiercest of enemies, I give you and yours my protection under my name." He took a step back from the boy and looked down upon his startled features. "I cannot offer you more than that as yet, but perchance for now 'tis enough," he declared. "Still...the choice must be yours."

Dristan watched Aiden chew on his lower lip in indecision as the boy was likely wondering what choice he really had. *'Tis the only home the boy has ever known,* he thought to himself. *Where else on this earth could the lad in truth wander, when all he knew and loved was surely held within these walls and the lands he had roamed all his life.*

Aiden gave a brief nod to those loyal men who waited for a decision and heard a few grunts of annoyance on what the clan now faced. Turning to face the Devil's Dragon, Aiden gave a soft sigh of resignation to their fate and stared up at Berwyck's new liege lord.

Finally, Aiden knelt on one knee and took a deep breath with hands held out in complete submission. Dristan reached out and clasped them, awaiting the pledge of loyalty that would bind the MacLaren clan as his vassals.

"I, A—Aiden of Berwyck and of Clan MacLaren, do so swear on my faith in God the Almighty to serve thee as my liege lord, Dristan of Blackmore. I promise in the future to be faithful to my lord, never causing you harm, and will observe my homage to you completely against all persons in good faith and without deceit."

"I accept thee as my vassal," Dristan proclaimed, nodding in satisfaction then motioned for Aiden to stand next to Riorden, whilst each of the lad's guardsmen in turn made their vows. The deed did not take long, since there were only seven of the boy's guard left alive.

Dristan folded his arms against his massive chest and stared down the length of his nose at Aiden once more.

"I will see to your training myself to ensure 'tis done proper-ly. Some may think I do you no favor as training with me is most brutal, but 'twill possibly keep your head attached to your shoulders someday," he said sternly then watched as the boy's eyes darted back and forth in further concern. "But now is not the time to fret about such matters. 'Tis more important we see to the burying of our dead than worry about your training."

"Aye, my lord."

"See you to your family, Aiden, so they know you yet live, and whilst you search the dead for your lord," Dristan said as he turned to his guard, "my captain, Riorden de Deveraux, will see that a detail assists you in laying your clansmen to rest and also ensure your safety. Although I can vouch for my personal guardsmen, others under my command are mercenaries. There is naught I can do about their lack of knightly virtues and the hatred they feel towards the Scots."

Dristan watched Aiden give a slight bow afore taking his leave. It appeared the boy left with a heavy heart, as the young knight put one foot in front of the other whilst slowly ascending the stairs to the upper floors to seek out his remaining family. Dristan could sympathize with the lad's plight. For years in service to his king, he had seen for himself those who had lost their homes to his conquering army. Most had chosen to swear fealty to King Henry. He did not like to think on the alternative outcome for those who did not. Change was in the air, and only the whim of fate would tell which way the winds would blow to determine the life course Aiden MacLaren would soon follow.

THREE

T HE YOUTH CALLED AIDEN, closed the wooden portal of the
solar door with a soft click, cutting off the frightened
words from Patrick, the youngest member of the family. The
child inside was aged only eight summers and had been petrified
with fear 'til the calming voice from his eldest sibling had offered him comfort.

Turning into the passageway, the young knight noticed Ian
leaning up against the stone wall with his arms crossed over his
chest. "The bairn's are alright?" he asked.

"Aye...at least for the moment." With the affirmation that
the family was safe, they walked silently, side by side, down the
long dimly lit corridor 'til they reached the MacLaren heir's
chamber.

Ian opened the door, allowing his charge to enter. The sound
of the portal shutting and the bolt sliding into place gave them
a sense of privacy they had not had in some time. The youth
stood still as Ian went about his business to assist with the re-
moval of armor once they entered the chamber. 'Twas some-

thing that could not be accomplished alone without some difficulty.

Raising both arms at his command, 'twas with a sense of relief when the heavy metal was slowly removed. Ian could be quite demanding when he felt the need, but the young knight was too tired to reprimand the man. In truth, what would that really accomplish? Ian had been by the twins' side since the first time their sire had put a sword willingly in their hands. His opinions and grumbles were something they had gotten used to over the years.

With a heavy sigh, the one dubbed Aiden turned and removed the chain mail coif from a head covered in deep red with coppery tones. With a firm but short tug, a long braid of the same hues came free from its confines. 'Twas a welcoming relief to feel the hair about one's neck that had been stuffed and hidden within the armor and garments worn for more days than could be remembered.

Where but a moment afore stood a young, confident, and justifiably exhausted lad, there now revealed in one heartbeat a young woman, holding her own against life's turmoil's and the chaos her life had become. As if a heavy weight had been lifted from her weary shoulders, Amiria at last turned towards her captain.

"Ah doona ken how weel continue this farce," Ian commented with a scowl. "Never mind yer da weel haunt me fer the rest o' me life!"

"Careful Ian...you're Scottish brogue is coming out. Just give me a moment, my friend," was all she could manage to whisper. "'Tis the first bit of privacy and rest I've had in days it seems."

"Ye'll need more than a moment tae put this aright, lass," Ian mumbled.

Looking down at her figure, Amiria could only shake her head as she stood afore her captain. No one in their right mind would mistake her for a lad for any length of time, so she was puzzled how their ruse would be to their benefit. For only being ten and nine, she was an exact replica of her brother but with her features more delicately refined and body slighter of frame. She could also wield a sword as no other woman she had ever come across, although she knew she needed more training.

Amiria had previously only fought for the pure joy of it and to prove her worth to her sire. Her lessons were never intended to produce such skill to slay her adversaries as she had done this past month. If she were to continue this path, her training needed to reach a new level, for hesitation would be her undoing on the field.

"You should have just let me say my name instead of using my brothers," she hissed. "I know you meant well, Ian, but now I have pledged my life to a man who thinks I am a boy and my brother at that! No good shall come from this deception. Mayhap he would have offered me his protection if he but knew I was a maid."

"Harrumph...or taken ye right thar in front o' all ta witness so yer maid no more. Ye know o' his reputation, Amiria, and he shouldna be trusted."

"'Tis too late for that now as we owe him our fealty; I do not, howsoever, like the lie that has fallen from our lips," she said, feeling aggravated.

Ian came to stand afore her and bowed. "My most humble apologies, Amiria, but 'twas out of my mouth afore common sense could stop my words."

Amiria gawked at her captain in amazement as she realized how he readily changed his accent to suit his mood. There certainly was no hint of a brogue that she could detect now. 'Twas her mother's doing, she thought, as her father had married an English noblewoman, hoping to bring peace between two countries. Lessons had always seemed to include Ian. He had been eager to learn since her sire had demanded the twins be always within his sight. It did not leave the man much of a life other than to guard them, but perchance he, too, had been resigned to his fate.

Gazing at him, Amiria could understand why all women from the highest born to the most menial serving wench would willingly fall into his bed if he but asked. He was tall with an unusual color of reddish brown hair graced with golden highlights kissed from the sun. Its length fell to his shoulders in soft waves many would envy. Eyes of hazel with brilliant green flecks had countless maids sighing with just one look from him. Years of training with their laird had his body muscular and almost as intimidating as their new liege. At a score and five he could easily have any lass of his choosing.

Amiria had frequently thought of him as most handsome but had kept the affection she felt for him to herself for many a year. She always knew what they had between them could never be more than mere friends, much to her deepest regret. Her lot in life was to marry a man of standing in order to procure more lands to add to the family wealth and to ensure an alliance in times of need. This was the way of the nobility, and she did not see that changing even with the new circumstances in which she now found herself.

Looking up into his eyes, the intensity she saw there made her more than aware that he had the same thoughts and longings running through his mind. With a heavy sigh, she held up her hand to stop any words that would be forthcoming from him. She was not sure her heart could stand it.

She crossed the room that resembled nothing of its former comfort, afore the enemy came to lay siege to the castle. All items having any semblance of femininity had been stripped away and, in truth, 'twas really nothing within the chamber giving evidence 'twas anything more than what would be used for a guest. The room itself was not overly large but was more than adequate for her needs, especially since she spent most of her time outdoors and hated the stuffiness of a closed chamber. She was lucky she did not have to share the place with her two younger sisters, Sabina and Lynet.

'Twas here in this very room that she had come up with the scheme with her twin brother Aiden that she would dress as a lad to help defend their home. Aiden protested and argued with her, but in the end, Amiria had won her way as she always did. If their father had known her thoughts and actions, he would have enclosed her in the dungeon. She would have been lucky to ever see the light of day again.

She went to the alcove, holding a most comfortable window seat, and opened the shutters with little difficulty. Her breath caught when the crisp ocean air assaulted her senses. She breathed in deeply, feeling a peacefulness run through her body to calm her frayed nerves. This had always been her favorite place to come and collect her thoughts and now was no different, although she knew she could not tarry long. Although she knew that others had been dispatched to search the dead and dying, Amiria felt 'twas her duty to find her father and brother herself. She knew they must lay somewhere beyond the outer bailey and there was some slight chance they yet lived.

She could sense Ian's stare, boring into her. Inhaling deeply once more of the salty sea breeze, she closed the shutters and returned her attention to her captain. "You should find yourself a wife, Ian," she said calmly.

"Ach, you know 'tis the farthest thing from my mind, Amiria."

She smiled at him warmly. "All the same, 'tis sure I am there be a fine Scottish lassie who would be more than willing to share your life."

"There is but one bonny lass who I would give that honor to, and you know of whom I speak."

She came to stand afore him quickly, placing her finger tips on his lips. He took them just as swiftly and kissed them afore she could take her hand away. Seldom did they give in to the pleasure of each other's touch, knowing the danger of where it might lead.

"Nay, please, I beg you...do not speak of it."

"Amiria...you know that I lo—"

"By the Blessed Virgin Mary Ian, I beseech you in the name of all we hold dear...please do not say those words to me. You know we can never be...

"We could run away," he proposed, and she knew 'twas said with an earnest heart.

She placed her hand hesitantly upon his cheek and began caressing it with her thumb. She had never dared such afore. The wetness from a single tear rushed down her cheek, giving evidence to the turmoil of her emotions. She felt a small bit of comfort as he covered her hand with his own.

"You know as well as I," she said with a touch of sorrow to her words, "we could never do something that foolish, without care for my family, our clan, or even our pride and honor. We would never truly be happy if we did so."

"I would give everything I have just to ensure your happiness, lass," Ian declared quietly. He took her hand and placed a gentle kiss upon its back.

Her smile was timid at best. "Aye, Ian, I know you would, but you know my father did not consent to your petition for us to wed. I would not dishonor his memory, if God forbid he has passed from this earth, by going against his wishes."

"Given enough time I could have persuaded him to change his mind," he mumbled in frustration.

"Aye, I suppose in time you may have done just that, but now we are not free to make our own choices in life. Somehow, I think the beast below would send out his minions and hunt us 'til the end of time itself, if we were reckless enough to make such an attempt of leaving. We are his vassals now and have no choice but to serve his every whim."

"Ah lass...you know not how that tears at my heart," Ian said solemnly as he brought her closer into his embrace.

"Please Ian," she whispered, frantic at the intimacy, not only of their gazes but also his touch. "We canna do this, for I know 'twill break my heart."

"I know 'tis not within my right to ask, but somehow I must," he said as he caressed her hair. "Just once sweet lassie...just once let me taste your sweet kiss that I may say at least for one small moment you were mine. I would treasure that kiss all my days and for the rest of my life, Amiria..."

"Oh, Ian," she moaned and began to tilt her head back as she closed her eyes to give in to this one small pleasure. She sensed, for a fleeting second, their breaths become as one, as he lowered his head but inches from receiving the gift of her very first kiss. She could not help the sigh of bliss that escaped her lips.

The sudden pounding on her chamber door broke the spell that had but briefly surrounded them. Ian whirled towards the door with sword in hand whilst Amiria once more disappeared into the guise of her brother. She rushed to the hearth and quickly rubbed cool ashes upon her face. With her mail coif firmly in place on her head, she tilted her head just so, allowing her features to remain somewhat indiscernible. It had taken hours practicing with Aiden afore he was satisfied she had perfected the movement for it to become a habit to her. She turned and saw Ian nod in approval that all appeared as it should. He slid the bolt and opened the door.

Killian and Finlay of her guard stood without, and Amiria placed her finger to her mouth to ensure they kept their silence from possible prying eyes and ears. With a brief nod, Killian stepped forward. "The devil below beckons we make haste tae see tae the dead an' wounded; seems as though a storm might be a brewing, so we best hurry."

"So be it Killian. Lead the way," she ordered.

As the two knights left down the passageway, Ian continued to hold the portal open for her. When she came aside him, she lingered momentarily, placing her hand upon his arm and giving it a gentle squeeze.

"I am sorry, Ian, for what can never be," she said so quietly, he surely must have strained to hear her words.

"As am I, Amiria...as am I," he returned, with a tense smile.

Looking up into the depths of his eyes, Amiria could have sworn a tear hovered on his lashes, for the look he gave her must surely have been mirrored in her own. With unspoken words, they both knew their one moment they could have shared was not to be. This was somehow much more upsetting to them both, knowing that such a moment would never be allowed to happen ever again.

FOUR

DRISTAN WIPED THE DRIPPING SWEAT from his brow and took a moment to assess the progress being made.

Kenna, the clan's healer, had her toil still ahead of her. She continued without complaint the impossible task of giving what aid she could to those wounded men who yet lived. There were so many. Unfortunately, more men than Dristan would have liked were beyond her healing powers.

The words of a priest competed with the moans of the dying whilst he persisted in his vigil of administering last rights to those who had passed on...warriors all, both of Dristan's own men and clan MacLaren's, who had fought for a cause each truly believed.

His guardsmen toiled alongside serfs and clansmen alike, attempting to get the dead in the ground afore the storms began. Dristan recalled how Riorden had been brought to Blackmore to foster as page for his sire, and the two young boys of similar age had become inseparable. Brothers Taegan and Turquine were but a few years apart and quite the handful when they were deep into their cups, especially without a willing wench at their sides. Nathaniel had joined their group during his travels in France. Rolf, Ulrick, Morgan, and Geoffrey had been with him since his first days, when he had squired with Fletcher's sire. The remaining three, Drake, Bertram, and Cederick, he acquired at one tourney or another whilst he made a name for himself, by acquiring his riches and lands all in the name of King Henry II.

All were specifically chosen because of their uncanny ability to train and fight to the death when needed, black dragons all. They were an exceptional group of men to have by his side and guard his back. No one could mistake who their master was as they were an impressive sight with all their darkness riding the countryside, leaving villagers trembling in their wake. He had lost count of the times he had been challenged over the years by some whoreson who wanted to have the privilege of saying he had slain the Devil's Dragon of Blackmore. Since he yet lived, 'twas obvious all failed in their quest for glory.

He looked in the distance and saw Riorden slowly following Aiden, whilst he picked his way through the bodies in search of his lord. 'Twas clear the boy and his men had yet to be successful as they carefully made their way amongst the dead.

Dristan came to stand above Kenna as she closed the eyes of yet another man who would not live to see another day. He offered his hand to the woman, although he was still leery, not knowing if she were in truth a healer or mayhap a witch. One could never be too careful when crossing the Scottish border, since he had heard tell anything was possible this far north. He watched her hesitation 'til she finally took what he offered.

As she rose, she refused to let go of his hand and clutched it in a firm and steady grip. She closed her eyes as if pondering something then opened them to look him directly in the eye.

And then she did the unexpected...she smiled, and he knew not what to say.

"I see you, my lord Dristan," she began knowingly. Her green eyes were the color of the sea, and they bore into him, as if looking for his very soul.

"And what do you think you see, woman?" he said, with disinterest.

"I see a man craving a different life than what you now lead."

"Truly? I have all I desire in my life."

"Think you?" she asked with a touch of surprise.

"Aye! I have my sword...an extension of my arm; my guards and my steed both loyal to a fault; and I have the favor of my king. I have more lands than I know what to do with and riches beyond your wildest imagination. What more could I ask for or want from life?"

"Mayhap you should ask yourself that very question."

"I need nothing more than what I now possess," he grumbled offhandedly.

Kenna let go of his hand, picked up her satchel of herbs, and turned to see who next she might aid. He fell into step beside her, 'til she turned once more to stare confidently up at her new lord.

"Are you a witch?" he questioned lightly, not wanting her to put a spell on him if she were in truth and felt offended by his question.

"Some may think so." She gave a small laugh. "But since I prefer not to roast upon a stake any time soon, I do not consider myself as such. Sometimes, not everything you see is as it appears, my lord. Is this not so?"

"You have the sight then?" he said, choosing to ignore her question.

Kenna looked at him again, and he became somewhat un-comfortable for all his reputation of fierceness.

"Sometimes, I know of things afore they happen. I do not know how...I just do. Mayhap 'tis why I know you would live a normal life if you but could."

"Ha! Normal...what is normal?"

"Normal is a loving wife to tend your needs, your children's laughter surrounding you in your hall, and a family to call your own...my lord."

"A wife?" he roared. "What need do I have of a wife? I can have any willing wench I want in my bed without the headache of having a wife harping at me day and night!"

She flashed a knowing smile. "You have spent too much time at war, my liege, if you do not know the difference between a wife and a wench."

"Bah...you are a most annoying woman," he declared off-handedly.

Kenna but laughed at him again. "You are not the first to tell me so, nor shall you be the last."

"Be about your business, Mistress Kenna, and save your helping hands to healing those who need your aid. The way in which my life is run is none of your concern."

"Of course, my lord..." Kenna gave him a short bow. "I but told you what I saw. What you make of my words is for you to decide."

Kenna looked up ahead and saw a group of clansmen form a circle with heads bowed, and watched as Aiden knelt down up-on the ground. "I am afraid the young one has found who was sought. Perchance I am needed there posthaste."

"Come with me," Dristan said urgently, as he ushered her through the lingering mayhem and wreckage of what his army had left behind. He had a foreboding they would be too late to offer what Aiden would need from the clan's healer.

Amiria knelt down next to her father and watched as her guardsmen Cameron, Thomas, and Nevin attempted to remove their laird's armor to see to his wounds. From the amount of blood she saw seeping into the ground, she knew the wound was severe, if not fatal. His breastplate removed, they all watched the ever so slight rise and fall of his chest and heard his ragged breathing. How he still lived, they knew not, but they did not question their good fortune.

'Twas at the sound of a deep booming voice, heard above the wailings of the village people, demanding they move, that she became aware her new lord approached. She saw him move aside Devon, her newest guardsman, with a slight push, whilst he made way for Kenna, who came immediately to her father's side. Amiria gave her new lord but the briefest of glances, afore turning her attention, once more, to her sire. She took his hand in hers and tried to warm the coolness from his fingers.

"Tell me Kenna," she whispered hopefully.

"'Tis most grave Aid—," her words cut off when she looked up, and she quickly masked her surprise by who she saw. 'Twas not often she was caught off guard, as she obviously was now. "I will endeavor to do my best," she said gravely.

Kenna set to work and lifted her laird's tunic to see the wound beneath. "Laird Douglas...my laird can you hear me?" Kenna asked.

When there was no response, Amiria tried to reach her father with her own familiar voice. "Father, 'tis me; come back to us, father!" she pleaded, with tears coursing down her face.

All watched as Douglas's eye lids fluttered open. If he saw all those who stood around him, they could not guess, but they could see the delight at seeing his offspring by his side. "Ach, 'tis me wee bonny la—."

"Father!" Amiria cut off his words afraid he might speak her name. She leaned down and kissed his weathered cheek. Taking his hand she brought it up to her cheek. "Save your strength, my laird."

"There's naught to savin me, darlin," he said softly. "Ye must be braw now without me to lead ye."

"Nay! Dinnae leave me Da..."

"Ian will keep ye safe now...he vowed it for always."

Ian stepped forward into his laird's vision. "I swear to you as I did afore, my laird, I will always see them safe." He made a quick glance at Dristan whose brow furrowed at his words.

Douglas gave a slight smile afore he began to cough, causing blood to slowly ooze from his mouth. "'Tis a good lad...if only I could have promised ye to me beautiful Amiria."

Amiria broke down in sobs, and she leaned over her sire to carefully hold him close to her heart without causing further pain. Those around them shared her heartache, knowing Kenna could do nothing further to aid the man from dying. She was only vaguely aware when Dristan made a motion to his men to retreat to give the clan their last remaining time with their lord without interference.

Whilst she tried to calm her fears, a steady stream of tears continued falling from Amiria's eyes. Ever so softly, she told her sire she loved him.

"Do ye see her, my sweet bairn?" he whispered for her ears alone.

"See who, Da?"

"Why yer ma o' course...me own sweet Catherine comin' to take me to her side. She's been awaitin' a long time, ye know."

Amiria looked up at Kenna who only gave her a reassuring smile. "Is she as beautiful as I remember her, Da?" she asked breathlessly.

"Aye that she is. I will tell her ye love her I will," he said quietly then turned his head to look proudly into Amiria's eyes. He gave her that smile she always cherished 'til she heard him take his last breath. Douglas MacLaren knew no more.

Amiria brushed one last kiss on her sire's cheek, gently closed his eyes, and shakily rose. "Garrick," she called to the piper standing by a nearby tree. He came to stand behind her as he waited for her words that shook with sorrow. "A song if you will Garrick...something sweet and pleasing to the ears to send our good laird on his way to the heavens."

Amiria stood beside her fellow clansmen whilst the mournful sound of the bagpipes filled the air. 'Twas fitting a slight rain began to fall from the sky. At least with the rain, the English could not see the tears stream down the faces of the vanquished, whilst they mourned the loss not only of their chieftain, but their very way of life.

FIVE

AMIRIA STOOD IN THE SOLAR once used by her mother and spoke in hushed tones to Thomas and Devon as they guarded the locked door. She continuously looked to the other occupants of the room in the hopes they would not over hear their conversation. 'Twould not bode well to have her family any more frightened than they already were.

"You are sure?" she questioned softly.

"My lady, we were most diligent in our search," Thomas replied in equally subdued tones.

"Then why has my brother not been found? I saw with my own eyes his fall beyond the outer bailey. Surely it does not take the whole garrison to find his body," she said in irritation.

"Mayhap the English saw him buried," Devon suggested.

"Hush you fool," Thomas interjected. "Do you want to cause our lady to be ill?"

"I was just trying tae help," he replied.

"'Tis not help you are giving," Thomas argued whilst rolling his eyes at Devon who was the youngest of Amiria's guards. "Now remain silent."

"Cease your bickering, both of you, afore you alert the others aught is amiss," Amiria said and took a moment to clarify her thoughts. "Are you allowed free movement about the keep and grounds?"

Thomas nodded, "Aye, so far, but the Dragon already talks of time in the lists to see how we have been trained. I think he waits for the storm to pass afore he begins to test us."

"He is the Devil's servant," Devon replied, as he crossed himself. "'Tis best we stay in his good graces, or we may end up serving his master residing in hell! Or, mayhap, even cursed fer all eternity..."

"Enough of your nonsense," Amiria spat, "he is naught but a man." She was still trying to get used to having Devon as part of her guard instead of a childhood friend she had gotten into mischief with in her youth. *I will need to exert an extra dose of patience where he is concerned*, she thought with a heavy sigh.

She noticed how Devon gazed at her with his doubts clearly written upon his face. He once more made the sign of the cross and then, for good measure, spat over his right shoulder. Amazed at his audacity, she could not resist asking, "Mayhap, you should do the same over your left side just to be extra cautious?" Afore she could tell him she but jested, he did just that, but twice more to be safe. "Deliver me from imbeciles, Thomas."

"You cannot fault him his beliefs, my lady. I've done the same myself a time or two."

"I suppose spells and curses from the underworld should not be taken lightly," she replied quietly, and crossed herself, as well, for good measure, then looked upon Devon, smiling in satisfaction to appease God above. "I've had enough of this speech of hexes and that dragon below whom we must serve. I must think of finding Aiden at all costs.

"Do what you must, as discreetly as possible, and see if any of the serfs have by chance seen where he has been buried. I cannot rest 'til I know he yet lives or where his grave lies. Somehow, if he were in truth gone from this world, I think I would know it within me, and yet I still feel a cold numbness of hope surrounding my heart," Amiria said in weariness and gave her men a brief nod of dismissal.

The two men bowed to her and left the solar, and Amiria went to sit on a vacant stool next to her sisters and brother who were also near the blazing hearth. Sabina, who was ten and seven, had her mother's dark brown hair, but had inherited none of the sweet disposition their dame had possessed. Her features were sharp and her eyes, which were too often filled with the look of hatred, were an eerie golden brown, almost like that of a hawk. She had oft wondered how Sabina came to be so bitter. Amiria found her sister callous and demanding and spent as little time in her company as was possible.

Lynet was the complete opposite at only ten and four. No matter the circumstances, the young girl always saw the bright side to things with the innocence of the young at heart. A smile could readily be seen on her face, with the exception of these past months and now as their sire had been laid to rest. Even so, she looked up at her sister with adoring eyes. Her golden blonde hair shone from the reflection of the flames and her clear blue eyes held a radiance few could hope to compare. Amiria smiled at the sweetness of the young girl's demeanor.

Her gaze at last fell on the forlorn little boy of only eight summers with shiny black hair, who could only stare into the fire with a lost look upon his face. His dark brown eyes held no joy. Amiria knew that no comforting words could alter the fact his laird was dead and older brother missing amongst the departed. Her heart sank at the loss of his childhood, as no boy should lose both of his hero's in one bad stroke of fate. She knew 'twould be sometime afore she once more heard Patrick's cheerful laughter ring out as he pretended to save her from evil with the forgotten wooden sword now lying on the floor near his feet.

What a mismatched group of siblings we are, for we are nothing alike, she thought to herself. *Looking at us, one would think we had different parents than the two that bore us all.* Amiria gazed reflectively again at her siblings and then shook off the horrible thoughts of her mother possibly straying from their father. She would not be the first wife to do so, and yet she hated thinking of her mother in such a manner.

Pondering the memory of her mother only brought more sorrow to her already broken heart as she had been very close to her. 'Twas giving birth to Patrick that cost her beloved mother her life and she watched as her father grieved for his love as she had never seen afore. Amiria could only envision the wonder of having a husband whom she could love in a like manner and have that love returned tenfold. Since her father never found a betrothed worthy enough for her, she had her doubts she would find the man on her own. Those who had come in the past only saw her for her dowry and saw nothing of the woman who they would take to wife.

Taking a poker from the hearth, she plunged it into the crimson, fiery coals then turned and poured herself a mug of wine. She sprinkled a few calming herbs into her cup and plunged the red hot iron into the brew to mull. A sweet aroma filled the air and for a moment the aroma reminded her of when her mother would perform this small act for her father. 'Twas almost as if she could feel her parents' calming presence in the room.

Closing her eyes for a brief respite from the hell her life had become, she envisioned her parents and Aiden standing afore her. She and her twin had been inseparable as youths and could be counted on to finish each other's sentences, to the irritation of Sabina. Of course, her poor younger sister had suffered terribly from their pranks. Amiria had to admit she had been prone, just as badly as her twin, to put a squiggly worm or two down her sister's dress or slimy toads into her shoes. They had never had the heart to do such to Lynet, and perchance this was the cause of Sabina's growing abhorrence of her youngest sister. Thinking of her twin, she knew in her heart, if he were in truth gone from this world and in heaven with their parents, she would have felt it with every fiber of her being. Since she could feel nothing but dread, she could only pray he yet lived.

As Amiria remembered her childhood, she could still see her father's face when he had come across Aiden teaching her how to use a sword. Aghast that his son would allow his sister to use a sharpened weapon of war, he had scolded Aiden 'til even her ears had felt burnt from the heat of their father's words. 'Twas only through her mother's gentle coaxing that evening as she soothed their sire, that he had decided to see to her training himself. He was amused by her skill at such a tender age, but Amiria could also remember the pleasure in his eyes at her progress. Never one to disappoint her father and always looking for praise from him, she had doubled her efforts to learn as best she could. It had been clear, however, the only chance she would ever use such a weapon was for practicing with her father, Aiden, or Ian. Her father never allowed anyone else to train with her and had made it perfectly clear her sword was never to be used for the defense of their home. That would only be done by well-trained seasoned warriors of the clan.

Amiria opened her eyes, looked at her siblings, and thought on the words she had given them but a while ago. Patrick was equally confused by his older sister's dress and could not understand the ruse of portraying her twin she had deployed for their new liege. Amiria was determined to do whatever it took to protect her clan and those she loved. She could almost feel the horrific omen sure to crash down over her head with the tale she had told, and knew the amount of penance she would pay for the sin of lying. Her knees ached at the very thought of the hours ahead of her on the hard, cold chapel floor.

Her time for day dreaming came to an abrupt halt with the opening of the solar door. Ian and Nevin entered with looks of displeasure. Clearly 'twas not a good sign of what was yet to come.

"He asks for you, Amiria...or I should say he asks for Aiden," Ian growled. "I dare not say him nay."

"Then let us be on our way to see our lord dragon, Ian," she declared, setting down her now cool wine.

"He requests all of you to come afore him," Nevin added. "Why he wants to see the bairn's, I know not."

"'Tis not surprising, Sir Nevin, since my siblings are now his charges and he will see to their best interests, or so I hope," Amiria answered quietly. "Come, children. We must pay homage to our new liege lord."

"He is no lord of mine," Sabina answered snidely, "and I am certainly no child!"

"Watch your shrewish tongue sister, afore you bring the wrath of yon dragon down upon our heads," Amiria replied sharply.

Sabina looked at her with hatred pouring from her eyes. "Who are you to tell me what to do? You are not lady of this hall, nor are you my mother. You have no right to speak to me so," she yelled.

Ian at last stepped forward between the two young women, who now stood toe to toe and looked ready to pull each other's hair out. "Cease your caterwauling and think of your younger siblings for once in your life, Lady Sabina. Do you want them cowering afore their new lord? You are the proud descendants of clan MacLaren and have their blood flowing through your veins! Remember my words and your station in life that you do not disgrace those who have already left this world afore you. I believe your father would rather look down from heaven and see you all standing afore the English with honor than trembling with fear."

Sabina stared with open mouthed wonder at his words. She shook with anger that he would speak to her so, especially in front of others. "How dare you!" she exclaimed once she found her voice.

"I will dare much to guard and protect this family, as I swore to our laird. 'Til I am told otherwise by our new lord, I will continue with my duties as I have done these many years," Ian chided. "Now come...you must pay homage to our liege, so do not further test my patience this day, wee one."

Sabina's mouth snapped shut, and she threw Ian a cold glare of hatred whilst she strode through the door Nevin held open for her.

Amiria took Patrick's hand in hers and followed behind Lynet. She chanced one small look in Ian's direction as she passed his way. The anger she saw in the depths of his eyes all but told her something was afoot, and 'twas not to his liking. She had a hunch she would not care for what she learned either, once she made her way down to the Great Hall to confront the dragon below. Giving a heavy sigh of weariness, she wished just once she could put off the inevitable.

Hugh squinted into the dimness of the pit whilst he felt something slither for what seemed like the hundredth time across his legs. He was cold, wet, and tired of the mire that continuously seeped through his hose, leaving him chilled to the bone. Having lost track of time, he had tried to climb the walls of his slime-infested prison, but to no avail. 'Twould be no escaping his tomb 'til someone at last remembered his location and lowered a ladder so he could escape to freedom.

Yet 'twas only a matter of time 'til said freedom was granted, and 'til then he would plot his retaliation against Dristan of Blackmore. With thoughts of vengeance running rampant through his head, Hugh smiled for the first time in days, and his malicious laughter echoed off the walls, declaring impending misfortune of what was yet to come.

SIX

A ND I TELL YOU, THE WENCH was more than happy to bed with me that night," Taegan argued with his brother.

"Hah...as if you could remember you were even capable of the deed, you were so far gone into your ale," laughed Turquine, thumping his mug on the wooden table to be filled by a nearby serving maid. The replenished brew sloshed in his mug when the girl jumped to miss his eager hands but still managed a squeal of protest as his palm landed affectionately on her bottom with a smack. "'Twas with me the girl had such a memorable night to remember! Believe me, mate's, when I tell you, she was not complaining!"

Bertram wiped his mouth on his tunic sleeve and gave a loud belch of approval of his meal. "You, and the entire company, had her boys!" he chimed in, and laughter resounded from several of Dristan's knights.

"Aye, I seem to remember plenty of noise coming from the stable's loft that night. She was a feisty wench that one was, despite her saying she was a virgin!" Ulrick reminisced with a chuckle.

"Virgin my arse!" Morgan yelled out.

Dristan laughed along with his men whilst the squabbling continued, in between bites of food and swigs of ale and mead. The fare had been the best he had eaten in some time and he was more than pleased with the cook of the keep. Pushing back his now empty trencher, he wiped his hands on his tunic, grabbed his goblet of wine, and rose from his chair.

Riorden and Fletcher joined him as they made their way to stand by the hearth with their own mug of ale in hand to quench their thirst.

"So will you marry the youngest maids off?" Fletcher asked quietly, taking a long pull of his brew.

"Perchance you might take a fancy to one of them and take her to wife yourself," Riorden added.

"You know that is not my intent with the younger girls, so why do you even bring up such a notion?" Dristan growled, looking at his captain with anger.

"Mayhap he thought you changed your mind," Fletcher suggested. "'Tis rumored no man will have the oldest, she is such a shrew!"

"As if I had a choice in the command I have been given." Dristan dragged his fingers through his hair, showing his frustration. "This time, the price is almost too high for the taking of this keep."

"I daresay you could tell the king nay," Riorden proposed.

"You must believe you are speaking to some other fool if you think I would just sit back and watch whilst I forfeit everything I have worked for and have it be stripped from me. I do not relish having to justify my actions to an angry king in order to keep what I have gained from the strength of my arm and sword!"

"Lands, wealth, and title are not everything, Dristan," Fletcher said lightly.

"Aye, 'tis not, but I do not wish to have my head sitting on yonder pike outside these gates either! I have cheated death one too many times to have my head lopped off because of King Henry's whim."

Riorden took a sip of ale. "Surely 'twould not come to that, *mon ami*. Are you not in good standing with our king?"

"Aye, today I am such...who knows what the morrow shall bring," he declared gruffly, hoping any further conversation regarding his decisions was closed. He watched the hall and his men with the eye of an eagle and thought mayhap he had been too lenient with them, that they indulged in drink too readily. *A little time in the lists will change that*, he thought smugly to himself.

A commotion on the stairway brought his attention to the group following Aiden as they made their way to Dristan's side. "*Mon dieu*, I am saddled with mere babes," he whispered in despair to Riorden.

"They hardly look related, they are so unalike," Riorden said just as faintly.

The family came to stand afore Dristan, and with a slight word from Aiden, they knelt together, giving him their pledge of fealty. One by one, they rose as they were commanded whilst Dristan took his time inspecting each of the children. He watched as the young woman with dark hair gazed at him as if he were a tasty meal about to be devoured. He had seen such a look afore on many a maid and knew this girl to be trouble. He dismissed her with a stern look whilst she lowered her head, even though she continued to do her own inspection of her new lord through lowered lashes.

The youngest boy could barely stand, he trembled so in fear. Perchance 'twas best if he started with him.

"So, young Patrick, you, too, have remained with your laird it seems. He did not wish to see you fostered at another keep and learn the duties of page?" he questioned with a scowl.

Patrick quaked in fear at the sound of his lord's voice and, most likely, had wild thoughts of being roasted alive by a fire breathing dragon running fiercely through his mind. He reached for his older sibling's hand. Instead of finding it, Dristan watched as Aiden gave the boy a gentle nudge, forcing Patrick to take one step forward closer to his new lord. "Na-Nay, my lord," was all he managed to yelp.

Dristan crossed his arms on his massive chest and looked down upon the boy. "Perchance he did not feel you capable of the job, do you think?" He saw the stubborn Scottish pride rise up in Patrick's small body and a spark light his eyes at Dristan's words.

"Nay, my lord; I could do it and do it well if but shown how!" he replied, with a confidence he probably only half felt.

"Hmmm...I am not so sure," Dristan replied as he stroked his chin, giving it further thought.

Dristan could only imagine what was going through the young boy's head, as Patrick stared at him with frightened eyes, assessing his liege's height. He hid a smile when the lad gave a mighty gulp, attempting to shake off the panic surely about to set in. But he had to give the boy some credit as he watched the boy's chin raise, as though he did not wish his recently deceased sire to think poorly of him.

"You could teach me," Patrick announced, and clapped his hands over his mouth in sudden alarm. 'Twas perfectly clear even the boy had not meant to have such words escape his lips.

Startled gasps of surprise came from his sisters and those other souls standing nearby. It echoed in the once quiet hall. Dougal even went so far as to suggest mayhap a curse had unknowingly been placed upon Patrick to so foolishly suggest such a thing to the Devil's Dragon. Devon frantically whispered he had heard from one of the passing serfs just this morn that the dragon afore them ate little boys to break his fast and young Patrick was doomed!

Dristan dismissed the gossip running rampant in his hall and held up his hand to silence those around them. His gaze leveled on the boy, who stood trembling afore him. "'Tis possible I suppose, and has merit. I have not taken a page in some time, however. 'Tis a big responsibility," he pondered. "What think you, Riorden? Mayhap the lad will serve me well?"

Riorden reached down and firmly took the boys chin as though to examine him further. "Well my lord, he will fit in with the rest of your men with his dark hair and eyes...we could not take him otherwise now could we?"

Dristan placed his hands behind his back and rocked back on his heels. "'Tis true, Riorden, and a trait required of any man who would ride with me. Hmmm," he mused with a scowl, as if deliberating the worth of the issue. He slapped his hand on his thigh with his decision. "'Tis done then...I will take you since you yourself made such a convincing proposition. Your training begins now, Patrick. Do not fail me!"

"Aye, my lord," came the weak reply as the lad stepped back next to his sisters.

Dristan took in the rest of the group, who stood there with nothing but shock showing on their faces. He looked down, feeling the youngest daughter's gaze come to rest upon him. "You are Lynet?" he asked gruffly.

"Aye, my lord," she replied quietly but with a smile upon her youthful face. "Do you have some task that I could also perform to aid our home?"

Dristan folded his arms again upon his chest and noticed how the girl seemed eager to also be assigned some small service to her new lord. "Perchance some mending. Can you sew a straight seam, Lady Lynet?"

"Aye, my lord, I can."

"Then mayhap you could assist with mending some of my soldiers clothing and blankets. That could keep you busy for some time, and would be most useful especially with winter upon us soon."

"I will see to it, my liege," Lynet replied most satisfied, knowing she, too, could serve her new lord to his liking.

He nodded his head and placed his arms behind his back. "The morrow brings us a new beginning," he addressed not only the family but the serfs also gathered in the Great Hall. "Obey me, and you will find me agreeable to most things. Do not mistake any kindness I may show for weakness, as I will punish those who go against my wishes and commands. A messenger will be sent to Edinburgh to fetch the eldest daughter home where she belongs. 'Til then you, Sabina, as the next female descendant, will serve as chatelaine of the keep 'til your sister's return. I expect the place to be kept in order enough to please our king if he deems to visit such a remote lowly place as this. A warm meal to fill the stomachs of my hungry men should also be at the ready. Do you feel capable of such a duty as this?" he asked, with authority.

Sabina looked him full in the eye and gave him her most seductive smile. She was obviously more than pleased with her new role. "Aye, my Lord Dristan. I have been well trained," she answered, and her voice, as she spoke his name, sounded like that of a caress.

Dristan ignored the implied invitation and continued to speak to the family afore him. "Your meals will now be taken in the Great Hall. If you feel you cannot break bread with me, then you can go hungry, as I will not cater to your whims of dining alone."

He turned his full attention to the oldest lad, who hovered in the shadows. A frown marred his features whilst he looked at the boy. *Merde*! 'Twas it just his imagination, or did the lad seemingly look more womanly with each glance he took? Perchance 'twas the lighting of the hall or he was just overly tired. Aiden's training could not begin soon enough, he decided.

"Follow me," he ordered to all within his hearing. He grabbed a torch from a wall sconce and strode from the hall into the cool evening night.

Clansmen and serfs alike walked outside not knowing what was to come as they followed their lord to the outer bailey. Villagers had also been summoned and had already gathered. Smoking torches had been lit and illuminated the area with a golden flickering glow. They watched as several of their lord's guardsmen stood in a long line and, as they parted, they saw Hugh of Harlow stretched out on a pole with back bared. 'Twas then they knew what they would witness this night.

Dristan motioned for Aiden to step forward to stand beside him whilst he handed a coiled whip to one of his men. The rope was released with a mighty snap that cracked into the evening air, causing those within its hearing to cringe and flinch. They stared in horror at the rope made of many lengths of braided leather, each holding a ball of metal tied to its end. 'Twould ensure that hideous pain would be inflicted on one's back. Only a fool would not learn his lesson after even one taste of such a lash landed upon one's flesh.

Dristan watched the boy's face turn ashen whilst his man readied his arm, awaiting his command. "Someday, you, too, shall have to issue the settling of scores so all under your care are treated fairly," he whispered for the boy's ears alone.

"Stand forth and witness the punishment of this man and understand justice will be swift," he bellowed loudly. "Know whether you are English or Scot, in the eyes of my laws I set forth, all will be dealt with equally. I expect loyalty of my subjects as I claim these lands in the name of King Henry II. You are now subject to the King of England. As you serve me, remember you are serving him, as well."

Dristan took a moment to rest his eyes upon his people to ensure his meaning was clear to all. "Hugh of Harlow, I find you guilty of one of many transgressions; speaking on my behalf without my leave, not following directives in the taking of this keep, and striking one of my vassal's with no right, to name but a few," he declared, so all could hear his words. "A score of lashes."

The Devil's Dragon of Blackmore gave a brief motion with his hand and the whip unleashed with the first blow. Hugh remained tight lipped, yet fury at this public display blazed in his angry eyes. As the leather struck Hugh's flesh for the fifth time, he finally gave way to the agony and began to scream in a torment that echoed eerily into the cool night.

When the last stroke had been laid, Kenna was allowed to see to the man's back. For Hugh, it made no difference by that time what the count had been. Long afore the executioner's whip had made the halfway point in its lashing of his flesh, Hugh had succumbed to the torturous pain being inflicted on his bleeding, raw skin. Beyond caring, he had slipped mercifully into a total state of unconsciousness where he felt the sting no more. The same 'twould not be said with the rising of the sun the next morn.

SEVEN

D RISTAN JERKED AWAKE INSTINCTIVELY reaching for his sword in reflex from years of living on edge. He was prepared to meet any unknown danger afore him even subconsciously, thus the soft feather mattress of the bed beneath him surely gave him pause. He had not felt such comfort in quite some time. His gaze searched the grand chamber he found himself in and relaxed once he realized where he slept and for how long. Since the fire within the hearth had long since died down to but a few red glowing embers, he presumed he had slumbered several hours.

Laying his sword aside, he rose naked from beneath the warm coverings still unsure of what had caused him to rouse at such an early hour. Kneeling afore the hearth, he took bits of dry kindling and placed it on the small embers of coal. It took but a few breaths to have the wood ignite with a crackle, and Dristan at last was able to put several logs upon the flames to take the chill from the room.

'Twas then he heard the faintest of sounds. He stopped to listen to the distant and bewildering melody of bagpipes playing somewhere outside the keep. Going to the shutters, he opened them and realized 'twas later than he thought. As his eyes strained to see in the early morning gloom, he began to ponder if the sun ever dared to show itself this far north. 'Twould be a most welcome change.

He inhaled deeply of the fresh salty sea air, even as his eyes searched the strand below and beyond the castle walls for the source of the tune coming to his ears. As if he conjured the sun out himself from the bleakness of the skies above, the clouds parted and rays of sunlight shone upon the lone figure of a woman surrounded in the morning mist. He blinked his eyes to ensure she was in truth really afore his vision and not just some mythical faerie he had imagined since the scene appeared so enchanted and surreal.

Dristan's breath caught at the sight of this solitary lady, staring off at the ocean waves. Although her back was to him, he took note of the length of her long, flowing red hair, reflecting coppery hues from the sunlight shining down upon her. The breeze caught and tangled her wild and riotous curls in a tantalizing dance about her unknown face, enticing him further.

Desire coursed through Dristan's veins with a need so compelling his only thought was how he wanted to pull the woman to him and bury his hands in those disheveled tresses. Her features were a complete mystery to him and yet even from the distance separating them, he felt he would recognize her anywhere. His hands began to tingle with the thought of them encircling her narrow waist. The color of her windswept gown appeared to be of a lavender bluish hue. It flowed about her body, adding to the spell wrapping itself around him. He felt himself harden whilst he envisioned the woman writhing beneath him in his bed.

The sounds of the mournful melody ended abruptly, and he watched whilst the woman sharply turned her head, looking up towards the castle. With the last notes of music echoing on the wind, the sun went back into its place of hiding. He watched in dismay as the mist began to thicken and all but swallowed up the lady upon the sand within the breath of a heartbeat. If he had not witnessed for himself what had been but moments ago afore his eyes, he would have thought he had dreamed the whole illusion and still lay abed, slumbering.

He shook his head, giving a snort of disgust at where his fanciful thoughts had taken him and wondered where such undisciplined feelings had come from. Mayhap he would have speech with Kenna after he had broken his fast. Dristan surmised a curse had been cast upon him and his healer must surely be about some mischief with a potion or two. He would be more careful henceforth of what mayhap was put into his wine.

Amiria carefully slid open the door to the hidden compartment and peered into the passageway to ensure the way was clear. Since no sound could be heard and no person seen, she squeezed herself through the opening and quietly closed the door. She quickly made her way along the flooring with soft footfalls. Surprisingly, her steps made little sound as she rushed towards her chamber.

She looked to and fro to safeguard her deception whilst she hurried down the corridor, giving only the briefest pause afore sadness overtook her when she scurried past the oak portal leading to her parent's old chamber. 'Twas somewhat difficult having the knowledge of whom no longer resided within. With haste, she quickened her step as her own chamber door loomed afore her then she silently slipped within. She leaned her forehead upon the closed door, slid the bolt home to ensure her privacy and let her breath leave her body with a heavy sigh. She had made it!

Turning, she let out a gasp of fright. Sabina yanked a fistful of her hair and pulled her into the center of the room.

"Have you lost your wits?" Sabina hissed at her sibling. Her eyes took in her clothing with disgust. "What game do you play now that you must put us all in peril with your latest ploy?"

Amiria lifted her head and stared her younger sister in the eye. "I owe you no explanation nor do I put us in danger. I will dress as I wish since 'twas by my arm and sword that at least kept us safe but a few weeks longer. You have no right to question me and my motives further!"

"Ha! You started this ploy to dress as our brother and now you put on your finest gown to roam where you will. How come you think this does not put us in danger Amiria?"

"I was discreet," she stated simply.

Sabina looked at her sister coldly. "Mayhap you play another game...one of a more womanly nature," she prompted.

"What do you mean?"

Sabina strode about the room and went to sit by the hearth, combing her fingers through her long brown locks with a dreamy expression on her visage. "He is most handsome is he not?"

"Who is this you speak of now?" Amiria questioned irritably.

"Why, our Lord Dristan, of course," Sabina smiled calculatingly. "I could have him if I so willed it, and have seen the desire in his eyes when he gazes upon me."

Time seemed to stand still. Amiria looked upon her sister, who now had this far off look in her eyes. "Surely you jest, Sabina?"

"Jest? Why no, Amiria, I do not jest and will do all I can to please our new liege lord," she taunted. "Mayhap I will even take him to my bed."

Amiria gasped. "And you dare to ask me if I have lost my wits? In truth you must be mad to suggest such a thing and such vile talk will have our beloved parents turning in their graves," she chided, making the sign of the cross.

Sabina tossed her hair with a flip of her hand. "I but speak the truth...I could have him if I choose to pursue the matter. Besides...what better way for me to remain the lady of this hall?"

"Sleeping with our lord will not make you lady of this keep, Sabina, but only his whore," Amiria said solemnly.

"I will be no whore, but his wife, if I but have my way," she reflected aloud, and continued with a dreamy expression on her usually angry face. "Oh, to have one such as he as a lover. Truly, he would know how to please a woman such as me."

Amiria looked at her sister as if seeing her for the first time. "I am horrified you would speak so sister and know you not at all. Perchance 'tis best mother is long since in her grave. With speech such as this, she surely would have taken you by force if necessary to Habersham Abbey and leave you with the good sisters to repent your evil talk and ways. Mark my words, Sabina, no good shall come if you pursue this course rattling around in your head," Amiria scolded.

"Bah! You are jealous I will call that handsome man my own one day."

"Mayhap you should get yourself to yonder chapel now to spend some time upon your knees and repent your wicked thoughts instead of thinking of our lord in such a manner."

Sabina only looked upon her elder sister with malice shining in her eyes. "I have better things to do than have my knees ache from hours kneeling upon the hard floor," she sneered, rising from the stool and heading towards the door. "I must see to the meal to break my lords fast. Since you have always enjoyed wearing men's garments, I suggest you get into them without haste and once more look the boy, Amiria. After all...you play the part so very well."

Amiria watched her sister leave the room, a smug smile still shining on her face. She fondly gazed down at her dress and smoothed the fabric beneath her trembling fingers. She rarely wore this gown, afraid of ruining the linen. A moment of sorrow overtook her as she remembered when her mother had chosen the cloth when a merchant had come to show his goods to the lady of the keep. Her mother had said the lavender color would bring out the violet in her daughter's eyes. Amiria and Lynet had lovingly sewed the garment many months after their mother's death and the gown had become one of her favorites.

The truth of Sabina's words came back to haunt Amiria, and, with a heavy sigh, she began the process of carefully taking off her gown and donning hose and tunic once more. Perchance soon she would be able to put the guise of a boy behind her and become the lovely young woman she was in truth supposed to be. As she took some dirt she had hidden away, grimacing as she rubbed it upon her face, she prayed with all her heart her charade would end soon, else she forget how to act the role of a lady forevermore.

EIGHT

DRISTAN SAT AT THE HIGH TABLE, observing not only his men but also the MacLaren clansmen as they finished breaking their fast. Their bellies full, they sat next to each other within the Great Hall, content and lazy although still wary of one another. 'Twas time he took his new men into the lists and showed them a true master with the sword and shield. Mayhap they would learn a thing or two that would serve them well in future times of battle.

His brow furrowed into a frown as he watched Sabina make her way amongst the men. When she looked up to the high table where he sat and noticed his gaze upon her, she cast a seductive smile his way and began striding in his direction. *'Twas more of a stalk*, he fumed, uninterested in the proposal her look suggested.

She finally came to stand behind him and a cold chill ran up his spine as she began caressing the back of his neck beneath his hair. She leaned over him to whisper into his ear. If not for his armor he was certain he would have felt her breasts against his back.

"Did the meal please you, my lord?" she said huskily.

"Aye," he declared briskly, shrugging off her advances and rising from the table.

"Perchance there is aught else that I may do to satisfy thee?" She came to stand afore him, almost begging him to take her.

"Nay! See to the keep. 'Twill be enough!" His tone was sharp and anyone with matter between their ears would have concluded the issue was at an end. Such was not the case with the girl afore him as he removed her hand from his breastplate.

"Mayhap, another time then," she murmured, keeping an open invitation in her voice.

"I think not," he exclaimed, dismissing her from his mind and thus did not see her look of disappointment and anger. "Patrick...get thee to the stables and see to Thor's needs this morn. You men," he called, "to the lists in full armor...we train this day!"

Dristan heard his men groan at what they knew would be a most strenuous day of training.

Only one dared voice his thoughts, since he had traveled with Dristan for many a year. "Should we not wait 'til the rain ceases, my lord?" Drake called from his comfortable spot by the roaring fire, obviously hoping Dristan would change his mind.

"War does not wait for the weather, nor shall we. For your cheek, you shall go first this morn, Sir Drake. Now everyone move, else I must think you wish to train long into the midnight hour!" he yelled, and watched the chaos ensue when they all scrambled out of their chairs to do his bidding. They made for the door swiftly as if their feet were aflame, much to Dristan's amusement.

Satisfied with their haste to be about their training, Dristan thought perchance this was a sure sign of hope for the new guardsmen after all. He noticed one lone knight sitting at one of the lower tables. As the man at last rose from his now finished meal, Dristan scowled at his blatant disobedience.

Ian hesitantly made his way towards Dristan, giving a slight bow.

Dristan scowled that the man had the nerve to still be within the keep walls.

"My lord," Ian began, "a moment of your time, if I may?"

"We have business outside. Do you think 'tis beneath you to train with your lord and his men? Mayhap, you feel there is naught I may teach you for those who you will protect?"

"Nay my liege...I would not presume such."

"So...as captain of Aiden's guard, what do you wish to have speech about that cannot wait?" Dristan said, already irritated to be delayed.

"I have but overheard your plan to make Aiden your squire," Ian began cautiously. "Is this true?"

"You dare to now question my motives regarding the boy?" Dristan could not believe the gall of the man afore him. "You do indeed presume too much, sir."

"Your pardon, my lord. 'Twas not my intent," Ian spoke in exasperation. "I have guarded the twins for so long 'tis become a habit of mine, along with concern for their welfare."

"They are no longer yours to worry about, as they are now my wards and my responsibility. 'Twill be I to decide who will be part of their guard when I know those who will protect them are capable of the task," Dristan said sternly. He could see the man had more on his mind than just Dristan acquiring Aiden as a squire. "I can see by your expression you have more to say, regarding this pair of siblings. Come...speak your mind, Ian, since I can tell of your sincerity as to their safety."

Ian ran a hand through his hair afore he chose his words. "All I ask, my lord, is you take into consideration that, for the most part, the pair are innocent children and have been greatly spoiled by their sire. They have been sheltered from the evils of this world and truly only know of this keep and their way of life. The girl, Amiria, had her father wrapped around her finger and could do no wrong in his eyes. Laird MacLaren cherished the twins above the others, although he loved all his children as best he could. I ask that you have patience, my Lord Dristan, when dealing with them."

Dristan looked upon Aiden's captain and saw the truth in his words reflected in his eyes. "You have given me much to think on, Ian, and I have heard your words. I am, however, disappointed young Aiden chose not to heed my words and join the company for meals."

"I am sure he will just need some time to readjust to your ways, my liege."

Dristan pondered that for but a moment and nodded his head. "We shall see. In the meantime, word will be sent up for Aiden to join us in the lists to begin his training, although I am sure he will regret not being allowed to break his fast when his belly begins to growl in protest," he said. "But come...let us be about the field and see what you are made of. Mayhap you could show me how to wield that claymore strapped upon your back. 'Tis a most fearsome weapon of choice you Scots prefer."

"As you will, my lord," Ian returned, with a bow.

Dristan gave a slight chuckle and a hard slap upon Ian's back that would have felled a less powerfully built man. He could tell Ian was taken off guard by his lord's unexpected moment of merriment. Dristan wondered what the day would yet come to hold as they made their way out into the rain drenched lists.

Whereas the garrison hall had but moments afore been filled with knights, it took but a few words from Riorden to clear the hall of all the men who had been lounging about in the slightly smoky room. Apparently, the guards did not want to be the last ones to get themselves to the lists and feel the wrath of the Devil's Dragon.

There was another besides the serfs, however, who lingered within the garrison hall, although 'twas most unusual to find a woman within its walls. Near the hearth where the light was better, Kenna rose and stretched as she looked down upon the man, who now rested upon a pallet that had been provided for him. He would never have made it up the stairs to the upper floors on his own.

It feels good to at last stand, she thought to herself, after having been bent over for what had seemed like hours. It had been a long process of removing the caked on dressing and applying new ones to Hugh's ravaged back. The man had awoken during the cleansing of his wounds and had screamed as if the flames from hell were scorching his flesh. Given the state of the man's hide, perchance that assumption was not too far from the truth.

Taking her satchel of herbs and ointments from the serf who was left to attend Hugh, she bent down one last time and felt the man's forehead. 'Twas only slightly warm, so for the moment no fever yet raged within his body.

"Watch over him closely and fetch me if you notice he begins to have a fever or take a chill," she ordered the servant, and confirmed his consent before leaving the knights' hall.

Kenna wrapped her cloak about her head to keep off the rain as best she could. 'Twas a difficult task as the water seemingly came down in great sheets. Despite the downpour, she heard undeterred men already about their training. Change was in the air for those who dwelled here, she reflected to herself. Only time would tell how all would cope with its coming.

Under the cover of her garment, she watched Lord Dristan and Ian emerge from the keep and noticed their ease in conversation as they made their way to join the other men in the lists. She smiled to herself with the knowledge that after much turmoil these two would someday become close friends. They would have a rough road ahead of them, however, to get to that point, if they but survived the journey.

Kenna was so deeply into her thoughts, she was inattentive to where she put her feet as she tried to make her way to her hut, residing inside the inner bailey. She stumbled and fell into mud, watched in dismay as her satchel spilled about her, and some of her precious herbs landed in murky puddles of water. She tried to rise to her feet only to find that her cloak had become entangled in her legs, causing her to once more fall to the ground with a mighty splash.

Distracted by the wetness beginning to chill her to the bone, she did not hear the distinct sound of armor as it clanked in time to someone rushing to her side. 'Twas not 'til a hand appeared through the tresses of her drenched black hair, offering assistance, that she knew her life was about to take a different direction than the one she had planned.

"Let me help you, Mistress Kenna," the voice reached her ears in a soothing caress.

She took the proffered limb and felt a shiver go through her entire body as she rose. She swayed unknowingly into the knights arms as her eyes closed and a vision flashed afore her.

She had not even as yet glimpsed the man's face and yet she could plainly see the two of them together like a memory playing in her mind as they were laughing, walking along the strand, and sharing an intimate moment she had never dared afore with another. Just as quickly as this vision came to her, another darker one followed closely, and her eyes opened quickly, searching the man's face. She smiled at him and although he had not offered it to her, she knew his name.

"My thanks, Sir Geoffrey," she whispered in awe, whilst staring into his dark green eyes.

He looked at her in puzzlement but also delight, whilst he held her in his arms. "Are you hurt, mistress?" Geoffrey inquired courteously.

"I am much better than it appears my herbs are, to be sure," she answered, with a light laugh.

"I fear they cannot be salvaged, but I am more concerned with your welfare," he said kindly, picking up her sack and handing it to her. "May I escort you somewhere to see you safe?"

Kenna dared much, as she patted his arm with familiarity. "I have traveled this path many a time, Sir Knight, and done so without fear for my person. 'Tis sure I am that you have more important things to do than to see the keep's healer to her humble hut."

"Nothing would give me more pleasure than to see you safely home."

Kenna smiled at his simple request, as the ending of her vision but moments ago briefly flashed afore her eyes yet again. She grabbed his arm and spoke more sternly than she intended. "You must guard your master well, Sir Geoffrey, for 'tis his safety that I stand in fear of."

"Have you not heard, the Devil's Dragon of Blackmore is invincible," he jested, "and, of course, so are his men?"

She let go of his arm, not amused by his cavalier jest of her beliefs and hurt that he made fun of her.

"Do not make light of my words, Sir Geoffrey, as you know not of what I have seen."

"I do not mean to cause you sorrow, my lady."

Kenna gave an embarrassed smile at his words. "I fear, Sir Knight, that I am no lady of a Great Hall, but just a lowly born woman trying to heal the hurts of her clan."

"I fear you must humor me...my lady," Geoffrey said honestly. "I can be most persuasive when I must needs be."

Kenna was halted from replying by the shout of their liege across the yard.

"Geoffrey!" Dristan called, through the pelting rain. "Do you dare to dally this day at a woman's side?"

"Nay, my lord!" he replied over his shoulder, and gave her a sheepish smile.

Kenna continued to stare at him most strangely, as her heart did a tiny flip when his eyes began to twinkle. As he lingered at her side, she quickly came to realize 'twas not an unpleasant feeling when it appeared he showed an interest in her.

"I must leave," he said simply, although 'twas clear he did not wish to depart. He took her cool hand and kissed her fingertips.

A soft sigh escaped her lips.

"Duty to your liege calls," Kenna replied warmly. "I beg thee please heed my words I have spoken this day, regarding our Lord Dristan."

"I shall always guard my lord's back Mistress Kenna—"

"Call me Kenna," she all but whispered to him, offering him leave to use her given name.

"Kenna...'tis a lovely name. I but wish..."

"Geoffrey!" Dristan bellowed with more urgency, for apparently, he would tolerate no further dalliance with the fairer sex this day.

Kenna gave Geoffrey a small understanding smile, which he returned then bowed over her hand and reluctantly released her, before he hurried to join the men in their training. She turned and quickly made her way through the rain to her home. As she reached the doorway, she turned just once more to stare through the barbican gate, knowing her knight had but moments afore passed under its portcullis. For the second time that day, she pondered the thought about change in the air, and mayhap for her, 'twould be most welcoming. She opened the door to her dwelling and entered its warmth with a most endearing smile.

NINE

THE WEEKS THAT FOLLOWED BECAME routine for those under the care of Dristan of Blackmore. Day in and day out,
the Devil's Dragon drilled his men in the lists with a ruthless-
ness and expertise that had been learned from being in mortal
danger and battle. There was no mercy given and no man asked
for it in fear of retaliation for their laziness. From sun up to sun
down, the ring of steel resounding against steel echoed throughout the castle walls as all trained to impress their liege lord.
Some excelled at the tasks they were given; others would require a bit more time with a broad sword in their hands to meet
Dristan's high standards of defense. By the time the evening
meal was finished, the men retired exhausted to the garrison
hall to rest their weary bodies 'til the ordeal began all over
again the next day. Even a willing wench to ease their comfort
was far from their minds.

For one, the training was the most tiring task that had ever
been undertaken in her young life. Amiria's entire body ached
as she longed to put aside her armor and sword and return to

being a lady. That, of course, was also the most pressing reason of the stress placed upon her weary shoulders. 'Twas only a matter of time afore the runner returned from Edinburgh and, with his return, her ruse would fall down upon her most likely in the harshest manner. She gave a shudder, for she did not relish spending time in the castle's ghastly pit.

"Aiden!" Dristan bellowed quickly, drawing her attention back to the present.

She watched in horror as Dristan checked the swing of his blade, having nearly taken off her arm. Her foolish negligence for the task at hand had almost cost her dearly.

"What ails you, boy?" he yelled, continuing his tirade. "Do you mayhap not wish to keep your limbs upon your body? Or mayhap you would like to lose your head instead? Stop your daydreaming, lad, and be about your training."

"I am sorry, my lord," Amiria apologized, lowering her voice to hopefully sound as a lad. She was finding playing the boy was becoming more difficult with each passing hour, especially being under the close scrutiny of her liege lord.

"I care not to hear your pitiful apologies, you fool! I demand the best, hence you shall give me your best, if I have to keep you here all night," Dristan snarled loudly. "Now proceed again and show me what I have been trying to instill in your thick skull for the past hour!"

Amiria lifted her sword and tried to not over think her movements. Each time her sword met Dristan's, she felt as if the force of their meeting vibrated throughout her whole body with jar wrenching results. She did not know how much more she could take.

"*Merde!*" Dristan roared in complete frustration, as he once more dropped his sword at his side and took off his helmet in anger. "You are about as useless as an old woman, Aiden.

Riorden! Ian! Come show this insolent pup how 'tis supposed to be done!"

Dristan shoved the back of her armor. Stumbling from his force, she made her way with him to the side of the lists. When they reached their destination, Amiria made as if to sit on the lone stone bench located against the wall. 'Twas a most welcoming site, if she ever saw one. Hearing the clearing of Dristan's throat, she raised her eyes and through the slits of her helmet, she noticed his brow rise as if daring her to finish her movements. Realizing she had no choice in the matter, she came to stand next to her liege.

"Now watch closely and let us see if you can learn anything this day!" Dristan instructed, apparently satisfied with her decision to remain standing.

At his request, Amiria turned her attention to the two men, who began to fight sword to sword. She had to admit 'twas an impressive sight, and she was most thankful Ian held his own against such a seasoned warrior as the Devil's Dragon's captain appeared to be. She watched in fascination whilst Ian swung his claymore time and again, performing the exact move Dristan had tried to encourage in her, whilst Riorden countered with the same precision. The two men's expertise far outweighed Amiria's own feeble attempts at such a skill, and she knew she in no way would ever be half their equal.

The sun chose that precise moment to make an appearance from above the cloudy skies and its rays reflected off Dristan's armor, causing Amiria to squint through the visor of the face plate of her helmet. As she watched him and how the sun reflected off his shiny crop of dark black hair, her breath caught and she could understand Sabina's infatuation with the man's good looks. Amiria observed his chiseled features; the square jaw hidden beneath a well-trimmed beard and mustache, the steel grey of his eyes rivaling the color of his blade, and a nose with the slightest crook, giving the hint it had been broken at some time in his life. Somehow it just made him look more attractive in a rugged sort of way.

He was a warrior in every sense of the word, standing tall and proud as he watched his men perform to his satisfaction with a gleam in his eye. His lips were well formed and although they usually showed a grimace, they now gave way to a smile, showing the white of his teeth when his grin increased in pleasure at the men's performance. His whole continence changed afore her eyes, making him appear as though several years younger than the age of a score and eight she guessed him to be.

His armor was molded to his skin and showed the ripples of his stomach muscles like a Roman gladiator's, and she had the notion that beneath the metal frame his form would be just as true. His body was all powerful, exuding pure vigorous physical strength from years of training and fighting to stay alive. Amiria could only admire his dedication to exercising himself, his guards, and the male members of the MacLaren clan.

As she continued reflecting on the man who stood beside her, she came to the shocking realization she had watched him most intently for these past many weeks. When the hatred and loathing she had first felt for Lord Dristan, relating to the death of her father and clansmen, had subsided, she could not say. He trained relentlessly; there could be no doubt of that, she mused. However, she had also been privy to times when he listened to the village people who came afore their lord to pass judgment on matters of dispute amongst themselves. She saw his anger rise many a time, but she also concluded he was fair in dealing with all under his protection. There could be no question in anyone's mind he guarded well all within his care.

Amiria, had begun to perform duties of squire, although Dristan seemed, for the most part, more concerned with furthering her training with a sword than teaching her other knightly responsibilities. She had given a sigh of relief more times than she could count and was thankful she had not been ordered to perform more menial tasks, bringing her into closer contact to Dristan within his chamber. She had been asked to join him, in what was now his solar, whilst he taught Patrick his letters several times. She had wisely declined, stating she had other matters to attend to. 'Twas better to keep herself, at a distance or in the shadows, than to have her true gender be found out when not in her armor.

Perchance, 'twas just such a night, whilst Dristan sat afore the hearth in the Great Hall, that had begun her heart's downfall. She had been hovering in the shadows of the stairway and watched as the flames of the fire brought out the richness of his hair. He had been idly strumming the strings on his lute when he had begun to sing an all too familiar tune. The deep rich vibrato of his voice called to her soul and had sent her heart beating rapidly in a sorrowful reminder that she was indeed a woman dressed as a boy. As she still pondered that evening, her cheeks flamed beneath her helmet and where her thoughts had taken her.

The dark green of his tunic had been slightly open at the neck, and she had glimpsed his furred chest whilst watching the muscles of his arms as they hugged the instrument to his chest. She could almost imagine the feel of his warm calloused hands touching her instead of the lute. Even from her hiding place, she wanted to go closer to him in order to see the blue specks, usually hidden in the grey of his eyes, sparkle from the candlelight of the room.

Devilishly handsome could only be her description of him. For all his reputation of fierceness and usual gruff exterior, she observed a softer side to his disposition. He may not have shown this side often, but 'twas there all the same, if one cared to take notice.

The sound of clanging steel ringing in her ears brought her out of her reminiscences with a jolt. Amiria shook her head, as if to clear the memories and the thought that madness must surely have overtaken her to have such imaginings coursing through her head. Better to concentrate on pleasing her lord with her sword arm than thinking on him in a womanly way. She had already witnessed Sabina's growing infatuation of Dristan with her constant fawning over the man. 'Twas wiser to exceed acting the boy and be praised for her masculine deeds than to receive the rejection her lord was wont to give her feminine sister. At least in this way, her woman's heart would be safe from the hurt and sorrow that surely plagued Sabina, for 'twas clear, Lord Dristan had no use for her sister other than the running of the keep.

The knight of her recent musings clamped a strong hand down upon her armor, causing the metal to dig into her shoulder. 'Twas perchance in her favor Dristan could not see her grimace of pain else he sentence her to additional hours in the lists for her unmanly show of soreness. Feeling another slight nudge in the direction of the two captains, who now took their ease, she faltered briefly and was able to regain her feet afore she shamed herself by falling into the dirt.

Her moment of rest at an end, she heard Dristan give out the call for Ian to take up sword against her. She hid her heavy sigh and took up her stance, praying she would not humiliate herself by falling on her exhausted sorry arse.

Dristan made a motion with his hand and Riorden joined him against the wall to observe the pair, who now raised their swords to begin the lesson. To his mind, there was no improvement to the boy's strokes than afore his brief rest.

"I am not pleased with the lad's progress," Dristan remarked gruffly after they observed the two for a time. "What think you, Riorden?"

Riorden clasped his hands behind his back whilst Dristan folded his arms upon his chest. "Look there...did you see it?" he questioned his lord. "Ian does the boy no favor by holding back. 'Tis not obviously done, but 'tis done all the same. In time of war, 'twill see the boy killed by a greater swordsman."

"Aye! I have noticed it, as well. Having just finished watching the two of you hack away at each other, 'tis plain to see Ian does not put in the same effort with the boy."

"You'd best stop them now, my lord, afore the lad is injured. He's just about spent I think."

Dristan nodded in agreement, much to his disappointment in the young man's showing. Although for the most part he did well with his sword, he did not feel that Aiden would ever become a master with his weapon.

"Aiden," he yelled across the lists, "'tis enough for the day! Come, men...let us sup!"

A cheer arose from the guardsmen, who sheathed their swords and slapped one another upon their backs in comradeship. All were ready for a respite from the drilling required of them, and the men made quite a stir as they made their way off the list and headed towards the Great Hall. A good day's training deserved a good evening's meal with a draught or two of strong ale to quench their thirst. All were ready to indulge in a fine meal. 'Twas something to at last look forward to 'til their misery began again with the dawning of the new day.

TEN

THE GREAT HALL WAS SWARMING to capacity with men and their overly loud conversations as the evening meal was brought into the room. Serfs scurried to bring heavily laden trenchers of steaming roasted boar, fowl, and venison to the tables. The platters were barely set down afore greedy hands began to tear at the meat as the knights filled their hungry bellies.

Serving maids made their way amongst several of the tables, pouring ale or mead into tankards waved in their direction to be filled. The lusty laughter of the whores who had accompanied the conquering army also filled the air, as they showed their wares with low bodices and a promise in their eyes if a man had but the coin to make it worth their while. 'Twas apparent some of the guards were in the mood to partake of what the wenches had to offer and their rowdy banter echoed off the walls of the hall.

'Twas into this mayhem that Amiria finally entered, dragging her feet as she made her way through the now repaired portal of the keep. Confusion seemed to reign as she looked about the crowded room with more people than usually filled its walls. She had become used to seeing the unfamiliar men from Dristan's army outside in the lists, but she had yet to become accustomed to seeing so many within her family's home. She was unclear why many of these knights were not dining at the Garrison Hall, but 'twas none of her business since she wished to make herself as invisible as humanly possible.

Everything seemed disorganized. 'Twas never so whilst under her care after her mother's passing. With a quick critical assessment for Sabina's duties, Amiria noticed how barking dogs roamed freely. Scraps of food were tossed their way or thrown upon the floor for them to fight over. The rushes were filthy, and she was thankful she wore not the woman's slippers she would normally have worn if she could but dress as a woman. They would have been rendered useless with just one pass across the floor.

As she looked about for an empty bench where she might break her fast in peace, she saw Ian stand and beckon to her from across the room where he sat at one of the lower tables near the kitchen entrance. Her guardsmen were there, including her piper, and Ian made a place for her next to him. He filled the trencher for them to share and Amiria quietly began to eat her fill. She glanced occasionally at her men, who ate in relative silence compared to the clamor resounding from other occupants of the room.

Dougal picked up his tankard and took a deep draught of the cool brew. He wiped his mouth with the back of his tunic sleeve and looked at those around him, who still ate. "They stick us here, boot they dinnae realize we get the best o' the meat as it leaves the kitchens," he smirked knowingly. Amiria listened as a chorus of "aye's" agreed with his words.

"Ach, look at 'em," Finlay said shortly. "Willna be long afer they become the mongrels they be actin' like! They growl after the bitches as if they be in heat."

"Hush now," Amiria scolded. "You do not wish to be over-heard by one of them do you?"

"As if they could hear us! They are so boisterous." Thomas sounded annoyed, apparently presuming all the attention of the whores were being given the Englishmen.

Amiria made no comment since he obviously forgot that he was more English than Scot.

"Weel, widnae ye think his men would be better trained in knightly ways?" Killian said, not to be left out. "Or mayhap not, since they are, after all, his men an' come from the depths of hell."

Although he did not speak, Devon crossed himself and his eyes darted to and fro as he assessed the room. He was about to spit over his shoulder when Amiria's silent glare instantly halt-ed his movements. With a satisfied nod at his refrain, she con-tinued on with her meal.

"Mayhap, if I play me pipes 'twill soothe the beasts," Gar-rick offered kindly.

"Doona ken ye be wasting yer time, lad, nor would they ap-preciate the like?" Nevin protested most convincingly. "'Tis clear to all they have the manners o' pigs!"

Amiria glanced at the high table where Dristan sat with his guardsmen and an obedient Patrick, hovering behind his lord. In her opinion, 'twas clear his personal guardsmen were differ-ent than his army.

"They all do not appear so," she said softly, and with one last fleeting look of longing at Dristan, she returned her atten-tion to her meal.

Silence fell once more around their table but, from her pe-
ripheral vision, Amiria saw how Ian continued to stare at her.
She began to fidget beneath the bench whilst his close scrutiny
all but laid bare her emotions of what she had been feeling for
their liege of late. She could feel his censorship for 'twas as if he
knew where her thoughts had taken her. She finally could stand
no more of him inspecting her as if she were some prize to be
won like a bloody coveted trophy! She raised her head to look
him boldly in his face. For the briefest second, his soul seemed
open for her to see what plagued a man who, at times, knew her
better than she knew herself.

He was jealous! There was no doubt in her mind from such a
clear revelation, and she quickly snapped her lips shut to halt
the tart reprimand she had been about to give him. Just as
quickly, he blinked, and the moment was gone, almost as if she
had imagined the whole thing. Mayhap 'twas better this way.
'Twould spare both the hurt that would surely have followed
any words spilled forth from bitterness of what was never to be.

Her perusal of the hall continued, 'til Amiria paused with
food half way between the trencher and her mouth.

"I'll kill her. I swear I shall kill her for her audacity," Amiria
sputtered angrily. She tossed the roasted venison back onto the
trencher and wiped her greasy hands on her tunic sleeves as she
tried to form coherent words to voice her fury of what she was
witnessing.

Her guardsmen, noticing that which had disturbed their mistress, grimaced.

Sabina had at last descended the stairs to grace all with her
presence, although this is not what caused the men at the table
to scowl. What caused their outrage was the gown she wore, for
it did not reveal the poise and charm on her scrawny form as
well as it did its true owner.

Her anger coming to full boil, Amiria rose afore any could stop her. Pushing her way through the crowd, she stormed across the floor 'til she gained her sister's side. She grabbed Sabina's arm and refused to let go.

"How dare you take my things," Amiria hissed in her ear. "Take yourself upstairs, sister, and change afore you regret this!"

Sabina arrogantly raised her head higher, evidently feeling superior to her sister for the first time in her young life.

"I know not what you speak of, *Aiden*," she sneered knowingly as she clearly enunciated their brother's name. "I but dressed in my finest to please my lord. By the look he cast me, I can tell he is well satisfied with my choice of gowns this eve! 'Tis only a matter of time 'til he takes me to wife and then where shall you be in my household? Mayhap I will deem you only fit to be a scullery maid, or, if I feel generous, I will at the very least allow you to attend me as one of *my* ladies," she pondered snidely.

Amiria jerked her sister's arm harder and spun her towards the stairs. "Our Lord Dristan is not that big a fool, so do not test me further this day. You know what this dress means to me. Now go and change afore I rip it off your skinny frame!" She gave her sister a non-too-gentle push.

"Aiden!" Dristan shouted from across the room.

Amiria turned and watched as Dristan shoved his chair back from the table and made his way to her side. She chanced a glance at Sabina and saw her satisfied, I-told-you-so smile. Amiria turned to give her full attention to her lord and made him a low bow.

"Aye, my liege?" she questioned, her head downcast.

"What goes on here?"

"Nothing, my lord," Amiria replied sourly, "'tis just a small squabble between siblings...no harm has been done here."

"Mayhap I have been remiss in your teachings of knightly virtues and have spent too much time training you in the proper use of a sword. Chivalry to all women must always be adhered to, Aiden. You shall never earn your spurs if you treat a lady thusly," he chided.

"Perchance if she were a lady..." she muttered under her breath.

'Twas a mistake he overheard, and she regretted her words for Dristan was sorely vexed. "I heard that. Sister or not, she is still a lady. As such, she deserves your respect. Get yourself to the stable and see to Thor. Mayhap you will begin to think differently with such a menial task of shoveling manure."

"As you will, my lord," Amiria consented. Her mood soured even more, seeing the smug look on her sister's face. She left the hall, making her way to the stable, stomping her feet as she went, and muttering under her breath about the sorry state her life had become.

Dristan saw, with a grave frown, Sabina's look of smugness as she stood afore him. The dress she wore looked vaguely familiar, but that was all that reminded him of the lady in the mist from his memories that early morn hour when he first had glimpsed the unknown woman. She examined his gaze on her and her smile brightened with obvious pleasure as she adjusted the wimple around her head. Perchance 'twas time he took his leave of the meal, afore he was once more assaulted with Sabina's unwelcome company.

With a flick of two fingers, he motioned to Patrick, who came rushing to his side. "See that water is taken to my chamber so I may bathe. I will be up shortly," Dristan commanded, sternly, as he watched Patrick run towards the kitchen to see the task done. He redirected his attention back to examining his hall, and his brows furrowed by what he saw. He did not miss Sabina's smile fade, nor her look of discontent when his attention went elsewhere.

Dristan moved to return to his guardsmen and his meal 'til he felt Sabina place her hand in the crook of his elbow as if to accompany him about the hall. He stopped and looked down into her once more smiling face. 'Twas not a smile that reached her eyes, but one he had seen countless times from the women he came in contact with who only saw his wealth. They all had the same notion and 'twas to either wed with him or to say they spent a night or two entwined within the Devil's Dragon's embrace.

He gently removed Sabina's hand from his arm and gave her a slight nod of his head. "You wished to have speech with me, my lady?" he brusquely inquired.

Sabina batted her eye lashes with a come hither look. Since he had seen it afore many a time, being a knight most favored by his English king, he was immune to its implications and the lady's charms.

"I could not help but notice you were pleased with my attire this evening, my lord. 'Tis true, is it not?"

Dristan gazed down the length of her and saw that the dress, although comely, seemed to hang unattractively on her slight frame. "It but reminded me of another."

Sabina frowned slightly yet gave a cheery confident reply, "But you are pleased all the same?"

Dristan was not sure if that deemed an answer and waited for her to continue her ploy that was so easily read. He could tell Sabina was racking her brain to think of something that would keep him at her side.

"I thought mayhap you and I could share a trencher to fill our fast, my lord."

"I have already eaten," was all he answered as he scanned the hall again, as if seeing it for the first time.

Sabina's once bright smile dulled to one of lackluster and lines of irritation appeared in her features afore they were yet again carefully masked. "Mayhap, there is aught else I can offer to give thee pleasure?"

Dristan looked down upon her and scowled.

"Lady Sabina," he began quietly, so as not to be over heard. "You have spoken these words to me afore and I have said thee nay to what you propose. You are the second daughter of the old lord and as such, you should know I will not avail myself to what you cheaply offer. If I desire my needs to be serviced, then any one of the castle whore's would do. In truth, I will endeavor to find you a wealthy husband as I am sure your sire would have done in my place."

He raised his hand to stop her speech and watched as she clamped her mouth shut whilst fury flashed in her eyes.

"I had asked if you were up to the task of seeing to the keep, but mayhap I have erred, as this is not how I saw this hall prior to your overtaking this duty. Mayhap, 'twas run in an orderly fashion by your sister, Amiria, but 'tis clear you are incapable of doing the same."

"I have been well trained, my lord," Sabina scoffed. 'Twas evident she did not care for the praise he had given her sister.

"Again, you have said these words to me afore, and yet you have not demonstrated such to me."

"I can prove you wrong!"

"Then do so, and I will hear no more talk or suggestions that I would welcome you into my bed. 'Tis clear to you then?" he rasped, and watched her grimly nod her assent. "Good! Then we need have no further speech on the matter. Now fill your fast and then see to this hall once and for all. It offends me."

Dristan left her standing there alone, giving her no further thought. He made his way past his men, who raised their tankards in a silent salute, and took the stairs two at a time up to his chamber.

He may not have felt so at ease if he had but seen the outright leer Sabina threw in his direction. If he had known the young woman's thoughts, he would not sleep a wink this night or any other night hence forth.

For such were the musings of a woman intent on snagging the man of her choosing for her future husband. 'Twas only a matter of time afore Sabina brought the Devil's Dragon of Blackmore to his knees.

ELEVEN

IN THE DIMLY LIT STABLES, Amiria worked hard grooming the massive black stallion of the new lord of Berwyck Castle. Though such a task was to be expected as part of the drudgery to be learned during this period, the normal routine of an everyday squire was not to her liking. Her labors were not that of an ordinary young lad...Nay, 'twas not so. For Amiria only pretended to be a lad who wished to be able to show her true self once and for all. The castle inhabitants who knew her best had so far guarded her secret well and kept it close to their hearts. She was not sure how much longer her ruse would last.

In truth, Amiria toiled only somewhat as she ran the brush through Thor's magnificently splendid, black-as-coal mane. The horse was as massive and glorious as his master, if she pondered the matter hard and long enough. Why she continued to contemplate her lord in such a manner was beyond her comprehension. She knew better, and was continually aware no good could come from her romantic musings.

Amiria gave a long sigh at her predicament, for she could not say how much longer her subterfuge would hold out. If anything, she reflected sadly, 'twould be her young woman's heart that betrayed her in the end. Oh, how tired she was of pretending to be other than what she truly was...a young woman ready to fall in love if such a magic love would but find her. How she longed to trade in her sword and have to lift nothing heavier than needle and thread. Although sewing was never one of her strong traits, she was more than capable of stitching a straight line, and 'twould be a most welcome relief...at least 'til she grew bored with the task, as she unfortunately always did. Such was the bane of her life.

Her mother, of course, would never have approved of her running around in hose and boots as she had of late. Torn between the memory of her sweet dame and the pride she had once seen in her sire's eyes when she learned a particular move with a sword, Amiria gave a long drawn out sigh. She was stuck in a deception with an outcome that could only have a terrible ending. No matter how long she contemplated her problem, she knew within her heart that one of her parents would not approve of the choices she had made of late. And to fall in love with the very enemy who stole her land? Well...her Da would roll in his grave at the thought of such an occurrence.

With one last stroke and pat of Thor's neck, she made to step from the stall, and was rewarded with an affectionate nudge from the huge beast. Her bubbly laughter gaily rang out, resounding with unabashed joy, afore she quickly stifled her mirth by clasping her hand to her mouth. With a fast look about the stable, she assessed that no other had been about to hear her laugh. Considering there had been nothing boyish about it, 'twas for the best that no one was there to question her.

Her solitude once more her own, Amiria reached for an apple and took delight in Thor's obvious pleasure at this unexpected, yet special, treat. Sounds of him munching the fruit quickly ceased. Thor gave her another nudge and nickered, quite clearly a request to feed him more. She smiled at his antics and reached for another piece to reward the large warhorse.

"You shall spoil him if you continue so," Ian's voice came from the shadows and echoed off the stable's walls.

A clear gasp of surprise escaped her lips and expressed her startled emotions whilst her eyes searched the darkness for Ian's whereabouts. She stretched out her hand, offering the horse the second apple which he gladly accepted.

"If 'twas your intent to frighten me to my wits end, you have succeeded, sir," she chided then closed the door to Thor's stall.

"I but came to see if you survived your punishment and to offer my assistance," he replied, as he came into the dusky light after closing the stable door.

"Somehow I do not think our Lord Dristan would welcome you coming to my aid, Ian," she answered, and observed his careless shrug.

He continued to stare at her, as she did the same to him. The unrelenting silence stretched on between them 'til it became awkward. She had never become tongue tied in his presence afore and she worried their one moment they had tried to share had ruined the friendship between them.

Ian came to stand beside her and made as if to reach for her hand. She furthered her distance from him and watched as he quirked his brow in an unspoken question. Since Amiria did not have an answer to give him, she stepped back 'til she stood with her spine against one of the interior poles of the stable. A shiver ran down her body.

"We must have speech, Amiria," he began honestly.

She shook her head in denial and began to gather the brushes to put them in their place. The task took her but a moment, and with nothing further to occupy her, she finally raised her eyes to meet his. "There is naught we must speak of, Ian."

"Ach lass, you did not think we were finished did you? In all truthfulness, did you think I would not at some point wish tae continue where we left off in your chamber?" he fumed in frustration.

"'Twas a mistake that should never have happened," she began, "you know that as well as I."

"A mistake you say? How can you think we are a mistake, Amiria, when I love you so?"

"Oh, Ian. How many times must we remind ourselves that we can never be?"

He watched her closely and came to stand afore her 'til she had to tip her head back just to see into his angry hazel eyes. "'Tis him, isna it?"

"Who?" she inquired softly, although she knew within her heart whose name he would utter next.

"Let us play no games between us, lass. I have known you far too long for us to begin such," Ian declared roughly.

"I know not of what you speak," she replied, with a stubborn flip of her head.

"You think I have not noticed, Amiria, where your attention goes these days? You have been under my care and I have guarded you for how many years now, and you think I do not see what is happening in your heart?" Ian yelled. "You have watched Lord Dristan most earnestly these past many weeks, Amiria...even I can see that!"

"Lower your voice lest you wish to bring others into this discussion," she chided coolly.

"I care not who hears us! 'Tis time all know who you are and that you are mine," he declared, and reached out to bring her into his embrace.

Amiria struggled against him and for the first time felt uncomfortable in his presence. He ran his hands all over her and she began to panic. Without thought, she swung back her arm and slapped him as hard as she could across his cheek. The sound cracked sharply, echoing loudly off the stable walls. 'Twas not hard to observe the red impression of the mark her fingers left on his handsome face, nor when his eyes glossed over with a rage she had never afore witnessed. She could not believe she had acted so rashly, and yet she fumed that he would act thusly with her.

"How dare you touch me so! Do you think me some lowly whore that you could make free with me here in the stables?" she demanded with tears in her eyes. She placed her hands on her hips, waiting for his answer, although in reality she was frightened by what flashed in his eyes. Ian rubbed his bruised cheek and inhaled to calm himself. He gazed at her closely, and Amiria knew that trepidation flashed in her violet eyes. 'Twas an expression she seldom showed to anyone, especially her captain.

"You are afraid of me. 'Twas naught my intent." His harsh tone echoed in her ears as she watched him shake his head, most likely baffled by what he had almost succumbed to.

Amiria knew not how to answer, as his words were really not a question.

"We have spoken these words afore, Ian," she voiced quietly, with a hint of sorrow in her words, "and they should not have to be repeated. We can never be anything more than friends."

"I am still your captain, and I gave my oath to your sire to guard you."

Amiria straightened her head gear to ensure everything appeared as it should to any possible observer. Then, she raised her misty eyes to him.

"Then guard me, Ian, but do not ask for more." She stood her ground and watched as the resignation to their situation registered in his hazel eyes. "I cannot in truth give what you would have of me."

She knew she had hurt him, but did not know what she could do to change anything. Amiria watched Ian nod to her. Just as he turned to leave the stables, the door was wrenched open. They quickly broke apart as a silhouette clearly appeared in the entrance. They watched in silence as the form came into the light. Amiria held her breath, for what she knew not was to come.

Riorden scrutinized the pair afore him with a scowl and approached them without words. He looked Ian up and down. "Leave us," he ordered with a nod of his head towards the doorway. Ian gave a brief bow and left without further comment.

He came to Aiden's side then circled the youth several times afore coming to stand once more afore him. He had to give the boy credit, for he stood his ground during the examination and defiantly raised his chin to look him straight in the eye. Silence stretched between them whilst Riorden continued his assessment of the boy whose nerves surely must be strung taut. The only sound to be heard was the occasional neighing of the horses stabled in their stalls.

Riorden reached out quickly and grabbed Aiden's chin and the youth struggled for breath in surprise. He led the boy closer into the light of a nearby torch. He turned the boy's face this way and that, trying to determine only what in truth the lad knew for sure. Still, Riorden continued to study Aiden's dirty soiled features with his black brows brought together in a terrifying frown of perplexity.

"You are not what you seem, I think," Riorden determined sternly, "and bare closer watching." He at last released him as if he offended him in some way. "Get you to our liege's chambers. He has asked you join him there." Riorden stared at the boy, who seemed unable to move his feet. "That does not mean you go at your own whim. Now move, Aiden!"

Apparently, those orders were all that were needed to get the lad's feet into motion as Aiden all but ran from the room. Riorden went to the doorway and watched as the young boy disappeared into the evening night in the direction of the keep. Aye...watch the boy he would, and closely, 'til he figured out what 'twas about the youth that disturbed him so.

Amiria made her way into the keep, pushing and shoving her way through the throng of men and serfs alike, who still gathered in the hall. The tables were in the process of being removed 'til needed for the next meal. Some of Dristan's men grabbed blankets and took themselves off to find places to sleep upon the floor since the garrison hall was near to overflowing with his army. Her family, it seemed, had already retired for the evening and was no longer present in the Great Hall. She saw her men near the hearth and they rose as if to follow her upstairs. With a slight shake of her head, they ceased their movement and returned to their conversation, with the exception of one.

Killian made his way to her side and halted her progress up the stairs. His kindly eyes looked upon her like a daughter and all Amiria wanted to do was rest her weary head upon the shoulders of a man who was considered part of her family.

"I dinnae like this, lassie," he whispered, for her ears alone. "Ye shouldna' be serving him alone in his chambers."

She only shrugged. "'Tis not such an unusual request to ask of one's squire. Aiden must needs obey the dragon's bidding."

"Aye, Aiden mayhap, if ye were in truth a younger version of yer brother. Ye must put an end to yer deception afore it blows up in yer face, lassie!" Killian hissed.

Amiria patted his arm, not that it provided the man any comfort. "I know not how," she whispered softly and watched him take his leave to return to the men.

Climbing the winding stone steps to the upper floors, Amiria passed numerous torches giving off a slightly smoky haze in the stairwell and corridors. Upon reaching the third floor landing, the passageway veered both to the left and right, leading to the family's private chambers. Her normal path would have taken her along the stone flooring leading to the left towards her own chamber, but this night was different. She took a brief breath and turned right instead to obey the summons she had been given. Her feet, trudging along the passageway, felt heavier than ever afore from the weight of the lie she continued to take part in.

It took her what seemed only a moment 'til she came afore the chamber door that once housed her father for as long as she could remember. Without further delay, she knocked on the solid portal then opened the door when she heard the command to enter.

As the door swung inwards, Amiria felt as if the world as she knew it now traveled in slow motion. Her eyes beheld a sight she had never seen afore and caused her mouth to hang open in a silent O of startled surprise. There afore her, the Devil's

Dragon rose in all his naked splendor from the wooden tub. The water ran from his glorious body, causing it to glisten from the candlelight with a sleekness that left her breathless and reminded her in truth of an all-powerful dragon ready to take flight. Her heartbeat quickened and she at last remembered to draw breath since it had been taken from her at the sight of such magnificence. Yea, he was indeed most handsome, especially since his face was now completely shaven and she had a full view of his visage. If a man could be described as beautiful, 'twould certainly suit the man standing afore her now.

Dristan turned in her direction, and surely her expression could only be called stunned. "Hurry and come in, boy. And close the door. You are letting in a draft." Amiria did as he directed but took her time whilst she tried to collect her thoughts. "Come, Aiden, and help your brother raise the pail to rinse me. He is having trouble lifting it."

She turned her gaze back into the room and saw Patrick was indeed trying to haul the bucket, containing the rinse water, to their lord. He raised his eyes and Amiria knew he was not pleased his sister was in her current predicament. Even at only eight summers in age, Patrick knew 'twas not seemly that she was in the presence of a naked man. Their father would have never approved. Although assisting in the bathing of a guest was a regular routine and usually performed or directed by the lady of the castle, this ritual was always forbidden for Amiria to take part in by her sire. 'Til this moment, she thought never to see a man in such a state 'til her wedding night.

"Aiden! I grow cold," Dristan bellowed and she could only imagine his thoughts as to what had befallen her to act so sheepish around him. After all, as far as he was concerned, they had the same parts.

Amiria came farther into the chamber and took hold of the pail in Patrick's hands. Apparently, her brother had other ideas in mind and a pulling war commenced between them whilst he refused to give up the handle. Amiria gave one final tug, and her sibling at last released his grip with a decisive plea in his eyes, which she ignored whilst water sloshed from the pail. Her gaze averted from the man, who was patiently waiting, she slowly made her way to the side of the tub.

Standing upon a stool, she raised the bucket and dumped the contents of warm water over her lord. Stepping off the stool, she watched through lowered lashes whilst Dristan shook the water from his hair. He came out of the tub, took a drying cloth that Patrick now handed him, and began to rid himself of the water that dripped from his hard muscular body.

'Twas only when Dristan turned, dropping the now wet cloth to the floor, that Amiria's situation finally penetrated her slow working brain. He was glorious to the eye with a body sculpted as if from stone. Her gaze raked in his body, noticing the broadness of his shoulders and the strength bulging in his arms. Moving her view lower she looked upon the ripples of rigid muscles stretched firmly across his stomach. She could not take her eyes from him, and blushed crimson when she glanced even lower to his manhood.

Amiria made as if to speak, but found herself unable to do so as her mouth became suddenly dry. After several attempts, she took one last look into her lord's grey eyes and bolted for the door. Her cheeks, she knew, must be flaming red in embarrassment. Slamming the portal closed as she fled, she began running as fast as her feet would carry her.

As she dashed down the corridor, she could hear Lord Dristan's voice roaring Aiden's name. She halted briefly at her chamber door, but knew no solace would be found there since 'twas the first place he would search. Her mind quickly made up as she sprinted to the end of the hallway, Amiria gave only one brief hesitation afore she fitted her fingers between the rough worn stones and felt the catch to open the hidden doorway. Closing it softly behind her, she slipped into the darkened stairwell leading to the strand below. She did so cautiously, since she brought no torch with her to light her way in her haste to leave the castle. She changed her clothing for one's she kept hidden in a chest far below afore she ventured out into the ocean air to clear her head.

The sea spray upon her face did much to lighten Amiria's mood and she could only wonder what had caused her to become so soft. She had always been made of sterner stuff, or so her father and Aiden had oft said of her, especially when most women would fall into a swoon given what she had had to endure.

Amiria was sure, however, that no peace would find her this night, as the sound of Dristan's voice continued ringing in her ears far into the still night whilst she walked the lone beach. Perchance, though, 'twas nothing compared to what her mind would remember if she but chose to close her eyes and ponder the matter. 'Twould take a miracle, she supposed, to erase the recent vision of Dristan from her memory. She did not think God above, in his infinite wisdom, would be so kind as to grant her that kind of a reprieve or favor any time soon...mores the pity.

TWELVE

WITH THE DAWNING OF THE NEW DAY, Dristan rose, dressed quickly, and made his way down to the Great Hall. There were not many who stirred as yet this early. He went to the kitchen, grabbing but a loaf of bread and some cheese to break his fast. He had much on his mind this morn and did not relish company.

Making his way to the stables, he went to Thor's stall and noticed the exceptional job Aiden had performed yester eve. His critical gaze took note of Thor's shining coat and he assumed the boy had brushed it to its now lustrous sheen. He grabbed Thor's bridle and trappings and had his horse ready in no time. Leaping into the saddle, Dristan left the security of the castles walls and made for the beach. 'Twas something he had longed to do for weeks since he had first seen the lady in the mist gazing out serenely upon the ocean waves. Thor seemed to sense his master's need for a taste of freedom, and tossing his head he lengthened his stride, putting the castle far behind them. His hooves thundered upon the sandy shore, and clumps of the disturbed sand marked their way across the strand.

Dristan let the stallion race along the shoreline with no thought of attempting to slow the steed to a slower pace. He became one with his horse whilst the scenery of the countryside flew by his vision in a blur. 'Twas the first time in a while he felt at peace, with no thoughts to his future or the responsibilities of the new castle and lands to now hold securely in the name of his king. With the taste of the salt air on his lips and the wind whipping through his hair, he was content to have only his own thoughts inside his head. At least there, no other would harp at him or try to tempt him into their bed.

The unwelcomed thoughts of Lady Sabina made him realize how far in truth he had traveled in such a short time and he could only marvel at Thor's stamina. He should breed the steed to a fitting mare so the line could continue with the blood of newborn colts. With only a slight tug on the reins and a slight pressure of his knee, Thor slowed his pace. Dristan turned his mount into the direction from whence he came and took in the view.

Sitting there, he fully surveyed his surroundings for the first time. The castle was well in the distance now, but still appeared impressive situated on a high cliff. If it had been anyone other than him and his army, they would have been hard put to penetrate its defenses. He planned to reinforce the walls where he had found weaknesses so no other would ever take by force what now belonged to him.

Thor stamped his hooves in the sand impatient to be on the run again, but Dristan only gave him a pat on the neck and continued holding the reins loosely in his gloved hands. The sun chose that moment to peek from beneath the clouds and the sand came alive as if 'twere covered in sparkling diamonds as far as the eye could see. The water shimmered whilst the waves crashed into the shore and even the trees of the nearby forest looked as if they, too, were shining a little brighter from the dew drops caressing each leaf.

Dristan was about to let Thor have his way and let the beast fly his way back to the security of the castle, when a slight movement by the edge of the forest caught his eye. He blinked once and tried to refocus his vision 'til he noticed a person lying wrapped securely in a MacLaren clan's tartan. He watched in fascination as the person stretched and unfolded and the unmistakable form of a woman became abundantly clear.

Apparently, the woman had not realized she was no longer alone. She rose from her bed on the sand and began to shake the tiny granules from her clothing and hair. Finally, in frustration, she grabbed both ends of her tartan, which she had used as a cape of sorts, and raised it above her head, shaking out the contents that had found every fold to hide in. 'Twas only as she settled the garment around her head and fastened a broach to keep everything in place that she chose to at last look up, and a startled expression crossed her face.

Dristan gave a brief smile as he took off his gloves, dismounted, and made his way towards the woman, knowing Thor would remain where he was left. The closer he came, the more pleasantly he was surprised, 'til she pulled the tartan close about her features. Although only allowed the slightest glimpse of her face, this woman appeared as an angel with porcelain skin, a neck as graceful as a swan's, and high cheekbones. A small pert nose and lips begging to be kissed were now hidden by the plaid she used to conceal her appearance.

His hands would no doubt be able to span her small waistline; her breasts were not overly large but he knew they, too, would fit well within the palm of his hands and then some. Her hair was the color of flames or the sky just as the sun was about to set as a few loose tendrils blew in the ocean's breeze.

She shifted her feet in the sand in indecision, and he noticed no shoes covered her feet, which even appeared perfect to his eyes. *Surely there must be some flaw with the girl*, Dristan thought to himself but he could find none. First the lady in the mist had consumed his thoughts, and now this woodland nymph had come to confuse him even more. Mayhap he could hope the damsel was not wed or spoken for.

"A good morn to you, *mademoiselle*," Dristan said, with a slight bow. "You are far from the village so early. Mayhap I can offer my assistance and see you back to your dwelling?"

A negative shake of her head was all Dristan was awarded, and he watched as she took several steps backwards towards the haven of the trees behind her.

"Come now...I mean you no harm, mistress, as I am lord of yon keep," he declared with a wave of his hand towards the castle. "As a knight of King Henry's realm, I fear you must humor me as 'twould be most unchivalrous to leave one so lovely unprotected to the elements of both man and beast alike. May I escort you to the village perchance?"

Once again, her hooded head gave no answer whilst she clutched the tartan closer to her, as if it offered the security she stood in need of.

"No? Well, I cannot in all good conscience leave you here to fend for yourself. A name then," he encouraged, "tell me your name?"

"My n-name?"

Dristan heard her whispered words softly teasing his senses. "Aye, mistress, your name. Surely you have one?"

He stood fascinated as the head of the woman swiveled quickly in his direction. For one brief moment he beheld eyes of violet, reminding him of the heather on the Scottish moors. Still he waited patiently for her answer and yet she provided nothing to give her identity away.

Merciful heavens, what was she to do? His words hung in the air between them, and her consciousness frantically screamed to find an answer to give him and quickly! Yet, no rebuttal came to her frozen mind as Amiria stood there in total indecisiveness. She knew she could not allow him to get too close on the off chance he might recognize her, even though her face was clean from the grime and mud usually gracing it these days. 'Twas the words he uttered, haunting her as he had spoken them to her once afore, although she was now in a different guise.

"Somehow, I do not think giving you my name would be in my best interest, my lord," she said quietly and took but an instant more to gaze at him afore her eyes became downcast. Her mind was racing, thinking of only how to escape the predicament she now found herself in with no horse to hasten her journey.

Dristan gave a soft chuckle at her words. "Mayhap not, but 'twould please me to know it just the same."

"It matters not to me if you are pleased, so I will keep it unto myself I think," she retorted sharply.

"I see a task afore me that I might coax it from your lips," he prompted, taking a step in her direction. For each footstep he advanced, Amiria took one in the opposite direction towards the forest 'til he halted.

"Call it as you see fit, but 'twill still not gain you what you seek." Amiria watched as he laughed out loud, but she could not find the humor of the situation from her words she had spoken.

"I do so love a challenge," he argued humorously.

"Do you?" she asked sarcastically. "And what, pray tell, do you achieve if you should know my name, my lord?"

Dristan looked on her with a slight smile set upon his handsome face. "Why I achieve the name of a beautiful woman I would like to know better."

She contemplated him again, wondering at his ploy. "And how know you I am beautiful with just one glimpse of my face?"

"Anyone with eyes in his head could tell, fair damsel, you are indeed a fine looking woman."

"They say beauty is not everything, my lord Dristan. Perchance I have a shrewish nature, as I have been told such afore."

"Somehow, I think not."

"Do you?" she repeated the same words of but seconds ago.

He interrupted her. "Besides, 'tis not fair you should know who I am, but I am not granted the same."

"Any and all would be a fool not to know the Devil's Dragon of Blackmore now claims his lair in Berwyck Castle."

"Then you have heard of me and my reputation has proceeded me," he cajoled.

"Aye, my lord, I have indeed knowledge of you."

"I see you do not fear me, as some do upon first encountering me. Why is that, I wonder, when you in truth do not know my nature?" he questioned honestly.

"I fear no man," she answered, as she raised her head defiantly with a flip of her head, "or beast for that matter!"

Dristan threw his head back and laughed. It sounded pleasant to her ears. "Well said, damsel. Mayhap in you I have finally met my match! Still you have me at a loss mistress...besides not giving me your name, that is."

She tilted her head as she pondered his question. "How so, my lord?" she whispered softly. Her breath left her in a sudden rush as he began to make his way towards her. She could not breathe, and she could not move. Her sanity left her as she waited for what was to happen next.

Dristan came towards the vision afore him whilst she stood her ground this time. He was impressed how she gazed at him directly, as if she in truth feared no man as she had said. He smiled at her again, noticing the unusual color of her deep violet eyes and saw her startled expression. He hesitated, if only for a second, afore he carefully reached for her hand holding the tartan in place to cover her features. He felt it tremble as the cloth fell away, and he brought her but a step or two closer to his side.

For once in his life Dristan could form no words as he stared down at the treasure afore his eyes. She was indeed more lovely than he had first thought, upon closer examination, and he was not sure how he would be able to let her go now that she was almost within his arms.

She closed her eyes, and he felt the heat of their body's as he moved her closer 'til they were but a heartbeat away. "*Carpe Diem,*" she spoke tenderly, as if she were savoring this moment, however brief it may be. She opened her eyes, noticing his further bewilderment at her words. "'Tis Latin...it means to seize the day."

"Aye, I know its meaning. I am just surprised you do, as well."

"My lord?" she questioned breathlessly.

Dristan continued to view the beauty of the woman, who watched him just as intently, almost as if she knew him. He cleared his musings inside his head and smiled once more at the fair maiden afore him. "You dress with clan MacLaren's colors and that of a peasant, yet your speech is of a lady," he answered. The mystery intensified as he felt the slight calluses in the palm of her hand he yet held, giving evidence she was used to hard labor.

"Not all peasants are unlearned, my Lord Dristan, even though 'tis most unusual," she said, as if stating the obvious. His brow once more furrowed in puzzlement, and he had the distinct feeling she was poised to take flight.

"You give no hint of a Scottish brogue which seems out of place if you are but a peasant from the village, and yet you somehow seem familiar to me as if we have met afore," he continued tentatively, and saw her give the slightest of smiles. "Surely this is not the case, as I would be hard pressed to forget someone as charming as you."

"I suppose, coming from the Devil's Dragon, I should consider your words a compliment, although I find it hard to believe that you give them often," she teased and gave him an expression that told him she was surprised she had found the nerve to do so.

Encouraged by her words, Dristan urged her closer and was pleased when she came readily into his arms, resting her hands upon his chest. "Tell me your name, *ma cherie*," he whispered, bending his head and inhaling the scent of her hair, a smell of the fresh sea air. "'Twould give me great pleasure to have it pass from my lips as we converse together."

She gave a sweet laugh, making his smile broaden in encouragement even as she shivered at his touch. "Converse, you say? Since you have already mentioned your reputation precedes you, my lord, 'tis hardly likely conversing is all you have in mind this day."

"I would be lying if I said I do not desire to have a taste of your sweet lips beneath mine and all else you would offer," he told her truthfully but watched in dismay as the spell that had been woven between them was broken with his words. She stepped away from him, covering her face once more. "Surely you would not deny your lord a simple kiss."

The woman pondered his words and took a hesitant step back as if she knew she had stayed too long. "A kiss is not so simple to a woman's heart, my lord, hence I would not give them lightly and without thought."

"Surely you are not wed?"

"Nay, my lord, I am not."

"Then I do not see the problem if we but share a moment or two of pleasure this morn." Dristan reached for her again, but to his irritation found only empty arms as she dodged his out-stretched hands. Still he persisted in his efforts to know the maiden further. "Come now, do not be shy. I but wish to know you," he said, trying again, and got no further than he did but moments afore.

"To what end, Lord Dristan?" she queried tartly, as he watched her become annoyed with him. "I will be no whore for you or any other man nor shall you make me your lady wife. I am but one woman among many to have crossed your path and surely there will be more to follow as you travel about on the king's business. I will not be used and tossed aside with mayhap a babe in my belly for allowing you to, as you said, share a moment or two of pleasure," she answered angrily. "Somehow, I think I am worth more than that, although you may not think so."

Caught off guard by the bitterness in her words, Dristan was about to reply when the sound of racing hoof beats came to his ears and he turned to see the cause. He was put at ease as several of his guardsmen came into view and dismounted with swords drawn as if protecting him from some unseen enemy. He turned back to have further speech with the woman only to find her gone from his sight with only a brief glimpse of her tartan as she disappeared into the forest.

Dristan swore to himself, afore turning towards his men with an enraged glare. Geoffrey sheathed his sword with a knowing smirk set upon his face as did Ulrick and Morgan. Taegan and Turquine began to chuckle but soon stopped with a glare from their lord.

Only Fletcher braved the dragon's wrath and came to stand next to his lord. "We thought mayhap you made leave of your senses to go riding without your guard. 'Twas most unusual for you to do so, Dristan, but perchance you had a meeting of a more intimate nature," he dared with a grin.

"I but wished some time unto myself," Dristan replied sternly."

"I do not think my eyesight was mistaken by taking that form to be anything other than of a pretty young woman. To chance an attack alone is not worth the price for a bit of a romp with a comely wench, my lord," Fletcher chided knowingly. "Bring her to your chamber if you must or avail yourself to one of the whores already housed at Berwyck. 'Tis much easier to watch your back when we know where you are than if you are missing, and we know not which direction to seek you out."

Dristan tossed Fletcher a scathing look, causing the man to laugh harder. He dared much and would only have taken the jest from him or Riorden and none other. Knowing he had not heard the last of this, Dristan went to Thor, grabbed the reins, and vaulted into his saddle. As he donned his gloves, he turned to his men with a smile they could only interpret as retribution, coming their way for making sport of their lord.

"Since you men are so concerned with my safety and some-how feel I could not hold my own, we shall ride back to Berwyck and commence to sweating out some valuable time in the lists. Perchance then you will remember who your master is and learn some respect," Dristan promised dryly.

No one dared to groan, with thoughts of the coming after-noon's training, with one who would show no mercy, and in unison, they turned their mounts towards home. He allowed himself one brief glance towards the trees where he had last glimpsed his woodland sprite of the forest. He smiled at the memory of how she had felt in his arms and vowed he would somehow find her. What he would do with her when he located her he knew not, but he pledged to himself he would not rest 'til she was his.

THIRTEEN

"YOU DID WELL, LYNET," Kenna praised the young girl, who held the newly made poultice in her hands. "You will do admirably with further tutelage to heal the ailments of the clan or your own family when the time comes."

"My thanks for your help, Kenna, and for all you have taught me," Lynet said, her eyes alight with happiness from her efforts and knowing she had pleased MacLaren's healer.

Kenna gave a slight chuckle at the look of innocence in the young girl's eyes. "Now go and remember to tell Dougal to keep the poultice on his arm as long as possible to draw out any poison from his cut. I do not relish having him lose a much needed limb!"

"Aye, Kenna. I will remember."

Kenna watched the youngest daughter of the old laird leave her side and hurry towards the lists where the sound of the men's training was already in earnest. Crossing the courtyard, she made her way to the outer bailey so she, too, could perchance catch a glimpse of the knight her heart sought after.

'Twas not hard to have him stand out from all the other men in armor, who were busy training this warm afternoon. She could only marvel the heat of the summer's day did not seem to dull their enthusiasm to show their liege their skill.

Sir Geoffrey was currently on the jousting field, waiting for another lance to make up for the one that had shattered on his opponent's armor. *What skill he has*, Kenna thought to herself when she noticed the ever so slight pressure of his knee to turn his steed in the direction he wished the beast to go. Afore she could draw breath, Geoffrey, shield in one hand and a new lance firmly gripped in his other, set his horse into motion. It lunged forward with its huge galloping hooves, and Kenna watched as both knights lowered their lances in unison.

Their two horses met midfield with lances splintering on the breast plates of both knights. Kenna had not realized she had closed her eyes at the contact of both men 'til she heard the loud thud of clanking metal as one knight toppled to the ground. Opening her eyes, she realized that, alas, 'twas her most gallant knight, who now graced the dirt. It took every-thing within her power not to rush to his side. Their eyes met across the distance between them 'til Kenna blushed at the lazy grin Geoffrey cast her way.

Dristan jumped off Thor's back and came to Geoffrey's side with a mighty laugh. "And here I thought you held such prom-ise you would remain topside awhile longer and give me a good day's sport," he announced merrily. He held out his hand and assisted Geoffrey to his feet.

"'Twas distracted, my lord," Geoffrey muttered hoarsely.

"What perchance could distract you so?" Dristan wondered. His gaze searched the yard 'til his eyes came upon Kenna near the wall. "Ah...I see. I suppose you must needs rest a spell afore you begin again?"

"Mayhap just a short respite, if my lord would indulge me."

"Make not a habit of it, Sir Geoffrey," Dristan retorted.

"Aye, Lord Dristan, and my thanks," Geoffrey said as he quickened his pace to reach Kenna's side.

"Do not thank me overly much, Sir Geoffrey, for you will train doubly hard upon your return!" he called laughingly.

Dristan shook his head, realizing how his humor had improved since this morning's encounter with the unknown beautiful young woman from the beach. 'Twas certainly not the norm that he would allow a knight to delay his training just to have speech with a woman who appeared on the lists. There was no doubt he would need to ensure that women be kept to a minimum during these daily rituals or he would be standing alone with no one to train, having his entire garrison seeking out a comely wench or two as they saw fit. He must be getting soft.

His eye's searched the combatants who practiced and noticed the MacLaren clan was coming along nicely with the moves he had further instilled in their handling of their broadswords. He even had enjoyed swinging Ian's mighty claymore and had commissioned the blacksmith to forge one for himself. He looked forward to feeling the hilt in his hands so he might, too, become proficient with such a weapon of war.

'Twas while his eyes were scanning the lists that he came upon the form of Aiden, finally emerging from the barbican gate to join the men in practicing their skills. The lad was met by Ian and the two were having fierce words, seemingly not pleasing to Aiden's captain. 'Twas clear Ian was not about to be silenced by the boy's argument. Still, their words amongst themselves were not what perplexed Dristan; 'twas the manner in which they spoke, as if they were about some intrigue that was not to be shared.

Dristan was irked due to the lateness of the day, to see the lad so tardy and keeping hours that seemed to suit only himself. The boy finally placed his helmet over his filthy face and then had the gall to raise his fist at his captain while still continuing their argument. *Merde*...did not the boy ever wash himself? He swore he had yet to see Aiden with a fresh face to actually make out his features clearly.

With thoughts of reprimanding the lad for the filth he continually lived with on his body and to get to the heart of the matter between those two, Dristan reached for his sword. Swinging it afore him, he marveled at the speed in which he did so. It seemed as light as a feather in his hands today, although he knew most would not even be able to lift such a blade as this. 'Twas as if the sword sang to his senses, spinning a web of magic over him so that he might remain victorious. 'Twas a song within him he had heard many a time afore. Even as the sun reflected off the engravings on its blade, it seemed as if the large ruby placed in its hilt winked at him. It whispered to its master to continue seeking the glory due him as the king's favorite champion and knight.

Sheathing his blade in its scabbard at his side, he went to make his way to Aiden but was distracted by the site of yet another woman on his lists. *Mon dieu* was he to be plagued all the long day with women who were where they did not belong? He called to Lynet and motioned for her to join him, and saw her slightly crestfallen face as she rose from her aid to Dougal and came to his side.

"My lord," she whispered shyly, bobbing a short curtsey.

He looked down at her with her bent head. "Follow me," he ordered harshly, and she fell into step behind him.

He sauntered across the field, whilst his men cleared a path, not wanting to fall prey to his ire. A piercing glare in an unspoken command had all returning to their work with now eager abandon in the hopes their lord would not find them lacking. He strode past Aiden, who quickly turned from him and all but ran to the lists to start his training. Still Dristan continued on past his garrison, who continued to train with various weapons of war. 'Twas not 'til he came to stand afore Kenna that he halted his stride, and with a brief flick of his hand, Geoffrey returned to the lists, as well.

Kenna gave a slight curtsey and stared at her liege lord but said not a word. She did, however, notice Lynet's unease that perchance she had done something to displease him. Kenna knew for the young girl there could be no greater punishment than to have some unknown offense hurt her feelings, for she was tender hearted. She gave a brief motion of her eyes to the young lady, who did not hesitate to comply with Kenna's unspoken words as she came immediately to her side.

"How may we serve you, my Lord Dristan?" Kenna asked contritely.

"Harrumph...that is indeed a mystery is it not Kenna?" he drawled in irritation.

"Something offends you my liege?"

"That, too, seems an understatement."

Kenna gave him a smile of understanding whilst he looked out upon his men. "What pray tell can we, as your most humble servants, do to change the disposition of such an ominous mood of the castle's dragon lord?"

"You dare to mock me?" he said, aghast, his brows furrowed in fury.

Kenna's laughter rang out in the air, causing a curse from the Devil's Dragon to spew forth from his lips afore they formed a grim line across his features.

She knew he waited for some form of apology to come from his healer, but she gave him none. She was not sure how much more she should tease him.

"You do not help my sorely vexed mood, Kenna." His answer was enough for her to realize she should not push him too much further.

"Somehow I do not think any words that may part from my lips will change your poor humor."

"I am displeased," he answered sourly.

"All can clearly observe that, my lord," she merely replied, "hence your knights scatter afore you so they, too, may not be within your path and feel the scorching heat of your temper."

She knew her liege still had an expectation of her request for forgiveness. Kenna only continued to smile at him 'til he focused his gaze instead on Lynet and frowned, further showing his dismay. She gave a gentle nudge to the girl at her side and watched as Lynet's smirk of humor upon her visage quickly vanished.

"I do not care for women on my lists, Kenna. They create an unnecessary distraction for my men," he revealed finally.

Kenna nodded her understanding of the situation. "I hear your words, my liege. 'Twas just that Dougal was in need of a poultice for his injury and Lady Lynet needed the practice."

Dristan's brows rose in surprise. "You have the gift of healing, girl?" he inquired.

Lynet's eyes seemingly sparkled in delight. "So 'twould seem, my Lord Dristan."

He pondered her for some time 'til he came to a decision. "Mayhap your talent then lay in another direction, *ma petite*, than mending blankets for my army, although I am sure the men appreciate your assistance," he declared. He saw her enthusiasm yet held up his hand to deter her words. "However...women on my field causes my knights to have their thoughts turn elsewhere besides their training. Lest called, I will send the men to you, Kenna, to tend their ills."

"As you will," Kenna replied, with a slight bow of her head.

"See to teaching Lady Lynet all you know," he continued. "If she in truth becomes half the healer you appear to be, Berwyck castle will be twice blessed."

"I will see to it," she declared, and whispered a few words to Lynet, who curtsied to Dristan and scurried away in happiness to do Kenna's bidding. Kenna herself turned to leave 'til she heard Dristan's words.

"Another moment, Kenna," he said with familiarity. "How is Hugh progressing with his healing? Is he well enough to begin training again?"

"Aye, he is, my liege," she said carefully, "and even now ready's himself to join you hence."

"But...?"

Kenna sighed as she observed Dristan earnestly and then spoke frankly. "I have seen things, my lord, and beg you to be careful with Hugh of Harlow. I do not trust him and feel he will do more harm than good once he is fully recovered."

"He is no threat to me, Kenna. Do not worry," he replied smugly. "If you must worry, then worry what I shall do if you continue to put strange herbs in my wine."

"My lord?" she questioned warily.

"You know that which I speak of. Why else would my thoughts be wandering to else but to the training of my garrison and the clan?"

Kenna was surprised he believed she would actually drug him. No longer able to mask the puzzlement that he would think such of her, her face turned to mild curiosity as to his own thoughts. She surprised him when she reached out and touched his arm. With her eyes closed, she swayed slightly and tightened her grip to prevent her falling while multiple visions raced across her mind. She stood there for some time 'til she at last opened her eyes and gave him a look that she could tell immediately put him on edge. She was not shocked he gazed at her warily, for 'twas a look she had become accustomed to from those she read. He became uneasy when she seemed to be able to see into his very soul.

"Eyes of violet," she said meaningfully, "a most unusual shade is this not so?"

"You know of her then and where she resides in the village?" he asked, startled she knew of whom he thought. 'Twas apparent he wished for her help in finding the lass.

Kenna's eyes sparkled in merriment afore she spoke quietly. "I see two women that have been crossing your dreams and mind of late, my lord."

At a loss for words, Dristan grumbled to himself about his healer not knowing her place, causing Kenna to laugh at him again in jest, further irritating him. "How is it you have no respect for your master, Kenna, and yet I still tolerate you?"

She bowed her head slightly and answered truthfully, "Mayhap 'tis the answers I give that pleases our clan's dragon." She saw him lift his brow at her question. "Well...are you not Berwyck's own dragon since you have claimed the lands for your king?"

"You evade the question I asked of you, Kenna," he replied gruffly. "Do you know of her?"

Kenna thoughtfully perused her answer. Of course, she knew who haunted his waking hours lately. His visions of the woman on the strand and the one found near the forest edge were clearly shown to her as if the woman now stood afore her. Even though the mist had swirled around one woman and the other had vanished into the woods, Kenna knew 'twas Amiria he searched for and that both women were one and the same. Still, she could not in truth reveal that which he sought. Whilst she had the answer that troubled him, 'twas not her place to divulge the knowledge that could only be done by the lady herself. Unbeknownst to Amiria, her time in disguised as her brother was quickly running out.

"Well?" he demanded loudly. "Do you know of her?"

She did not answer him, much to his disappointment. He was even more than stunned when she turned her back on him and began to make her way off the lists. She could not miss the furious sound of his voice when he began cursing loudly, especially since he had not given her permission to leave, let alone that she had not given him the answer he sought.

"Kenna!" he bellowed. She slowly turned back to face him, gave a small sigh, and returned to his side. She stood there silently, waiting for his words. When he spoke, 'twas in a tone of barely contained anger. "Do not make me ask again Kenna. You have tested me more today than most would dare and my patience is at an end. I will not follow in your wake like some well-trained dog for you to give heed to my question when it suits you!"

Kenna considered her words afore she finally gave him his answer. "Although I have said these words to you afore, perchance you may not have heard them or understood their meaning at the time they were spoken. Sometimes, not everything you see is as it appears, my lord, for that which you seek may be closer than you know," she whispered, and left Dristan standing there, sputtering curses of how that was no answer at all. Unfortunately, 'twas all the words of advice she was able to bestow upon him for now.

Hugh made his way to the lists and brushed past Kenna as she went towards the inner bailey. He sneered in her direction and then spat, for he did not like feeling beholden to a witch. He could think of her as nothing else, since the healing of his back in such a short span of time was nigh unto a miracle. As far as he was concerned, she should burn at the stake and good riddance to her no matter what she had done for him.

Despite the feeling of hatred that had been festering inside him for the past month, he was at least grateful he could once more heft a sword, however gingerly. God's blood, he felt as weak as a newborn babe and disliked the feeling!

Hugh's eyes scanned the field 'til he espied his nemesis, and yet another, who lingered close to the stone wall, caught his interest. He could not remember her name, but knew 'twas one of the daughters of the old lord, apparently lusting after the newest liege of the castle the way she followed Dristan's every move. Mousey brown hair and not much to look at, but perchance she would serve a purpose that would suit his needs.

But first things first, he thought confidently. 'Twould still take more time, much to his distaste, afore he would at last be able to fight as he once did. Then, and only then, when he was back to his normal self, would he exact his revenge on the Devil's Dragon and take the castle that should be his own. Smiling with the future vision of himself as lord of the keep, he began his day of training in the lists with more enthusiasm than he had felt in some time.

FOURTEEN

A MIRIA RACED HER HORSE CALIANA with Ian and her guardsmen as if Hell's demons were fast on her heels. Perchance fiends were less of a threat to her piece of mind than the dragon haunting her every waking hour. No matter what she did or where she roamed, he was always there in the forefront of her mind, training her to be a great and noble knight by day and invading her sleeping dreams with a kiss she had never felt during the restless night.

Several days had passed since Amiria's latest fiasco with her liege lord, as she continued to try to forget the feel of her hands set upon his muscled chest. 'Twas with an appreciative sense of relief that afternoon when Dristan called a halt to the day's torture and selected but a handful of his garrison to accompany him to places unknown. To her, it mattered not where he had gone, so long as she was free from the dreaded beast for a spell.

'Twas when she called her own guardsmen to her after Dristan had departed that she caught the eye of his captain, staring at her most earnestly. Riorden had called her to join him, but she chose to ignore his summons. Amiria was sure that she, or at least Aiden as 'twere, would pay, and pay dearly, for the slight come the evening hours. For now, she cared not what price she was to forfeit for her insolence this day. Her only thought was to feel the wind on her face, her steed beneath her, and to arrive at the destination she had in mind so she could enjoy the remainder of the day.

Amiria slowed her pace when her guards entered the forest and made their way at a more leisurely pace. There was in truth no other option due to the density of the trees as they rode in single file. A sigh escaped her, and she began to enjoy the small respite from the rigorous routine that had become her life of late. She chanced a glance backwards towards Ian and knew in her heart he was well aware of where she led her faithful loyal group of clansmen. From the grimace on his face, 'twas clear he was not pleased with her choice.

She pressed ever onward whilst she continued to soak in the rays of sunshine, peeking through the leaves above her. 'Twas surprisingly warm for this time of year, and she was thankful for the warmth of the late afternoon hours, considering what she had in mind for herself. She raised her face to feel the heat of the sun as her mare continued forward. A sudden peacefulness she had not been able to sense in a long while came over her. The day was truly lovely, and she would enjoy it fully for as long as the moment was allowed to last. She knew 'twould not be for long.

As they rounded a bend, her group came upon a glade filled with tall grass and blooming flowers. Amiria halted her horse with a smile of pure pleasure and slid from the saddle to the ground beneath her. She gave the animal a well-deserved pat of affection and was rewarded with a gentle nuzzle begging for more. She gave a joyful laugh and obliged Caliana, for it had been some time since she had been afforded the luxury of riding her horse with no other purpose but the sheer thrill of it. She was especially fond of the dark brown mare with its black mane and tail for she had been a gift most recently given from her father. Amiria treasured every opportunity that presented itself for her to become one with her horse.

She viewed her men as they dismounted, and they began to talk amongst themselves.

Ian came to her and stood silently at her side. "I like not what you have in mind," he protested sullenly, giving her a thunderous look.

She ignored him, tired of his constant disapproving looks lately. It seemed she could do nothing right anymore in the eyes of her captain.

"No harm will come to me with you and my guard to keep watch," she replied confidently.

"We know not where he is, Amiria. 'Twould be wise to exercise caution 'til—"

"Nonsense, Ian," she interrupted, throwing her helm from her head and reaching for a leather bag attached to her saddle. "Our beastly dragon will not find us here so far removed from the castle, for how would he know of such a secluded place as this hidden on his lands? For just a while, Ian, I want to enjoy my God given right to be female, and I intend to do just that. 'Tis tired I am of acting the boy and on such a fine day. For once, do not pester me with questions or my motives. Just please, I beg of you, let me have peace to enjoy this moment unto myself, would you?"

"I still do not like the risk you take, Amiria," he grumbled and she flung him a stony, mutinous expression. He threw up his hands in defeat. "Very well...we shall do as you ask to ensure your privacy. I only hope you shall not regret it!"

Amiria rolled her eyes, turned from her men, and made her way through the dense flora and fauna 'til the woods once more opened up to reveal a piece of heaven on earth. She had come here often as a child with her family, and for just a few seconds, she closed her eyes in memory of those who no longer were with her. With a sigh, she returned to the present, since she refused to give in to the melancholy mood that had descended upon her. Instead, she took in the view afore her.

She feasted on the sight she beheld and lost her breath in dreamlike awe. 'Twas a magical place to her, where flowers grew in abundance, encircling her in a magnitude of vivid shades of red, pink, yellow, blue, and purple. She knew not how they still bloomed this late in the season, but she was indeed happy she would be able to enjoy their essence. But the foliage was not the only reason she wanted to escape to this haven, and with one last look to ensure she was truly alone, she began to strip the filthy disgusting clothing from her person. Leaving them in a dirty heap in the green blades of grass, she ran naked to a rock ledge, climbed atop it, and leapt into the air, plunging herself into deep warm water. With sure long strokes, she swam in the pool fed by a nearby bubbling spring. A waterfall from high above the mountainside completed the backdrop of perfection, although the water from that source could certainly take one's breath away from the coldness that rained down in a constant cascade.

To say her swim was refreshing was an understatement, and afore long she swam back to retrieve her leather bag, took out a chunk of soap, and scrubbed herself clean. Her initial thought had been to take delight in a fragrant bar she kept hidden from Sabina's greedy hands. But thoughts of smelling like roses might cause some eyes to rise in concern, considering her masquerade as her brother. 'Twas a bitter disappointment she could not indulge in such a luxury. At least for this afternoon she could fulfill her desire to be a woman!

Reaching behind her for her long braid, she began the tedious task of uncoiling its length so it, too, could be cleaned of the grime it contained. It took a bit of work 'til 'twas completely lathered and she swam to the waterfall to rinse the soap as she watched the bubbles disappear in front of her. Amiria smiled broadly for 'twas wonderful to feel her hair free of its plait whilst it fanned out behind her in a red shimmering wave as she began to swim again.

For her, time stood still and although she knew she should don her clothes once more, she ignored the promptings of the little voice inside her head, whispering to hasten at her task. Again and again, she dove under the water, enjoying her freedom of splashing around in childlike abandon for 'twas a decadent indulgence she could not resist. On such a glorious day as this, Amiria would take this precious time for herself since only the good Lord above knew when she would have another moment as this to relish the life he had granted her.

Climbing out of the water slightly breathless, she looked at her forgotten soiled garments and could not bear the thought of donning them just yet. Instead, she laid down in the soft blades of grass and stared above, watching the fluffy white clouds, in an otherwise clear blue sky, take shape in her imagination. The sun beat down, warming her skin 'til she felt her eyes begin to flutter in sleep. Her sweet dreams took her deeper and deeper within its waiting arms and bequeathed Amiria a vivid vision of naked limbs intertwined in an intimate lovers embrace. She would awake, unfortunately, to her worst nightmare.

She bolted upright at the unmistakable sound of arguing men. Disoriented from her slumber, she hurriedly surveyed her surroundings and the direction of the disturbance. Ian's voice was raised in a warning shout along with several of her guards. There was no mistaking the argument that was ensuing whilst they attempted to restrain at all cost whoever was about to invade her solitude. Broadswords being released from their scabbards now echoed throughout the forest. She cursed at her stupidity of not listening to Ian for once in her young life and for falling asleep.

Leaves on the shrubbery began to rustle quite loudly. 'Twas a clear indication that unwelcome company was upon her and someone finding her naked certainly did not bode well. Looking to the ground for her sword, she recognized her own foolishness since, feeling she was safe, she had carelessly left it in her saddle in her haste to swim. No help would apparently be found there. Having no time to climb into her clothes, she ran for the water and dove in, swimming fast towards the waterfall. 'Twas the only place she could somewhat conceal herself.

Her hair was plastered annoyingly to her face and she brushed the wet tresses from her eyes. She began to shiver from the cold, as the water did not seem as warm since the sun had begun to set. She looked at her arms and swore at her idiocy once more as her skin was an ugly shade of red from being burnt by the sun. No wonder the water was cooler than it most likely was.

She waited, scrunching her toes in uncertainty with the sand beneath her feet. She held her breath 'til it left her in a loud whoosh that was only masked by the torrents of water coming from above and splashing in front of her. She blinked her eyes several times and could not believe who she saw come striding into the clearing as he had done so a hundred times afore. He did not look pleased whilst he scanned the area with a practiced eye 'til he sheathed his sword, seeing no imminent danger. She began to pray he would leave and quickly. Unfortunately, for her peace of mind, her prayers were about to go unanswered!

Horrified, Amiria saw how Dristan all but sauntered over to the water's edge and noticed Aiden's clothing piled in a repugnant mound. If she but listened hard enough, she would surely have heard his thoughts of how he was anxious to see what the boy looked like afore he was once more covered in dirt. His piercing gaze swept and searched the water in the growing darkness and Amiria knew the moment when he espied a brief glimpse of her red hair behind the waterfall.

Amiria watched in gut wrenching fear as Dristan removed his belt and dropped his sword to the ground. He unfastened the clasp holding his cape in place, and it floated to the earth somewhat near her own discarded garments. His tunic soon followed along with his hose. With a full view of his tautly corded stomach and well-formed long legs, she closed her eyes tightly as he reached for his braies', hoping against hope he would not soon be diving into the water with her. The sound of a splash too close to her current whereabouts caused her to open her eyes in dread. She had nowhere to go or hide, for the pond was not overly large.

She ducked down into the water 'til only her head was still above the water line. She prayed the darkness of night would descend upon the glade to help conceal her form. Looking up into the sky, she knew this particular request would also be denied her. She tried to steady her breathing but failed, especially when she saw Dristan swimming in her direction.

He came to where she was scrunched down in the water with only the veil of falling wet spray separating them. She attempted to make herself invisible through the cascading waterfall but surely 'twas not the case.

"Come, Aiden," he called urgently, "the hour grows late and we must away afore the night falls completely."

"Nay, my liege, I cannot."

"'Twas not a request. I can see you shivering from here and would not have you catch a chill or you shall be useless on the field come the morrow."

"I must respectfully refuse, my lord, lest you leave so I may don my attire."

Amiria could not mistake Dristan's chuckle to what would appear to be a young boy's unease. "Best you get over any sense of modesty soon, Aiden, for when you are in the king's service, privacy is a luxury not afforded a knight most times. Besides, you have nothing I myself do not possess."

"Do not be so sure of that," she muttered under her breath.

Amiria fathomed she had spoken louder than she had thought whilst Dristan shook his head in disbelief. He swam to the other side of the streaming water and Amiria moved as far as she could possibly from her lord and still remain submerged up to her chin. Panic settled in her heart for surely he was not such a fool that he would not now realize that she was in truth a lady.

"You, too, will someday have a form such as mine and our knights, Aiden," Dristan proposed, trying to allow *the boy* to feel more comfortable. "Do not be ashamed or embarrassed of that which your youth cannot change 'til you grow a bit more."

"I am not ashamed, so be gone dolt!" Amiria yelled harshly and watched in dismay the determined mindset of her liege lord.

"Enough of this nonsense," Dristan exclaimed annoyingly. She instantly knew she had pushed him too far in her refusal to obey his commands. Her cry of alarm rang out into the suddenly quiet air.

Dristan made an attempted grab for her arm and instead he received a punch for his efforts. Amiria recognized it barely had much force to it nor did it make much of an impact on her determined lord. Again he reached out for her, and this time was rewarded with a screech of outright rage. Amiria quickly realized her ruse was up and her fists flew in a hundred directions, landing several blows 'til Dristan gave a grunt of surprise.

His arms came around her chest in a deathlike grip. For several moments they stood there thusly, neither one moving 'til Dristan came upon the realization of what surely must have mystified him in puzzlement. There was no mistaking his right hand was cupping her well-formed breast.

"*Merde!*" he growled, and the loudness of his voice caused even the birds above to fly from their resting places in the tree tops.

Amiria dared not move lest she reveal more to Dristan than he had already encountered. All sense of struggle left them instantaneously as their ragged breathing synced in perfect unison. His chest was firmly molded to her back side, trapping the length of her hair between them. There could be no oversight of what he now held lest he was a fool. *Surely such would not be the case*, she thought.

"Release me!" Her demand burst forth from her lips. She hated how her voice quivered as she spoke. She waited impatiently and started to squirm 'til he finally let go of her breast. He did not, much to her dismay, release her so she could distance herself from the man who would surely not be pleased with her deception of the past months. She felt his hands on her arms as he slowly turned her trembling body around. She met Dristan's eyes with a lift of her chin and a glare of defiance born of her stubborn Scottish pride she inherited from her father. 'Twas the blight of her existence to be sure and would surely be her downfall this night! They stared at one another in stunned silence, and she marveled he controlled the rage she knew was hiding just underneath the surface of his look of disbelief and simmering fury. She held her breath, knowing she was about to feel the scorching fire of his wrath!

Dristan held his anger in check and was amazed at how calmly he was able to do so.

"Aiden?" he questioned aghast his voice sounded not like his own.

"Amiria!" Her voice crackled with hostility that she had been found out.

It explained so much, he thought, but to be duped by a mere woman was beyond his comprehension. Bloody hell, 'twas not only her doing but the entire inhabitants of the castle and clan that partook in her ruse! Surely all knew this mere slip of a girl had made a fool of him. He took hold of her arm as they swam whilst he all but dragged her to the small remaining bit of light still found in the middle of the pool. Taking her chin in hand, he lifted her face and saw angry eyes of violet returning his gaze in a rebellious manner. 'Twas the eyes of a woman who had haunted him for days.

Dristan released her with a look of revulsion and left her there, for where else was she to go naked as she was? He made his way to where his clothing lay on the grass. Dressing quickly, he turned his back and offered his cape for her to cover herself. It did not take long for Amiria to dress. Then, Dristan lengthened his stride to return to their men.

'Twas not hard to miss the gasps of surprise coming from his guardsmen as they stood at attention with their mouths agape at the sight afore them. One did not mistake the obvious sight of a woman, who followed their lord as she was draped in his cloak, reaching down past her feet. The MacLaren clansmen were positioned next to their horses as they uncomfortably shuffled from one foot to the other, trying to figure out how best to help their mistress.

Dristan glanced back to Amiria whose wet hair fanned down over his cloak. This sight alone could have tempted a saint to sin. 'Twas when his gaze settled on her captain, however, that at last broke the damn on his tolerance of being duped and made the fool. One look into Ian's hazel eyes silently told Dristan that Ian knew he would bear the brunt of their charade.

Dristan raised his arm, pointing to Ian, and spoke a command that was not to be dismissed. "Bind him."

"Nay!" Amiria yelled, trying to put herself between the two men whose eyes blazed furiously at one another.

"You will not speak lest spoken to, woman, else you may not like what happens to you next," Dristan voiced coolly with unmistakable authority. He pushed Amiria aside and headed towards his horse. He could no longer stand the sight of her, no matter how much he had wanted to find the woman from the beach, learning they were one and the same.

Amiria was helpless whilst Ian allowed his wrists to be tied He was assisted onto his steed, his reins were taken, and he was led from the glade in a manner much like an ill behaved child whose privileges had been stripped from him. What had been an afternoon filled with a sense of much needed independence, had turned into an afternoon of regret. 'Twas just as Ian had predicted.

Tears silently fell down her cheeks as they made their way slowly back to Berwyck. 'Twould be some time to come afore she would be able to right the wrong she had done her captain.

FIFTEEN

A SENSE OF UNEASE AND DARKNESS CREPT over the people residing within the silent stone fortress of Berwyck Castle. Whether they were serf, knight, or lady, all scurried out of the path of the Devil's Dragon in fear his growing wrath would fall down upon them, dooming all to a warmer clime in the hereafter. In the past se'nnight, it had become uncommon to pass someone who was not crossing themselves to ward off the evil looming in the air. Even the chapel seemed to hold more souls, of late, who came to pray for salvation from the priest, who welcomed their devotion to a higher being. All feared their liege lord more than ever afore and dared not incense him further. No man, woman, or child wanted to seal their fate in such a dreadful manner.

Blasts of lightening filled the lord's solar, casting eerie flickering shadows upon the walls of the chamber. 'Twas followed seconds later with the deafening boom of thunder, resonating across the rain drenched countryside. He heard and saw nothing as he stared with unseeing eyes into the dancing orange flames in the hearth. Within the depths of the blaze, where the fire was at its hottest, were vivid shades of violet. 'Twas a grim reminder of a woman he had been trying to forget for days. It had become a nigh impossible task.

Torrents of rain had been bombarding the land for the past several days, causing rivers to form where they should not exist. Having to stay indoors did not help improve Dristan's temperament but only seemed to enhance the resentment consuming him. A chalice of now cooled mulled wine remained untouched in his hands. He was unsure how long he had sat thusly on the stool but if the ache in his back was any indication, then 'twas time to rise and come out of his foul and ominous mood.

Placing the mug on the floor, he rose and stretched his arms above him afore dragging his fingers through his hair in frustration. He began to pace the chamber 'til he felt as if he were a caged animal. He went to a nearby table holding various parchments he needed to peruse but felt no inclination to do so, knowing he would not be able to give them his full attention. His mind could only make out hair the color of flame and a pair of eyes the shade of azure seas, which held him mesmerized against his better judgment. A snarl of rage came forth, and he raked his arm across the table, watching the contents of the table top go flying across the room. He slumped down in the chair as scenes from the past several days, a living nightmare, played themselves afore his eyes.

The ride back to the castle had been done in silence but at a pace that was almost frantic. Dristan had cared not, as they rode through the forest, what his men thought whilst branches whipped at his face. The sting had mattered little to him for 'twas a welcome distraction from his mindset of outrage. If he could have put his hands around Ian and Amiria's necks, he surely would have strangled them both for the part they had played together.

Dristan could only wonder if their relationship went further than just captain of the guard and daughter of the now deceased lord. She was, after all, a very beautiful woman. Thoughts of the two of them spending time alone together ran amuck in his head.

They had entered the inner bailey, and stable lads had readily come to take their horses. He had briefly glanced at Amiria, who stood there, trying to assess her situation. 'Twas not 'til he ordered her knights to the dungeon that he at last had a reaction from her. She had snarled her rage and grabbed her sword from the saddle to protect her men. 'Twas a futile effort, at best, as her sword had sailed through the air after making contact with Dristan's own.

Ian had attempted to come to her defense but struggled against the ropes binding his hands. Dristan had stood between the two and hissed between clenched teeth at Ian that he had erred in his service to his mistress. Amiria had hung her head with guilt 'til she heard Dristan order ten lashes as Ian's punishment and that he be put into the stockade afterward. Afore any could halt the madness that had overtaken her, Amiria pulled a dagger from her boot and lunged at Dristan, who easily side stepped out of her way.

She had fallen to the ground with blinding tears in her eyes whilst she watched Ian being led away. With a cry of anguish, she had pulled at her hair stuffed into her tunic and raised the dagger to cut her tresses as her own self-made punishment. Dristan had been upon her afore she knew what had happened and had held her wrist in a painful grasp 'til the blade had fallen from her numb fingers.

He could still remember whispering in her ear the harshest words he had ever spoken to a lady...for every single strand of her hair she cut from her head, he would retaliate with a lash of the whip.

Amiria had risen from the ground, cursing him to hell and back as no other had ever ventured. She had then turned her back to her liege, as if she dismissed him from her mind like some mongrel dog, and went to pick up her fallen sword. Dristan had followed close behind her, not wanting to underestimate the ire of a woman who felt scorned. He remembered reaching for her sword and disarming her afore she acted rashly and regretted her actions this day. 'Twas only as she finally turned to face him with a furious glare that he realized she had been but taking what moment she could to try and compose herself. From the look set upon her face, 'twas clear she had failed miserably.

Dristan rubbed his eyes, hoping the vision he still held in his memory would fade from his mind or, at the very least, change for the better. Yet still the image's plagued him. He remembered how they had stood there, toe to toe, although she had tilted her head back so she could look him boldly in the eyes. He had ordered her to her chamber. She had stood there staring at him, assessing the worth of such a command. Dristan could still picture the expression in Amiria's beautiful eyes whilst tears coursed down her face as clearly as if she were standing afore him now. She had left him standing there in the courtyard, feeling as if he himself had erred.

A woman's tears had always been his downfall. Rarely did he put himself into a position to care enough about a woman and whether the lady shed them or not. Why he felt differently about Amiria he knew not, but 'twas most likely because he knew her to be the woman who had haunted his dreams. If he had been able to offer her some form of compassion, he would have wiped those tears away with a gentle caress and kissed her lips 'til she sighed in pleasure. 'Twas not a reality he could foresee. Their fates seemed to now be sealed on a course he could not change, for she would bear him nothing but hatred for some time to come.

Since Amiria had become his ward and he was responsible for her welfare and future, mayhap 'twas for the best she hated him. Her ploy still bothered his peace of mind, since she had pledged her fealty to him. However, he continued to ponder what steps he would need to take as the lord of the keep. 'Twas no small wonder he lacked sleep and could no longer think rationally.

Dristan came out of his reminiscing at the persistent rattling from the closed shutter window. It gave evidence to the fierceness of the winds of the late summer storm that continuously blew across the castle, making the rooms uncommonly cold. The flickering candlelight proved there was indeed a breeze in his solar and he would need to mayhap add a tapestry to the window seat to assist with keeping out the chill.

Rising from his chair, he returned to the hearth and stooping down picked up his wine and tasted of it. Even though the wine had become chilled, 'twas still refreshing and he took another swallow, enjoying the heady flavors. His moment of peace did not last, however, as a gust of wind slammed the shutter open against the walls. Parchments swirled around the room as he rushed about collecting them afore they inadvertently ended up in the hearth. Placing a heavy tome on the stack so he did not have to gather them again, he went to the window where the rain soaked the floor and the cushion on the window seat.

His hand briefly made contact with the shutter only to have it wrenched from his grasp yet again by the gale force winds.

After another attempt, he finally had the wood firmly in his grip and was about to shove the portal closed when something caught his attention whilst he peered out into the night. 'Twas only the ever so slight movement in the outer bailey, catching his eye, that gave him pause whilst he was getting soaked down to his skin. He squinted to see through the sheets of rain and could barely make out Ian even now in the stocks with the flickering torches somehow remaining lit. But Ian was not what caused him to pause in bewilderment. Nay! 'Twas the sight of another figure beneath a cape of sorts, trying to hold her cloak and one more around her captain for protection against the tempest, that caused his wrath of fury to explode.

Apparently, the woman had no common sense to listen when told to stay in her chambers. Once again she had defied him and most deliberately. Indignation against the stubborn girl renewed within him. Dristan closed the shutters with a loud bang, slapped the latch in place, and left the room with an enraged, furious stride.

He paid no attention to those souls who scurried out of his path as he made his way down the winding turret and through the Great Hall. He only had one purpose on his mind and for once that temperamental red haired vixen would obey the commands coming from her lord and master. Since she gave no heed to the instructions he had issued her, 'twas apparent she felt herself above such menial objectives and was in need of a well learned lesson. Two could play this game of hers and if she wished to play with fire and feel the wrath of the Devil's Dragon, so be it. Only time would tell if she would be able to survive the flames!

Amiria sat in a puddle at Ian's feet, trying not to shiver from the cold. 'Twas this blasted rain, making it a near to impossible feat for there was not a part of her body that was not drenched. Yet here she sat and so here she would remain to protect her captain against the elements at any cost. 'Twas her doing that found him in his current predicament since she had not listened to his counsel. In her heart she felt, at the very least, she would share in his agony against the storm.

She tried to stifle the persistent cough she had been trying to hide from Ian, but such a task had become more and more difficult as the hours passed. In truth she had no knowledge of how long she had been out here with him. At some point, she remembered how Garrett had shown up, offering what assistance he could. He had continuously played sweet and pleasing melodies on his bagpipes, reminding them of days gone by. Yet as the rains began to worsen, Amiria told him to put his pipes away and find a warm fire. He could do no more for her than what she asked.

Is it just my imagination or does this infernal downpour come at me from all sides? she thought. No matter which way she turned her body or moved her cloak, the wetness penetrated her attempted defense of trying to remain dry and seemed to mock her. Even the muddied water splashed her face from the ground beneath her. The puddle she sat in was now beginning to widen to the size of a veritable river and Amiria contemplated how long she would be able to remain vigilant in her resolve to stay with Ian. She would do him no good if she was carried away with the floods growing around her.

She chanced a glance at Ian and realized he had been watching her beneath his reddish hair, hanging limply from his head in long wet strands. 'Twas as if he read her thoughts and he knew her resolve to stay with him was breaking and weakening.

Raising her head, she dared him to speak his thoughts aloud and was rewarded with the smallest of smiles.

"Go inside, Amiria," he said thoughtfully. "Ye've doon enough lass."

She rose slightly and adjusted what she could of the mantel she had draped around him and the stocks that had kept him standing for days. "Ach Ian, dinnae try tae be such a braw laddie," she chided in Gaelic, "'tis boot a bit o' a drizzle annoyin' us fer a spell."

"English, Amiria, as I find it more pleasing to my ears to hear it from your lips," as he, too, switched back to a language to which they had become accustomed.

"As you wish, Ian."

"I am glad to see you still can muster up a bit of humor though, my lady...a bit of a drizzle indeed," he laughed gruffly for the first time in days, as she made a grab for her cloak whipped from her head by the wind. He continued to study her so she gave him the tiniest hint of a smile to put him at east. She failed to hide how she trembled from the cold. "Truly, Amiria...enough is enough. Lord Dristan will release me soon, and I'll not have you watch when he does so. I'm sure my legs will give way and I'll end up in the mud on my sorry arse. 'Tis not fitting you should witness a knight so."

"I stay 'til you are released, Ian," she retaliated somberly. "I have vowed it upon my soul so do not ask me again to leave as your words will fall upon deaf ears. I already have much to repent of in the chapel come your release."

Ian clamped his lips shut, apparently not having the strength to argue with her further, and Amiria once more settled herself at his feet. How long they were there thusly she could not say as time had no meaning when they were just trying to bear the brunt of the storm.

She must have dozed off but quickly awoke with an anguishing scream as she was lifted from her vigil by Ian's side. Her arm was pulled roughly by none other than Lord Dristan as he began pulling her through the bailey. Ian shouted her name but to no avail as the sound escaped on the wind, and she quickly lost sight of him. She called out for her captain, feeling helpless that he should remain out in the elements because of her stubbornness.

Amiria clawed at Dristan's arm and hand as he dragged her through the mud towards the keep. Yet still he continued onward, tugging her farther and farther away from Ian's side. She cursed Dristan's soul to hell and heard a faint mutter from him, saying he was already there thanks to her schemes. They had reached the inner bailey when she used her last remaining strength to kick and punch any part of Dristan she could come in contact with. His patience came to an end when she heard him grunt in pain as her fist landed squarely in his left eye. She felt herself being lifted up in his arms with not even a pause in his stride as he carried her as if she weighed nothing.

"Continue as you have been behaving, and your men and Ian will stay where they are 'til you come to your senses. I do not care if they are there through winter. 'Tis your choice!" he voiced sharply.

Amiria finally calmed at his words, not wishing her men a longer sentence due to her actions. She felt Dristan shift her slightly, and her head naturally came to rest comfortably on his shoulder. She would have sighed if she could have, but her body decided it had suffered enough abuse and began to shiver uncontrollably. 'Twas followed by a deep agonizing cough she could not control.

They entered the keep and several paused at the sight of their lord carrying Amiria close to his body. She turned her head into his shoulder in embarrassment with thoughts that some might think Dristan was off to have a bit of pleasure between the sheets. Apparently, any misinterpretations of his actions did not bother him in the least as he lengthened his stride, calling for Kenna and Lady Lynet to follow him to Amiria's chamber.

He hurriedly took the steps two at a time and called for a serf to open Lady Amiria's door. Several other women followed them into the chamber, stoked the fire, and pulled down the coverings on the bed to ready the room for its mistress.

Amiria felt the warmth of the hearth as Dristan began to peel the soaking wet garments from her freezing body. 'Twas a task greatly hindered by Amiria's own feeble attempts when her weak hands slapped him, thinking he would not take her thusly. She cried out in frustration when the only remaining cloth covering her was a flimsy chemise, molding itself to her young lush body. It revealed more than any other man had ever seen afore.

Looking down, she was appalled to notice the material was indeed almost transparent and she used her arms and hands to cover herself as best she could. She watched, fascinated and surprised, when Dristan noticed her embarrassment and at last turned his back whilst one of the serfs came and a sleeping gown warm to her chilled skin was thrown over her head.

The fabric barely ceased its motion at her feet afore she felt a blanket wrapped around her and she was once more deposited into Dristan's arms. Amiria began to struggle 'til she heard Dristan murmur to cease. 'Twas not a command nor an order, but just a quietly whispered word that put her immediately at ease. All fight left her and she thought it surely must have been her imagination when she felt her lord caress her hair and seemed to rock her gently in his arm as her coughing began again. His soothing words spoken in Norman French reached into her soul against her will and wrapped itself around her torn and confused heart. With a single tear gently falling from her eye, Amiria allowed sleep to finally claim her.

She would have been astounded if she had been aware when Dristan wiped away that solitary tear as several of his own fell in concern for her welfare from his deep grey eyes.

Hugh watched Dristan and Amiria disappearing up the stair well. *Damn his soul to hell*, he thought, fuming with his anger rising to new heights. Who would have known such a beauty had been hiding beneath that filthy face and boy's attire? Were they all such fools not to see for themselves she was in truth a girl? He looked around to those who still occupied the hall, hoping to find a willing wench to take care of his needs. Where was a castle whore when you had need of one in this God forsaken place?

Not seeing a serf who would be able to service his baser desires, he espied the daughter with the lanky frame. She stood staring up at the stairs with a look of bitterness upon her sharp features. He smiled calculatingly and made his way across the hall. When he reached her side, he leaned towards her, whispering words of flattery in her ear. It had the desired effect, which was to have her blushing and nodding her head in agreement to his suggestions. *Foolish girl*, he thought, escorting her out of the keep to find a secluded place for them to while away the hours. *She would suit my plans to perfection*, he reflected as he cast her a smile that any other would have recognized as pure evil.

SIXTEEN

DRISTAN STOOD IN THE GREAT HALL with Riorden and Fletcher. Leaning over the large oaken table, he perused various parchments etched with the improvements he desired to have constructed on the castle walls and grounds. He weighed the merit on the words of the two men closest to him when they voiced their opinions with possible changes and gave them credit for seeing a few flaws in his theory of change. They were details he should have thought of for himself, but he had been distracted of late. He glanced up once again and swore for the hundredth time when serfs headed towards the stairs, carrying yet another stack of linen and several pails of water. His brow furrowed with worry. 'Twas obvious Amiria was not improving as he had hoped.

"Scowling will not cure what plagues her, Dristan," Riorden commented dryly.

Dristan's concern focused on the now empty stairwell. "Use any other word but not that one, Riorden," he replied sharply.

"Last thing we need is something as deadly as the plague running rampant throughout the countryside."

"'Tis becoming a lovely shade by the way, my lord," Riorden said with a smirk, apparently trying to lighten his foul mood.

"What is?" Dristan questioned snidely, trying to pay attention to their conversation and failing terribly.

"Your eye, of course," Riorden answered. When Dristan cursed it only made the obnoxious man laugh louder. "'Tis a shade of purple that would not look well on others but it seems to suit you most splendidly indeed, my lord."

"You risk much to further sour my foul humors, Riorden. If I was not so worried about the girl, I would take you to task for your cheek with a quick trip to the lists so I could show you a thing or two about respect," Dristan grumbled, giving his captain a warning look that this conversation would continue at a later time.

"I am still perplexed on how such a wee bit of a girl managed to fool us all into thinking she was in truth her brother," Fletcher marveled. "Considering she is a woman of such small stature, she handles a blade most admirably."

"God's blood, I knew there was something about Aiden that was not right! I just could not figure out what was wrong with the lad...er...girl," Riorden continued, clearly annoyed he had not been able to solve the mystery where the boy was concerned.

"So where do you suppose her brother is?" Fletcher inquired.

Riorden waited a moment for their liege to answer. When none came forth, Dristan gave a brief nod and Riorden began to recall to Fletcher all he had learned. "Her men claim to believe he is buried in some unmarked grave since they saw him fall by their lord. They had hopes that perchance he yet lived and have searched everywhere. There is no word this has come to pass."

Dristan continued his unapproachable stance. He heard Riorden's words but they in truth did not register that he needed to offer further comment. All his thoughts were with a small slip of a woman, who lay in her chamber with an illness Kenna had not been able to heal. Since he was so preoccupied, he missed the looks given between his two closest guardsmen.

Dristan barely acknowledged Riorden as he began to pace. 'Twas clear his mind was elsewhere and not on the task at hand of perusing the parchment afore him. His captain strode to a sword leaning against the wall near the hearth and grasped the hilt, feeling the weight in his hand. Only a fool would leave their weapon unattended whilst under the close scrutiny of their lord. Visions of a lad hefting such a sword swam through Dristan's mind.

The sound of metal scraping against stone tore Dristan out of his internal turmoil coursing through him and back to the present.

Riorden began swinging the blade back and forth afore him.

"'Tis hers," Dristan muttered hoarsely.

"Aye, I see that now upon closer inspection," Riorden replied as he handed the sword to Dristan.

Dristan took the offered hilt and studied the blade for several moments. "'Tis too heavy for her."

"I agree, which would explain her utter lack of progress on those moves you were trying to instill in her," Riorden exclaimed.

"'Twould appear so," Dristan voiced coolly. "'Tis still a fine blade despite the weight."

Silence stretched on between the men 'til Kenna appeared, rapidly descending the stairs. She halted afore the three knights, her brow heavily furrowed with worry lines. She swayed slightly and Dristan reached out to steady his healer afore she fell from fatigue.

"What news do you bring, Mistress Kenna? Will she be well?" Fletcher asked hopefully.

She raised tear filled eyes to Dristan but clearly 'twas plain to see she would not bear them glad tidings. "I fear I have done all I can, Lord Dristan," Kenna said quietly with downcast eyes. "I am afraid 'tis in God's hands now."

"Nay! I refuse to believe 'tis so!" Dristan voiced in exasperation as his words resounded off the walls. He bolted from the room, taking the stairs two at a time just as he did when he carried Amiria up them but recently.

He heard the others following him up the stairwell, leading to the third floor housing the family members. Upon reaching the landing, he turned left and raced in the direction of Amiria's chamber. He halted at her door when he noticed young Patrick, sitting on the floor in the passageway, crying. Taking a moment, he squatted down to his page and patted his shoulder, offering him what comfort he could.

"Please, my liege, I beg of you...make her well," Patrick hiccupped, wiping his tear filled eyes with the sleeve of his tunic. "I canna lose them both."

"I am no healer, Patrick, but I will do what I can," he said gruffly, and the boy nodded his head.

Entering the room was akin to walking into the scorching heat of a raging fire. A serf knelt at the hearth with her sleeves rolled up, busily setting wood to the flames to further heat the chamber. A pile of linens were being collected by another, who all but ran from the room. The skin of those who remained glistened with sweat as they mopped their overheated brows. With much reluctance, his eyes went to the bed. He was prepared to see the worst. 'Twas not far from the truth as his eyes scanned the slight form, lying motionless upon the bed. Amiria lay under multiple coverlets, shivering with cold. Her ashen face caused the color of her hair to appear an even darker redden hue. Lady Lynet knelt by the bed with a rosary in her hands. Her nimble fingers moved from bead to bead as she mouthed a noiseless prayer for her sister over each. She glanced up when she felt his presence at the edge of the bed but remained silent.

His expression grim, he came to sit upon the edge of Amiria's bed and saw how her breathing was shallow as if each breath she took cost her a bit more of her life. He reached his hand out to her brow and felt the beads of cold sweat running down her face. Perplexed she should feel chilled to the bone with the chamber a furnace of heat, he placed his hand down between the coverlets on the bed and felt the cool wetness of the mattress. Growling his aggravation, he threw the linens from her drenched body and heard the gasps of shock coming from the occupants of the room behind him.

"What madness are you about, my lord, that you would disturb my sister when she is so ill?" Lynet voiced, worried for her sibling. She rose on wobbly legs from spending time upon the floor in prayer.

Dristan's piercing gaze briefly met the young girl's, subduing her words. He ignored any further protests from the others, as well, and silenced them with a single glance. He leaned down and scooped Amiria up into his arms. Worry crossed his brow as he carefully held his charge, feeling as though she weighed no more than a mere babe. Tenderly, he cradled her unresponsive form, bringing her shivering body closer to the warmth radiating from his own.

He began shouting orders afore he even left her room. A serf scrambled to open the heavy oak door. Others rushed down the passageway to Dristan's own chamber where they proceeded to stoke the fire in the hearth and turn down the bedding. He cared not who he left in his wake. His only concern was to break the chills consuming Amiria's tormented body. Most would not approve of his methods he thought to use, but he could think of no other option.

"Leave us," he commanded to those who had followed him to his chamber. All but one fled in haste.

"My lord, I beseech you, perchance—" Kenna began.

I said leave us!" he shouted, still holding the trembling girl to his chest.

"I think only of her reputation, my liege. 'Tis not proper you should be alone with her even though she is ill," Kenna dared. "I fear I must speak on her behalf since she is unable to do so herself, although those who remain outside may also have cause to echo my concerns for her welfare."

"You have nothing to fear on that account, Kenna."

"Be that as it may, others may not agree, and then who would see fit to wed a woman who is soiled? Whether you touch her or not, her reputation will still be sullied," she answered gravely. "Not all would believe your words, given your reputation, my Lord Dristan."

"There will be no others to worry about asking for her hand."

"My lord?" she questioned with concern, afraid Amiria would spend her life alone or be sent to a nunnery.

"I have been given my orders from our king and obey him I must without question." Dristan looked at his healer and let out a deep breath he seemed to have been holding a lifetime. "Amiria of Berwyck and clan MacLaren will become my bride, forever sealing the fate of this land and its people to England."

Her alarmed expression of shock showed on his healer's features and 'twas apparent from her reaction to his words that for once she had not seen such an event coming. 'Twas obviously the first time her sight had failed her and it took several moments of staring at him afore she at last found her voice. Her words were not very reassuring but he would have been surprised if they had been.

"If this is so, then tread lightly and with care, my lord, or you will find yourself saddled with a hellcat. She will not take it well she is used as a pawn in a king's game for power. Lest she comes to love you of her own free will, I am afraid you will truly learn what hell on earth really means."

He nodded to her only once. For now, 'twould have to be enough and he would deal with the repercussions of his actions when Amiria was healed. He gave a silent prayer to God above, hoping his meager offering would be enough to appease a higher being.

Kenna's mouth remained in a grim line of disapproval but she was powerless to do anything further for Amiria. Moving towards the hearth, she left some warm broth and herbs she hoped would help cure the young woman. Against her better judgment, she assisted Dristan with removing Amiria's wet gown from her body. She took the garment to have it be laundered and turned to leave the room whilst Dristan laid the young naked girl down in his bed. She caught one fleeting glimpse of her liege as he, too, stripped the clothes from his body and joined Amiria, wrapping his arms around her and bringing her close. Embarrassment heated her cheeks to be witness to something so intimate between two people.

Quietly closing the door, she leaned back against the oaken portal, giving a huge sigh of distress. Her sight had failed her! She had known Dristan and Amiria were connected by some invisible bond but she had no inkling that the king had demanded Dristan was to wed her. They may not as yet know it, but their destiny would be linked together for all time. Knowing Lady Amiria and her stubborn nature, 'twas perchance best any choice to her future would be taken from her. Their liege would have his work ahead of him to convince the woman he had their best interest at heart. She did not want to be around to witness such a battle of wills that surly would be put to the test.

Kenna made her way out of the keep, across the baily, and into the chapel. She was not surprised to see it filled with not only Amiria's guardsmen, who had been released, but Dristan's, as well. As her eyes became accustomed to the darkness of the room, she espied other clan members as they, too, knelt on the stone floor, offering petitions for the daughter of their deceased laird.

With a quiet stride, she went towards the front of the chapel 'til she witnessed Geoffrey slide over to make room for her. With his hand held out to her, Kenna took hold of it and knelt down next to him. His thumb made a slow lazy motion across her skin 'til he at last gave one last reassuring squeeze afore he let go and returned to his prayers. She bowed her head and began to humbly make her plea, fervently hoping that God above would hear and grant her wishes. She was not sure 'twould be enough for what she knew was yet to come.

SEVENTEEN

SABINA SAT ON THE FALLEN OAK LOG, swinging her bare feet back and forth and enjoying the bit of sunshine finally gracing the land. In her hand she held a clear glass bauble recently given to her as a gift from her brave and mighty knight. It had been strung into a necklace with blue and green beads, and she marveled at the reflections shining from it as the sunlight came to rest upon it. She hoped this would be the first of many such treasures to come from time alone with an attractive knight of the realm.

A nearby splash from the river caused her to look up as Hugh rose from the water. He was not as handsome as Dristan but he was still easy on the eyes. His blonde hair hung down around his shoulders and fell across his forehead. Sabina had a most urgent desire to drag her fingers within its length as she brought his head closer so she could eagerly savor his kiss.

Her greedy and hungry eyes took in his naked torso and the muscles that bulged from his arms and chest. Indeed he was a fine specimen of male ruggedness with a stride of someone who was confident in his desires. She knew those desires included her. Such was the pride she had in herself for she was aware of her worth as a daughter of the MacLaren clan. She had no doubt of her worth that included a huge dowry and any man would be lucky if she but graced their company.

Hugh came to stand afore her, and although she tried to read his thoughts in his dark brown eyes, she became confused by the look of disinterest in his features. Sabina gave him a smile that surely was seductive, but watching the frown appear on his brow caused her yet another pause. *Surely he wants me as much as I want him*, she thought haughtily. Jumping down from the log she perched upon, she went to wrap her arms lovingly around his neck only to have her hands slapped away as if she were naught but an annoying bug to be squashed beneath one's feet. Afore she could voice her concern, he spoke harshly, causing her to grimace in uncertainty.

"Why is it you follow me? Did I not satisfy you enough last eve?"

"I but missed your company, Sir Hugh," Sabina said huskily.

"Bah, you do not know me well enough if you think I will believe such drivel after a few brief romps in the stables."

Sabina gave him what she hoped was a brazen stare and licked her lips in a silent invitation, causing his brow to rise in question. "Perchance now is as good a time as any to remedy the situation between us." She took a hesitant step forward, not knowing if he would reject her offerings. When he remained calmly looking down his nose at her, she timidly placed her arms around his neck and leaned the length of her body against his. His reaction was instantaneous. Encouraged by what she felt growing beneath her skirts, she nuzzled his neck in response to his growing desire for her.

"My, you are such a lusty wench aren't you, my pretty?" Hugh replied whilst his hand roamed at will up her thigh beneath her gown. He cupped her buttocks and her moan caused him to chuckle. She had a moment's hesitation that perchance she gave herself too cheaply 'til he pressed his manhood against her. 'Twas her undoing as she remembered their night together and the pleasure she had found in his arms.

Her thoughts racing ahead to finding herself wed to a knight of the king, she was startled when Hugh grabbed her none too gently and backed her up against the solid trunk of a nearby tree. He tore at her bodice and she listened at the near deafening sound whilst the garment ripped beneath his questing fingers. Delving further beneath the fabric, he grabbed at her breasts, painfully pinching the nipples. A started gasp escaped her but she was not sure whether 'twas from discomfort or pleasure for the two were so closely related.

Pleasure quickly turned to pain. Sabina cried out when the abrasive bark from the tree tore into her flesh as Hugh continued his assault on her body. She called his name, asking him to stop. He dismissed her plea and only continued his pursuit to shed her of her garments. She heard him begin to mumble. Her ears strained to hear his words that sounded almost as if he were speaking of Amiria. She gave a brief laugh and held onto his head as he began to nuzzle her breasts. She must have been mistaken. Hugh was hers and hers alone, and no one would come between them especially her sister!

'Twas not 'til Hugh heard the distant rumbling of approaching horses that he finally raised his head, eyes glazed over. His vision of the beautiful red haired vixen promptly vanished to be replaced by the unremarkable and harsh features of a crow. He made no attempt to hide the look of disappointment when his eyes fell upon Sabina.

"Dress yourself, lest you wish to offer your services to my army," he scoffed, adjusting his hose and giving the wench no further thought.

Hugh retrieved his tunic from the ground and continued dressing. He had just fastened his sword about his waist when a group of men advanced. A sly smile lit his features. He went to meet them, further distancing himself from Sabina so she would not overhear their speech.

Hugh approached the leader, who jumped down from his steed. Each stood facing the other as if unsure if they should be reaching for their swords. Hugh continued to view the chap afore him, who was of similar height and coloring. They resembled each other so much that they could have been brothers.

In unison, they both gave a short laugh and quickly embraced in a fierce hug. "'Tis good to see you this far north, especially in this God forsaken country full of Scottish swine. Since you are here, I assume you received my missive?" Hugh exclaimed in delight that his plans could now move forward.

Gilbert of Windermere gave his cousin a hard slap on the back. "All business I see, as usual Hugh. Some things do not change even with time."

"You have assembled more men than I had thought possible on such short notice. They are not averse to wreaking some havoc on the countryside I hope?"

"You of all people should know, as a hired mercenary myself, I work for what you will pay me. The men will expect the same," Gilbert answered smugly. "They care not what the job entails, so long as they have enough coin in their pockets and a willing or unwilling wench to service their needs."

"See to business first, cousin, and then you may worry about what crawls between their legs for their pleasure."

Gilbert gave a mighty laugh, slapping Hugh heartily once more on his back. He looked over his cousin's shoulder to see Sabina, adjusting her clothing. "I see you have been busy, as well, this day. Hopefully, you will not leave a brat in her belly as you did with that countess in France. I think I can still hear her shriek of outrage that you would not wed her."

"By God's bones...she was not worth the trouble, especially after I found out her father had lost her dowry and family fortune from gambling debts," Hugh answered with a short laugh. "How ironic 'tis that a lot of that fortune still ended up in my purse which is now funding this little excursion."

"So what is the story of the wench there?"

Hugh turned and gave but the briefest of glances towards Sabina afore giving his full attention back to his kin. "She's the old lord's daughter, or at least one of them. She shall serve my purpose for the time being, but she is not the prize I am after."

"You always did go after what was beyond your reach during every siege, Hugh. This one must have cost you dearly if you have sent for me to aid you."

Hugh thought on Gilbert's words afore answering, and yet his anger rose when he thought of the humiliation he had suffered at the hands of the Devil's Dragon. "Do not test my temper, cousin, as you may not like the results," he warned.

"I see I have hit a sore spot in your armor," Gilbert snidely replied. "Tell me, what is the merit of such a prize that had you so urgently requesting my assistance? Surely the wealth must be great that you will make this trip worth my while."

Hugh glared meaningfully at his cousin. "The castle should have been mine."

"Again, Hugh, you seek that which is not yours, especially given the fact you must serve Dristan of Blackmore," Gilbert said casually. "Did you not learn your lesson in France?"

"Damn you to hell, cousin! Do not remind me that I am but a vassal to that man!"

Gilbert continued with a wave of his hand as if he had not heard Hugh's words. "Besides, Berwyck Castle is but a pile of stones far removed from the wonderful delights London has to offer that I know you so enjoy."

"You would not scoff away my words so easily, Gilbert, if you but knew how long it has been since I've had the leisure to tarry in London for my pleasure," Hugh declared loudly. "'Twas by my blood, sweat, and the steel I carried that won this land for king and country."

"You know the way these things work Hugh. The castle and lands were destined to be held by Dristan for he is King Henry's champion. Come now and tell me you but jest when you say the lands should be yours?"

"Months of living in the muck and hacking away with my blade at worthless Scots, and what thanks did I receive for my victory?" Hugh bellowed to himself. "I shall tell you what my reward was and what it earned me; a trip to the stables to muck away manure like the lowest stable lad, time in a foul watery pit with creatures crawling at my feet, and twenty lashes 'til my back was raw and fever raged within my body! I earned this land, and I shall claim it as mine! I will have my revenge and to hell with Dristan of Blackmore!"

"You speak bravely now Hugh, but I would not attempt to declare ownership of anything once it has been claimed by the Devil's Dragon."

"Bah, the king has yet to venture here to award the lands to that beast," Hugh said viciously.

Gilbert gave a short laugh. "The king is a busy man. Think you he will travel this far north to publicly award Dristan these lands? I tell you now, Hugh, forget about the madness of your greed and leave here with us. We shall travel back yonder to France to enjoy what life has to offer there and indulge in all its pleasantries!"

Hugh could only stare at his cousin as if he had lost what little sense his dame had given him. "Leave here and lose favor with the king? Nay Gilbert, I cannot for I should like to keep my head firmly attached to my shoulders. Besides there is more to this than just a pile of stones, as you so call it, and afterwards I shall still remain loyal to the crown."

"Please tell me a woman is not involved with this plot of yours!" Gilbert snorted snidely. Hugh cast him a look and his cousin had his answer. "Nay, tell me 'tis not so...not again!"

"She is a prize above all others, including the lands. 'Tis just convenient she comes with the castle as its ward," Hugh conceded.

"Then her care will be determined by Lord Dristan and hence the girl will be unattainable to a mere knight of the realm," Gilbert said, hoping to convince Hugh of his logic. "Forget the wench! There is always a willing whore who can see to your needs."

"She is no whore so watch your words when you speak of her thusly!" Hugh warned menacingly.

Gilbert held his hand up, backing down from the fight that was but a word away. "Then if she be a lady from the keep, she now belongs to Lord Dristan and as such is beyond your reach," he declared logically.

"She cannot belong to him, however, if he is dead, now can she?" Hugh smirked knowingly as he watched his cousin come to terms with his words. "Come. Let me tell you of my plan and how we shall proceed in claiming my new lands."

Hugh began to weave his plot and smiled at his cleverness. 'Twas only a matter of time afore he would claim Berwyck Castle as his very own!

Sabina watched as Hugh and the newcomer knelt on the ground whilst Hugh began to draw something in the dirt at their feet. They began to laugh and as they rose, Hugh tossed the stick he had used up into the air and caught it with a gleeful smile set upon his face. Sabina wondered how her knight had gathered the small army she saw in the distance for 'twas not a common practice when one was a soldier to another.

With a worried look upon her brow, Sabina gathered up her cloak and necklace and made for her horse she had left standing near the river. As she mounted her mare, she only gave one brief glance at the men now surrounding Hugh and decided she would worry about what they discussed another day. After all, it had turned out to be too glorious a morning to be wasting her time on such trivial matters of what mere men had on their minds. She had more important issues to think about, relating to her future.

With one last look upon her lover, Sabina kicked her horse into motion and began to softly hum a tune as she made her way to the castle. Bringing her horse to a full gallop, she began to consider all the ways she might begin to please her knight come the eve and earn his undying love and devotion. She could almost see him now on bended knee, begging her to be his bride with all his adoration for her shining in his beautiful dark eyes.

Sabina would have been devastated with the knowledge that Hugh had not given her a further thought the remainder for the day. Instead, he was even now scheming of ways to have Amiria as lady of his hall and, more importantly, in his bed.

EIGHTEEN

A FREEZING BITTER MIST SURROUNDED her so she knew not where she was. Arms outstretched, she called for aid, knowing she was lost, but only the sound of her lone voice could be heard, resonating about her. None came to help her find her way home from the fog entrapping her. She continued crying out for those who were dearest to her. Yet no reassuring tone to calm her fears was heard to her ears. She called for Aiden, Lynet and even Patrick. She called for Ian and her guard, but none came to save her from whatever force held her. She was utterly alone.

The cold continued its assault on her senses 'til she felt arms of steel take her into their embrace. She attempted to claw her way from the pit of despair she had fallen into but to no avail. Surely sunshine and warmth could be found to coax soothing heat into her chilled body. Yet no relief came to her whilst she fought her way to what she thought was the surface where she might see clearly and escape the now frosty steel holding her captive.

She persisted to shout out her plea 'til she was hoarse and still hopeful that surely someone would come to her aid soon. As the mist began to clear, she shook her head, attempting to adjust her blurry vision. The barest hint of an elusive smile at long last appeared upon her beautiful face when she began to feel a comforting warmth seep into her very soul. 'Twas a heat she had seemingly craved for a lifetime. Soothing words of solace penetrated her world whilst memories of her father flashed across her mind. She called out for her laird, thinking surely it must be her da, who had rescued her from the abyss she had found herself in. Yet he, too, deserted her with a look of disappointment on his features.

'Twas then she began to realize her mistake, thinking a friendly ally had come to take her to safety. Nay, 'twas not so! Fire began to now devour her. Fire or ice...she did not know which was worse but thought she would rather die freezing to death than to feel the red hot flames of fire flickering at her toes.

Screams of terror spewed from her lips. Her eyes now beheld the Devil's own, coming ever closer to pull her down into the depths of hell. His minion began to take shape into the form of a sleek black dragon with glowing red eyes. Fire breathed crimson in the monster's nostrils. His mouth gleamed into a tooth filled sinister smile. She watched in horror as the back of the dragon's mouth began to blaze with an orangey fire ready to consume her. She attempted to scamper away but found that the Devil's Dragon quickly whipped out its tail to capture her in a viselike grip, refusing to release her.

Who would come and save her from this despair? She knew of only one soul who was capable of the deed of slaying the demon imprisoning her. 'Twas said he, too, was a loyal servant and in league with the Devil, so why would he assist her? Time and time again she had defied him, even though her heart yearned for things to be different between them. In her agony, she could feel the burning heat radiating from the tail ensnaring her. She could only wonder if he would put aside their differences to come annihilate the dragon that bound her.

And then she heard the gruesome sound of laughter coming deep from within the chest of the beast afore her or perchance 'twas the Devil himself. In her mind she could not differentiate between the two. Quickly, another image began to intermingle with her tormentors. For her, she only knew the reality that danger was fast approaching. The scorching fire came closer and closer towards her side. Her decision made without any further hesitation, Amiria called out a name and only one name over and over again...Dristan.

For nigh unto a se'nnight, Dristan hovered over the weakening young woman, lying in his bed, who seemed dwarfed in his eyes. He had become a mere nursemaid to the lass for he would let no other tend her. Sleep had become something of a novelty to him and he could not remember when he had last been able to close his eyes with a good night's slumber. At least for now, Amiria rested, although she had yet to open her eyes.

Kenna or Lynet saw his meals were brought to his chamber and he ate when he remembered that his body needed nourishment. Usually, 'twas the soft cry of his name coming from Amiria that would cause him to rush to her side, hoping her fever had at last abated. He still remembered how his body had flinched in reaction to hearing his name uttered from her lips for that first time in some desperate cry for help in her state of delirium. 'Twas a clear indication from her words, calling out to him, that whatever tormented her in her dreams, she at least felt he would save her from her fate. If only this would be true once she awoke. Her words, however, may not be of joy once she learned she had unknowingly shared his bed.

Sitting next to her, Dristan's eyes raked his charge for even the slightest of changes. Fever continued to rage throughout her body. He had alternated between cool cloths upon her head to placing her in a tub of tepid water. The latter seemed to help more, although she put up quite a fight even in her weakened state. He awaited new water to be brought up to be placed in the tub in another attempt to remove the heat tormenting her. Given the last attempt, he would bolt the door and remove his own clothing this time since the last endeavor caused him to become as drenched as Amiria when she fought him from the icy cold.

A brief knock on the door had Dristan rising, thinking the task would be at hand. Opening the door, he saw Riorden, standing there with a grim look upon his face. He opened the portal wider and his captain entered, although he did so reluctantly.

"Is there any change with our lady?" Riorden inquired quietly in concern.

Dristan gave a negative shake of his head. "Your news must not be pleasant for you to disturb me. You have continued training the men?" he drawled wearily.

"Aye, my lord, although 'tis not why I have come."

"Then tell me your news so I may continue to see to Amiria," he commanded with a sharp edge to his voice.

"A messenger has returned from the men sent to patrol the outer boundaries of your lands, my liege," Riorden uttered coolly. "The farthest hamlet to the north has been raided with the village burnt to the ground. All have been slain and the crops destroyed."

Dristan looked at his captain with fury glazed eyes. "None survived?"

"Nay, my lord. Even the livestock were slaughtered."

"Have another dozen men sent out to scour the country side. Instruct them to ride light in order to cover more ground. Include one or two of Amiria's guard. Perchance if the villagers see one of their own with us they might loosen their tongues if they know of any wrong doing," Dristan said meaningfully. "I will not let this go unpunished if we can capture those involved, nor stand for killing those who are under my care!"

"I will see to it Lord Dristan," Riorden said with a brief glance towards the bed. "We continue to pray for Lady Amiria's recovery."

Dristan only nodded, not trusting himself to speak further regarding her welfare. He opened the door, allowing his captain to exit and bid enter the servants, who brought several pails of water to fill the tub. After they left, he put the bolt in place, locking out the world beyond his chamber. He tested the water and noted 'twas but lukewarm, although to Amiria's skin 'twould feel like the coolest of springs found high in the mountains.

No sense in putting off the inevitable, he thought and gave a silent prayer that God would forgive him for his deed. He stripped off his clothing and left them neatly folded on a stool by the hearth. With a heavy sigh, he looked down upon his chest and saw the four strips of tender flesh where Amiria's nails had raked him the last time he plunged her into the tub whilst she fought him like the very devil.

He went to the bed and gazed down upon his beautiful lady. He could think of her as nothing else for she would in truth become his wife once she was well again. 'Twas whilst he stared at her that he began to notice the slight beginnings of a smile playing upon her lips, and he pondered what she dreamed of. She began to stir most alluringly and whispered his name as provocatively and sweetly as any lover could.

He pulled the coverings from Amiria and lifted her into his arms. She molded her body closer to his own and his heart began to beat a little faster. Dristan was caught off guard, feeling her silky limbs wrapping themselves around his neck. The warmth of her lips began to nuzzle his neck and she gave a sigh of contentment as his arms held her tighter.

"You came for me...I knew you would," she purred into his ear in a soft confident whisper.

"Aye, so it appears," he said as a tingle went through him with the feel of her breath in his ear. Carrying her to the tub placed by the fire, he slowly swung his legs over its rim to feel the water at his knees. "Brace yourself, Amiria." She held him tighter as he began to sink down into their bath. Water sloshed over the sides onto the floor the lower he brought them.

"'Tis too cold," she said groggily with a shiver, trying to get closer to the very heart of him.

"'Tis for the best, my lady, and will make you well again."

"I do not like it," she said with a pout and proceeded to turn in his arms.

Afore Dristan could cease her motion, Amiria lifted slightly away from him, moving both legs to either side of his own, and promptly sat down upon his upper thighs with a wiggle of her bare bottom. This certainly was not what he had intended whilst he watched in fascination her fixed glassy eyes take in his face. Her tongue moistened her lips. Smiling, she stole a quick fleeting kiss.

"Warm me," she demanded, molding herself to his chest and lowering her lips to receive another of his kisses as if she had done so a dozen times afore.

A part of him sprang to life against his better judgment and yet he could not for the life of him cease the intoxicating kiss she gave him. He breathed life into her as their tongues intertwined in a dance known to lovers for centuries. For just a moment longer would he indulge in what she offered, for he knew she would not remember what she did once she was herself again.

He cupped her head, bringing her closer and deepened their kiss. His fingers tangled themselves in the length of her hair 'til he could stand no more. His hands lowered themselves down her back in a gentle caress. She sighed in pleasure and Dristan heard the throaty moan that escaped her. He would have smiled through their kiss if 'twere possible for he had the notion he had awakened a temptress that would forever belong only to him.

She pulled away from his lips with a shake of her glorious red mane and gave a satisfying laugh. Her eyes widened in bewilderment from the hardness of him against her naked flesh. "I have roused my dragon, I see," she smirked knowingly.

"That you have my dear, but you must yield the day for I would not have you hate me come the morrow. I am, after all, just a man with a man's desires."

"You want me then as I want you?" she inquired shyly with a blush to her face.

Dristan gave a brief laugh and caressed her cheek as she leaned into the palm of his hand. "Aye, my lady, more than I should but we cannot continue this."

"Who are you to say we cannot?"

"I am your liege lord, Amiria. When we come together I would have you more yourself that you remember our first time together as husband and wife."

Her brows puckered into a frown as she pondered his words. "Are we not wed?" she whispered in puzzlement. Afore he could answer, she continued onward with a brazen look upon her features. "It matters not," she declared possessively, "for you belong to me!"

Dristan watched his lady as she for the first time hesitantly reach out and began running her fingers over his wet furred chest. Making small circles, she watched him through lowered lids and he shivered at her touch. He sat back amused at her expression since he could tell she was enjoying the feel of his skin beneath her fingertips. Her hushed words confirmed his suspicions.

"I somehow thought a dragon such as you would be smooth to the touch and not covered with so much hair. I believe I like it better this way..." she declared, with a promise reaching her eyes.

Dristan took hold of her hand as she began to reach lower and tenderly placed a kiss to the inside of her wrist. She sighed again at his touch. "Nay, my lady, do not test my resolve further, I beg you. One of us must remember not to let this insanity overtake us, so behave, you vixen!" he said with a chuckle although he had to admit he enjoyed this playful side to Amiria. "Now sit back down that I may bathe you to bring down your fever," he ordered.

"I am not a child to be treated so."

"Then do not behave as one so I can do my best to heal your illness."

She ignored his words and rose, slightly kneeling with him between her legs. She took her hands and smoothed his tresses back from his face in a gentle caress. He gave a sharp intake of breath as she began to touch him at her leisure. 'Twas apparent she approved of feeling a power that she could affect him so.

"You are mine," she declared knowingly, "and mine alone."

Dristan stared back at the seriousness in her eyes. "Aye, as you are and will be mine."

"Then take me now, Sir Dragon."

"Not today and not like this Amiria."

"Please Dristan...I want you and only you."

"You know not what you say, *mon amour*," he said, trying to calm his racing heart. God help him but his need to be inside her was beyond anything he had ever felt afore.

If Dristan had known her better, he would have realized from the stubborn tilt of her chin that Amiria would not have him gainsay her as she was wont to have her way. She leaned forward 'til her breasts caressed his chest. Enjoying the sensation it created, she captured his lips again in another searing kiss even whilst she began to lower her body to meet his own.

Dristan was so distracted by the enchantment she had woven around him that he did not realize what Amiria was about in her determination to carry out her desires had been met. 'Twas not 'til he felt himself entering her and breaking through her maidenhead, making them one, that the comprehension came to him full force. He heard her cry of pain and cursed his foolishness at what he allowed to happen. It came crashing down upon him like the fiercest of storms.

"Amiria!"

Too late, she wrapped her arms around his neck. She held on tightly almost in some attempt to protect him from the pain she felt. Her breathing slowed whilst she became accustomed to the sheer size of him. Dristan feared to move since he did not wish to cause her any further pain, so instead he held her close and whispered words in French to sooth her.

She at last raised her head and loosened her grip about his neck to look into the depths of his eyes. The smile she gave him melted the ice surrounding his heart. He only hoped and prayed she would one day forgive him.

"Now you are in truth mine, Dristan of Berwyck, and we are mated for all time and eternity like the dragons of lore, who but take one true mate for their lifetime," she said with conviction. "Now make me burn for you, my dragon, as I know only you can and claim me as your own!"

His resolve broken since the damage was done, he told Amiria to hold tight as he rose with her still in his arms. Her legs fasten themselves securely around his hips. They never once broke contact whilst he carried her to his bed with her words to make her burn seared into his heart and, more importantly, into his very soul. Seeing the woman beneath him that had consumed his own dreams for days, he lowered his head and sealed his fate with a hungry kiss. She returned it just as greedily and clasped him tightly to her as if she would never let him go.

Dristan took the remainder of the day and far into the evening to do just as she had asked somehow feeling that he, too, had been burnt into her very soul. 'Twas not 'til the moon was high in the midnight sky that they at last were both completely sated and at long last slept peacefully still entwined in each other's fierce embrace.

NINETEEN

A MIRIA BEGAN TO ROUSE from one of the most incredibly delicious dreams she had ever experienced in all of her ten and nine years. Oh, to have such a night in truth as she had spent with the phantom of her dreams. Heat rose to her cheeks in a becoming blush at the remembrance of how she had lost all inhibitions by behaving so wantonly. She never would have dared such had she been awake.

She snuggled deeper, bringing herself closer to the warmth beside her and inhaled deeply of a scent that, although unfamiliar, was most pleasant to her senses. Was it perchance just a figment of her imagination that it felt as if a well formed muscled arm embraced her to keep her in her current placement? As Amiria became more fully awake, she flinched. Surely 'twas a leg not her own that her naked toes were idly rubbing up and down against like a lover's caress.

Amiria suspiciously opened one violet eye and took in the sight of Dristan lying next to her. Her mouth hung open in a silent O of surprise of whom she beheld afore her. 'Twas true and not a vision! She was molded up against him if she were an extension of his own warm skin. One of her hands rested upon his chest and she felt the steady beat of his heart beneath her palm. He, on the other hand, lay upon his back with one arm extended above his head; the other held her firmly in place as if afraid he might lose something most precious to him. She could hardly believe what she beheld as a soft snore came from his slumber.

She was not sure if she was more outraged or embarrassed as she remembered her actions, knowing she had initiated her own demise of her lost virginity. She began to disentangle herself only to realize the length of her tresses were firmly trapped beneath her dragon. God's Blood, had she really uttered those words to Dristan, all but daring him to claim her as his own? She had obviously become her own worst enemy since she had encouraged him with her words and actions. 'Twas more than apparent, since she lay naked next to him, that Dristan had indeed laid claim to her long into the evening hours. If she remembered correctly, and she was afraid to admit it even to herself, she, too, had enjoyed their coupling 'til sheer exhaustion overtook them both.

Amiria attempted once more to rise only to realize in horrid fascination that Dristan automatically tightened his arm about her. His snores suddenly ceased and he opened a bleary eye to stare at her.

"Come, Amiria, and rest yet awhile," he whispered huskily, "'tis frightfully early to be about the morn after such a night as ours! I am still most weary."

Amiria watched in fascination as he closed his eyes, expecting her to obediently obey him. He had all but dismissed her! Unable to hold her temper any longer, she released her outrage with a well-aimed fist into his rock hard belly. His eyes flew open with a grunt of unexpected disbelief. She was momentarily satisfied 'til he moved with lightning speed and she quickly found herself pinned beneath him with her arms extended over her head. She tried to find her voice and the anger she had felt but a moment afore yet failed given the delightful intimacy of her situation.

"What was that for?" he demanded sharply.

"How can you ask that of me?" Her chest rose and fell rapidly, as she looked into the depths of his steel grey eyes. Desire coursed through her veins for a taste of what he had given her the night afore. She was further undone when he began to caress her hair ever so gently.

"You sorely test my patience, Amiria," Dristan murmured, "especially when I had planned to give you time to get used to the idea of us as husband and wife."

"Surely you jest, my lord, if you think we shall wed," she said defiantly.

He gave her a smirk that she had come to know all too well, usually when they were out in the lists. "And surely you realize that I would do nothing less than wed thee once I took you to my bed."

She quickly gazed around the chamber and saw that she was indeed not in her own room. Still, this changed nothing to her thinking. "I know you not well enough that I would pledge my troth to you."

"You know of me," he drawled lazily with another smile that spoke more than any words could reveal.

Amiria frowned in puzzlement. Was that a hint of hurt she detected in his words or just conceit, thinking how she must be pleased with him? She was so very confused! "Nay I do not, my lord. I know you not at all."

Apparently conceding the battle of wills at least temporarily, Dristan rose from the bed and began to don his garments. Once he was fully clothed, he built up the fire to take the morning chill from the room. The task did not take long and Amiria watched his every move with uncertainty, not wanting to admit where her course in life would now lead.

He at last turned his attention back towards her, and Amiria's breath caught in her throat from the intensity of his gaze. Dristan stood afore her as the embodiment of a champion knight favored by his king. Any woman in her right mind would be lucky to have a man such as him to call her husband. Yet, her stubbornness refused to allow another to make a life's decision for her whether 'twas reasonable or not. She refused to remember that if her sire yet lived, she would have obeyed his commands of whom she was to marry without question. She gazed at Dristan, carefully trying to assess what was crossing his mind when he remained staring at her from across the chamber.

He moved in one fluid motion. She was his prey and he stalked her with a precision and a determination she had never witnessed afore. She could only imagine he was the same when it came to planning a strategy upon the battlefield. She drew the fur blanket up to her chin, as if that alone would save her from his steady gaze. He came and sat next to her but did not touch her.

"You know me better than most know those who would wed together," he clarified. "Resign yourself to the idea that you shall be my wife."

"How can you want me as your lady wife when you've only known me as a lad?" she protested.

"Surely even you know that is no longer the case, *ma cherie*," he said as he reached out to touch her.

Amiria jerked away from his hand in distaste at how easily he thought she would comply with his demands. "Do not think that after one night you can be so free with me again. I will not allow it!"

Dristan gave a slight chuckle of amusement. "Your destiny has been decided Amiria and one that was truly never yours to control. You have a most fiery soul, my lady, and I would be hard pressed to find a more perfect match even if I searched 'til the end of time."

"You still canna be free to touch me at your will!" she protested, knowing Dristan would do whatsoever he pleased.

He reached again towards her and although she slapped his hand away a second time, he gave her a devilish grin and tucked a lock of her hair behind one ear. "Touch you I will whenever I so wish it. Again I tell you to resign yourself to your fate, for we shall indeed wed."

"But you must give me time," Amiria pleaded. "Several months at the very least."

"Take care of what you ask of me, my lady, for I will be honest with you...after what we have just shared, I will be hard pressed to get you afore a priest with all due haste."

Amiria blushed crimson at his words. "You cannot plan to hold me to that which I thought was but a dream!" she retorted hotly.

"Aye, my sweet Amiria, I can and will do so," he said, feeling her forehead and finding it cool to his touch. "Your fever has left you. 'Tis a good sign."

"How long have I been sick, my lord?" she inquired hesitantly.

"'Twas longer than to my liking." Dristan once more swept her with his intensive gaze. "Stay abed this day. I will see that food is brought to you so you may break your fast."

Amiria allowed him to softly run his fingers through her hair once more. Memories of their night together flashed across her mind and she knew her cheeks blushed most furiously yet again. He seemed to know where her thoughts had taken her as his smile broadened. With another satisfied glance at her features, he at last rose from her side.

She watched his every move as Dristan strode about the chamber 'til he finally took up his sword, fastening it to the belt about his hips. He gave her one last satisfied look afore he took leave of the room.

'Twas not 'til her air had left her with a sudden whoosh that she realized she had been holding her breath. With a muffled groan, she threw the covers over her head and pondered the mysteries of her sorry life. She was beyond angry with herself for allowing her deepest most thoughts to become a reality even whilst she thought it all but a pleasant dream. Oh, how she hated that insufferable man!

'Twould be well into the afternoon afore she came to the realization that against her better judgment, her dragon had indeed made claim to her as his mate and had branded himself into her very soul.

TWENTY

I SWEAR, IF I MUST STAY within this chamber one moment longer I shall scream from sheer boredom loud and long enough to bring down around us the walls of this keep," Amiria ranted sullenly.

"Mayhap if you resume your stitchery, sister, 'twill soothe you," offered Lynet whilst her fingers worked at the cloth in her lap.

Amiria quit her pacing to stare in annoyance at her sibling. "You know better than anyone that there is only one thing that will calm my nerves and taking up needle and thread is not it."

"'Tis forbidden...besides, you are to rest."

"I have rested enough."

"Mayhap 'tis so, but our Lord Dristan has ordered you to stay within your chamber so you must obey his will," Lynet reminded her. She frowned in concentration as she began to loosen another botched attempt at mending the garment beneath her usually nimble fingers. "He would not be pleased to find you wearing hose and tunic instead of gown and wimple. You should not test him so."

"I will wear what I choose as I have always done!"

"Be prepared then to pay the consequences when you are staring up into his angry eyes, for I do not believe you will like the view," Lynet predicted, focusing on trying to undo a knot that appeared in her unraveling of the mess she had made. "Please sit, Amiria, for you are distracting me with your frantic stomping about, and I must now start this over yet again."

"I am restless, and the pacing helps my already stretched nerves."

Lynet ignored her sister's words and continued her chiding. "Your behavior and rambling about Lord Dristan's untimely demise has been far from ladylike. I can almost hear mother's voice taking you to task for it."

"I need fresh air," Amiria complained, as she continued traipsing from one end of the room to the other.

"Then go to the window and open the shutters for goodness sake," Lynet proposed in irritation of being cooped up with her sister.

"'Tis not enough."

"'Twill have to be for that is all Lord Dristan shall allow you."

Amiria whirled around at her sister and threw up her hands in frustration. "Say his name just one more time Lynet and I swear by all I hold dear I shall thrash you for it. I will not be held prisoner in my own keep!" she yelled.

"Surely you are not a prisoner, Amiria. It also does you no good to take out your irritation on me," Lynet said, calmly putting down her mending. "I have seen the way he looks on you when he comes to see how you fare each eve. He only means to ensure you are healed from your illness. Besides...I like him."

Amiria merely grumbled quietly about the nerve of the man that he should dare to order her about as if she would listen to him. 'Twas not as if they were already wed, and even if that miracle came to pass, she was not sure she would give him the satisfaction of obeying him. Lynet's words, however, still hovered in the air like an unforeseen shadow of what was yet to come. She made her way to the window seat and opened the shutter as her sister had suggested. The slight amount of fresh sea breeze wafting its way to her senses was like a welcoming balm to her troubled soul. She soon became lost in thought as the past se'nnight's flashed across her memory.

Dristan had come each eve to bring her supper, assuring himself she had eaten her fill and was on the mend. The silence stretched between them had been deafening and, if it had not been for Lynet and Patrick's chatter, there would have been no conversation at all. Her hand trembled in recollection on how each night as he left, he lifted her numb fingers and placed a tender kiss upon them. If she closed her eyes and willed it hard enough, she could still see how the torches held in the wall sconces reflected the light onto his black hair whilst he looked down upon her from his towering height. She gave a hearty sigh and wondered when she had become such a dewy eyed imbecile, who could no longer put more than two words together once in his presence.

She slammed the shutter closed in disgust. "I've had enough of this confinement," she decided and went to her chest at the end of her bed. Lifting the lid, she began to haphazardly throw gowns up over her head 'til she reached towards the bottom and found what she had earnestly sought. "Help me don this," and she began to pull her armor out with a loud clank of metal as it hit the stone floor.

"He will not like it," Lynet advised with a grim expression.

Amiria silenced her with a stony glare of warning 'til her sister held up her hands in defeat and began to help her with the tedious task of settling the heavy armor on her small frame. 'Twas not 'til the mail coif was placed on her head that she began to feel a bit of her old self. Her scabbard missing a most vital element, she began to search every corner for her sword.

"'Tis not here, Amiria," Lynet said carefully in answer to the empty sheath Amiria all but shoved in her face.

"'Tis mine and I shall not allow him to take that which our father gave me," Amiria retorted, as she reached for her helmet, pushing the mail coif from her head and pulling out her braid. "Why did he see fit to take my sword of all things?"

"Given your reaction, I believe he did what he thought best in his own behalf. I think he must care for you, Amiria," Lynet chimed in. "He declared he would keep it so as not to offer you the temptation of sending him to keep the devil company and thereby depriving you of a husband."

"I'll send that horses arse to the devil alright and enjoy the pleasure of performing just such a task to rid me of that vermin!" she raged.

She left her chamber and sibling behind her in a huff of righteous determination to set things straight with the lord of the keep. She would begin by finding out where Dristan had put her sword. With her helmet under her arm, she made her way down the spiral turret and through the Great Hall with an unwavering stride to begin her search for her dragon. God help his sorry hide when she found him.

TWENTY-ONE

"SWORD!" DRISTAN SHOUTED at Riorden as yet another blade was tossed into his eagerly waiting fingers. Never taking his eyes off his two opponents, he swung both blades now gripped firmly in each hand. Now this was a challenge he would prefer instead of that sulking bit of a female who confused his thoughts at all hours of the day.

"*Mon ami*, I believe you have grown weak since you have tended your young *mademoiselle*," Nathaniel taunted, assessing his lord for where he might strike to win a victory in his name.

"You would have thought he would have learned a thing or two from Fletcher's sire," Rolf added with a gleam in his eye whilst he also swung his blade. "Mayhap he must needs return to the duties of squire!"

"'Twould be fitting, since he cannot remember to don his armor or even chain mail," mocked Morgan. "Just look at him, strutting about the lists, bare chested as he is."

"Don your armor, my lord, or the castle whores will be of no use to any of us but you," ridiculed Taegan. "'Tis no wonder they laze about lusting after such as he."

Raucous laughter filled the lists from Dristan's guard, along with a number of silly giggles from those same lusty wenches who dared much to be in the lists just to gaze upon him as he trained.

The men had all halted their own individual training to watch the spectacle and skill of Dristan hefting two blades at once. The whores only licked their lips with hope that he would take notice of them and have him beckon unto at least one of them to share an evening of delight in his arms. Much to their dismay, he was too preoccupied with the task at hand and that was to relieve the garrison knights of their swords and perchance a bit of pride in their own worth. There could be no doubt, to those who viewed his performance, that he demonstrated his superior prowess and ability with his weapons. Even Ian and those of Amiria's guard appeared impressed upon the site afore their eyes.

"A wager! Aye! A wager, Rolf will be the first to find his sorry arse in the dirt," Turquine forecast whilst he continued watching his three companions fight. His grin only broadened from the glare tossed in his direction from Rolf, who advanced on the field again towards his target. "Come now...surely one of you will take my bet, or are you all cowards?"

A groan went up in the air from those on the sidelines as they watched Turquine's prediction come to pass afore any coins could exchange hands. Nathaniel closely followed with a grunt of pain as he, too, landed on his backside.

Dristan looked over at his men, giving them a silent demand to join him. Ulrick took up the challenge next. He let down the visor on his helmet and Drake followed closely on his heels.

'Twas an impressive site as Dristan engaged another two opponents. On and on, he continued his assault with sure steady strokes, taking on one of his guard after another, including dispatching Ian and his men. 'Twas not 'til he was left standing alone on the field that he stabbed both blades into the dusty earth in front of him as he looked to see who he could take on next. 'Twas a good day's training, but he was ready for more as he had hardly worked up a sweat of much merit to his thinking.

"Perchance, now that you have had a small warm up, you would care to take on someone more experienced to challenge you," Bertram called confidently.

Dristan laughed. "Well come hither if you dare, Sir Bertram, and let us see what skill you have this day. I shall endeavor to give you aid by only using one blade, if you think it shall help with your feeble attempts to actually heft your sword upright."

"No need. I will not be coddled like some babe!" Bertram called, advancing to the center of the field.

Once more the sound of steel connecting with steel rang out in the air, surrounding the two men, who stood toe to toe in combat. Bertram gave an impressive effort as Dristan labored at least slightly harder to keep him at bay and at arm's length.

'Twas only when a slighter figure dressed in armor, with her long red braid swinging behind her to and fro, came into the corner of his vision that Dristan faltered in his stance. One sword went flying as 'twas torn from his grasp. He hissed seconds later, feeling a nick from Bertram's blade skimming across his arm. *Merde, that woman will be the death of me,* he thought.

He watched Bertram back off a pace or two, aghast that he had actually somehow managed to penetrate his liege's defenses and draw blood that seeped down his arm.

"My lord I—," Bertram began appalled at what he had inadvertently done, which was no small feat.

Any further words of apology were silenced and Dristan waved off his efforts, as the mistake was of his own making. As her liege lord and soon to be husband, he assumed Amiria would obey him and stay off the lists, remaining in her chamber as he had commanded. His stupidity knew no bounds for 'twas obvious by her determined stride as she advanced towards him that he was to suffer a lifelong battle of keeping the upper hand where she was concerned. By the look upon her face, her Scottish pride was in full fury mode. She stopped afore him and gazed at him with blazing violet eyes. *God, what a beauty*, he thought silently.

"Where is it you vile excuse for a man?" she said and made to give his chest a shove to drive home the depth and point of her anger. She became further annoyed when he did not budge even an inch. He folded his arms over his massive chest and began to smile.

"My lady," he replied casually.

"Do not belittle me with useless titles. I am certainly not yours!"

"You are mistaken if you think differently, Amiria," Dristan replied for her ears alone.

"How could you take that which is mine to protect myself...my sword of all things?" she yelled furiously.

"You have no further need to carry a blade, as you now have me to protect you. Do you not agree 'tis only fitting I should do so, given the status of our new relationship?" he asked smartly.

"You had no right to take my blade, Dristan!" Amiria retorted hotly between clenched teeth, ignoring the gasps heard around her when she addressed him so informally.

Seeing the men listening intently to their conversation, he made light of the situation for their benefit since he would not have them think he had become soft, as he dismissed her words.

"What is it you want of me that you interrupt my men's training? Do you not perchance have something to sew to keep you occupied 'til you can attend me this eve?" he joked more loudly than he intended, as his men joined in with their own laughter. He did not miss the quick look of hurt that flashed in her eyes afore it quickly transformed into hot blazing ferocity.

A snarl erupted from Amiria's lips. She threw her helmet onto the ground and swirled around to look upon her men, who stood nearby. She noticed Devon and advanced on him, since he was shorter than the rest of her guard. Amiria held out her hand and waited for her guardsman to release his blade over to her.

"I beg o' thee milady, dinnae ask such o' me," he pleaded, crossing himself furiously and glancing back and forth between his lady and his lord.

Amiria only continued her grim assessment of Devon and once more thrust out her hand in a silent command. 'Twas only with the greatest reluctance when he finally placed his own sword within her reach.

Turning, she marched her way back to Dristan and he knew from her expression she was not pleased he had just ridiculed her in front of the entire garrison. As if to prove her point that she was more than worthy to guard his back instead of whiling away her hours at stitchery, she lifted her blade. Dristan should not have been surprised to see her determination to swing the weapon towards his head. Only at the last minute did Dristan react as he brought up his own whilst the two swords met with a thunderous clash.

'Twas at that precise moment, that God above voiced his displeasure at the two opponents and rain began to pour down from the heavens. Lightening lit the sky and 'twas not long afterwards that the once dry ground began to turn to mud as the two strong willed people continued to hack away at one another.

Dristan made a motion of his hand, dismissing the garrison to seek shelter. Sheer rage drove Amiria to the brink of exhaustion as she lifted her sword time and time again. She would not yield to him nor concede defeat, but neither would he. He continued to marvel on how well his soon to be bride was handling the blade she held and looked forward to when he would present her with the sword he was having forged for her.

On and on, they engaged one another in a fight that was more than just the raising of swords. Their footwork remained sure despite the mud that would have made the ground tremendously slippery to a novice swordsman. After a few more jabbing efforts on her part, Dristan could surmise Amiria began to tire and made the decision for her that she would fight no more this day.

He achieved his objective of maneuvering her during their sword play from the lists to the inner bailey. She was so determined to win their match that he knew she had no inkling as to her whereabouts. A quick glance into the courtyard showed that most had stopped on their way to find cover from the storm to watch the exhibition afore them. Others hid in the shadows of the buildings to watch in fascination their display, whilst buckets of rain fell from the sky.

Dristan gazed at his lady, who still met his sword stroke for stroke and had to admit that for a woman of such small physique, she had held her own against him better than most young lads her age would have done whether they had been ill recently or not. Impressed with her skill, a smile of pleasure escaped him that this woman would be his wife. He had met his match and with Amiria at his side, he would never be bored.

Amiria witnessed the gleam in Dristan's eyes whilst the memory of their time within his chamber flashed unexpectedly across her mind. She watched him advance as his sword swung out as if to proclaim its master would not be defeated. Transfixed on the movement of his blade, she came to realize too late 'twas just another ruse to the unknowing opponent to become distracted whilst the blade flashed afore her with lightning speed. Her hand numb, she watched in dismay when her blade went sailing up into the air.

He came to her in all his manly glory and crushed her to him in a massive embrace. They stared into one another's eyes, both breathing heavily. Trying to catch her breath, he did not seem to mind her armor digging into his flesh. Afore she knew his ploy, his head swooped down and claimed her lips in a fierce and hungry kiss. 'Twas almost as if he rewarded her for a job well done, when his mouth became possessive and demanding, she yielded to him.

Her resolve to remain angry crashed down around her, much like the tempest swirling furiously above their heads. His grip tightened around her waist, and then she knew no more other than the intoxicating headiness she felt as the magic of him left her wonderstruck. Her ability to think clearly became dull, including everything around her, but him. All Amiria could manage to ponder was how he continued to delve into her weakening senses, leaving her mesmerized whilst she was effortlessly lifted and carried into the keep.

She clung to him never wanting to let go. One moment she was outside with the rain pelting down upon her head and the next the door to his chamber slammed shut with the bolt thrown into place. She knew not how he had divested her of her armor and garments so quickly, but ceased to worry about aught else but the man who caressed her hot skin. Instead, she lovingly wrapped her arms around his neck, welcoming him whilst she was pressed down upon the feathery mattress of the bed.

The storm pressed on around them, but they cared not what was happening to the world outside the chamber. For them, nothing existed but this moment in time as they took the remainder of the afternoon to while away the hours in a diversion known only to lovers. If there was cause for regret, which surely there would be, they would come face to face with that misfortune another day.

Hugh sulked out of the darken passageway and glared at the door closing upon the woman he wanted for his very own. Cursing, he made his way to the garrison hall and his quarters. Taking parchment and ink, he set to scribbling a message to his cousin, even though his writing was hardly legible. Sprinkling sand on the document to dry the ink, he blew the granules away, folded it, and dripped hot wax upon the edge, placing an unrecognizable seal in its place. None other than Gilbert would identify it belonging to him. A small coin was pressed into the hands of his most reliable servant, ensuring his missive would reach its intended destination.

His patience at an end, he leaned back in his chair with a grim smile, knowing soon he would have all he desired.

Twenty-two

SABINA DESCENDED INTO THE GREAT HALL with the attitude born of a queen. Her head held high, she stood on the last step so that all might view her beauty. She waited in silence with the hope one gallant knight would come to her, offer his arm, and escort her to break her fast. The longer she lingered, the more agitated she became, knowing that none, including Sir Hugh, would extend such a service.

The hall itself was swarming with men who consumed their food with gusto and those who trained hard and had empty stomachs to fill. 'Twas apparent a majority of Dristan's original army had departed for places unknown to her. Mayhap with their purses full of coin, they traveled elsewhere now that the battle had been won for England. They had been mere mercenaries and of no worth and, as such, were beneath her. She cared little of what had become of them.

Her gaze drifted to the high table where Dristan sat upon the raised dais as if he held court. His captain, Riorden, was placed to his right along with several of his closest guardsmen.

Amiria sat to his left along with Lynet and Patrick. A lone chair sat empty that she assumed was meant for her. Since food was already laid out afore them, 'twas evident they would not wait for her arrival afore they decided to partake of their meal.

With narrow eyes and a troubled frown across her brow, Sabina continued her observation of Dristan and Amiria as they ate. *Just look at them*, she thought furiously. *They sit as if they were in truth already wed.* She inwardly snarled whilst Dristan offered her sister the choicest meat from the trencher they shared. With a flick of his wrist, a servant rushed to fill the chalice of wine held in his hand. Dristan took a small sip then turned the chalice towards Amiria. *A lover's gesture*, Sabina reflected with a scowl. With a small smile, Amiria placed her lips where her lords had just a moment afore been pressed, as she, too, partook of the heady wine. Disgusted with their affectionate display, Sabina could watch no longer and looked upon the hall to see what else might intrigue her.

Sir Hugh sat with a group of men at one of the lower tables and although she attempted to catch his gaze, he continued his conversation as if he did not see her gesture for him to join her. Feeling slighted, Sabina began to wonder if mayhap she had erred by bestowing this particular knight with the gift of her virginity. 'Twas not as if he had been gentle with its taking or any other time he had bedded her. Still, he seemed to be the best of what this hall of late had to offer, with the exception of Lord Dristan.

As her gaze continued to sweep the large smoky room, she looked upon one of the tables near the kitchen and espied Amiria's guardsmen. *Now here is something to briefly hold my interest*, she thought wryly. One lone knight in particular did not eat his fill of the food placed afore him. Nay! He, too, had eyes for only one individual within the hall. From the stern look upon his face, he was none too pleased whilst he watched Amiria's movements.

Sabina began to weave her way across the filthy rushed covered floor, not that she cared the silk slippers she wore would be ruined beyond repair. They were, after all, Amiria's, so why should she bother to worry about their care. Coming up behind Ian, she felt him flinch when she placed her hands upon his shoulders and leaned down to whisper in his ear.

"She makes a spectacle of herself, does she not, Sir Ian?" she questioned him snidely whilst she planted the small seed to take root inside his head.

"You are not to judge her, Lady Sabina," Ian replied through clenched teeth, apparently guessing at her ploy.

"She will be with him again tonight in his chamber, Ian. Mark my words 'twill be so!" Sabina gave a short laugh. Moving her hand across his shoulders in a slight caress, she left his side.

Her work done with Amiria's captain, she walked with swaying hips through the middle of the hall, knowing that all male eyes watched her every move. Sabina saw how Dristan watched her most intently and smiled towards him regardless of the frown he bestowed upon her. She watched in fascination when he crooked his finger, beckoning her to his side. *Now this is most promising*, she thought.

"You asked for me, my lord?" Sabina said quietly, bowing her head ever so slightly.

Dristan's perusal swept around his hall and apparently, he did not like what he saw. "Is there perchance something wrong with the victuals served here in my hall, Lady Sabina, which causes you to be late?" he questioned irritably.

"Nay, my lord."

"The company then," he proposed. "You do not care to break bread in my presence?"

"Again, I say you nay."

"Then take your place at my table and do not be late again or you shall forego eating 'til the next meal is set," he exclaimed smartly. Dristan beckoned to her once again and she made her way to his side behind the table. He turned in his chair to face her, clearly showing his displeasure. "The keys to the keep, Lady Sabina," he said, holding out his hand. "'Tis clear you require further instruction on how it should be properly run."

"As you will, my lord," Sabina said quietly. She undid the link from about her hips with fury raging within her. A quick look about the hall gave evidence everyone had witnessed her mortification and disgrace. Any power she had held, however briefly, was gone when Dristan now handed those same set of keys to Amiria.

"You would do well to listen and learn from your sister," he ordered, giving her a nod towards the vacant chair.

Sabina realized she was dismissed since Dristan turned his attention to the conversation going on with his men. As she made her way passed Amiria, her jealousy got the best of her and she leaned down to whisper in her sibling's ear.

"Looks to me like 'tis you, dear sister, who has become his whore," she taunted.

Sabina took her place and watched in satisfaction whilst all color drained from Amiria's face. As she began to eat her fill, she saw that where once Amiria had enjoyed her evening, it now appeared Sabina's work was done at the high table, as well. Even Dristan could no longer coax a smile upon her sister's face. *Ah yes*, she pondered snidely to herself. *Sometimes 'tis indeed the small things in life that gives one cause to smile and brings so much pleasure. You just have to pause and savor such a moment whilst it lasts.*

Hugh waved to a serving wench, who rapidly came and poured more mead into his empty cup. In return, his hand reached out giving her bottom a hard squeeze. With a squeak, the girl rushed off towards the kitchens and Hugh returned his attention to gaze on the beauty of the woman who sat not far from him. He continued to watch and wait, although he was unsure if what he had been waiting for would come sooner rather than later.

As if he had willed it, the door to the keep burst open and a messenger rushed to Dristan's side. *Wait for it*, Hugh thought, watching in disguised amusement as Dristan listened to the lad's words.

Hugh did not have to tarry long for Dristan's reaction. After reading the missive, Dristan immediately rose, shouting for his men to mount up to ride to one of the villages under his care. Hugh knew 'twould not matter how hard and fast the army rode, for there would not be much left for Dristan to save once he arrived. 'Twas interesting though that he planned on taking Amiria's guardsmen with him, leaving the girl most vulnerable. Hugh had not thought Dristan would be so careless, but 'twould be to his advantage. Hugh cared only that he was left behind.

Keeping his eyes upon Amiria, Hugh watched in amusement when Dristan leaned down to have speech with her and she shied away from his touch. Dristan threw up his hands, downed what remained in his chalice, and stomped from the keep, firmly slamming the portal closed behind him.

Vastly pleased, Hugh took a long draught of his drink and wrung his hands together in anticipation. Perchance this was going to be much easier than he thought.

TWENTY-THREE

THE MOURNFUL MELODY from the lone bagpipe player vibrated off the rafters of the stable. Garrick leaned up against a hay bale serenading Amiria with a Scottish tune as old as the Highlands itself. He had a look about him that said he would have smiled had he been able to and not miss a note. Amiria took up the song and sang with a purity most could not compare to. Her father would have been proud to hear her sing the song of her ancestors in perfect Gaelic.

For Amiria, she simply had come to tend Caliana when she noticed her piper on the way to the stables. He had seemed somewhat lost with the majority of the castle knights riding off with Dristan. She motioned for him to join her and, as she took up her brushes and began to coax a shine into her horse's mane, she listened joyfully when Garrick took up the tunes from days of old. She smiled happily whilst a part of her childhood played for her listening pleasure, for 'twas a humble reminder of when days were simple and she was able to just be a child.

Memories flashed afore her of when she and Aiden shadowed their father and Killian with their little wooden swords. She had thought when she and her brother had grown that her sire would appoint Killian as their captain, for 'twould have been a logical decision. She had been surprised of his choice in Ian, since he was younger by several years. It had not seemed to bother the older man though and she was thankful to have Killian to watch over her like a relative. There were not many who could be considered so devoted that he would willingly lay down his life for her and her twin.

Her thoughts for some reason turned to Devon when he had first been brought to the castle by his father. The lad had been terrified to be sent to Berwyck as its newest page. Yet still he knelt with an unknown confidence of a boy of only eight summers as he pledged his fealty to his new laird.

Caliana nickered and brought Amiria out of her musings as Garrick continued playing much to her delight. She continued brushing her horse 'til the slamming of the stable door made her jump anxiously. She was not thrilled by whom had entered.

"Cease that infernal caterwauling!" Hugh demanded as the sounds of the pipes abruptly became off tune.

Amiria nodded her consent and with a brief nod of her head, Garrick took himself and his pipes from the stables in haste.

"Do you never dress as you should, woman?" Hugh asked, disgusted as his eyes raked her up and down.

His distaste at her hose and tunic had little impact on her as she continued on with her labor. "'Tis none of your business how I deem to dress myself."

"Perchance 'tis time someone makes it his business. Remove yourself from the stall and come hither, wench!" Hugh ordered.

Amiria arched her brow at his words and cursed to herself that once again she was without her sword. She did not relish the fact that Dristan had left her defenseless, especially from the gleam she noticed in Hugh's eyes. She knew that look and what he wanted from her, which did not bode well for her person. She could only pray she would be able to reach the knife she had safely tucked into her boot, should the need arise.

"You forget yourself, sir, as to who I am if you think to order me about. You are not my lord that I must obey you," Amiria replied with a sneer of loathing. With another brief glance towards Hugh, she looked him up and down much as he had done but a moment afore. She found him lacking and not worth her time. She turned her back on him and resumed her brushing.

A growl rent the air, and Hugh pressed forward in a rush. He opened the stall door, startling Caliana, who began to prance at this intrusion to her grooming. Ignoring the horse, he made a grab for Amiria as she tried to distance herself from him, only managing to take hold of her long plait of hair. 'Twas enough to get her immediate attention. He ignored her shriek of outrage, as he forcibly pulled on her tresses, yanking her from the stall. Her feeble attempts to keep his hands off her person only amused him, if his chuckle was an indication of his mood. Slamming the stall door, Hugh pressed her up against the solid wood, staring into her mutinous eyes. Her hands were held in a viselike grip.

"You, my little hellcat, will do well in the future to heed my words when I have speech with you," Hugh promised. "The alternative will not be pleasant, I assure you."

Amiria saw into the black depths of his eyes and only had a moment's hesitation afore she replied boldly. "As I just said, you forget yourself. I belong to Dristan."

He laughed maliciously. "You poor young delusional fool! Do you honestly think you are so different than any of the other whores he has taken to his bed? You are only one of many and surely will not be taken to wife."

"Think you are so dissimilar?"

"You will be well pleased once in my bed. I guarantee it."

Amiria squirmed, trying to break his hold on her without success. She liked not what she saw in his visage, nor did she care that he began to press the length of his body against her own. "Release me you insolent filthy whoreson! Think I would welcome you to share my body after I have known Dristan of Blackmore?" She gave a short laugh, not caring as she watched his anger rise. "You are an even bigger fool than I if you believe such drivel."

"And you seem to be under some misconception that I care whether I take you willingly or not!" Hugh fumed as his face flushed red with fury.

Beyond caring, Hugh plunged downward, taking her lips beneath his own. Amiria clamped her mouth shut as he attempted to pry her mouth open by biting hard into her lip. If he thought she were in truth a hellcat afore he tasted of her, 'twas nothing compared to what he had now unknowingly unleashed.

Amiria fought him against the violation he attempted as best she could and when he at last tore his mouth from her own, she let out a mighty scream of outrage. As she struggled in earnest, she sank her teeth into his arm, since this was the only part of him she could reach. Apparently, 'twas enough but, when he released one of her arms, 'twas only long enough to swing back his arm, slapping her hard across the face. Her head reeled from the impact and she fought against the pain of her cheek, even as stars danced afore her eyes.

The sound of her tunic ripping caused her to come somewhat out of her stupor. When the intrusive feel of his calloused hand roughly kneaded her breasts, causing pain to penetrate her head, she struggled fiercely to somehow reach her dirk. She had just managed to feel the tip of the hilt when the distinct sound of a sword pulled from its scabbard halted Hugh's progress to further divest her of her clothes.

"Release the liedy if ye have any care fer yer sorry hide!"

Hugh pushed Amiria away and she fell to a heap on the stable floor. She cringed, whilst he took a moment to view her naked breast with a lick of his lips. She quickly retrieved her torn garment and pulled the fabric about her, protecting what she had left of her modesty.

Hugh turned to face an extremely angry Scotsman whose claymore was drawn and menacingly pointing the weapon in his direction. He was obviously surprised Dristan had not taken all of her guard as he might have thought. If being interrupted in his play had not been enough, then the sight of her piper standing behind Killian with a smirk of satisfaction on his features caused Hugh's anger to further heighten.

Hugh must have known to yield the day for he held up his hands in at least a temporary show of surrender. He began to back his way out of the stables even as Killian continued to bare his blade in his direction 'til he at least came to stand afore his mistress.

"'Til later...my lady," Hugh mocked, taking one last view of Amiria. He began to whistle a merry tune as he left on his own accord.

Humiliated, Amiria tried to keep her composure 'til she saw a helping hand come into her vision. Her body shook whilst, holding her tunic together, she held out trembling fingers 'til they were taken in a firm grip. Once pulled to her feet, she found herself wrapped in a comforting embrace. 'Twas not 'til she felt Killian's hand caressing her hair that she finally gave into her fear as heart wrenching tears poured from her eyes. He held her as her father would have done with a slight swaying, giving her the reassurance she stood in need of.

She allowed herself but a few moments of letting another comfort her 'til she at last regained her composure. Clearing her throat, she took a step back, wiping the tears from her face with the sleeve of her tunic. Her features once more showed that of a woman holding her own, even though inside she knew this false bravado would crumble once she gained the privacy of her chamber.

Amiria watched both Killian and Garrick for any signs of pity and thankfully saw nothing in their eyes to show what they were feeling. "We will not speak of this," she declared hoarsely.

"Ach, I doona ken how ye figure tae keep this silent, lassie," Killian predicted. "Not tae Ian, and certainly ne'er tae Laird Dristan."

She raised her head proudly. "All the same, I will endeavor to keep this from them both."

"If ye say so, milady."

Amiria fetched a small woolen blanket from a hay bale and wrapped it around her shoulders. "Remember...not a word. Do not betray me."

Amiria left them in the stable with that final reminder. If she had taken the time to look back upon her men, she would have seen how they watched the proud young woman make her way to the keep. With whispered words, they each made a vow to keep their eyes on their mistress and, more importantly, the ever dangerous Hugh of Harlow.

Twenty-four

FOR NIGH UNTO A FULL DAY, Dristan pushed not only his men but their horses to their very limit in order to reach one of the farthest hamlets upon his land. He had at last called a halt to their flight the night afore and camped under the stars, knowing they could travel no further that eve. With the rising of the morning sun, they resumed their course.

As the day waned, Dristan held up his hand, and the men reined in their horses. Momentarily stopping upon a small rise, Dristan looked down upon the devastation with his dark brows drawn together as he scanned the area. The livestock had been slaughtered and left to rot around the once green fields. The huts had been burnt to the ground with only a few showing what remained of the timber that had once made up their frames. His lip twitched in rage. He pinched his eyes closed, trying to erase the horrible sight he viewed.

Dristan sighed and motioned his men to continue on. They proceeded slowly down the hill then dismounted once they reached the remains of the first dwelling.

"Rolf, Morgan, split up and scout the area." They nodded and ran off, cautious of what they might find. Whilst he had the notion that none of the villagers would yet be alive, Dristan still held some small sense of hope that his first impression of the situation would not be so.

He motioned for his men to keep an eye out as they continued towards the center of the tiny village. A grim and grisly scene awaited them in the center square, making even the seasoned warrior's cringe; the memory would be forever etched in their minds. The villagers had been bound and burnt, their bodies scattered around the square. The pungent odor of burning flesh lingered in the air around them and several men covered their noses with their hands.

Dristan observed Devon's eyes grow wide as he crossed himself afore turning aside, retching. He was not to blame for his weak stomach, for even a stronger man would barely stomach such a sight and smell.

"Thar's a guid lad," Nevin said, as he helped the poor guard to his feet, patting his back. Although Devin stood upright, he did so on wobbly legs and with a pale face.

"Who could have done such a thing?" Riorden asked quietly.

Dristan gave no answer. Instead, he scanned the square in thought, knowing the violence on these innocent people was a personal attack against him. *All these souls*, he bemoaned; 'twas a sad sight to behold even for a man who had been in countless battles. Watching a man die beside him, after he fell defending what he believed in, he could take, but not this...never this.

He was pulled from his thoughts at the sound of his name being called.

"My lord," Morgan shouted, running into the square out of breath.

"What news?" Dristan asked, their eyes meeting.

"I found a hut on the edge of the forest. 'Tis a gruesome site. A dozen or so bodies are hanging from the rafters. Women and children, my lord," he finished reluctantly.

Dristan ran a hand through his hair in frustration. "For God's sake, Morgan, cut those poor souls down. Bertram, Drake, go with him," he snapped.

They followed Morgan, and Dristan looked over at Nevin as Rolf approached equally out of breath.

"My lord, there are riders spotted on the edge of the forest. They have been watching us."

"How many?" Dristan demanded quickly.

"Mayhap eight. They entered the woods as I ran to get you."

"May the bastards who did this pay for their transgressions," he vowed and with a battle cry well known to his men, they turned as one from the square.

Mounting their horses, they kicked their steeds into a full gallop. As they passed the last hut, the men whose job 'twas to retrieve the innocents' bodies ran out of the dwelling, hastened to retrieve their horses, and joined the group.

Dristan led the way, his face contorted in rage. He saw the three riders, who lingered on the edge of the forest on horseback. They quickly fled into the shadows of the trees as Dristan and his men fast approached. As they took to the forest, the light grew dim except for small rays of sunshine cutting through the treetops to reach the forest floor. And yet they rode on after these men with a determination to right the wrong done to his vassals.

The density of the wooded terrain opened up to a small clearing. Dristan brought his horse to a halt, keeping alert to a possible ambush. If he were to plan one himself, this would be just such a place he would lay in wait for his enemy. His men quickly filled the once empty space with impatience. Looking about, they saw no one around them in the darkness.

Dristan kept Thor firmly in place as his hooves pranced to be about some actively. Well trained, the stallion did as he was bid, although he shook and quivered to be about the oncoming battle.

"Where are you?" he yelled. "Show yourselves, you cowards!" There was no answer to his demands. "Show yourselves," he attempted yet again with the same results.

Dristan looked at his men and with the briefest of nods, they pulled their swords from their sheaths. He watched in alarm when Devon foolishly dismounted his horse and made his way to his side.

"They wouldna just disappear, milord, would they?" Devon inquired hesitantly.

"Fool! Get to your horse," he bellowed. Afore Dristan could further voice his concern with Amiria's youngest guardsman, who had unknowingly put himself in danger, a warrior rushed from the darkness of the trees and thrust his sword completely through Devon's stomach. Devon fell to his knees, tears spilling from his eyes whilst his cry of agony rang out in the once still forest.

Everything began to happen at once as Nevin leapt from his steed, letting out a yell to defend his comrade. Men rushed from the woods in a wave of humanity as now Dristan's men also jumped from their horses to join the fray. Nevin engaged the man who had harmed his friend whilst Devon crumbled to the ground in pain. Perchance, 'twas the recent training with his new liege lord, but at last Nevin defeated his enemy and the man lay dead on the ground at his feet. He spat on him with a sneer, wiped his lip with his sleeve, and then looked about him on whom to take on next.

Scanning the area around them, Dristan could see a dozen or so men engaging his guards as sword rang against sword, allowing the sound to echo throughout the woods. Dristan's brow twitched, anticipating the attack of one lone man, who charged him. He was about his own height and as the man gazed at him with a dirty toothed smile, Dristan raised his sword to defend against the attack.

Time and time again his sword sang out and he viewed the enemy begin to fall in defeat. During the skirmish, he swore he heard the distinct sound of laughter coming from the shadows. His sword slicing through the air, he felled his opponent only to have another take his place. This man took a swing at Dristan, who blocked it with ease. 'Twas a battle of strength and the man broke from the hold and stumbled back.

With a swoop of his sword, the unknown man crumbled to the ground dead. He looked around as his men conquered their enemy but he could see one standing off at a safe distance. He leaned against a tree, his arms folded across his chest, watching the fight. Dristan could see his demeanor was merciless, for he smiled in amusement whilst he watched the destruction of his own men. Some of the cowards began to flee and Turquine let out a roar of victory. Dristan saw his target take a step forward into the small light falling to the ground. Their eyes met across the field of fallen bodies and Dristan knew this was only the beginning of more bloodshed to come.

Distracted by the revelry of his guards, Dristan lost sight of the man, who took to the shadows once more. He pushed forward to follow but to no avail. The man was gone. Riorden had followed and laid a hand on his shoulder, as Dristan stood, staring off into the forest.

"What is it?" Riorden queried, his brows drew together as he looked at his friend.

"There was a man here. He stood, leaning against the tree, watching us fight his men. He smiled with their defeat," replied Dristan, startled that one could be so callous towards those he rode with.

"Should we follow?"

"Nay. We still have much to do what with the burying of the villagers." He turned and began making his way back to the center of the circle. He gave a sharp whistle and listened as Thor whinnied in the distance.

"And what of the men just killed?" Riorden asked, as he followed, looking for his own horse.

"Leave them as a warning to those who dare to raise arms against me," he returned sharply. Dristan leapt into the saddle and twisted the reins to head Thor through the forest.

The men began to look to one another 'til finally Finlay spoke up. "But what o' Devon, milord?" he asked sadly. "He yet lives."

Dristan pulled the reins but kept his unseeing eyes in front of him. "Bring him," he said quietly in sorrow. "Perchance by some miracle Kenna can as yet save him." He knew he would not be able to bare the look upon Amiria's face if Devon passed on.

He scanned his men and for the most part they had come through the battle unscathed with the exception of a few minor cuts. The most noticeable injury to his men was to Geoffrey, who was being helped to his horse with an arrow protruding from his left thigh. Kenna would have more than enough work to occupy herself and Lynet once they returned to the keep.

"Geoffrey?" Dristan called with a silent question to his guardsman.

"A clean shot through my lord. Besides the pain and a stiff limb I should heal well enough I suppose to meet you upon the lists again another day," Geoffrey said with a crooked grin despite his wound.

"We shall see..." Dristan grumbled, kicking his horse and moving forward. His men began to mount up and all were solemn. There was no cause to be jubilant with their victory, not knowing the plight of Amiria's youngest guardsman. Her guard was the last to follow. Ian took the responsibility for Devon as Cameron and Thomas helped place his body on Ian's horse. Ian put his foot in the stirrup and sat behind Devon as he groaned in pain. They began to ride very slowly as Dougal brought up the rear, leading Devon's own steed.

'Twas not a long way back to the village and as Dristan broke into the light he shielded his eyes from the heat of the sun. The afternoon began to wane and he left a small detail of men to deal with the chore of burying the bodies of the dead villagers in a nearby field. 'Twas a somber group that began to make their way back towards the castle, knowing their progress would be slow for they could not hasten their journey due to Devon's injury.

Dristan nodded his head to the dead, giving his last respects when he rode by the villager's burial place. He began to pray he would make it back in time to Berwyck Castle. He did not relish the thought of digging another grave.

TWENTY-FIVE

THE LONE FIGURE OF A WOMAN high on the battlements gazing out upon her land gave those at their posts reason to pause at the unusual yet beautiful sight. In days past, she would not have been found in such a precarious place without her armor and sword for the high parapet was narrow and dangerous.

Today, however, found her dressed in her second finest gown. 'Twas made of the finest linen colored in a soft pale shade of green and flowed with ease upon her frame. A blue, green, and red plaid bearing the MacLaren colors was held about her shoulders with a broach to ward off the chill from the ocean's breeze. A golden chain holding the keys to the keep hung low on her hips, attractively complementing the garment. Golden bangles jingled upon her wrists and rings of the same design adorned her delicate fingers. Mayhap the most flattering asset the young woman had besides the beauty of her face was her hair. 'Twas left unbound in a riot of curls and flowed about her as if alive and just begging to be caressed by a lover.

Her gaze this day did not as usual look over its usual position of the ocean that she so loved, however. Nay, not today...today her view was captured inland towards the horizon where she could clearly see dust rising up as horses drew ever nearer. The portcullis and drawbridge had already been drawn up to prevent entry, in the event yet another enemy drew near.

Her deepest hope was that Dristan had returned, hence, her current attire. She had dressed to please him despite the nervous knots in the pit of her stomach. Uncertainty consumed her with doubt, thinking he may not be pleased with her gown. Despite their differences, she felt she and her family were safer when he dwelled within the castle walls. At least she had not had the misfortune to run into Hugh again. She was sure she would not be able to resist the urge to slip a dagger in between his ribs for the liberties he had dared, should they come face to face this day.

Her eyes lit up with a smile of delight when the riders drew close enough that she could at last see Dristan's standard. She had not realized the depth of her heavy sigh of relief 'til she heard Killian tsk tsking as he came to stand beside her. From the look on his face, she assumed she would be hearing a reprimand from the man she considered an uncle.

"Ye shouldna look so eager tae see 'im," he said quietly.

Amiria's smile faded when she turned to meet his knowing glare. "Does it show so clearly then?" she asked, looking down the road again.

"Ye show yer feelings all tae well, lass, I'm afraid. Ye should take care, lest anyone figure it out, especially Ian. He willna like it," he predicted as he smiled at her. His blue eyes twinkled as she met them.

"'Tis not easy," she said quietly, looking around and hoping that none of the guards overheard their words.

"It never is, milady," he said sadly.

"I canna help how I have come to care for him, Killian," she remarked shyly.

"Yer father wouldna approve ye share his bed without so much o' at least a simple 'and fasting. Nor do I, if'n that matters tae ye," he grumbled.

"Lord Dristan does not seem the type who would honor such a Scottish tradition of hand fasting." Embarrassed that all knew she had become no better than one of the castle whores, she began to wring her hands. "You are right that my father would not be pleased, nor my mother I suppose. All the time repenting on my knees in the chapel will not erase the mark and sin against my soul."

Killian patted her shoulder. "God is forgivin' child...'twas not yer fault I am sure."

Amiria shook her head, knowing she could not pass a lie to the man next to her. "Mayhap my parents and God will forgive me if they watch over me from the heavens above," she pondered and continued hopefully. "He has said he will take me to wife when I am well."

"Ye seem fine tae me, Amiria, and from the looks o' things, ye dress tae catch 'is eye."

She shrugged off his comments but dismay again shook her confidence in her choice of dressing so obviously feminine. She placed her hands upon the gown as if to ensure the fabric was not creased. "He has been busy with training and seeing to the land and our people."

"Aye, 'e 'as at that but thar's still been plenty o' time tae see the priest and wed thee. I feel 'tis me duty since yer da isna wid us to take 'is place to see ye properly settled," he said with a fatherly tone.

Amiria smiled at his words and rested a hand on his folded arm whilst gazing up into his familiar face. "I give you my thanks for watching over us all these years. You knew my father better than anyone and were his most trusted friend and valued guardsman." She stared into his kind blue eyes and stifled the urge to weep upon his broad shoulders. "You remind me so very much of him," she sighed with a small catch in her voice from her loss.

"I couldna do anything less, child," he replied with a note of regret.

"I suppose I must resign myself to the fact that Aiden has passed from this earth. I must needs pray his soul rests in peace and is not destined to roam the earth with unfinished business."

Silence stretched on between them. They watched the drawbridge and portcullis being lowered to allow the returning men to enter the inner bailey. The procession was long and 'twas certain Dristan would bring up the rear. Amiria's brow furrowed in concern by the events unfolding afore her gaze. Chaos turned the once silent courtyard into a hectic sea of bodies bumping into one another to aid those in need. Knights dismounted hastily, horses whinnied and nickered as they were being taken by eager stable lads, and voices rose in volume calling for aid from Kenna.

With a brief glance to one another, they quickly made their way to the tower stairs and upon reaching the Great Hall, moved with haste to see what help was needed. Amiria threw open the doors, stood on the stairs, and awaited one man in particular's attention to turn in her direction.

Killian put his hand up in greeting to their liege that was quickly answered in kind. Amiria took the rest of the stairs, pulling up the hem of her dress as she ran towards the one whom she sought in earnest. As Dristan dismounted, she went to stand beside Thor and rested a hand upon his neck. She gave the briefest of smiles 'til Dristan finally met her gaze. He looked down at her grimly, but did not return the welcoming she had hoped for. He simply stood there, giving her the slightest of nods, afore he took his leave of her and entered the keep.

Amiria stared blankly at the ground in front of her, her brows together in thought. She turned her head, the wind catching her hair, and looked after him only to hear the slamming of the keep door. Confusion ran wild within her head 'til she realized there was more commotion in the bailey requiring her attention. Her men formed a half circle whilst Kenna rushed to the man lying upon the ground. She turned to see Ian standing only a few feet away, looking grim, and quickly made her way to his side.

"What has happened, Ian?" she asked in a breathless whisper.

"The village was burnt, everyone murdered," he replied quietly. He watched her closely whilst she covered her mouth with her hand. "There is more Amiria..." he began only to have his words cut off by a scream as she caught the sight of Devon.

She ran over and fell to her knees beside him. Grabbing his hand, she leaned over him and noticed his blue eyes staring up into the sky, his breathing eerily shallow. With a look from Kenna, Amiria sadly knew there was nothing her healer could do for Devon. There was no point in halting her from attending Geoffrey where she could do some good.

"Oh, my dear friend," she whispered with a small anguished cry.

Her words seemed to penetrate his mind in recognition, for Devon turned his head to gaze at her. She took his hand and wiped the hair from his face and watched as a small trickle of blood came from the corner of his mouth.

"I-I wish it w-wasna like th-this, my l-lady," he sputtered.

"Shh. Be quiet now, Devon," she said, tears forming in her eyes. "All will be well, you shall see."

"At least I made it home tae see ye if only fer one last time," he breathed.

Amiria could not suppress the tears that escaped at his words. "You have done well as my guardsman, Devon, and also served my father well."

Devon gave a small smile in satisfaction at her words. "I w-would 'ave s-served ye forever, milady," he said ever so quietly. His eyes fluttered but once afore he gave his last breath, staring at her now through sightless eyes.

Sobs shook Amiria to her very core as she grieved over her guardsman. "Oh, Devon, my dear, dear friend. May God keep you safe. I pray you are in a better place." She brought his hand to her lips and placed a kiss upon its back afore letting go. Quickly she turned away from the sight of his skin becoming an ashen grey. She would not remember Devon this way but alive with life.

Ian held down his hand for her and she took it. He gently pulled her into his arms, as she wept her sorrow. He continued murmuring words of comfort for her ears alone. He caressed her hair and in the back of her mind, Amiria kept the knowledge that this would be the one and only time Ian would ever hold her this close again. She continued her weeping not only for Devon's death, but also for the feelings she had once felt for this man, who only wanted her to love him. She felt his arms tighten around her protectively whilst his lips brushed her forehead in a fleeting kiss.

"Hush now, Amiria. Dinnae fash yourself, lass. Our Devon wouldna wish tae see you so overwrought," he spoke calmly to her in such a loving tone.

She shuttered at his words as reality slammed her back to the present. Drawing back from him, she was remiss that she had let her emotions get the best of her whilst everyone watched her every move. Where once afore stood a woman frail with regret, now stood a woman of determination. After all, she was a warrior at heart and had no time for such foolishness like falling in love or showing signs of weakness.

Amiria called to Garrick, who once more took up his pipes and played a tune that had unfortunately become all too familiar in the past few months. Everyone halted in their duties and bowed their heads in sadness for a boy who had barely known manhood afore he had become an honored guard of the MacLaren clan.

She watched as Ian took up the detail to see that Devon's body would be laid to rest. She nodded only once to him afore she walked silently into the keep. None stopped her in her misery and she trudged up the flight of stairs to her chamber with a heavy heart.

There was no mistaking the distinct sound of the slamming of neither her door nor the bolt being shoved harshly into place. The sound of her weeping far into the night tore at the hearts of those who cared for her most, and they could only wonder if their mistress would ever be the same again.

TWENTY-SIX

FOR A FULL SE'NNIGHT, AMIRIA had chosen to remain enclosed within her chamber, no doubt coming to grips with the death of her guardsman. She refused to admit Dristan, or anyone else for that matter, into her self-imposed sanctuary, nor did she descend below to the Great Hall to break her fast in his presence. 'Twas apparent she felt Devon's death was his fault, although she, as much as anyone, should know that death is the price one must pay for the cost of war, securing of lands, and protecting one's people.

His patience at an end, Dristan climbed the spiral stone stairs and made his way along the passageway towards her chamber. He was not surprised to see her captain standing guard at her door as if some harm might befall her whilst she resided inside her room. He glanced at Ian and felt a hint of jealousy rear its ugly head, causing a mighty scowl to appear on his brow. Aye, he had been told how Ian had held Amiria within his arms and Dristan's irritation with that small measure of knowledge caused his temper to rise with each step he took.

Dristan strode to stand afore Ian, who looked him in the eye. Was that perchance a hint of anger or arrogance he saw mixed within the younger man's hazel eyes?

"My lord," Ian said with a slight bow.

"There is no need to stand guard whilst I am within my keep," he voiced coolly. He slapped his gloves against his leg, trying not to let his anger get the best of him.

"'Tis a habit," Ian replied, just as inhospitably with a shrug of his shoulder. "Besides...there is always mischief afoot surrounding Amiria."

"No harm will befall her as she has me to defend her now."

Ian hesitated only momentarily afore he found his voice. "Do you mean to release me then from my vow to protect her?"

"Aye. She and the other children are now my concern and I will see to their welfare," Dristan declared, almost daring Ian to challenge him.

Ian opened his mouth but no sound emitted and he shut his lips with a snap. "I see."

Dristan watched a multitude of emotions rush across Ian's features. 'Twas clear he felt more for the woman he guarded than just being her captain and suddenly it dawned on him just how much Ian cared for Amiria.

"Bloody hell," Dristan grunted hoarsely, "you are in love with her!"

Ian's crestfallen look spoke for itself. "What is there not to love, my lord?" he asked quietly with a strained smile.

"This poses somewhat of a difficulty. You have heard Amiria will be my wife, have you not?"

"'Tis hard not to hear the goings on of the castle gossip, my liege," Ian answered glumly. "Her parents would not be pleased you have made her nothing more than your whore."

"You dare speak to me thusly or are you just a fool, who speaks with no thought to your life?" Dristan roared.

"'Tis the truth is it not? I, at least, would have made her my lady wife already if only I were more than just a guardsman," he said gruffly. "Without lands of my own or a title of merit and worth, she is far beyond my reach no matter the feelings I have for her."

"You were charged to guard her Ian, not fall in love with her. You should have known nothing good would come from such a situation. Does she know of your feelings for her then?"

Ian pondered his answer as he crossed his arms over his chest. "Oh, I suppose she does, but that is of no consequence at this point. What is more important is what you feel for her."

"'That, Ian, is none of your concern," Dristan huffed in annoyance.

"No disrespect intended, my lord, but who else would champion her cause if I do not do so myself? You have made it abundantly clear you care not what others think of her situation by not making her your wife. You may release me from my vow to protect her and my service to you for there is nothing I can do about such an occurrence. But I shall not rest 'til I am sure my lady has been properly wed, and you will care for her along with the other bairn's," Ian threatened.

"You dare much."

"Aye, I dare much, my lord! I made a vow to her dying father and will not besmirch his memory by not keeping my word. It means all to me, for I have nothing left but my honor. 'Tis at stake if I do not make every effort to keep my oath made to a man who took his last breath at my feet. Surely you would not ask such of me, or would you?"

Dristan took in the younger man afore him and had to admire his determination to see Amiria settled and to uphold his honor. As a knight of the realm he understood. He shook his head that he could be so blind in the treatment of the woman he would take to wife.

"I hear your words, Ian, but tell me this...do you plan to just stand aside and watch her wed another considering how you feel for her? To be honest, even I myself would find such a task most difficult."

Ian sighed and relaxed his stance. "All I ask is that you do what is proper, my lord, and make her a whore no longer. Then, and only then, will I ask you to release me from my pledge of fealty," he promised calmly. "I love her most deeply, wishing only her happiness, and yet I fear I must leave this place. I do not believe I could endure the torment of seeing her love another."

Dristan was surprised at his words. "You believe she loves me then?"

"Open your eyes, my Lord Dristan, and see what is afore you," he said. "All the world can see the love she has for you shining in those magnificent eyes of hers."

Dristan nodded at Ian's words as their meaning began to take root inside him and slowly sink in. He patted Ian on the back, cleared his throat, and stood afore Amiria's door. He knocked for entry. He was not surprised when silence was his only answer.

"You might as well get used to your patience being tried at every turn, my lord. She is most stubborn or even persuasive when the need arises," Ian drawled wryly. "I myself would not have her any other way."

Dristan glared at the man, 'til Ian laughed smugly and made his way down the passageway, leaving his liege glaring at the solid wood portal. He stared at the loathsome door as if 'twas an enemy to be conquered.

He grabbed his sword and banged the obnoxious object afore him with its hilt. The sound echoed off the walls, and yet still it stood firmly shut afore him, barring his way from the woman within. 'Twas only the threat he gave her that he would break the wood down if he must that Amiria at last conceded and opened the door.

Her appearance gave him pause, for she was utterly disheveled. She slowly went to sit afore the fire lit in the hearth, and he swore to himself whilst watching her hands shake. Red puffy eyelids from her tears nearly rivaled the color of her hair. He was not surprised to see her in hose and tunic, although her garments would be beneficial to the outing he had originally had in mind for them this day.

Amiria began to run her fingers through her glorious mane of hair and quickly made fast work of threading her tresses into a fat braid. With a complete look of disinterest thrown in his direction, she turned back towards the fire, clearly indicating she planned to ignore him.

Dristan, on the other hand, only leaned upon the doorframe, crossed his arms, and took in the view of perfection that was afore him. Aye, perfect she was for him in every way, and, at last, he could admit that truth if only to himself. He was still unsure if he could trust her as yet with the tender care of his much guarded heart.

Only the crackling of the fire, as the wood snapped and hissed, broke the deafening silence of the chamber. When Amiria could at last stand it no more, she turned to face the one who had been tormenting her every waking hour. She would not even begin to give way to what agony her dreams gave her during her sleep. It only irritated her further to see a charming grin plastered on his handsome rugged face.

"Something amuses you?" she inquired sharply.

"Aye."

Ach, she thought; a simple, annoying answer that grated on her already stretched nerves. "I have no desire to have speech with you, or any other for that matter."

"That means naught to me for we will have speech together, Amiria, among other things," he declared knowingly.

"I think not, my lord. Besides...I am in mourning."

"Aye, you are in mourning for the lad, and yet Devon would not wish you to grieve for him so," he drawled grimly.

"You dare to tell me how I should mourn the loss of my guardsman? Devon died in front of me. I grew up with him. Are you so callous and heartless, Dristan, that you do not mourn him, as well, no matter that he only served you most recently?" she screamed at him.

"*Merde*! Amiria, we were ambushed. 'Twas nothing anyone could do," he thundered. "You yourself were among those soldiers who helped to defend this castle. The price of war is high, Amiria. You know that! Sometimes that price is costly. By Saint Michael's wings, woman, I should not have to explain this to you."

"You could show some remorse, you heartless bastard!"

He pushed off the doorframe, threw his gloves in frustration upon the bed, and came to stand afore her. "My birthright is not in question here. Aye, I mourn the lad, but in my own way. If I showed such weakness afore my men, I would lose their respect, so I keep those feelings unto myself. You would do well to do the same."

Amiria had no words of reply and only continued to stare off into the flames of the fire. 'Twas not 'til he thrust his hand in front of her that she glanced up into his stormy steel grey eyes.

"Come with me," he commanded.

She gazed at the proffered limb and felt a weariness overcome her. Not having the energy to fight with him further this day, she could only stare at his hand as if seeing it for the first time.

"You are a most annoying man," she proclaimed softly. "Will it always be thusly with us do you suppose?"

"Aye. I'm afraid ours will be a stormy relationship with a constant battle of wills waged between us," he said gruffly. "Better that than the alternative of being bored, *ma petite*!"

"I will cower afore no man," she said boldly. "You should know that by now."

"As long as you know the same holds true for me, Amiria. I am lord here and no woman, you or any other, will ever lead me about by the nose," Dristan said with a stern warning look. "But know you this...I would rather you stand beside me willingly and accept me as not only your lord but as your husband. I do not relish a lifetime of war between us, my lady."

"Accepting you as husband may be easier said than done, my lord."

"Perchance 'twill not be as difficult as you may think," he said huskily as he once more extended out his hand for her to take. "Now, as I said, come with me. Such loveliness is not meant to be stifled between the walls of our keep, but instead should be outside where it may thrive in nature's glory."

His compliment took Amiria by surprise, especially when he referred to the keep as their home. She finally placed her hand within his, and he gently pulled her to her feet. She felt a tremor pass between them, leaving her slightly breathless and in awe of how she felt when she was with this man. From his startled expression, Amiria knew, without any doubt, he had felt it too. She saw the edges of his mouth lift in an ever so slight smile, and she returned it with one of her own.

Encouraged the day may yet be salvaged with the thought of being outdoors, Amiria willingly walked alongside Dristan. 'Twas not 'til he captured her hand, with a twinkle in his eyes, and placed it on his arm as they reached the Great Hall that she began to enjoy the sensation of being in his company. Perchance, if she but wished hard enough, there would be hope for their match after all!

Twenty-seven

SABINA'S MOANS, COMING FROM THE HAYLOFT, echoed off the walls, 'til she realized they might be overheard. He was quite the lover, not that she had another to compare him to. Stifling a giggle, she looked down upon his head whilst he went about his business. A smile lit her face in excitement from his touch. Such a fine amorous knight was he and she was thrilled he was hers and hers alone.

Sabina suddenly gasped and flinched in jealousy. She pushed with all her might at the man who she had, but moments afore, clasped to her bosom. "What did you call me?" she screeched angrily.

"I know not what you speak of," Hugh muffled as he went back to nuzzling her breasts.

"Get off me, you misbegotten cur! How dare you utter my sister's name whilst you take me to your bed?"

Hugh raised a brow in irony as he scrutinized their surroundings. "You are mistaken and err mightily if you believe you would ever be worthy enough to enter my bed."

"Ha! I at least was born a lady, expecting those to honor me since my birth, and did not have to bribe my king to earn his favor!"

Hugh's smirk seeped with condescension. Rising, he began to adjust his hose. "No lady would be caught alive without her garments in a hayloft, my dear, especially without the benefit of wedlock."

"But you will wed with me, Sir Hugh, of that there is no doubt," Sabina said confidently.

A small laugh escaped his lips as he looked down upon her whilst she attempted to remove the hay tangled in her long straight hair. "I think not," he replied and strapped his sword to his side. "You would be the last woman I would care to wake up to for the rest of my life!"

Sabina began to sputter her outrage. Quickly she began to claw her way out of the straw, which seemingly clung to her from every direction. The loud creaking of the opening stable door caused Hugh to reach down and place his hand none to gently over her mouth to further silence her protests.

"Bloody hell, Hugh! Are you not yet finished?" hissed his cousin.

"Aye, most assuredly," he called from above.

"Then what is taking so long?" Gilbert said impatiently. "We must away and without further haste. I do not relish being caught within the bailey's walls!"

"I'm coming," he exclaimed without care for the hurt that crossed Sabina's features. "I have no further business here."

"But what if I am with child?" she whispered in dismay that he would not take her to wife.

"That, Sabina, is your problem and not mine," Hugh drawled callously, giving her a final look of cold distain.

Sabina stood there motionless and horrified whilst Hugh's words began to take form in her mind. She reached out for him only to have her hand slapped away as he took his leave without so much as a backwards glance.

She began to shake uncontrollably. The silence of the stables was deafening to her ears. The horses whinnied and snorted occasionally as horses were wont to do, but she did not hear their sounds. Nor did she see the dust molts as they danced and floated in the air from the sunlight penetrating the cracks in the ceiling. Nay...she only stood there alone and frightened with her thoughts.

Her hands at last came to rest upon her belly for she knew that a child had indeed taken root within her womb. *What to do? What to do? What to do?* Her troubled thoughts repeated the same question over and over in her mind. No answer seemed to be forthcoming. *He must wed me*, her way of thinking demanded no matter how irrational those demands might be. Surely he would come to love her and the child she carried!

She adjusted her clothing and began to slowly climb down the ladder, ensuring her skirts did not trip her on her way down. She was just removing the last remnants of straw from her hair when two lads entered to grab bridles and tack.

She made it appear she had been tending one of the steeds housed there. A quick glance at the youths proved that mayhap Hugh had not been as careful as she assumed, for the young lads tossed her a knowing look. She glared at them for their gall, but they turned from her without so much as a by your leave. How dare the whelps treat her so as if she was not a lady at all? The slight burnt like a fever within her as she gathered her thoughts to give the boys a piece of her mind.

She collected her words to voice her displeasure but choked them back when they entered the stall where Dristan's horse was kept. Thor seemed to be as displeased with the louts as much as she was. They approached the stallion cautiously and tried to not get beneath his massive hooves when he pranced in anticipation of his freedom. After some difficulty, they at last managed to have the steed saddled and led him from the stall to receive his rider.

'Twas not 'til Sabina heard her sister's voice saying she would retrieve Caliana that a feeling of utter resentment consumed her. Her sanity snapped as easily as a dried twig beneath one's foot. With her sister's approach, Sabina knew only one thing for certain...she would die a thousand deaths afore Amiria would take the father of her child from her!

Amiria entered the stable with a smile set upon her face, 'til she espied her sister hovering in the shadows of the room. Sabina slowly came into the light and Amiria was startled by the somewhat crazed look upon her features. She began to reach out towards her sibling, to find out what had befallen her, when Sabina snarled at her.

"You willna have them both, you witch," Sabina cried out in anger.

"Are you daft? Whatever do you speak of?" she questioned somberly, noticing Sabina did not look well. "You have no reason to turn your wrath upon me."

"He is mine. You willna cast some spell upon him so his favors fall from me!" she bellowed, raising her fist. "You willna have him too. If you think to take him from me then I will kill you just to keep him unto myself!"

Amiria tried to comprehend exactly what Sabina was trying to tell her, since she made no sense. They had always argued amongst themselves but somehow hearing her sister threaten to slay her was more than just sibling rivalry. 'Twas when Sabina began to mutter to herself that Amiria truly did worry if her sister had gone mad.

She reached out her hands to console the troubled younger girl. "I know not what has caused you to hate me so, but you are my sister and I love you."

"Love me? You do not love me but have always made my life miserable. You and Aiden were always the favorites in father's eyes," Sabina screeched. "I was never good enough, but I will show you, and everyone else, that I will have my way. You will not win this battle, Amiria."

"What battle? Why are you so distraught and angry with me? Talk to me, Sabina."

"You willna have them both," she repeated with tears shimmering in her eyes. Crying out, Sabina burst into tears, gave Amiria a mighty shove, and ran from the stables. Amiria made to follow but was halted when Dristan joined her. Sabina's cries continued to be heard by all as they echoed off the bailey walls.

"What the devil ails that woman?" Dristan asked sharply.

"I am not sure, but it cannot be anything good. I fear for her as I have never done afore," she replied softly in concern for her sibling.

"I know she is your sister but she and her ways vex my nerves," he said in annoyance.

Amiria smiled slightly whilst one of the lads brought out Caliana and began the task of saddling her. "I am afraid, my lord, that Sabina tends to irritate all within her path, usually on a daily basis."

"Then she bears watching so she does not harm those around her, including herself," Dristan answered sternly.

"I am most worried, Dristan," she said in a hushed tone. "Perchance I should go and check on her."

Dristan came to her and took her hand, placing a gentle kiss upon the inside of her wrist. Her surprised look at this small display of affection gave him pause and yet still caused a devilish grin to light his face. "She will be fine. Let us away Amiria and at least for a while enjoy a carefree day. We shall see how long it can last, which I am sure will not be for any prolonged amount of time."

Her horse ready, Dristan waved off the lad and assisted her into the saddle himself. Once settled, he handed her the reins. She blushed when his fingers brushed her own and she could tell it took much on his part to leave her side.

Amiria admired Dristan's handsomeness, as he effortlessly leapt into the saddle. With little effort, he easily controlled the massive stallion beneath him. She took one last worried look in the direction of the keep before she turned her mount and followed behind Dristan's warhorse. Once past the outer walls and drawbridge, they took flight and raced as if trying to catch the wind. With the opportunity to enjoy a day free from the restraints of the castle, Amiria took Dristan's words to heart and began to enjoy their day, praying for many more to follow.

The fading laughter of the departing couple seemed to hang in the air like a promise of good tidings to come from the heavens above. Those who had been lucky enough to have heard such happiness occurring from their mistress, now went about their duties, feeling light hearted that all would be well at Berwyck Castle.

For one, it only added to the distress on her frantic thoughts and already tortured mind. As she stood high upon the parapet, watching the dust disappear from the jovial couple, Sabina could only wonder if she would be missed, even in the slightest, if she flung herself off the wall to her demise.

TWENTY-EIGHT

"BUT MY LORD, HOW CAN YOU WED with her if she does not have dark hair like the rest of us?" Patrick ventured to ask as he put down his quill. The lad appeared quite full of himself now that he was in possession of a tunic bearing Dristan's crest and wore the garment with pride. "I thought all must have black hair, if they are to bear your coat of arms?"

Dristan reached out and ruffled the boy's hair playfully. Leaning over, he viewed with a practiced eye the parchment on which Patrick had been writing his letters. Picking up the near-by quill, he demonstrated the letter the lad was having difficulty with. "See you here? It goes in this direction," he said. "Try again, Patrick."

"Aye, my lord," Patrick sighed wearily. He began muttering underneath his breath about why he must needs always be studying his letters and such, especially when he would rather be learning sword play.

Amiria grinned, admiring Dristan's patience with her brother. 'Twas quite the domesticated scene, if she was to ponder upon it for any length, and one she had not thought would come to pass given her lord's reputation. Normally the lady of the keep would be required to teach a squire his letters, and yet Dristan had insisted he take over this task with her brother. Seeing the tip of the poker was now red hot, she pulled it from the fire and plunged it into a chalice of wine. Allowing the herbs to steep a few moments, she at last reached out and handed the cup to Dristan.

He came to her and took it with a nod of thanks. By the expression on his face he was pleased with her efforts to see to his comfort. Turning back to the lessons at hand, he placed the cup down upon the table to review Patrick's work again and placed his hand over the boy's to help him with the correction of his letters. Another weary sigh escaped Patrick from the difficulty he was having.

Amiria let out a brief laugh at the concentration on her brother's face and caught Lynet's eye as she looked up from her stitchery wondering at the cause of her mirth.

"I can remember Aiden doing the same thing when mother was trying to teach him his letters," she declared with a smile. "He never could seem to get them to go in the right direction either."

Lynet smiled with the memories of their mother as few as they had been. "I do miss her at times, especially when I could use her advice on a particular stitch or even with learning about the healing herbs found in the garden."

Dristan rose from leaning over Patrick and came to stand beside Lynet. "Kenna tells me you are doing exceedingly well, Lady Lynet, with all she is teaching you. You are a fine addition to my household, and I am glad to know that Berwyck is twice blessed to have two healers in residence."

Lynet beamed from Dristan's approval. "Thank you for your kind words, my lord," she whispered, and resumed her needlework.

Dristan gave her sister a small reassuring pat upon her shoulder. Their gazes met 'til Amiria felt as if he were stripping her of the dark blue gown she wore. Her breath left her, and she smoothed her unbound hair that fell down her back in a riot of red curls. She bit her lower lip and saw how his eyes followed her movements 'til she swore she could almost feel his lips beneath her own, teasing her to allow him entrance. *Was it just her, or did the room suddenly become stifling with heat?* she wondered.

Finally taking her eyes from his mouth, she raised her gaze to stare up into his twinkling grey eyes. He returned her look with a mischievous grin. *The rogue*, she mused. He knew exactly where her thoughts had taken her. She attempted to think of some way to save face in front of this over confident man but decided to yield to him at least for now. She sat back in her chair and just enjoyed the sensation of having his full and undivided attention.

Amiria lounged in her chair with the confidence of a woman who knew the effect she was having on him.

The little vixen! he mused. She returned his playful smile with one of her own, and he wished not for the first time this day that the solar was empty save the two of them.

"My lord," Patrick called from across the solar.

"Aye, Patrick?" Dristan answered, never taking his eyes from Amiria and the picture of perfection she offered him. She was going to make him daft. Perchance they should wed without further haste. He reluctantly dragged his eyes from his lady and turned his attention to the young lad, who motioned for him to come closer. He humored the boy by striding across the room and leaning down next to him.

"She doesn't have black hair my lord," he whispered in Dristan's ear.

Dristan chuckled. "Aye, she does not, does she my boy?" he paused and held out his hand to show a ring he wore on his finger. "But see you here this dragon on my crest? See the flame spew forth from his mouth? Somehow I think the red of her hair will compliment us. Do you not think 'tis so?"

"Well...I suppose," Patrick answered softly still not completely at ease that 'twas right. A sideways glance upward and Dristan knew the boy would not argue with his lord.

Dristan's mirth could no longer be contained as a laugh escaped him from viewing Patrick's expression. "Perchance now is as good a time as any to present my lady with a small pre-wedding gift. 'Tis mayhap not the most normal gift one would bestow upon a lady one is to wed, but I thought it most appropriate."

He went behind his desk to the corner and removed a tarp that he began folding, hiding from view the rather large box residing up against the wall. With a quick peek over his shoulders, he hid his smile as he watched Amiria, Lynet, and Patrick return to their tasks at hand. In Amiria's case, she continued to lounge there, looking quite fetching. Lifting up the box, he came to stand afore her and presented his hand for her to rise.

"For you, my lady. I hope you like it," Dristan said, offering her the present. "If you but lift the lid, I shall hold it steady for you."

She gazed at the size of the box with a look of puzzlement upon her face. "It appears heavy," she said. Her creased brow led him to believe she was mystified of what could possibly be in the container of such considerable size.

"Hurry, Amiria, and open it," Patrick said excitedly as he came to stand next to his siblings.

"Aye, do hurry, Amiria! I just love presents," exclaimed Lynet.

Amiria began to lift the lid whilst Dristan looked on his lady's face. He smiled in satisfaction whilst she seemingly pondered the thoughtfulness of his gift. As she peered inside to see her present, her mouth opened silently, for no words could be found apparently to express the joy at what she beheld. She looked at Dristan and a single tear slid down her cheek, for nestled in a bed of purple velvet was the sword he had forged for her.

He watched her joy as her fingers wrapped themselves around the golden hilt of the sword. Pulling it from its velvet bed, she brought it in front of her and gazed upon its flawlessness. The blade had been engraved with two dragons; their tales intertwined as if they were in truth one. That in itself should have spoken more than any words Dristan could ever say to her, for 'twas a reminder of their first time together. She took a quick glance at the hilt that fit her hand perfectly and admired the enormous purple gem winking at her from the firelight.

"The stone's color reminded me of your eyes," Dristan spoke, reading her thoughts.

Setting the blade carefully down, Amiria launched herself into Dristan's arms. He caught her easily and held her close.

"'Tis magnificent," she whispered softly in his ear, "as are you!"

"Harrumph! 'Tis about time you noticed, my lady," he said playfully, although he still felt slightly embarrassed at her words.

"'Tis a very thoughtful gift, and one I shall treasure all of my days," she declared sweetly. "I did not think you would care for me to lift a sword again."

Dristan looked into her eyes captivated by the depth of emotion he could see shining there. "How else are you to guard my back if you are not properly trained, my lady?" he answered with a sparkle in his eyes. "Besides, I believe this one will suit you better as 'tis lighter. I still have the sword your father gave you and, perchance one day, if we should be so blessed, you can bestow it to our son."

Amiria could no longer contain showing her happiness. Reaching up, she pulled his head down in order to reach his lips. Dristan clasped her to him, for she kissed him with all the emotions she had held in check. He felt her tremble beneath his hands whilst she held onto his arms. He deepened their kiss just to prove that he would leave her weak-kneed, necessitating his support to keep her upright.

"Come Patrick," Lynet prompted. "Let us leave them some privacy for a bit."

"But Lynet, I want to look at Amiria's sword," he whined.

Dristan reluctantly pulled his mouth away from Amiria but did not loosen his hold of her. Placing a kiss upon her forehead he called to her siblings. "Lynet, go see what cook has in his kitchen. He can put everything into a basket and we shall away to the strand and enjoy the afternoon there."

"Me too, my lord?" Patrick asked hopefully.

"Aye...you too, Patrick. Mayhap you could see that our horses are ready along with blankets to take our ease on the sand," Dristan said humorously and saw the enthusiastic smile that lit the boy's face.

"Hooray!" Patrick exclaimed, jumping for joy and running from the solar with Lynet fast on his heels, calling down the passageway for him to slow down.

As the door closed softly, Amiria turned once more into Dristan's arms. "We will have no peace once Patrick's feet hit the sand you know. He just loves the ocean."

Dristan chuckled. "He's a good lad and in truth had more patience than I ever would to sit as long as he did. I thought he deserved a reprieve."

"You are good with him, and Lynet of course."

He reached out and smoothed her fallen hair back from her face. "Well, they are to be my family, are they not? I could do nothing less than see to their care, now could I?"

"Aye, my lord," she whispered and closed her eyes as he again pressed a kiss upon her lips.

"Now...did you in truth like the gift?" he said hopefully and watched her nod. "Good! Then go change. We will away and see how you improve with a lighter blade."

"As you wish, Dristan," she said happily and leaned up to receive another of his kisses. He tightened his arms around her yet again, for he did not want to let go of this moment.

Dristan finally pulled away but saw the look of regret in his lady's eyes. "Go on now, you saucy wench, afore we disappoint the others and retire to my chamber for the afternoon instead." He watched as she tossed him a look promising more to come later and with a light pat upon her bottom, Amiria laughed gaily, running from the solar.

Dristan joined in her laughter, although he was now standing there alone with his idle thoughts. Raking his hand through his hair, he went to the door to head down to the stables and caught a fleeting glimpse of blue gown as Amiria entered her chamber at the end of the long passageway. God...what a woman.

The day could not have been any more spectacular if she had planned it herself...well with the exception of her current task at hand. Amiria once more sat in Dristan's solar, only this time she was making an attempt at mending his hose. That she would indulge in such a mindless endeavor said much for her change of heart of late. True, darning was not her strongest asset but 'twas either mend the small hole or sew an entire new garment. 'Twas really no other choice as the latter would indeed take much longer.

So here she contently sat in a comfortable chair on top of a very lovely cushion Dristan had provided for her comfort. Who would have ever thought such a thing could happen from a man with the fiercest of reputations, spanning both England, France, and possibly farther abroad? But here she was, sitting next to Dristan, who was busily sharpening a dirk he had found to his liking from the armory. From his expression, he appeared as if he was about finished with the task, for he began to repeatedly flip the blade end over end, testing its weight in the palm of his hand.

Returning to her mending, she smiled in remembrance of their afternoon sojourn to the beach. It genuinely had been a lovely day, although it had turned out that others had joined their party at the seashore. She should not have been surprised that Dristan's guard had joined them along with her own. Apparently, even this close to the keep, the loyal knights, were determined to guard those whom they had vowed to protect.

Amiria had taken special care to look for Sabina but she had been nowhere to be found. Her disappearances had almost become the norm these days, so her grumbles had not soured or spoiled their outing. Although she did worry about her sister, Amiria was resolved she and her family would take pleasure in the afternoon.

Lynet and Patrick had immediately dashed to the ocean's edge and Amiria still laughed at the memory when Patrick's little boots went sailing into the air as he made a leap towards the waves. Ian had not been far behind the boy, and between him and Lynet, they kept Patrick out of trouble, much to the dismay of her brother. Still, 'twas a refreshing change to hear his squeals of delight whilst he raced along the shore, trying to catch the tide.

Cook had provided a most adequate repast for them whilst she and Dristan sat and spoke of small things about each other's lives. Sometimes, Amiria's eyes darted to and fro with the hope no other had overheard her words to the man sitting beside her on a blanket, behaving as if he absorbed her every word. With their privacy ensured for the most part, considering their guards were standing vigil not far away, they had whiled away the day at one another's side.

They had walked the strand for some time, and she felt a wonderful sensation, holding on to the strength of his arm. Dristan had brought her new sword. She had kicked off her boots, much like her brother, and felt the sand between her toes. Then she had brought the blade up, and they had taunted and challenged one another playfully. On more than one occasion, she had noticed, he stared at her most attentively, causing her to blush repeatedly. A continuous smile had lit his features and 'twas a welcome change from his usually gruff demeanor whilst in the presence of his men. The happiness he must have been feeling reached into the very depths of those incredibly mysterious eyes of his that constantly fascinated her. For the moment, she had been content, and so, it appeared, had he.

When they had returned from their stroll, the others were beginning to gather their belongings to return to the keep since dusk was fast approaching. With Kenna at his side, Geoffrey had been gently assisted onto his horse. Dristan had said earlier that day he would not coddle a knight of his, and Geoffrey should begin to exercise his leg lest he cared to only have a stump to limp about on. Amiria had caught Ian watching her as he kept close watch on Patrick but noticed the resolve now imbedded in the hazel of his eyes. It had saddened her to observe such a look, but she was determined to move forward with her future, a future that would forever be entwined with Dristan's.

She felt the intensity of Dristan's gaze come upon her as she returned to the present and looked up from her stitchery. 'Twas most mesmerizing, and she quickly felt the heat of desire rushing to her face. The room once again seemed overly hot but it had nothing to do with the flames in the hearth for they were at their lowest. Her cheeks burnt along with the rest of her body. He spoke no words as he rose and came to her. Perchance none were actually necessary. Taking hands, they left the solar and made their way to his chamber.

As she was ushered gently into the room, she turned back towards him and gave him her most warmhearted smile. He said not a word but firmly shut the door, closing out the world behind them. After all, there were more important matters that required his immediate, and most assuredly, complete attention.

Dristan came to her side with a powerful stride that was overwhelming to her already shaky senses. Amiria more than willingly met him half way with a promise shining in her own eyes as she welcomed him most affectionately into her arms.

Time had no meaning and stood still. Nothing existed but the two of them as their limbs became intertwined together in a dance of love. They became as one, for it seemed that where one ended the other began, as they were consumed in the pleasure of the spell that had been woven about them.

For unbeknownst to Dristan, his heady kisses whilst he took her gave way to a sensation as if Amiria was soaring up like an angel taking flight into the heavens. Higher and higher did he send her 'til the world as she knew it shattered along with any barriers she held around her heart. She cried out his name, breaking the silence from the still of the night.

Ever so slowly did she drift back down to the reality of her earthly form, and the peacefulness surrounding her was found in the man whose comforting arms held her close to his side. She leaned back to view his face and smiled upon him. His returning grin sealed his fate as she snuggled deep into the very warmth of him. With a heavy sigh of happiness, Amiria now readily accepted him, not only into her heart for this one evening, but for all time. Aye...she was indeed most willing to now become his wife.

Twenty-nine

"TAKE THIS TO KING HENRY and hand it to no other," Hugh ordered the knight standing afore him. "Do not fail me!"

"Aye, Sir Hugh," the man said with a short bow afore running towards his horse. He leapt into the saddle with a mighty swiftness like the devil himself was chasing after him. The messenger never gazed back as he galloped out into the cold starry night.

Hugh turned to the group of men who huddled near the fire, trying to find some warmth from the flames. He stooped down, grabbed another couple of logs, and threw them into the pit. The small sparks flittered upwards, disappearing into the evening sky. A mug was given to him and he downed its contents whilst his cousin stood beside him, perusing him warily in silence.

"What?" Hugh asked, clearly annoyed at the silence between them.

"The king, Hugh?" Gilbert questioned shortly. "Are you out of your mind? Why would you get the king involved?"

"The keep should be mine. I shall show King Henry how Dristan is not fit to see to such an important holding as Berwyck," he declared sullenly.

"Damnation Hugh! I swear you shall see us all dead with this scheme of yours," Gilbert protested.

"Do not question my motives again. Cousin or no, I will let no man stand in my way in my desires to have the keep!" Hugh warned, and flicked his wrist to dismiss the irritating man afore him. His patience at an end, he began to pace back and forth, muttering all along about life's injustice and how he would prove his worth to the king and earn himself a title.

There was only the briefest of an instant where Hugh's thoughts went to Sabina afore turning to her sister. With the coolness of the evening sharpening his senses, he went to sit and warm himself by the fire. His demeanor sparkled in pleasure, thinking of all the ways he envisioned taking Amiria once she was beneath him in his bed.

Aye, Berwyck Castle would belong to him, and all would be calling him Lord Hugh afore the fortnight was over. He could hardly wait 'til he took the keep as his own, but more importantly made his claim on a certain red haired hellcat. With his vile mirth ringing out into the forest, he turned from the fire and bedded down most contently for what remained of the night.

Gilbert threw up his hands in disgust and went to find a place to make his bed whilst trying to digest what he had gotten himself into. He scrutinized Hugh whilst his cousin at last quit his frantic pacing and lay down next to the fire. He groaned out loud. There was nothing to gain from sending a missive to the king except mayhap a noose stretched tight about one's neck!

His unrelenting scrutiny of the dilemma gave him no answers, as he tossed sticks into the quickly disintegrating red hot orange flames at his feet. *Mayhap I should head to France*, he mulled over to himself. At least there he would have a ready wench to serve his needs and no cousin grumbling about the unfairness of his sorry life.

Good Lord above! May the saints save and preserve me from my imbecile of a cousin, he thought, cringing. *A message to the king indeed.* A cold chill blew across the back of Gilbert's neck and raced down his spine like the forewarning of an executioner's axe in his near future. With a bit of luck and fortune on his side, mayhap they would show some leniency and he would not, at the very least, have to dig his own grave.

"Sabina, come to bed." Lynet stifled a yawn as she called to her. "'Tis late."

"Leave me be!" Sabina cried out. "I need not you or any other telling me what to do!"

"I was only trying to help, so suit yourself. I care not if you do not rest properly," Lynet said, turning on her side, away from her sibling. She punched her pillow and closed her eyes.

"Go to sleep," Sabina muttered, annoyed she still shared a chamber with her sister.

She began to rock back and forth on the stool she was perched upon as if that would help solve the problem of having a child growing within her and still being unwed. She must have speech with Hugh afore any further time comes to pass. Wringing her hands together, over and over again, brought her no answers. She was aware Hugh had left the keep for parts unknown. Surely someone must know of his whereabouts.

Tomorrow, I shall find him, she thought, as her mind schemed to bring him to heel and do what was right by her and her babe. He was a knight after all. Surely he would keep his oath to protect those under his care. Did knights now make such a solemn vow upon their knighthood to do such rot? She scratched her head in indecision on what path to take to bring him to wed with her.

As she crawled between the covers next to her sister, it never occurred to Sabina that Hugh would not want to claim her as his bride. She closed her eyes with visions of Hugh as her husband and the joy she would see in him when he learned of their child.

THIRTY

FIRELIGHT LIT THE CHAMBER and warmed the room to the occupants within whilst the logs in the hearth crackled and hissed as they burnt brightly. Dristan's deep rumbling chuckle erupted from the bed where the flickering shadows of the couple who sat there reflected upon the nearby wall.

"Aye, you may laugh, my lord, but I did not find the jest humorous at the time," Amiria said shortly. She watched as Dristan looked down upon their repast, spread out between them, then offered her a bite of cheese, mayhap as a peace offering. Her brow raised and then she laughed. "Well...perchance there was humor to be found after all."

"Think you Cook will ever again provide us another decent meal once he learns we have pilfered and raided the larder this eve?" Dristan drawled casually. "I have become quite fond of the fare to be found at our table. 'Tis the best I've ever tasted, truth be told."

"'Tis your larder, Dristan, so who is Cook to gainsay you?" Amiria chided. "What we should be worrying about is that the king does not learn such a marvel can be found in the kitchens at Berwyck. Otherwise, we shall have nothing left in the cellars to see us through the coming winter if he and his retainers come to grace us with their almighty presence."

She bit into an apple and offered him a bite, which he took. She licked her lips hastily as the juice threatened to run down her chin. Just as quickly, Dristan leaned over towards her and kissed her lips. Surprised, she sat there in wonder not sure how she should respond.

"Delicious," he replied with a glint in his eyes.

"Aye," she whispered softly," the apple is most sweet."

Dristan watched her for several moments 'til he reached up to toy with a lock of her hair. "Aye, that too."

Amiria blushed, for his words were like a caress to her very soul. "You tease me, my lord," she said ever so quietly.

He reached over and tucked the stray wisp behind her ear, as the covering that had been draped around his hips dropped dangerously low. Her heartbeat quickened. She tried to remain aloof to the feelings he stirred in her, especially since he made no move to alter the blanket. 'Twas obvious from his relaxed demeanor that modesty was not a problem for him, for he comfortably lounged there on the bed as if he cared not whether he was clothed or not in her presence.

Trying to distract her roaming thoughts, when he leisurely leaned back upon the pillows whilst still casually observing her, she began to tidy up their meal and took the remains to a near-by table. She poured wine into a chalice and took a sip to calm herself, knowing there was not much left to do but return to his side.

Dristan waited for her in silence. The intensity of his gaze scorched her to her very core like a fire tickling greedily at her feet. She was not used to having such admiring looks from men, yet his eyes seemed to smolder in his desire to have her yet again. She thought perchance a lifetime looking at this magnificent man may not be long enough to satisfy the yearning she felt for him. *But what of his heart*, her soul whispered of her own desire to have the one she wed love her. As yet, she had no answer to her unspoken question.

He leaned up on one elbow and pulled the coverlet down, holding out his hand for her to rejoin him. Amiria hesitated only briefly, and he brought her close to his side.

"I was not teasing you, *ma cher*," he said huskily, nuzzling her neck.

Amiria shivered at his touch but had the sudden urge to have him declare himself unto her afore this night was over. She gave a gentle push upon his chest and sat up whilst her hair fell like a veil in front of her face. With a frustrated sigh, she pushed the troublesome tresses back and covered herself as best she could.

Dristan gave her a troublesome look at her sudden change of mood. "Is their aught amiss, Amiria?"

"Perchance I am pondering the mysteries of my life of late," she muttered forlornly.

"Surely such musings can wait till the morn," he said brusquely. "I want you..."

Amiria shook her head to break the enchantment he attempted to weave around her. If he continued to distract her with his dizzying kisses, she would never know what was in his heart. "Aye, you want me as much as I want you, but what of the morrow or the day after? Will you tire of me and toss me aside or someday make me attend your lady wife?"

Dristan sat up, his ardor apparently cooling quickly at her words. "What nonsense do you speak? Have I not said we will wed?"

"Aye, but when?" she said, frustrated they should be having this conversation. She had thought mayhap he would take time to woo her in the manner her mother had said her father had done in times past. Mayhap she was being unfair since Dristan did gift her with a most wondrous sword, but she could not help the vulnerable feelings inside her, nor the catch in her voice as her confusing thoughts rumbled around in her head.

Dristan continued to stare at her, and Amiria knew he saw a thousand emotions play across her face. She was not good at hiding her feelings and, against her will, she could feel unshed tears begin to glisten in her eyes. If only she could make him understand something of her plight.

He pulled her into his embrace and ran his calloused hands down her hair. She pulled back to look at him, in silence. Mayhap he understood after all.

"When?" she asked yet again, longing to hear his answer.

"On the morrow if you but wish it," he declared. "You had asked for time to resolve yourself to our marriage. I but thought you wanted to get to know one another better. As it troubles you, we shall wed on the morrow, if that satisfies you."

"And what of you, my lord? Will that satisfy you?" she questioned hurtfully. "You have not declared your feelings for me. I hear no lays to my beauty, nor do I have flowers on my table. Will you be about wooing your future wife afore we pledge our troth?"

"I am not much for this wooing business, Amiria. I have spent my life as a seasoned warrior and have never afore had time or patience to worry about such fripperies. I did not think such pretties would make much difference," he said gruffly. 'Twas clear he felt out of his element.

"Mayhap not, but every woman wants the one she is to spend her life with to make at least a small effort. Besides, you play the lute most splendidly and have a most wondrous voice. Perchance if you took the time to play and sing for me, 'twould count towards a bit of wooing in my eyes."

"I would have thought the sword was more to your liking," he grumbled.

"You know it means all to me, Dristan," she said with a touch of apprehension. "I just wish to know what I see when I look into your eyes."

Dristan thought on her words afore answering. "'Tis said the eyes are the window to the soul, or so I've heard somewhere. Perchance, they are instead the window to my heart. I have kept it well guarded for I have never found anyone of worth to melt the ice surrounding it, for more years than I can remember."

Amiria leaned towards him and rested her hand on his chest, feeling a steady beat beneath her palm. "And if my heart could see you, Dristan, what in truth would it behold?" she inquired carefully.

He placed his hand over hers and took her cool fingers, bringing them to his lips. He kissed each one 'til she placed her other palm along his cheek. "Surely you know, I care for you Amiria," he declared honestly. "I would not take you to wife otherwise."

"Aye, well, 'tis rumored you have been ordered to do so by the king," she said sadly with indecisiveness carefully hidden beneath the surface of her trying to be brave.

"You have heard tell of that?"

Amiria shrugged casually as if what she had learned had not torn her heart asunder. "Servants gossip and I have ears to hear all whether I wish it or not."

"Then let us put an end to idle castle gossip, shall we?" he replied. "May I speak honestly without you thinking I am some sappy youth with no spurs on my heels and no knowledge of women and their desires?"

"Of course, my lord," she whispered hopefully. He took her hands and began rubbing his thumbs over the top of her knuckles as she waited patiently for him to gather his thoughts. His eyes rose to hers, and the look he gave her made her catch her breath in anticipation of his words. 'Twas more than just a gaze of desire hidden within those magnificent grey eyes of his. 'Twas an open invitation that reached out to capture her heart, if she would but let him into her very soul. She gave him a tentative smile and waited. She would not be disappointed that she did so.

Dristan took in the woman afore him and felt for the first time that his future would be bright if he could but keep Amiria at his side. A whisper of a conversation with Kenna skimmed across his spirit as he remembered her words, saying he sought a different life. At the time, he thought her words were nonsense and bore no merit. But aye...with Amiria as his wife, all things would indeed be possible.

"I have spent my entire life with a sword in my hand, most likely from the time I could stand," he began. "Riorden came to my parents holding to squire for my father at an age similar to Patrick. He has been beside me, guarding my back ever since. I have seen much death and killed many men for the sheer victory of a conquering hero, all in the name of a king, who has rewarded me most handsomely. Tourneys have added to my staggering wealth, which only enforced my reputation as the fiercest warrior to ever grace this earth. To be honest, I grow weary of watching those who shrink in fear, whenever I arrive at a castle gate, that I will invade their lands, lopping off heads as I kill all in my wake for the sheer sport of annihilating my enemy."

"Dristan, surely you know, I do not think such of you any longer."

"Let me finish, Amiria," he said, dragging his hand through his hair, and once more grasped her hand, bringing it to his lips. "My coffers are nigh unto bursting with enough gold to see me through all my days 'til I am old and grey and beyond even that. My holdings are numerous and vast, both here in England and in France. But gold is only gold, and not the treasure I now seek to claim for the rest of my days," he said, closing his eyes and taking a steady breath.

He felt Amiria caressing his skin beneath his eyes with her thumbs, ever so gently, 'til he once more opened his eyes to her. "And what treasure doth my dragon now seek to soothe his mighty temper?" she teased gently.

"You," Dristan simply answered with no hesitation.

"Me?" she seemed astonished at his declaration for, apparently, her thoughts ran true to his own heart.

"Aye, Amiria. 'Tis you," he repeated. "You are the true treasure I would have beyond gold, land, or title. You have captured my attention several times, my lady. The first was upon the strand as an apparition in a very fetching lavender gown. I thought for sure that a faerie queen was gracing me with a vision of loveliness. For just as quickly did I gaze upon you, did she just as rapidly take you by returning to the surrounding mist in those early morning hours at dawn."

"I did not realize you had seen me there. 'Twas after my father's passing, and I was feeling quite alone."

"And I am most sorry for his loss, Amiria, and that of your brother. If I could turn back the hands of time and return your loved ones, I would do so most willingly."

"Thank you, my lord."

Dristan reached out and fingered a lock of her hair again. "I had barely begun to get my senses restored when I met yet another girl asleep on the sand dunes. She made me laugh, that woodland nymph, and I searched for days trying to find her whereabouts, to no avail. Little did I realize, the young man I was training most ruthlessly each day was, in truth, the maid I had been searching for. Imagine my surprise that eve at the spring!"

Amiria blushed and gave him a timid smile which he returned.

"I see there is a fire within you, burning most vibrantly, somewhat similar to my own which is fiercely lit within me," he began again. "You are my match, Amiria, in every way. I cannot promise that all will be peaceful between us for the rest of our lives since we are both strong willed, but I do promise we shall live life to its fullest. We will learn to love one another as our time together advances through the years, we will have children to raise and watch grow to our delight, and I shall see your siblings are well taken care of."

"'Tis more than I could ever hope for." Amiria believed he spoke the truth.

"Then I earnestly pray your heart will tell you my words are true, and if you were to see mine, then you would know that it will beat for you and you alone. No other will I take, for you are mine, and just as you claimed me, I shall do the same for all of my days, however blessed those shall be," he vowed. He gathered her in his arms and laid her down upon the pillows. "So what say you? Will you be my lady wife? Not because our king demands it of me, but because I wish it for myself."

"Aye, Dristan. I will pledge you my troth forevermore," she whispered softly, and he claimed her lips in a fierce and hungry binding kiss.

And so, as the evening progressed, there were no longer whispered words or mingled laughter coming from the lord's chamber, only sighs of pleasure. On this night, they sealed their fate to one another 'til they could get themselves to a priest to give his blessing in the eyes of God above, and fortune could then smile down upon them.

'Twas not 'til the skies began to lighten in brilliant shades of pink and orange as the new day dawned, that Amiria and Dristan did at last fall fast asleep. Even as they slumbered, they continued to hold on to one another as if afraid to let go of what they had found.

For although 'twas most unexpected, and they were not as yet ready to admit it fully even unto themselves, they had found the rare gift of love in one another. After all...love, beyond any doubt, is life's true treasure transcending time itself. Beyond compare and if carefully nurtured, 'twould last them a lifetime and fulfill their hearts' desires. The miracle of love...Aye, they were most fortunate indeed.

THIRTY-ONE

THE EARLY EVENING HOURS had brought the majority of the Berwyck's inhabitants into the chapel to attend the evening mass. The priest stood at the altar, peering down from his lofty perch upon the souls whose heads were bowed in reverent worship as he continued preaching his sermon in Latin. The grey smoke from the lit torches had filled the room with a lingering haze, irritating the eyes of the occupants, although none dared to voice their discomfort. 'Twas a small enough penance to pay for the absolution of one's sins.

Amiria sat with fidgety hands, wondering when the priest would be finished so she could return inside the keep and once more don hose and tunic. She had dressed this eve to please Dristan in the lavender gown he had first seen her in and was thankful Sabina had not done it irreparable damage. It had taken longer than she thought 'til Amiria found the garment carelessly discarded beneath her bed in a wrinkled heap. Thanks to Lynet's help, the dress looked good as new.

Her hair she had left, at least temporarily, down in a cascade of shimmering loose red curls. From the look Dristan cast her when she entered the chapel, he had been most satisfied to see her thusly attired. Casting a sideways glance at him beneath her lashes, she noticed that he, too, had dressed resplendently this eve in a rich dark-blue tunic.

She began to silently tap her foot from boredom. 'Twas a bad habit of hers she had tried to still over the years whenever she was required to sit for long periods of time whilst indoors. Apparently, she still failed after all this time to cease the repetitive movement. To ease her mind, she thought about the past se'nnight and how time seemingly flew in a whirlwind of activities of living life to its fullest, as Dristan had made mention.

They still trained every morn after mass, although Amiria now took on the task of seeing to the keep. The men had been most pleasantly surprised that first eve when they had returned to sup and witnessed the miraculous condition of the Great Hall.

The dogs had been removed from the keep and no longer added to the filth of the floor that had been scrubbed clean. New rushes mixed with scented herbs were now in place having been strewn about the scoured stones, giving a fresh clean odor to the room. 'Twas indeed more agreeable, even to the hardened warrior's way of thinking, than its earlier condition. Nor could they complain when Amiria saw that food and ale were readily available to fill their hunger and quench their thirst upon arrival from their rigorous training.

'Twas only when Turquine bellowed for one of the whore's to come out of hiding and join him for a mug or two that they learned all the woman of that ilk had been sent to the village where they belonged. His voice rang out in annoyance as several others joined in to proclaim their displeasure. Amiria had come to stand afore them with her hands on her hips, daring them to usurp her authority. Her own temper flaring, she voiced, in no uncertain terms, that this was her home and they could very well take themselves off to the village to see to their needs, for those women were no longer welcome within the walls of the castle grounds.

Since Dristan continued to allow her to have her way and did not gainsay her, 'twas clear the knights stood no chance of swaying her decision on the matter. They had grumbled into their cups about the distance they now had to travel for a comely wench, along with what other unpopular changes may yet come.

Fingering the fabric of her gown whilst memories flooded her mind, an enchanting smile appeared on her face. After their last coupling, Dristan refused to have her come to his bed again 'til after they were wed and instead each night escorted her to her own chamber to take her slumber. She may have had doubts briefly flash afore her mind, but they were quickly put to rest when he opened the chamber door for her to enter that first eve. Her eyes had sparkled in delight, as she beheld what flowers he could find gracing the tables of her room. Given the time of year, she was astonished to know the time it must have taken him to find any at all that had not succumbed to the frost found most mornings. She had turned to face him, yet he had only taken her hand. Bowing low, he had pressed a chaste kiss into her palm afore he took his leave. When the door had pressed shut, she had given a heavenly sigh of pleasure.

The evenings had been just as splendid. Spending time in his solar with Lynet and Patrick, 'twas a most promising setting with her family about her, especially when he took his lute in hand and began to sing. The melody of his voice felt as if it sung to her alone whilst his agile fingers strummed the instru-

SHERRY EWING

ment. When he had finished each eve, the look he gave her
shook her to her very core. Aye...there was no doubt left in her
mind that he had properly wooed her to her satisfaction after
all!

"Cease, Amiria," Dristan whispered in a low timbre, "else we
must needs sit here longer in the eyes of the good father, since
you refuse to pay attention to his words."

"I canna help it, Dristan," her hushed tones were for his ears
only.

The priest cleared his throat and began again with his voice
raised louder, as if to reach into their very souls.

"Ugh! I was right," he moaned in frustration. "Now we must
listen to him drone on about the weakness of the flesh!"

"I am most sorry, my lord," she said softly as she bowed her
head again and made every effort to sit still.

Seeing her meekness must have appeased the priest, as he at
last finished his sermon with a loud amen. With those about her
rising to leave, Dristan took her elbow and moved her forward
towards the altar.

"A moment longer, Father Donovan, if you please," he said
as everyone halted their steps to depart.

"Aye, my lord?" the priest said, coming to stand afore the
couple.

"We ask that you would give us your blessing and wed us,"
Dristan declared as he brought Amiria closer to his side.

The priest glared at the two in stony silence 'til his gaze finally hovered on Amiria. "And what of you, my child? Will you
have him?"

Amiria looked up at Dristan and saw an instant where the
thought she would refuse his offer flashed in those steel grey
eyes. She smiled with the confidence of a woman who knew her
own heart. "Aye, Father, I shall have him."

A screech rent the air as Sabina ran, stumbling from the chapel, wailing at the injustice of life. Amiria shook her head and gave her attention back to the priest. "Please proceed, good Father," she said gently.

"Holdings?" the priest queried to Dristan.

"Scribe!" Dristan called out. A young man moved quickly forward and took out parchment and quill. "Take this down," he ordered, and with a short nod from the scribe that he was ready, Dristan quickly began to give an accounting of all his holdings and property he brought to the marriage.

Amiria's eyes widened at the amount of wealth Dristan would bring to their union. The scribe's quill made loud scratching noises upon the parchment whilst he continued to furiously take down all that was being said. Time and time again, the quill went from ink well to parchment 'til Amiria was afraid the bottle would run dry. From the accounting Dristan gave, 'twas clear she would not want for anything for the rest of her days here on earth.

The priest nodded his approval and once more he looked up-on Amiria to give her own reckoning of her dowry. Afore she could answer, another spoke on her behalf.

"She brings a full garrison o' knights along wi' gold," Killian said firmly. "Several 'orses will also add tae our liege's stable. Thar's property tae tha north in Scotland wi' a fine a keep you'd ever find and o' some worth belonging tae her Da's grandsire. 'er mother also bequeathed her a modest manor on tha outskirts o' London."

He continued to rattle off more of her holdings and worth. When he had finished with his speech, he crossed his arms and took up a stance slightly behind Amiria, as her own sire would have done if he had given his approval to their match. With a nod from Dristan that he was in acceptance of the accounts, the priest made a motion to them as they lowered themselves to their knees. He began the ceremony to seal them in marriage.

A cloth binding their hands together was tied around their wrists, and the final blessing was finished. They rose as one, and Dristan leaned down to give her a chaste kiss. A document was rolled out, and Dristan and Amiria each in turn took quill in hand, signing their marriage contract. With a nod of satisfaction, the priest gave them a final blessing, rolled up the parchment before tying it with a ribbon, and handed it to the scribe for safe keeping.

Making their way to the Great Hall, 'twas evident Dristan had given much thought to the day for a feast was prepared for the returning couple. Kegs had been brought up from the cellars and a spigot was being punched into one of the barrels. Ale began to flow to celebrate, and cups were raised to salute their union. Even musicians had been procured and began to tune their instruments to await their pleasure.

Amiria lightly squeezed Dristan's arm as he led her to the dais to take their place for the meal. "Thank you, my lord," she said, reaching up to caress his cheek.

He leaned down and kissed her forehead. "The pleasure was indeed mine, my lady."

Dristan pulled out her chair, and once seated, he began to fill their trencher with the finest of meats. She could only sit back enjoying her wedding celebration. She sighed in bliss knowing that today began the rest of her life.

Accepting a chalice of wine, she gazed upon her husband over its rim. He must have felt her stare. He looked upon her with his grey eyes capturing her own. The intensity passing between them caused her heart to flutter in anticipation of what was yet to come later this eve. With a promise in her eyes and a light touch on his arm, feeling his strength beneath her palm, she leaned back against her chair with the realization that all her hopes and dreams had been fulfilled.

"This just arrived for you, my lord," Rolf said, handing the missive to Dristan with reluctance of the bearer of bad tidings to mar the celebration that had been so carefully planned.

"*Merde!*" Dristan murmured. He tore open the seal of the King and scanned the parchment. His brow furrowed in displeasure as he read the contents.

"My lord?" questioned his knight. "Is there aught amiss?"

"Aye, Rolf. It seems I have been summoned to appear afore King Henry with all due haste."

"Surely we must not leave this instant, my lord."

Dristan looked about the inner baily courtyard and saw the merriment afore him. "Nay. The morn will be soon enough I suppose. Give word about the men, we ride with the dawn."

"Of course, my liege."

"And Rolf..." Dristan continued and watched his man pause in his stride. "Tell them we travel light afore you return to the dancing."

With a flick of his hand and a final comment to enjoy the festivities, Dristan dismissed his knight. 'Twas not long that his errand was finished and Rolf snatched up a comely maid and led the young lass to join the other dancers.

Espying his lovely wife among the revelers, a smile replaced Dristan's previous grim expression as he gazed upon her loveliness and wild spirit. A light rain had begun to fall and with it Amiria had dared all to come outside to dance amongst the mists emerging from the sky. Her laughter rang out and was infectious to all who came under her spell. Even the musicians began to play their instruments, beneath a hastily erected awning, to please Berwyck's mistress.

Shaking off his musings and needing to tell Amiria that he must leave with the rise of the morning sun, he was about to step down the stairs to join the dancers when Riorden came to his side, looking none too pleased.

"I have news..." he began.

"Not now, Riorden."

"'Tis of some import, Dristan, and should not wait," he said roughly. Receiving a nod to continue, he rushed on. "Sir Hugh is missing, along with a number of men."

Dristan turned towards his captain with a look that did not bode well for Hugh when he was found. "How long?"

"At least two days' time, my lord," he answered with a glint of anger.

The rain began to fall in earnest now and still the music played on, to the dancer's delight. "We shall speak of this in the morn whilst we prepare to leave for London. And I will determine who I shall leave to watch over all here."

"Aye, my lord," Riorden said as he watched Amiria detach herself from her guardsman Cameron and make her way towards them. "I see your bride shall demand your attention, as is fitting, for the rest of the eve." Dristan looked upon his captain and saw a teasing grin plastered upon his face. "Perchance you should make ready for the time honored tradition of the standing up?" he jested.

Dristan's reaction was immediate as he took a menacing step towards his captain, who held up his hands in mock horror and laughed. "Do not test me, Riorden. You are sorely mistaken if you think to strip me and my wife of our garments just in order to ensure our marriage is consummated!"

Riorden only laughed harder and bit back any further retorts as Amiria joined them. "My lady," he said with a bow, "if you will excuse me."

Amiria watched him leave and turned towards Dristan, noticing his frown. "Something troubles you, my lord?"

"Aye! But Riorden shall live to see another day as long as he remembers whom he serves."

Amiria only gave a small smile and his anger disappeared whilst he gazed upon her. She seemed to be pondering something, and he could only guess at the thoughts running through her head. As if she made up her mind and could resist no longer, she reached up upon her toes and placed a chaste kiss upon his lips. He felt her breath catch when his arm encircled her waist and she was crushed against the hardness of his muscled chest. He heard her sigh in pleasure at the contact of his body held against her own soft form. From the searing look he gave her, she knew 'twould not be long afore they adjourned up to his chambers.

Her arms wrapped around his neck and she played coyly with his hair. Still he felt her shiver as his hand caressed her back. He would not admit it to her, but he was just as affected by holding her close. His eyes lowered. She bit her lower lip and her tongue sneaked out to wet her lips. He swore he was becoming drunk from her beauty.

"Continue looking at me as you are, *ma petite*, and I'm afraid I will no longer be able to restrain myself," Dristan said huskily. "You, my dear wife, are too enchanting to be getting drenched by the rain. I think 'tis time you are properly bedded by your husband, who has waited too long to feel your touch."

Leaning down, he gently teased her lips with his own even as he tightened his hold, bringing her closer against him. Hearing her sigh only heightened his desire to get her alone in their chambers. He would have continued his assault on her senses by deepening his kiss, but she quickly pulled away with a delightful bit of laughter that shot straight to his soul. Good Lord, he must be bewitched. His eyes watched Amiria's every move as she held her arms up to the sky and twirled around in the rain. Totally mesmerized, he waited as she ran back into his arms and wrapped her arms tightly about his neck.

"Come...take my hand and dance with me in the rain," she whispered into his ear as he caressed her back, "for life is good if you but open your eyes to all the possibilities it has to offer."

Dristan thought he must have taken leave of his own senses when he allowed her to pull him to the center of the dancers. As if on cue, the musicians began a slower piece. Amiria came to him and all but molded herself to his body. Her touch caused his flesh to feel as if 'twere on fire. If this was in truth some new dance, he had no knowledge of such a one at court, and it should be limited to the bed chamber. He was completely aroused whilst holding her close as the rain fell down, soaking them both. They continued to sway to the music as she smiled up at him with a promise in those incredible violet eyes.

The dam of his desire, which he had held in check, faltered. He could take no more of the torture from his traitorous body and his desire to have his woman in his bed. His decision made, he scooped his wife up into his arms as Amiria burrowed her head against his chest, draping her free arm across his shoulder. He lengthened his stride as he felt her snuggle deeper within his arms. Feeling her shiver, he knew not whether 'twas from the chill of the rain or in anticipation of their destination. He hoped 'twas the latter.

Their guest's voices rose into the night air as their cheers rang out and resounded into the evening sky. Dristan, however, gave them no further thought since he had far more important matters to see to. For him and his bride, their evening had only just begun.

Thirty-two

THE NEW DAY DAWNED BRIGHT with sunny skies to appease those who would ride this day towards London. For some, the rays of sunshine were brighter than usual, since they had over indulged in the spirits that had flowed freely the eve afore.

For one lone knight, 'twas not the amount of spirits he had consumed causing his sour disposition. He could only have wished that 'twas so, but 'twas the agony of knowing the one woman he would have taken to wife had wed another. He knew this day would come, and yet his heart bled with the knowledge she was completely lost to him and out of his reach forevermore.

Contemplating where his life would now lead him, he rested his head back against the rough stones of the keep with closed eyes 'til he felt a presence near at hand. Turning his head, he espied Lynet entering the gardens. From her forlorn expression, there was no doubt left in his mind that all was not well with the young lady and she, too, had much on her mind.

She came to stand afore him with a silent look that spoke far beyond her years. "May I?" she asked, indicating the empty space next to him. With his nod, she sat arranging her dress afore turning in his direction.

"You are to leave us," Lynet predicted solemnly, as if his horse being readied in the bailey wasn't evidence enough of this fact.

"Aye, there is no longer reason for me to stay. My duty here is done." He was somewhat surprised his thoughts were so easily read by such a young lass.

"You could stay, Ian," she said with hope lingering in her words.

He looked at her aghast. The thought of remaining would shatter what remained of his already dispirited heart. At a loss for words, he leaned his head back against the wall again 'til he felt her small hand upon his own.

"My pardon, Ian, for that which you have lost," she said. "'Twas inconsiderate and thoughtless of me to request that which would be so unfair to you."

"You are not at fault, Lady Lynet," Ian declared. "There is no one to blame but myself for what plagues me."

"Aye...well...I am afraid I also know only too well how it feels to watch someone you love with all your heart turn to another."

He gazed at her wringing her hands in the folds of her gown. It seemed her mind raced to try to form words to say to him. What she uttered next was not what he expected from her.

"Sometimes that which you seek is right afore your eyes but cannot be seen because you are blinded by aught else," she spoke ever so softly.

Her words hung in the air as an uncomfortable silence descended upon them. Ian raised his head from the wall and turned to peer at Lynet, wondering if there was some hidden meaning in her words. Her face could only be described as lovely, not only in the perfection of her features, but also from the beauty that came from her innocence and being young at heart. She could not possibly have feelings for him, could she? Looking into her hope filled eyes, he was afraid 'twas true.

He reached for her hand and took it in his own. It trembled slightly at his touch and looked so incredibly small in his own large callused one. "Lynet, I—"

She gave a small laugh ringing with all the insecurity she must have been feeling. The sound was strained, leaving her emotions openly exposed for him to see. "Oh, I know what you must think," she declared bravely, even though her words shook with sadness. "I am nowhere near my sister's equal nor can I even begin to lift a sword to defend my home as easily and readily as Amiria can."

"'Twas not what came to mind, Lynet."

"Truly?" she asked in surprise.

"Nay. I was but thinking I am honored to know you have feelings for me. I can only pray, however, you have not felt I led you to believe those same feelings are returned."

She let out a heavy sigh from his words of rejection. "I know I cannot compare in any way to Amiria, for what is there not to love about my sister? Nay, Ian. You have done nothing to mislead me." Unshed tears glistened in her vivid blue eyes. "Even though I have my own guardsmen, you have taken it upon yourself to watch over myself and family just as you have Amiria. For that I am most grateful. I am afraid 'tis just my girlish wishful thinking that mayhap you could come to care for me."

"You should not compare yourself to your sister, Lynet. You are still so young but will make a fine wife to someone worthy of your love. Never settle for anything less than to have the gift of your love returned to its fullest potential," Ian said honestly.

"I am not that young at four and ten. Most girls my age are already wed with a bairn or two, as you very well know. Besides...you could be that very someone."

There was such hopefulness lingering in her voice that Ian was afraid to crush such devotion and yet he had no other choice. "Nay Lynet. For in this time and place, I cannot give that which you deserve."

"I would wait for you, Ian, if you think it could be possible."

"Sweet lass, what do you want with an older warrior like myself?" he said, chuckling. "You deserve someone far younger than I. Someone who has not been sullied by his past."

"Bah! What do I want with some younger man who sees me only for my dowry?" she declared in misery.

"I have nothing to offer you Lynet," Ian announced bitterly. "My sire died and left my brother head of the clan. I have not returned to the Highlands for more years than I can remember. I could not stand by hopelessly as a younger son and watch all my sire had built ruined by my brother's greed for gold and revenge. I have no place to call my home and would not have you living your life out of a tent as I travel to hire out the use of my sword. You deserve much better than that."

"I would follow wherever you lead, if I could but have your love."

Ian brought her hands to his lips and placed a kiss upon each. "Again, I am most humbled by your declaration Lynet, but please do not wait for me. I would not care to learn someday you were disappointed I never returned for you."

She raised her head to gaze upon his face, as if memorizing his every feature. Her wounded look told him in no uncertain terms that he had broken her heart and most likely her spirit.

He dropped her hands. There really was nothing more that he could say to mend her sorrow.

She rose gracefully from the bench to leave his side, 'til they noticed Dristan making his way towards them. Afore he knew what she was about, Lynet quickly leaned down, wrapping her arms around his neck to hug him close to her.

"Please, Ian...come back to me," she murmured in his ear.

Taking both his cheeks in her small dainty hands, she gently placed an innocent childlike kiss upon his lips afore she blushed in embarrassment. Her flushed faced registered the shock she must have felt for behaving so brazenly. Hastily, she spun away from him whilst lifting her skirts and ran past Dristan up the stairs to the keep.

Dristan came taking the place Lynet had vacated, his brow lifting in concern of what he just witnessed. Waiting for an answer, Ian silently shook his head, apparently just as amazed at what had just occurred. "Is there aught you must tell me, Sir Ian? You dare to dally with my sister?"

"Nay, my lord, 'twas not as it appeared," Ian said, standing afore his liege.

"Very well...I must ask a favor afore I release you from your oath of fealty."

"Of course, my lord, I am ever at your service."

"I would have you accompany my retinue whilst I travel to London. I thought perchance you may wish to take in the sights afore going wherever the wind would take you on your new course in life. I am leaving Riorden here to help guard those I care most about, along with a few others of our guard. I am sure it will keep the regular garrison knights in line to remember their duty during my absence. Will you ride with me?" Dristan asked.

"'Twill be an honor to be a member of your guard, at least 'til we reach London, my lord," Ian said, giving Dristan a bow.

Dristan nodded, placing his hand upon Ian's shoulder in friendship. "My thanks, Ian, for your companionship, at least for a little longer. I know what it costs you to leave Berwyck, but know Amiria's wellbeing is what is most important to me. That red haired vixen has become most precious to me and I would not leave her with any but my most trusted knight to protect her whilst I travel about the king's business."

"I understand, my lord, completely."

"Aye, I knew you would. Speaking of Amiria, I must needs go find her whereabouts. I know not where she has disappeared to, so I suppose in a way I have already misplaced her," Dristan snorted.

Ian laughed at the look on Dristan's face. "Then if I may offer a suggestion?" Ian proposed and saw his lord's agreement. "Look above, my liege. If I know Amiria, she shall be up on the parapet."

"Only she would find solace at such dizzying heights, but I suppose you know her hiding places better than anyone. Come, I will discuss a few things with you afore I speak with my wife. Our time grows short, and we must soon leave."

The two men began to make their way through the bailey. 'Twas not long afore their laughter could be heard ringing out between them.

As Kenna opened her door from her hut and saw the two knights afore her line of vision speaking as friends, she could only smile knowing some of what she had foreseen had come true. She picked up her herb basket and made her way to the garden, humming a fine tune, satisfied at the way the day was progressing. She only prayed the remainder of her dreams would not come to pass for those visions would not bear well for the occupants of Berwyck castle.

THIRTY-THREE

"MUST YOU GO DRISTAN?" Amiria questioned wearily as the wind whipped up a stray tendril of her hair. She waved her hand in front of her face as one lone lock misbehaved and flitted out of her reach. She gave up in her attempts to tame it into order. Raising her eyes to her husband, she hated to admit it, but she already missed him.

They had not slept long afore Dristan had woken and told her of his morning departure. In her haste to dress, she was only too glad to have at least managed to place her boots on the right feet. As an afterthought, she had grabbed a tartan to wrap around her shoulders when she fled their chamber.

Standing upon the battlements, the sounds of activities reached her ears. 'Twould not be long afore the group below would be ready to begin their journey to London. With thoughts of Dristan's impending departure, Amiria needed to be in the one place she always went when she was troubled. The knowledge that he would leave the very day after they wed had sent her scurrying up the tower stairs to breathe in the air from the sea to calm her frayed nerves.

"I know the timing is not at its best, Amiria, but I can hardly ignore a summons from the king," he declared. He reached for her to bring her close and captured her lips with his own. "You knew there would come a time when I must travel about his business."

She snuggled up against his warmth and breathed in the very scent of him, inhaling deeply the hint of spice lingering in his clothes, so she might remember the very essence of him. Looking up into his face from the protection of his arms, she smiled shyly.

"What?" he asked, espying her curious behavior.

"You will think me a silly child to ask this of you," she replied hesitantly. She continued staring up into his handsome visage, trying to form the words, but only blushed in embarrassment of her unspoken thoughts.

Dristan gave a brief laugh at her expression, and she pressed her lips firmly shut, refusing to now give voice to her question. "Come now," he continued, "I am but humored at your countenance, *ma cherie*. What is it you wish to ask of me?"

Amiria stepped away from him and grabbed the plaid that almost escaped from her shoulders. Tying a knot in the fabric to keep it firmly in place, she went to a nearby wall and picked up a basket. Bringing it to his side, she showed him the contents. 'Twas mostly coal and some rags, but she held them as if they were something to be treasured.

"My father used to tell me the stones here would screech in protest one day from all the scratching I did upon them in my youth. 'Twas just a release for me to draw now and then, plus I adore being up on the battlements," she said and looked at him quietly standing there, waiting for her to carry on.

"And..." He let the word linger whilst he waited patiently for her to continue as if he had nothing better to do with his time other than to linger at her side.

Amiria rushed on. "I was but wondering if perchance, since we have obviously not had time to hire a painter to come and do our portraits, if 'twas permissible for me to sketch your shadow upon the stones? I would then at least have a semblance of a reminder of you to gaze upon whilst you are gone and, of course, the sun is at least cooperating today."

She lowered her gaze and blushed in astonishment that she would give voice to such a sentimental request. He must think her such a fool, and yet he surprised her once again by reaching out to cup her chin. There was no teasing that she could see shining from the depth of his eyes and she was glad of it. Leaning down, he placed a gentle kiss upon her lips and gave her a devilish grin.

"Where would you like me to stand, my dear wife?" he asked quietly. Her whole demeanor radiated her happiness, for his words more than pleased her.

Amiria led him to one of the tower walls that had somehow escaped any markings or drawings from her past. She took his hand and positioned him just so. The sunlight lit upon him, casting the perfect shadow of his silhouette upon the weather worn stones of the tower. Taking coal in hand, she carefully traced his reflection whilst her hands became as black as the coal she held.

"Just hold still one more moment, my lord," she said, concentrating on making the etching just right to her eyes. "There! 'Tis perfect!"

At her words, Dristan hesitated no longer and gathered her in his arms. "I am glad you are pleased, but kiss me so I, too, may have something to remember 'til my return."

Dristan leaned down and captured her lips, and Amiria felt the heady sensation of their mouths joining whilst he breathed life into her very soul. He always affected her so 'til she lost all semblance of sanity. He made her forget aught else but the feelings he brought out in her. He deepened their kiss, and she moaned in pleasure. If they had more time, she would have begged him to return to their chamber so they might continue what he started. But, 'twas over all too soon, and she at last felt him reluctantly pull away. She placed her hands upon his arms to steady herself and felt herself sway as her knees all but buckled beneath her.

His amused chuckle brought her attention to the satisfied grin he had devilishly placed upon his fetching but arrogant features. Even his smug visage told her, in no uncertain words, he was fully aware of how he affected her. She raised her brow at him and realized she only mimicked his own expression he sometimes gave her. He laughed all the louder to her annoyance.

"Aye, I was right to wed you Amiria. We shall never be bored with one another," Dristan proclaimed knowingly.

"Be gone with you!" Amiria huffed with a haughty look. "I care not if you return."

"Oh, but I will return, my lady, of that you can be assured!"

With no more thought of jesting with him further, she rose on her toes to place a kiss upon his lips. "Then go, so you may return to me all the faster," she said sharply. "I will not add to the conceit you already have by watching you leave and spouting words on how I shall miss you!"

Dristan took her chin and raised her face to meet him. "I will remember last eve most fondly, my sweet wife. Besides, I, too, will carry a part of you with me," he said, showing her the prints of her coal covered hands, left upon his tunic from her embrace.

She gasped. "Let me get a rag and quickly clean the mess I made, Dristan, afore you go to the king!" she proclaimed with horror at the thought of his arriving at the king's palace thusly.

"Nay! I think I will keep them as a reminder of the beautiful woman who awaits my return." He gave her another sly grin. He kissed her once more afore landing a playful soft slap upon her bottom. Then he began to make his way from the battlements.

Amiria sadly watched him leave her side whilst she rubbed her backside, muttering about men and their self-worth. She had to admit his impending departure did distress her, for he would be taking a piece of her heart with him. It seemingly sunk with his parting. *I love him*, she thought and the realization almost brought her to her knees.

She watched Dristan hesitate with his hand upon the handle of the door whilst he debated something within him. She did not have long afore he turned and gave voice to her unasked question of why he delayed.

"You may wish to come below, Amiria, to say farewell to Ian. He rides with us this day." Dristan gave her a jaunty salute and shut the door to the tower behind him.

Her emotions wreaking havoc with the thought of Ian leaving Berwyck, Amiria went up onto the parapet and peered down, listening to the noise that met her ears of those who gathered below. 'Twas seemingly only moments later when she saw Dristan join his men. His gaze swept the perimeters of the bailey and, from his nod of approval, apparently all was in ready for their departure.

Her decision made, she flew from the battlement walls and down the narrow winding steps of the tower. The sound of her boots on the stone stairs echoed with her haste to reach those who meant the world to her. She almost ran into a maid, who rapidly gathered the linen she was carrying in her arms to keep it from falling to the floor. With a hasty apology, Amiria continued her flight 'til she flung open the oaken portal of the keep's door. It ricocheted with a loud bang against the wall and bounced back, almost hitting her, as it slammed shut behind her.

Her eyes quickly scanned those who were already seated upon their horses 'til she found one amongst the many knights dressed in Dristan's colors. He, too, had been honored with clothing to match but 'twas the red of his hair that gave him away. He was in the process of leaning down to take one last look to inspect his saddle and trappings when she saw him halt his movements.

He must have felt her stare, since he gave a sudden upright jerk of his head. He stood proudly straight and turned, meeting her eyes directly, as if no others stood between them. Amiria slowly descended the steps with Ian coming to meet her half way. He bowed low and she held out her hand to him. He took it with no hesitation and placed a kiss upon its back.

"My lady," Ian said hoarsely.

"Ian..." She could not lessen the hint of sorrow ringing in her voice. She knew not what to say, knowing she may never see him again. "I had not realized you would leave us so soon."

"I would not have thought 'twould come as much of a surprise to you, Amiria," he drawled carelessly.

"I suppose," she replied glumly.

"You are left in capable hands with Riorden here as captain now. Our Lord Dristan would not have left you otherwise."

Amiria nodded, not trusting herself to speak and peeked upon her husband to ensure he was not offended she had speech with Ian, even though 'twas his suggestion. With a wink from him, she returned her attention to the man who had been her captain. Ian had been with her family longer than she could remember. Berwyck would not be the same without him and yet she understood his need to leave the only home he had known these many years.

"I know not what else to say, Ian." Her voice cracked with emotion as she flung herself into his arms.

Ian held her close as her tears began to run down her cheek pressed against his neck. He gently held her at arm's length and wiped the moisture from her eyes.

"No crying, my sweet lass. I would remember you with happiness shining in those beautiful eyes and not that of sorrow upon your face," Ian said, forcing a smile upon his lips.

Amiria stifled a sniffle and wiped at her nose with the sleeve of her tunic. She tried to give him a smile, but it must have shown as more of a grimace, for both Ian and Dristan smothered their mirth.

"Well if that is the best you can do, I suppose 'twill suffice Amiria," Ian said.

Her stubborn Scottish pride reared up as she managed a look of what she hoped was cool disinterest. She must have looked much like her usual self for Ian's eyes began to twinkle with merriment.

"That is much better, my lady." He took his gauntlets from his belt and began to don them when the keep door once more opened. Lynet came to stand at the head of the steps with Patrick, looking lost with his departure. He raised his hand to them and bowed once again.

"Godspeed, Ian," she whispered to his ears alone.

"And to you, my lady," he replied softly. "Be happy, Amiria, and well."

He left her and made his way to his horse without another word spoken between them. With a nod from Dristan, the procession began making its way through the portcullis, leaving a trail of dust behind them as they rode from the castle and her sight. Ian never once looked back.

Amiria, however, stood there in stony silence, staring at the empty gate. 'Twas not 'til the dust at last settled that she came out of her trance like state. Ian's leaving had affected her more than she thought was possible. Apparently, he, too, owned a small piece of her heart and with both men she cherished most gone from Berwyck, the castle now seemed like a hollow heap of stones with no warmth to bring her comfort.

But castle life moves on, for with the winter months fast approaching, there was much to do. The normal sounds of daily living once more reached her ears and yet she could not shake off the eerie feeling that something was not as it should be.

She automatically reached for the hilt of her sword and felt the familiar feel of the handle as it rested in the palm of her hand. Amiria made a quick scan of the bailey, but saw nothing amiss. Perchance 'twas just her imagination, she mused, and with a careless shrug and a toss of her head she ignored the sound of the small voice inside her head begging her to use caution.

Tucking her braid into her tunic and with the sounds from the lists calling to her, she strode with a purpose in mind to perfect her sword arm. There was nothing like a good day's work in the lists to get her mind off her troubles. She should have listened instead to her instincts to be wary.

THIRTY-FOUR

SABINA LEANED LOW OVER HER HORSE'S NECK, urging it to quicken its pace as she rushed across MacLaren land. With the wind in her face and the feel of a brisk chill hanging in the air, 'twas clear that afore too long snow would blanket the earth. She hugged the beast closer, hoping its warmth might help keep the cold from her shivering body. 'Twas to no avail. Stupidly, she had given no thought to dress warm in her haste to reach her destination.

She had been waiting for what seemed like forever, after Dristan's departure, to finally hear some word amongst the servants of Hugh's whereabouts. Noticing a serf bragging to some of the other lads, she quietly had hidden behind a large barrel and heard the boy mention the coin he had received from Sir Hugh. He had continued to flaunt his wealth afore the lads, who had only sniggered at his foolishness and then left him, one after the other.

The boy had stood there, wallowing in humiliation, clenching his fist around the coin that only a moment afore he had been proud to receive. Shaking his hand in the air, he had left and made his way towards the stable. Sabina quietly had followed, knowing at last she would find her lover.

She had entered the stables and seen the boy idly lounging against a bale of hay, tossing his precious coin in the air. She had cleared her throat, catching his attention, and the boy hurriedly rose, the coin all but forgotten as it fell to the floor. She had gone to him and peered down into his face afore picking up the coinage and handing it to him.

"Tell me where Sir Hugh is, and I will give you another to match the one he gave you," she had said with a scathing sneer.

"I know not what ye speak of, milady," the boy had replied casually.

"'Twill not go well for you if you do not tell me what I wish to know. The Devil's Dragon does not deal well with traitors, or so I hear," she had replied coolly with a careless shrug. "'Tis up to you, but I would not like to be in your place when I tell him of your exploits upon his return."

Sabina smiled at the memory of how the lad's face had quickly transformed into terror at the mention of Lord Dristan. He had swiftly spewed forth all he knew and how he had been passing information to assist Sir Hugh. Finally receiving her answer as to Hugh's whereabouts, she had waited seemingly a lifetime for her chance to slip a horse from the stables and leave Berwyck Castle behind. Riorden had the eyes of an eagle, but when the opportunity came, she had taken it without further thought. Hence her flight in a dress meant more to impress rather than provide warmth and comfort. It did not help when the garment and flimsy shell of a cloak flapped behind her in the wind, furthering her discomfort from the cold elements of nature's wrath.

As if to further test her resolve to reach Hugh, she felt an icy snow flake against her cheek. As this one melted, another took its place, and then another and another. 'Twas not long afore the precipitation began to blanket the earth in a sparkling display of pure white snow. She must reach Hugh soon. Surely he would have a blazing fire in his camp to warm her.

On and on, she rode over the land 'til she became numb to the cold and all around her. At times she cursed her fate and wondered why God had forsaken her. Yet mostly she cursed her sister and her husband. *Husband!* Amiria had always gotten whatever she wanted and now she had become lady of the castle and wife to the most handsome man Sabina had ever laid eyes on. She should have been lady of Berwyck, and if she had her way, 'twould still be so!

Sabina slowed her steed when she entered a forest miles from her home. Although she had never ridden this far North, she knew she had passed over into Scotland and into the domain of the MacNaghten clan. Although they were the closest clan neighboring her own land, the MacNaghten's continued to cling to the old ways and her father had fought against the raiding of his land and cattle for many a year. The laird of the clan was mean spirited, to Sabina's recollection, and had tried to take over Berwyck castle many times in the past. 'Twas almost unsurprising and fitting that Hugh would be in league with a MacLaren enemy.

Suddenly, a man jumped from a tree and stood afore Sabina's horse, a crossbow ready and aimed directly at her chest. She raised her arms in surrender. Her reins were ripped from her hands by another, who appeared from the woods as she sat in the saddle confidently afore the ruffians. "Take me to Sir Hugh," she ordered.

"Who are ye?" the guard questioned, not lowering his weapon.

"He shall know of me. Now I insist you take me to him at once!"

Several other warriors appeared from the trees and Sabina began to panic. She was immediately surrounded and cursed, knowing she had nothing to defend herself.

One dared to reach out his filthy hand and yanked her from her horse. He grabbed for a lock of her hair. "Look 'ere lads! We've a fine liedy in our midst!

"Get your hands off me, you dirty oaf!"

"Ooh, and feisty too, just the way I's like me women," the guard guffawed, snatching Sabina's arm and drawing her close. "Not much tae look at but she will do, don't ye think?"

Sabina gagged at the smell of the man's breath as he tried to make contact with her lips. Her scream rent the air and echoed throughout the trees as the others chortled at her helplessness. They smacked their lips and pulled at her arm, knowing what danger she had put herself in. From the taunts they hurled in her direction, 'twas clear it had been some time since any of them had had the comforts of a woman. Sabina swore that woman would not be her!

She began kicking and screaming at the top of her lungs 'til she at last made contact with the man holding her. From his grunt of pain, he was none too pleased and he raised his fist in her direction. She cringed, waiting for the blow to strike. Thankfully, luck was on her side for once. Raising her head, she scanned the forest and her gaze gratefully came to rest on the welcoming figure of the one man she needed the most as he came to her rescue.

"Hold!" Sir Hugh yelled. His scathing look halted the men in their tracks. "Return to your posts."

The men scampered away to do his bidding. The man holding Sabina gave her one last leer, and she shivered in fear.

Hugh came to Sabina and wrapped his cloak around her trembling frame. Normally he would not care that she was cold or frightened, but he had heard rumors there might be a secret entrance to Berwyck Castle of which only family members were aware. The loose mutterings from that foolish boy Patrick just may have given him the advantage he was in need of.

He smiled as if he was glad to see her, and from her eager response, he gathered he would receive his answer in no time. The serf at Berwyck had been worth the coinage for he knew the boy he entrusted had faithfully informed Sabina of his location.

"Come, my sweet...let us away to the fire to warm you. You may also use my tent to rest your weary self. You have traveled far to see me, have you not?" Hugh purred in her ear.

Sabina smiled at him and snuggled into his arms as he led her away whilst she murmured how she knew Hugh would keep her safe.

They did not stroll far and he watched her face transform by what stood afore her. He watched in amusement as her mouth hung silently open whilst she viewed at least one hundred men, if not more, camped in the field where fires blazed in numerous locations. Tree's had been cut to accommodate the large army gathered here and pennants fluttered in the early evening air belonging to the MacNaghten clan.

"I have been busy as you can see, my pet," Hugh pronounced proudly with his arm stretched wide to show her his army. "They come to fight beside me whilst I claim Berwyck as my own, as it should have been from the start."

"But what plans do you have for me, Sir Hugh?" Sabina questioned, with a bit of apprehension ringing in her whispered words.

"Did you not wish to be lady of the castle?"

"Yes, of course but..."

"No worries, Sabina. You shall get your just rewards, and all shall be as it should," he said, nibbling at her neck.

Hugh led her to his tent to the jeering sounds of his men egging him on. Sabina did not care for the crude hecklings being thrown their way. She began to voice her displeasure, but he only silenced her with a kiss as they entered his tent. He began running his hands down the length of her body 'til he felt Sabina melt against him in delight from his touch.

Hugh began to mutter meaningless words of love whilst he quickly divested her of her garments. She truly was such a simpleton to believe the babbling he said to her. She wrapped her arms around him, and he began to encourage her to tell him of the entrance. As she moaned in rapture at what he was doing to her body, she at last relented and told him that which he asked. He laughed in triumph at how easily he had received his answer. None too gently, he finished the dreadful deed he had taken on himself and pulled out of her. His release was most timely for he was not sure he could have stood much more of listening to her spout her love of him.

He adjusted his hose and fastened his sword against his side, since he had not deemed her worthy to fully undress. He took her clothes and bundled the linen in a ball. Striding to the tent's entrance, he spoke softly to someone outside and returned to the task of putting on his remaining garb.

He watched as Sabina leaned up on her elbow from the makeshift bed, frowning in puzzlement when he took her clothing in his arms as if to return outside to his men.

"Come back and lie with me, Hugh," she whispered with a flirtatious grin.

Hugh ignored the invitation and went to a low table to look over the parchments that had been laid there for his perusal. His eyes narrowed. As far as he knew, the map of Berwyck Castle was most accurate, and he should find that which he sought from the information Sabina had given him. He patiently scanned the drawing, as his finger skimmed a line along the sheet. There! There is the entrance he would need to gain access whilst his troops attacked the front gate. He was most pleased.

"Sir Hugh?" Sabina cooed prettily, patting the coverlet next to her. "Surely you could delay just a bit longer, my Lord..."

He gave her a cold look and watched her flinch as if slapped. "I go to war you silly chit, and have no further need of you." His voice practically dripped with arrogance. He grabbed the pile of her garments and made to leave. Tonight he would have Amiria beneath him, calling out his name with passion, and he would be well rid of Sabina and her clinging ways. He had waited long enough to claim the true prize of his desire.

"Where go you with my clothes, Hugh?" Sabina demanded, rising up from the bed, pulling at the blankets to cover her breasts.

He tossed her a laugh filled with pure malice and with a sneer watched her face fall in worry. "You'll have no need of your clothing, my dear," he snorted.

Going to the entrance of the tent, he opened the flap and admitted the man from the forest. The man licked his lips, viewing Sabina's body ready for the taking, as Hugh watched Sabina's face quickly transform from seduction to complete horror.

"I believe I deprived you earlier of some sport, my friend, so enjoy the spoils of war," Hugh said with a lecherous grin. "See you that she does not leave this tent to alert those at Berwyck. I am sure you can think of some way to see she is kept entertained."

He laughed, and the man joined in his mirth and began divesting himself of his weapons. Hugh left the tent without another thought of Sabina. Hearing the sounds coming from the tent, he smiled in satisfaction that she would indeed be kept busy for some time. He heard her scream out his name 'til the sound was muffled but he cared not. Instead, he rallied his men. The time had come to lay siege to the castle.

He mounted his horse, gathering the reins in his hands, and surveyed his army as it began to move in the direction of Berwyck with a smile, reaching his eyes. 'Twas time he claimed Berwyck and his kingdom for his own.

THIRTY-FIVE

A MIRIA LOWERED HER SWORD and held up her hand afore she commenced in her lesson with Nevin once more. She thought she had been mistaken in what she had hoped would not be heard any time in her near future. But no...there 'twas again...the ever persistent sound of the tower bell ringing out in warning to secure the outer gates and drawbridge. The sound of crossing blades quickly diminished as knights rapidly sheathed their swords and ran to their designated posts. The garrison was well trained and knew their duty, unlike Amiria, who stood there silently in shock 'til her feet at last took flight, and she, too, made for the battlement walls.

She made fast work of the tower stairs mostly because she was unhampered by her armor that would have under normal circumstances slowed her ascent. Just this morn, Riorden had presented her with a leather jerkin for her to don, stating 'twas Lord Dristan's wish she learn to train whilst lightly dressed to improve her form. She had to admit, there were certain advantages, along with a great sense of freedom, to training without the additional heavy weight of several pounds of metal upon one's back.

Opening the tower door, she strode purposefully to the west battlement wall and made her way up another flight of stairs leading up onto the parapet. With no hesitation to the width of the narrow walkway, she made her way to Dristan's captain, who pondered the horizon with a heavy frown set firmly on his brow.

"What think you, Riorden? Are they friend or foe?" Amiria asked, dreading his answer.

"I hardly think they are friends, Lady Amiria." His reply was harsh, causing his dark brows to further deepen in thought.

She began to see the noticeable sign of dust rising in the distance. Riorden was right! This was no ordinary party and, at the rate they were moving, they could be at Berwyck's walls by late afternoon, if not sooner.

"'Twas good planning on the part of your ancestor's in having the foresight to build on such a high cliff," Riorden praised. "We would not have noticed their advancement this early without such a strategic advantage."

"My sire had always thought so, as well."

"The villager's will know what to do and come to the keep for protection?"

"Aye." She gave her hushed reply whilst a feeling of *déjà vu* came over her. 'Twas not all that long ago she stood in this exact spot, contemplating with her sire and brother whilst their attention scanned the distant horizon and the approach of an oncoming army. She did not relish the thought of more of her kinsmen's blood being shed. Her people had suffered enough this past year.

As she continued to watch the scene afore her unwavering gaze, she began to notice the first signs of villagers coming to the castle for protection. They carried in their hands what they could of their meager possessions. If another foe had come to claim the lands, all knew that any remaining crops would be burnt and the village ransacked of anything of worth. Thank goodness most of the crops had already been harvested. As if she had willed it, a light snow began to fall and Amiria knew she would once again need to raise up her courage to help with the defense of her home.

"I must go," she began, but her movements were halted by the steel grip of Dristan's captain.

"And just where is it you think you must go, my lady?" Riorden questioned with a stern look of disapproval upon his face. It appeared as if his features were made of chiseled stone with a look she had become used to only in another.

Amiria looked him firmly in the eye. "Why, to don my armor of course. Where else would I be needed at a time like this?"

"Do you honestly believe Lord Dristan would allow you to carry a sword into battle whilst you are on my watch?" he said with a ferocious roar.

She lifted her head defiantly. "Just try to stop me."

"Do not test my patience, my lady. You are in my care and will do as I bid you."

"I listen to no one's counsel but my own. My people need me just as they did afore," she replied tensely with a saucy toss of her head.

"Your clan may need you, but 'tis not to sacrifice your life on their account!" Riorden countered in aggravation, raking his free hand through his hair and staring down on her. "God's wounds...how does Dristan deal with such a defiant woman?"

Amiria continued struggling to free her arm from Riorden's grip but 'twas impossible. No amount of prying on her part was working. "I did my duty with the last siege, Riorden, and I must do so again!"

"And look at what the cost was to your clan from the last battle, Lady Amiria," Riorden bellowed. "I understand what drives your need, but I cannot allow you to put a sword to use. Dristan would see me drawn and quartered with my entrails scattered to the four corners of this earth, if I allow you to follow this course."

"Let go of me!" she cried out angrily. "You canna tell me what to do and soon you will be too busy to worry about my whereabouts." She stood there as defiant as she could be whilst raising her fist at Riorden, almost daring him to gainsay her authority. From the look he gave her, she knew she had pushed him much too far. She eyed him cautiously, not knowing what the man had in store for her. Whatever it may be, 'twas surely not what Amiria had in mind.

Riorden gave up trying to reason with Amiria for she was just as stubborn as her husband. He took by both arms and gave her a none too gentle shake in order for her to come to terms with his words. "You will go directly to our lord's chamber, bolt the door, and remain there 'til I say otherwise," he sternly ordered. "I will see your siblings are sent to you so I know you are all safe in one place."

"Nay! You canna force me stay in my chamber, Riorden. I can help," she shouted.

"If you will not go willingly, then you leave me no choice, my lady," he said in annoyance and with the promise of his words, he lifted her up by the waist, threw her over his shoulder, and carried her off the parapet like a sack of grain. Amiria squirmed and kicked but he held firm as she raged at him that he could not treat her like some child. It only made his resolve stronger as he tightened his hold on his lady.

As Riorden made his way down the tower stairs to the floor where Dristan's chamber was located, he halted a knight on his way above and bellowed for him to follow. Flinging the portal wide, he dropped his angry charge upon the bed and quickly stepped back afore she could draw her sword upon him. Her eyes blazed with fury more than likely that he would dare to treat her thusly, but he would brook no disobedience to her wishes, no matter her desire to aid.

Turning from her, Riorden made his way to the door, his armor clanking as he went. "Bar anyone from leaving this room once her siblings have joined her," he commanded, "and no other than myself enters or leaves 'til I say otherwise!"

The knight nodded his understanding and Riorden turned once more to Amiria, giving her a short bow. "I shall return when this skirmish is over, my lady."

"Rior—!"

Slamming the door and ignoring her when she called his name, Riorden made quick work of rounding up Lynet and Patrick, sending them to Amiria's room. 'Twas in his search for Sabina that he came to the fast realization he had failed Dristan for her missing horse was a clear indication of his lack in judging the girl. *He will have my head on a pike when he learns I have erred*, he thought.

Knowing he was unable to waste any further valuable time looking for the wayward wench, who should have known better than to leave without her guard, he hastened to secure the castle. 'Twas fast becoming nigh to overflowing, as the villagers continued to flock to safety through its gates.

Kenna suddenly halted her steps and held on to Geoffrey's arm. Aye, there 'twas again; that small tremor coursing through her body. 'Twas a sure sign she was about to have yet another vision. She never could get used to this feeling no matter how many years had passed by.

"Kenna?" Geoffrey asked quietly in concern. She began to sway and she felt him holding her close to his side.

Scenes of horror played afore Kenna's mind, as though the images had in truth already occurred and were but memories. Swords clashed; arrows flew; knights fell; the occupants of Berwyck screamed in terror as fires alit in the inner and outer baileys; a massive battering ram was in the ready to storm the massive barbican gate; men attempted to scale the outer walls, as those from above poured boiling water down upon their heads. Yet still the enemy forged on in order to gain access to the keep.

Two men stood apart from the battle being waged against the castle's wall. They were as different as night was to day, at least in their appearance, though their objective was the same...to win the battle and claim the land.

One dressed in full armor and that of a knight, although he had no honor within him. He lifted his visor and the black eyes of Sir Hugh were revealed. The other man was dressed as a Highlander in his clan's colors. The fabric fluttered in the winter wind as did his unkempt brown hair. He, too, lacked any sense of chivalry and his only thought was to dispose of the man next to him and take Berwyck for his very own.

'Twas the final scene of Hugh slipping the long slim blade of a dirk into the back of the unsuspecting Highlander and making his way up through the tunnel with a number of men that finally brought Kenna out of her vision. Her eyes flew open as she looked around hopelessly disoriented by her surroundings.

"Easy my love...I've got you," Geoffrey whispered against her hair as he held her. "All is well Kenna."

"Nay Geoffrey. 'Tis anything but well," she gasped. "There is trouble afoot!"

"What is amiss?"

"'Tis Berwyck."

"What about Berwyck?" he asked, holding her from him so he could peer into her face. She could see his worried expression for surely her features were ashen.

"'Tis under siege, Geoffrey," she wheezed.

He laughed at her words. "Surely you jest Kenna. We left there less than a hand full of days ago. How can this be happening now?"

Kenna gazed around the glade where they had camped so Geoffrey could take his ease in the warm waters of the nearby pool. It had helped to lessen the pain that caused him to limp 'til his leg could completely heal.

"I just know 'tis so," she said quietly, shaking her head. "Do you doubt my words?"

Geoffrey looked at her closely. "I would but have to see it for myself, my lady."

Anger flashed briefly in her eyes, causing her temper to rise. "Doubt me then if you must, but we shall get nowhere near Berwyck lest you care for a lengthy stay in its dungeon. I hear 'tis not a place one cares to reside!" Sarcasm dripped from Kenna's mouth for 'twas not the first time someone did not have faith in her visions. Her feelings hurt that he would question her words; she left the comfort of his side and made her way back to their camp where she busied herself with packing their gear. She cared not if he believed her or not.

Geoffrey came to her at a slower pace and waited 'til she rose from her task. Taking hold of her from behind, his arms encircled her waist, bringing her against the warmth of him. She felt his breath against her neck and for one moment she enjoyed the bliss of being in his arms.

"Do not be cross with me, Kenna," he whispered huskily in her ear. "We are still getting to know one another and I like it not when you are angry with me."

She turned in his arms and took in the boyish look in his face. She reached up and brushed back a lock of his black hair that had fallen across his brow. He smiled at her and she felt her heart melting at such a look. Quirking her brow, his smile only broadened as his green eyes sparkled with mischief. *How can I stay mad with him when he looks at me so*, she mused?

"You must have driven your parents mad by wrapping them around your finger if you gave them such a glance as you have just given me?" she managed to muster. "Has no one ever told you, nay?"

His deep chuckle rumbled in his chest. "I suppose someone may have said it a time or two." He leaned down to kiss her and only managed a short chaste kiss that was apparently none to his liking.

"Not now, Geoffrey. We must away to intercept Lord Dristan," she said hastily, as she swatted his hand and began again to pack up their gear. "He will walk into a trap otherwise. Sir Hugh knows about the tunnel."

Geoffrey roughly took hold of her arm and studied her features. They were full of concern that could not be doubted. "Sir Hugh? And what damn tunnel?" he growled.

"The escape route from the floor housing Berwyck's family," she replied just as harshly. "We are wasting precious time Geoffrey."

"You still say 'tis under siege?" he questioned.

"Aye, but if you still do not believe me, then see it for yourself. Just exercise caution so we may yet live to see another day."

Their horses saddled, they made their way from their haven and began their trek towards Berwyck. They had not traveled far afore Geoffrey halted their progress and tied their horses to a tree. They crept through the forest and crouched down low behind some bushes to remain unseen.

A twig snapped and Geoffrey quickly turned back towards Kenna, motioning her to remain silent. She gave him a look that wordlessly said she was trying. But a knight, hearing the sound, halted his progress to peer into the darkened forest surrounding him. Kenna took Geoffrey's hand as she held her breath whilst terror overtook her. The soldier continued his vigilant inspection at no particular point of reference. He took several steps in their direction 'til his name was called. Unsatisfied, the warrior took one final look about him afore he reluctantly moved on. Kenna's breath left her as she sagged against Geoffrey and trembled. He gave her hand a comforting squeeze.

In disbelief, they watched the tail end of what, she assumed, was a long procession heading directly towards Berwyck. There was no other destination, other than the castle, leading along this path. She watched as Geoffrey's head shook in disbelief, still trying to deny that which he saw. A look passed between them almost as if he said aloud that he never should have doubted her words.

Motioning for Kenna to return to her horse, Geoffrey turned and crawled back to the tree where their mounts were tied. Once certain that no others followed, they mounted then kicked their horses into a full gallop, making their way south towards London. As the miles passed, Kenna tried to get Geoffrey to slow his pace, but he ignored her. Blood began trickling down his leg and Kenna could only pray Lord Dristan was already on his way home. With his coming, she hoped her liege had acquired a few more men than those with which he had left. He was going to need them.

Thirty-six

CANDLES LIT THE LARGE ROOM in the west wing of the White Tower, filling it with a smoky haze that floated to the ceiling high above the heads of those gathered there. The richness of the room was evident everywhere one cared to look, and 'twas obvious King Henry II was in residence at the Tower of London. Wine flowed freely, and servants ran to fill empty chalices upon demand. There was no lack of food to fill their hungry stomachs, and 'twas all at the expense of the monarch. What was there not to love about being at court?

Overcrowded as they waited for an audience with the king, men and women mingled amongst themselves whilst a few musicians played for their amusement and pleasure. For the women, they could care less that the lute players performed most wondrously. They were too busy whispering in hushed tones the latest gossip holding their interest at court. In turn, the men conspired greedily with one another to form alliances in their quests to acquire more land and power. If their conversations waivered from this subject, 'twas to speak of their mistresses or on the recent turn of events in the latest war against the Welsh.

'Twas in this very room that Dristan and Ian kept close vigil of the intrigues playing out around them and running rampant like a plague to those not careful to evade its clutches. As Dristan gazed about the room, a small grin formed on his face. 'Twas not so long ago that he himself would have been amongst those enjoying the pleasures of court and what the ladies here freely offered for a night in his bed. Glancing about the chamber, he noticed one lady in particular whose favor he had tasted of. She waved at him, but Dristan did not so much as acknowledge that he saw her.

Much had changed at court, or mayhap, 'twas he who had changed now that he had a lovely wife waiting for him at home. If it had not been for the summons he had received from King Henry, Dristan would still have been happily enjoying wedded bliss with Amiria by his side. Now, looking around, he could only despise those at court and the games they played. The sooner his audience was over with the king, the sooner he could return back to his estate and Amiria. 'Twas only the thought of his wife and what he was missing without her nearness that surely kept his sanity in check. He had not thought that he would miss her so.

Two women passed by Dristan and Ian and, from their flirtatious stares, 'twas evident the two men would have been welcomed into their beds this night. Their giggles reached them when they stopped a short distance away. Snapping open their fans, their eyes raked over Dristan's body. His bored stance from their obvious antics did not deter their eagerness in attempting to capture his attention. One even dared much when she asked her companion loud enough to be heard if she thought Dristan of Blackmore was well endowed since the rest of him was so impressive.

"*Merde*! I am not sure how much more of this I can take," Dristan complained, wearily as he scanned the room again, ignoring the women's pouts. "How could I forget how annoying court life can be?"

"'Tis no small wonder I stay in the north. This is no place for me, my lord, no matter the offerings that are freely presented," Ian murmured as his eyes raked the two nearby women. He presented them a slight smile and was encouraged when they both returned it. "Mayhap a small dalliance with one of those fair ladies would appease my desire for a willing woman and ease my memories."

"Be careful, my friend, lest you take what belongs to another," Dristan warned. "One damsel, although quite beautiful, belongs to the Earl of Brindle. He is a close friend of the king, or so I have heard, and one not to anger. I understand him to be very possessive of his wife. 'Tis common knowledge a man or two has met their demise at the end of his blade for just the offense of a mere glance towards his lady."

"They both may still be worth the risk," Ian replied, ignoring Dristan's cautious words of advice.

"'Tis your head," Dristan returned and watched in amusement as Ian's face changed with the thought of his head being lopped off. "I thought you might change your mind," he continued with a chuckle.

"You might as well have tossed me in the Thames, my lord. I can almost feel the cold chill of an axe against my neck."

Dristan laughed and clapped his hand upon Ian's shoulder. "Do not despair, Ian. I am sure you will find your needs well met soon enough."

Ian grumbled something unintelligible and motioned for his chalice to be refilled. A servant obliged him and he began to drink his fill of the heady wine.

Conversations that were but a moment ago filling the room were quickly silenced as an antechamber door was opened to reveal King Henry and King William of Scotland entering the room. The women sank into a deep courtesy whilst the men bowed afore their king. The two men both bore solemn expressions whilst they made their way to a raised dais where chairs had been set aside for them to take their ease.

King Henry motioned for all to rise and the conversations resumed at a quieter level. He whispered to his man, who then straightened to scan the room.

"Dristan of Blackmore," the man called, the sound carrying throughout the room.

Dristan made his way through the crowd with Ian following behind. He bowed low, giving homage to his king afore rising.

"Ah, Dristan," King Henry said with his soft French accent. He leaned over to King William. "Dristan has been a most valuable knight to my cause in vanquishing those who rise up against me," he praised, watching King William's reaction to his words, who only nodded and kept his own counsel. Returning his attention back to Dristan, the king continued. "Allow me to introduce you to King William of Scotland who is my...guest."

"Your Majesties," Dristan said, bowing. "May I present Sir Ian, recent guardsman at Berwyck Castle?" He gave Ian a slight nudge, spurring his companion to bow.

"Aye...aye," Henry replied off handedly. He rose since he had a restless spirit and did not care to sit lest he was eating. "Come gentlemen and walk with me."

Dristan and Ian followed the king, who made his way from the room whilst all bowed when he left. They did not go far, and yet they found themselves surprisingly in a relatively large chapel inside the White Tower.

The king turned and clasped his hands behind his back, rocking to and fro upon his heals. "So tell me good sir...what brings you this far from Berwyck? I would have thought you to be enjoying wedded bliss by now Dristan with the fair Lady Amiria. Tell me I shall not be disappointed in you and the directives I gave you?"

"Nay, sire. All is well and we but wed recently."

"She is a fine match for you. Have you tamed that wild side to her nature then?"

Dristan looked stunned that he would think such a thing. "Nay, Your Grace. I find her most pleasing just the way she is."

Henry smiled as he stroked his chin. "Ah then 'tis now a love match. Good! I knew you would be the best Lord for Berwyck. Such good news. So what, pray tell, would take you from your lovely wife's side and bring you to court amongst all those vipers that bow, paying me homage, and yet still conspire against me behind my back? Speaking of vipers, I hope you have Sir Hugh in line?"

Dristan and Ian looked at each other surprised at the king's words. "My liege, I came at your bequest."

"I have not ordered you to come afore me."

"My pardon, Your Majesty," Dristan said, reaching inside his cloak, "but I received your missive stating 'twas most urgent I travel to London."

Henry reached for the parchment, turning it over. "I did not send this to you Dristan. The seal is a close resemblance to be sure, but this is neither my writing nor my scribe's." The king handed the parchment back and Dristan took it, frowning.

"I am a bit bemused then, Sire."

"Aye, well, I may not have sent this, but I did receive a message from your man Sir Hugh, stating how you were raiding the villages in your hamlets. I have been most suspicious of Sir Hugh's motives of late," Henry said with a wave of his hand. "I knew his words to be false and assumed you would handle such matters as you saw fit, since you have never failed me afore. Killing your own serfs is not in your nature, despite your fierce reputation otherwise."

"I am honored at your confidence in me, my liege," Dristan said humbly. "I fear that Hugh may be up to more mischief than I realized, since he went missing err I left Berwyck. With your permission, I shall leave at once to ensure all is secure in your name."

"But of course. I will send extra men with you just in case you are in need of them," the king replied. They began striding their way back to those milling around for his attention. He spoke briefly with his aid, who scurried away to relay the king's message to his soldiers.

Henry came to the raised dais and took his dress sword from his belt. "Afore you go, Dristan, I must bestow something upon you, if you would but humor me."

"I am ever at your service, my liege."

"Such service over the years should not go unrewarded. Take a knee my valiant and trustworthy knight, and forevermore shall you be titled Lord Dristan Blackmore, first Earl of Berwyck."

Dristan knelt afore his king and bowed his head as Henry tapped both shoulders with his sword. Stunned, he was told to rise, and he did so whilst attempting to mask his shock of what had just occurred. *Mon dieu,* he thought. *I've just been branded an Earl.*

"Now, my friend, get thee back to Berwyck and especially Sir Hugh," Henry ordered as he clapped Dristan on his shoulder. "I have confidence you will put all back to order, Lord Dristan."

"By your leave, Your Majesty," Dristan replied, bowing once again as Henry waved him on.

Dristan and Ian hastened to depart from the White Tower and more importantly the confines of court life in London. Looking around, he realized King Henry would be giving him an army of at least one hundred men to command. Time was of the essence. He made his way to Thor and vaulted into the saddle. Raising his arm, he signaled the knights to proceed. Slapping his reins, he put his horse into a full gallop.

Dristan felt a desperate urgency Amiria was in need of him and felt compelled to ensure for himself she was safe. May God help any who thought to take that which was his and that most certainly included his wife.

THIRTY-SEVEN

A MIRIA PACED HER CONFINED CHAMBER like a caged lion-
ess. That Riorden would dare restrict her to her quarters
infuriated her beyond words. Her nerves stretched to the point
of breaking in twain, her anger seethed that he would dare cast
her out like some witless female, ill adept in the protection of
her clan. She was more than capable of defending her home.
Had she not proven her worth once afore, she debated to herself?

"Ugh...I can stand no more," she fumed. "Lynet! Help me
with this armor afore I lose what little I have left of my sanity."

"He willna like it," Lynet predicted.

"Aye! You have said as much afore yet only about my husband," Amiria chided. "I cared not then, nor do I care now
about the orders of stubborn men. Our clan needs me."

"But, Amiria," Patrick interrupted, "how can this be? You
are but a woman."

Amiria whirled to face her young brother and came to his side. "Aye, Patrick, I am only a woman, but I am a determined one at that."

She heard him muttering to himself and took a moment to give Patrick a small hug of reassurance. Turning, she gave her attention back to the deed at hand. Despite its weight, Lynet proved most proficient at hefting the heavy metal onto her body.

"Have you forgotten the guard?" Lynet inquired with a lift of her delicate brow.

"Do not fret. The guard, I can handle."

"Then mayhap I will go to Kenna's dwelling. I am sure our people are in need of a healer."

"You must change your dress, Lynet. There is hose and tunic with a plaid in my chest that will be more serviceable to your mission," Amiria ordered and continued on at the shocked look upon her sister's face. "Just don it and quickly." Satisfied, she watched her sibling make fast work of changing her clothes.

"What of me?" Patrick gasped. "I want to help too."

Amiria came and knelt down to her brother and brushed her hand down his soft black hair in a light caress. She gave him a smile. "Nay, Patrick, not today, but soon will you train with our Lord Dristan and become a mighty warrior, just as he is."

"Do not leave me here, Amiria, by myself," he whined.

"'Tis the first place they will look if the curtain wall is breached. With our freedom, I want you to run to the garde-robe and bolt the door. Do not come out lest you hear my voice. Do you understand me, Patrick?"

"But it stinks in there, Amiria." He grimaced. She could not blame him his thoughts of being locked up in such a small place with the stench for possibly hours on end.

"Which is why they willna look there," she said gently and took the boy by the shoulders. "I need to know you are safe, little one. Will you obey me?"

Patrick gave a slight nod of acceptance, and Amiria placed a kiss upon his forehead. Her brother glowered at such a sign of affection, causing Amiria and Lynet to give a brief laugh, given their circumstances.

"Let me find you something more befitting a serf than a young squire," she said and went to the trunk to find a soft vest and shirt she had worn in her youth. She ruffled his hair and smudged some dirt upon his upturned face. She smiled in satisfaction at her sibling's transformation then turned to flee the room.

Amiria slid the bolt and opened the door. She was startled that none stood vigil at the door.

"I canna believe it. Where is the guard?" exclaimed Lynet.

Patrick whistled his own sense of amazement. "He is going to be in so much trouble once Riorden hears of this.

Amiria partially shut the door. "I am sure he must have been called away, but it matters not where he went; only that he is gone." She turned to look upon her siblings as if to memorize their faces. "Be safe and remember I love you," she said with a small catch in her voice. Life was short and she would not want them to ever think she did not care for them in the event she fell like Aiden.

Lynet gave her hand a brief squeeze afore scampering towards the tower stairs to make her decent. Amiria took a deep breath when she caught her last glimpse of Patrick as he, too, rounded the corner leading towards the garderobe. *May the Blessed Virgin Mary watch over them*, she prayed.

Amiria began to make her way down the passageway, but had gone no more than a few steps. She halted at an unexpected sound, catching her attention. She turned back in surprise to the see the hidden tunnel door being pushed wide open.

She would have called out for help, but none would have heard her voice above the distant sounds of the raging war. Instead, the sound of her blade rent the air as 'twas released from its scabbard. The noise carried an eerie echo off the walls, causing her eyes to narrow at the foe afore her. Her fingers gripped the familiar hilt of her blade, knowing she would face him alone.

"How many times have I told you, I detest you in armor?" Hugh grinned evilly.

Amiria gave no answer, for she quickly saw more than a dozen men begin to fill the narrow passageway. She held her stance firm and steadily brought her sword forward. Instead of words, she would let her blade speak on her behalf.

Sabina wearily opened her eyes, trying to focus on her surroundings, guessing the new day had yet to dawn. She lay abed and could hear the loud snores of her companion. She knew not how long she had been held at his mercy, as he had stubbornly ignored her constant pleas to be released. She had quit asking days ago, ever since a fist had been her reward for annoying him.

She tried to rise and fell back awkwardly against the coverlet. There was not an inch of her that did not hurt from his continual cruelty and misuse of her body. Filled with shame, Sabina tried again and made it to a sitting position, only to wait 'til the room stopped its swirling motion. She felt stickiness between her legs and reached down. Bringing her hand forward, she suppressed a startled cry. Her hand was covered in her blood. She had lost the babe, although mayhap, given her foolishness, 'twas a blessing in disguise.

I must flee, her tortured mind screamed. After several attempts, she at last stood on wavering legs. She glared down at the foul pig who had used her, over and over again. The offensive villain was flat on his back with spittle drooling from his mouth. She spat on him and felt a small bit of satisfaction when he did not so much as even flinch. She was not surprised, for he had consumed more ale than she thought a man was capable of drinking and still able to perform his worst on her.

She looked into a chest of Hugh's and found garments she thought she might manage to fit into. A dirk fell from one of the items she held. She smiled when she picked it up, feeling its weight in her palm.

She went to the side of the makeshift bed, glaring down at the vile excuse of a man who had harmed her. She gave a hasty prayer, hoping God would forgive her actions this day. Quietly, she straddled the mercenary, who then began to stir. She smiled into his eyes even when he looked on her most hungrily.

"Now this is more like it," he whispered, trying to bring Sabina closer. "I's knew ye'd come to favor me!"

"I have something for you, my brave soldier," she said huskily, almost retching at the smell of his breath.

"Do ye now? Well whatcha got fer me?" He began licking his lips. Sabina only wanted to wipe the smirk from his disgusting face.

"This!" She whispered her words in such a seductive manner that he did not react afore she speedily drew the dagger slicing his throat. *Men are such fools and only think of one thing,* she thought smiling in satisfaction. She watched the dying man beneath her gurgle 'til he took his last breath. A heavy sigh escaped her. Wiping the blood from the knife on the coverlet, she held it up into the dim light of the tent. "'Tis a most useful dirk to be sure. I think I shall keep it."

She rose from the man and pulled a blanket over him. 'Twould be hours afore anyone realized he was not asleep.

She carefully opened the tent flap to peer outside at the nearly deserted campsite. Cautiously, she made her way to her horse still corralled with several others. She was surprised to see no others lingered around the camp to detain her, but mayhap this was a testament to Hugh's conceit.

Sabina somehow managed to free her horse and spoke softly to the animal to quiet it. Finding a stump, she stood upon it and noticed her blood beginning to seep through her stolen clothing. 'Twas not a good sign and only weakened her already abused condition. Thrice she attempted to mount her steed and 'twas not 'til the fourth attempt that she managed the feat.

She struggled to stay atop the horse as it slowly made its way towards home. Sabina grasped its mane to ensure her hold on the animal. Her only thought was to return to Berwyck and right the wrong she had done to her family. If she made it, she would beg their forgiveness, and ask them to pardon her errant ways.

Her last thought was of seeing her siblings. She drifted into unconsciousness still atop her steed which continued forward at a slow pace careful of the burden it held, plodding ever onward towards Berwyck and home.

Thirty-Eight

To say Dristan was annoyed would have been an understatement. He raked a hand through his already mussed hair in irritation and adjusted his tabard that seemed to be choking the very breath from him. Whilst he appreciated the offer King Henry had given him for additional aid, he was puzzled on how he was to make haste and still remain undercover with well over one hundred men creating the rising dust. Fifty he could have concealed easier but the amount had tripled. He had left behind a good majority of men at court, who were still waiting for horses to be readied. Those men had now joined his army when they answered the call to rise to arms. All in Christendom must see there was a legion on the move towards Berwyck. They would be hard to miss.

Dristan turned as four riders came abreast of him. Nathaniel, Rolf, and Fletcher stilled their horses even though 'twas clear they, too, wished to quicken their pace. Ian sat, unmoving in his saddle, a grim expression on his face. Dristan had not thought Ian would accompany him straight back to Berwyck, but Amiria's former captain made it clear nothing would stop him from reaching the family's side. It seemed the two of them had only one thing on their mind and 'twas to ensure the safety of those they had left behind.

"We must ride ahead," Dristan insisted. "I will take no more than a score of men. Fletcher, you stay here in my stead, and half past the hour get this army moving again towards Berwyck."

"As you will, my lord," Fletcher drawled, "although I am not sure I can get them moving any better than you have done with any sense of remaining unseen for miles around. With this many men, 'tis a most improbable task."

"Do what you can," he said sternly. "I cannot waste any more time."

Ian moved his horse closer. "I come with you."

Dristan raised a brow at Ian's assumption that he would travel with him. "You could be of more use here with Fletcher."

"Aye, I suppose I could," he snorted decisively, "yet I know something that can be most useful. If I were to guess, Amiria did not as yet have time to tell you of Berwyck's secret."

"What secret?" Dristan roared.

Ian began somewhat sheepishly to tell Dristan of the tunnel that led down to the strand. His reaction was instantaneous and understandable. "You willna find it without me, my lord."

"I swear, when I get a hold of my wife, I shall throttle that woman within an inch of her life," he snarled. "It explains much on how she left the castle on the two occasions that I am aware of."

Dristan began muttering about all the ways he would make his lady's life miserable when he returned to Berwyck, 'til Nathaniel and Rolf began to laugh at his expense. He glared them into silence. A sound of thunder reached their ears. Then a speck of dust on the horizon caught Nathaniel's eye and he peered into the distance. As the riders came closer, they recognized their comrade in arms.

"Ho, Geoffrey!" Nathaniel called to his friend, wondering what caused him to be so far from the castle.

Strain showed on Geoffrey's face as he grimaced in pain and rubbed his leg when they came abreast of the group. Kenna came along side of him and he held out his hand to her. She took it and he placed a kiss upon its gloved back.

Dristan watched the pair with a bit of amusement afore his thoughts returned to the obvious fact they were far from home.

"Your news must be grim for you to travel this far from Berwyck," Dristan voiced coolly. "Let me guess...Sir Hugh is up to some mischief."

Geoffrey and Kenna looked astonished he had guessed so correctly. "How did you know?" Geoffrey wheezed.

"It seems my vassal has sent word to the king on matters that would be questionable if I was not in such good graces with His Majesty," Dristan chided.

Kenna looked about her at the mass of men who accompanied the group. "'Tis apparent you are still in good stead with him," she guessed.

"'Tis even more so," Ian proclaimed. "He has just been knighted an Earl."

"All the more reason you must hasten your journey to reclaim Berwyck," Geoffrey replied quickly. "Hugh will be laying siege to the castle. I have seen his army moving in its direction as we rode out."

Dristan's gaze went to Kenna 'til she nodded in answer. "'Tis true my Lord Dristan but there is more you should know."

"He knows the castle secret," Dristan guessed. "But who would betray us so?"

"Search your heart and you will find the answer, my liege," she replied with a hushed tone.

It did not take Dristan long in his pondering. "Sabina! That wench is more trouble than she is worth!" he rasped.

"I have seen much as we rode, my lord," Kenna said. "Trust me when I tell you, Lady Sabina has paid a price for her treachery. One that no woman should endure."

"What of Amiria and her guardsmen?" Dristan and Ian exclaimed in unison. They shook their heads at one another and waited for Kenna to continue.

Closing her eyes, 'twas clear another vision overtook her. Dristan continued to watch his healer from his saddle, although he did not wait long for her to once more come back to them. The look of sorrow was one he was not prepared for.

"Taken...it appears. Thrown into the pit and dungeon, my liege," she whispered. "The garrison continues to fight on in your name."

"We must go, and now," Dristan bellowed.

"My lord I—," Geoffrey began. His words halted from his lips as he slid from his mount.

"Geoffrey!" Kenna cried out the same instant Nathaniel leapt from his horse to catch his friend as he fell. Blood once more began pouring from his wound.

"Take care of him, Dristan ordered. "Ian, you come with me."

Their stallions reared in their eagerness to run as both men turned their steeds. Dristan called out to several of King Henry's knights, who were only too eager to join him as he rode off to claim what was rightfully his. 'Twould not go well for Hugh when he got him within the reach of his sword. Dristan pressed onward, knowing within his heart Amiria would not fare well in Hugh's clutches.

It had seemingly been days since Patrick had bolted the door of the garderobe. He had become immune to the putrid stench rising up to meet his nose, or so he thought, muffling a cough. Cut off from his sisters and any form of security, he was about at his wits end to this hiding business. He was, after all, a squire to one of the most notorious knights in all of England. Surely a squire such as he should not be hiding away, doing nothing.

He glanced through a crack in the frame of his confinement, but only saw the flickering flames of the nearby torch lighting the passageway. 'Twas time to take a chance for surely something must have befallen Amiria, since she had not come for him by now.

He quietly unlatched the door and peered without. Seeing nothing, he scampered down the corridor and made his way down the tower stairs. All was silent and frightfully so.

He slowed his pace at the entrance to the Great Hall and examined the number of men who lounged about drinking and eating their fill. To his dismay, he did not recognize any of Berwyck's garrison. The men's laughter grated on his ears whilst they boasted of their easy victory. Patrick could not miss how Sir Hugh sat at the high table, lording over all. *The traitor... What trickery is this?* He wondered. Patrick listened only long enough to hear Sir Hugh bellow to the men to get their sorry arses out to patrol his battlements. Patrick soundlessly quit the room. He had heard more than enough.

Keeping to the shadows, he made his way towards the kitchens and held his finger to his lips to silence the servants, who were surprised and overjoyed to see him. Cook led him to the back of the room behind some barrels of flour. He was joyful to see Lynet, although he frowned at her change in clothing. Dressed in a gown of coarse wool, she was frantically mixing various herbs together.

"Here, you but need put the potion into our enemies' ale and wine." Lynet gave the satchels to Cook, explaining, "to make them sleep." She turned to her brother and said, "Sir Hugh has thrown Amiria, along with Riorden and Ulrick, into the pit. You must continue to hide, Patrick. Be safe." With a look of concern in her eyes, she gave Patrick a quick peck on his cheek and rose. "Now, I must be on my way," she said softly and left to return to the healing of those in need.

Patrick, having learned of Amiria's fate, could not believe anyone, even someone as foul as Sir Hugh, would sink so low as to put a woman in Berwyck's pit. 'Twas a foul place and far worse than his most recent place of hiding.

Since Cook would see to serving those in the Great Hall, Patrick held out his small hands for another pitcher. "I will do my duty to my sister and descend below into the bowels of the castle and encourage the guards to drink their fill," he declared. With the pitcher in his hands, he gulped down his feeling of the sudden fear attempting to creep upon and consume him. Trying not to spill the contents of the jug, Patrick slowly made his way down the steep steps into the depths of the most dreadful place to be found within Berwyck's walls.

Reaching the final step, he moved into the light where three guards immediately came to attention.

"Who goes there?" asked the tallest guard.

He made an excuse as he held out the jug. "The ale is an offering from Sir Hugh for a job well done."

The men took the jug, taking turns as they greedily guzzled down the brew. With a loud belch, one went back to his post and waved Patrick away to fetch more.

Patrick took the pitcher and made it appear as if he returned above to fill their request. Instead, he waited in the darkness on the stairs for the herbs to work their magic. When he heard the loud thuds, as one by one the guards fell to the floor, he quietly came down the remaining steps to peer within the room. Snores met his ears, and Patrick gave a sheepish smile. Looking for the keys and finding them hanging from the belt on the tall guard, he gave a brief laugh at his cleverness and turned towards the first of several cells. 'Twas time to free his sister.

Thirty-nine

AMIRIA WAS FREEZING. Her legs and body exhausted from trying to keep herself out of the sticky slime beneath her feet. She swore when she was released from here, she would demand the pit be filled in forevermore. The dungeon itself would be punishment enough, since the cold penetrated down to one's bones at this level beneath the keep.

How long had they remained here in the darkness, she did not know. It seemed God had forsaken her, but still she continued to offer up prayers to save her and her guardsmen from the hellhole they found themselves in.

For she was not alone in her misery...nay, she was not. Riorden and Ulrick shared her fate as they huddled together, trying to find enough warmth between the three of them. Unfortunately, they were failing and would not be able to endure the extreme temperature much longer. They had attempted to climb one on top of the other to escape, but had failed to reach anywhere near the top of the slick and icy walls. Now they stood there shivering in the cold dampness of their prison.

'Twas almost ironic she would wind up in the pit of all places, and yet this was better than in Hugh's bed.

Images of how she had put up a valiant fight flashed within her mind. At least she had taken down two opponents afore Hugh had stepped in to take over, in his pursuit to become victorious. His remaining men had poured from the doorway and she could do nothing to stop them whilst Hugh had bellowed at them to get the gates opened. In the end, the narrow passageway had been her downfall when she inadvertently tripped over one of the fallen men. With nowhere to go when her feet flew out from beneath her, Hugh had brought his sword forward, knocking her blade from her hands. To watch his face light up as he grabbed her and then feel his lips viciously crushing her own, she did not know which had been worse.

Repulsed, she had done the only thing she could think of and, clenching her gauntlet hand into a tight fist, she had swung back her arm. Blood had oozed from the cuts she slashed across his face. Amiria had then been the one to smile in satisfaction. Her small victory had not lasted long, however, for he had retaliated in kind, knocking her senseless.

She had roused briefly at the sound of those coming to her aid. The feeling of a knife to one's neck tended to bring one back to their senses though. The sound of Hugh's voice, threatening to slice her throat if her men advanced further, had added to her disbelief and disappointment she had failed. Her eyes had met Riorden's and she had seen his displeasure from her disregard to follow his orders. 'Twould have made no difference, however, since deceit had won the day.

Left with no alternative since her life was in jeopardy, Riorden and the other guardsmen had surrendered their swords. They had been herded down the stairs of the tower at the point of steely blades. Turquine and Taegan had put up the biggest fight as they were led down into the depths of the dungeon whilst Killian and Nevin had followed suit, voicing crudely how the men would pay.

Amiria thought she was to have shared their same fate when her men had been thrown into their cells. But the iron doors had closed with a loud clang and the key had been inserted to lock the men in. The guardsman had then turned to Ulrick and Riorden, and, with a leer, they were shoved coldheartedly down into the castle's pit.

Hugh had advanced on her and she had felt his breath on her skin that began to crawl at his touch. He had told her in no uncertain terms she would be in his bed, but not afore Amiria learned her place. She had let out a scream in fear whilst she, too, was pushed into the murky depths below.

The rancid stench had immediately risen up to meet her, even as her feet sunk up to her ankles in slime. The two men had broken her fall, but she had gagged at the smell surrounding them. Once she had gained her balance, she came to the fast realization there was not much room to move between the three of them. 'Twas as the torch light faded above to only a glowing glimmer that she had turned to her companions. They had found themselves thrown into hell.

She had not been able to see her own hand, let alone the faces of Riorden and Ulrick, but they had made quick work of divesting themselves of their armor. At least it had kept the majority of the muck off their feet, but their holding was slippery to say the least.

So here they stood, since sitting was not an option. The men continued to try to warm her, for she had one in front and the other to her back. But 'twas to no avail. Amiria had tried to change position with her two guards numerous times, but Riorden and Ulrick only grunted their responses of nay. They would do what they could to keep her warm no matter the cost to themselves. Chivalry, it seemed, reigned on in Dristan's knights, no matter what ordeal they faced.

Numb from the cold and drained from standing for so long, Amiria became aware of a faint sound. She raised her weary head and listened again. Was it just her imagination, or did she hear a barely audible and familiar whistle? Aye...there 'twas again, and she squinted in the darkness as a light appeared from above her.

She saw no ghostly apparition beckoning her on towards the heavens, nor a frightening banshee claiming her to join the souls already doomed in the underworld. Instead, Finlay poked his head over the side and spoke softly, "Lady Amiria, can you hear me?"

Joy filled her heart when a rope was lowered. One by one, they began their climb 'til they reached the top ledge and eager hands reached out to their aid. Freedom had never felt so good, and Amiria looked around at all, who began to speak, asking of her welfare. It seemed that despite a few scratches and bruises, all had fared well.

Thomas stepped forward and offered her his cloak, which she accepted gladly.

"How is it you are free, Sir Thomas?" she asked in amazement and looked upon each of her guardsmen, who gave her a sheepish grin. Dristan's men were no better and began to laugh in earnest.

Their circle around Amiria opened 'til one small form came forward, shuffling his feet with downcast eyes.

"Patrick!" Amiria called, and looked about her men, who began clapping the boy on his back. His smile broadened and Amiria watched her young brother beam with pride at his accomplishment.

"Yer da would be proud o' this young laddie," Killian boasted, as if he were Patrick's sire. "'E 'n Lady Lynet put 'erbs in the ale tae make the guards fall asleep but 'twas the courage of yer brother that 'as freed us all!"

Amiria gathered her brother in her arms in a fierce embrace. "I am so very proud of you Patrick," she said quietly. She felt his arms wrap themselves around her waist and she was never more grateful for anything in her life than to know her siblings were safe.

She felt him loosen his grip and saw his embarrassment afore the men at such a sign of affection. Trying to regain his composure, he tugged on his sister's arm 'til Amiria leaned down so he could whisper in her ear. "I was so scared, Amiria, but I dinnae show it," Patrick muttered.

Amiria saw his chin tremble slightly and gathered him to her once more. "I would imagine you were, dear brother, but you have done well in obtaining our rescue."

Patrick beamed at her praise, and the guards began to gather around them in a protective shield of strength. 'Twas clear in their stance they were more determined than ever to keep them safe and secure as they reclaimed the castle in Dristan's name.

Riorden took control over the group and began to strategize their plan to return above, even whilst the men put in their own words of advice. Amiria shushed them when their voices began to rise in volume. She spoke quickly to Patrick, ordering him to return above to hide out in the garderobe once more. His grumbles reminded her of her husband and she ruffled his hair, telling him to scoot. He did so, even though he voiced his displeasure of where he must needs return.

Without haste, Riorden, Ulrick, and Amiria donned their armor despite the smell and swords were thrust into their willing hands. One by one, the men began to ascend the stairs from the core of the castle. Riorden halted Amiria, as her foot was placed on the first step, for they were the last to depart the dungeon area.

"You will stay behind me at all times, else you stay here where I know you shall remain safe," he demanded gruffly. "Your word, Lady Amiria."

"Aye, Captain de Devereux, you have it," Amiria agreed as he looked her up and down to assess the truth of her words. He must have believed her since he began to take the stairs two at a time in order to catch up with their men.

She trembled slightly as she made to follow him and gave a quick prayer that God above would be with them this day. She would not feel secure 'til she once more found her own blade in her hand instead of one that already felt too heavy for her to lift. She had the notion on just where she would search. Amiria knew the first order of the day would be to find that low life scum Hugh. God help him when he was at last afore her so she might exact her revenge for her trip into the pit! She began her steady climb up the steep steps to follow her new Captain with a look of sheer determination lighting her face.

FORTY

S ABINA CLAWED AT THE STONE beneath her face. Her vision blurred afore her eyes as she wondered how long she had been lying upon the steps beneath her. Her only thoughts had been to reach her family, even if she had to climb these retched stairs on her hands and knees. That assessment was not too far off what she had been attempting, for what seemed like hours. It could have been days for all she knew. With the darkness of the tunnel surrounding her, she could not even determine what progress she had made in reaching the upper floor housing her family.

She was not well. That much was clear, for the sickening smell of her own blood met her nose along with the mustiness of the cave itself. If she did not reach help soon, she would die here alone with no one to help her. She groaned at the thought of her soul lingering between heaven and hell. Surely God and his angels would not permit her to enter their garden in paradise without her sins being absolved by a priest.

Reaching out her hand, she attempted to pull her body up just one more step. 'Twas to no avail. She just did not have enough energy or strength to go any further. She closed her eyes even as she seemingly espied a faint light coming from the tunnel below her. Her lips slowly managed an offering petition for she knew her fate was now in the hands of God. She could only pray he would be merciful and not allow Satan to consume her soul.

Sabina cried out when she was gently lifted from the ground. Was she about to fall off the edge of one of the many drop-offs in the cave? Nay, she reasoned, since she felt herself warmed by a cloak being wrapped around her freezing body. She heard only somewhat the rumblings of displeasure against her ear and at last became aware she was cradled ever so gently in the arms of a man. She opened her eyes and gasped. Surely she must be in heaven to be held so lovingly by the one who clasped her to him as if she weighed nothing at all.

A sob escaped her. "I am dead!" She felt a tender kiss placed upon her forehead.

"Nothing is farther from the truth, my dear sister." The deep baritone of his voice speared her heart with its comforting sound for she never thought to hear it again.

"Aiden?"

"Aye, 'tis me, Sabina, and not some ghostly apparition coming to take you from us."

"But how...we thought you were dead!" She began to cough, and she could no longer manage further conversation.

"There will be time enough for explanations. We must needs get you above to your chamber and Kenna called to see to your injuries."

Sabina attempted to warn him of what he would find above, but somehow he must have already known as he began to give instructions to those men who followed behind them. How many there were, she could not say for she could barely lift her head any longer.

The soft click of the opening doorway signaled they had reached their destination and, without further ado, they entered the torch lit passageway. She could hear the metal of Aiden's loud clanking armor as he hastily made quick work at shortening the distance to her room. He came to a skidding halt when a childlike screech rent the air.

She barely recognized Patrick as he hurdled himself about their brother's legs. He began babbling about the goings on below and the ill that had befallen Amiria.

"You must help them, Aiden," Patrick sobbed. "They will be outnumbered and I fear for Amiria's safety no matter how well she has learned to fight. She is, after all, just a girl."

An amused chuckle erupted from Aiden. "Best not let her hear on your words, little brother, lest you wish to spend some time in the stables mucking out its stalls. But come," Aiden declared, rushing into Sabina's chamber, "you must look after your sister 'til I come back for you."

Sabina was laid down upon her bed with a covering hastily thrown around her shivering frame. She watched as Aiden began to bank up the fire in the hearth, asking Patrick to see to its care, afore he leaned down over her body. He brushed her hair from her face and she grasped at his hand.

"Please be careful, Aiden," she whispered reverently, "I could not bear loosing you a second time.

"I will be careful, sister." He leaned down and quickly kissed her cheek, and Sabina watched him leave. Patrick quickly rose and slid the bolt in place, locking the world without.

Time passed once more, and again Sabina had no knowledge of just how long she had lain there. Patrick's young head was bowed whilst he knelt at her bedside, offering what prayers his young heart could mutter. Time was slipping away from her and she knew she could no longer wait for help. Reaching out, she took her brother's hand.

"I must beg your pardon, young Patrick, to ask this of you. You must needs hurry and find Kenna or Lynet for aid afore 'tis too late." She began shaking uncontrollably and faintly heard her brother crying out her name.

Once again her vision blurred as she saw Patrick fly from her side and unbolt the door. Her last conscious thought was for God to have mercy on her soul.

FORTY-ONE

Dristan cursed when his foot came in contact once again with another unseen stair in his path.

"I warned you to be careful, my lord," Ian declared knowingly.

Dristan muttered to himself and tossed a glare at the knight ahead of him, not that he would be able to see such a look. He was not pleased and was becoming careless in his eagerness to reach his wife whilst he plodded forever upward on these never ending steps.

"I remember no such thing," Dristan complained, trudging vigilantly up onto another level 'til he reached what he assumed was a flat surface. Still...he suspiciously put out his foot, searching on where he would tread next. At least he was rewarded, once he heard several comparable curses from behind him, that those who followed were sharing a similar fate to their feet.

"I clearly heard your words to me, my liege," Ian continued irritably whilst he fumbled around in the dark. "You told me to shut my trap when I mentioned the curve that surely would be upon us."

"Has no one told you err afore, you are most annoying?" he inquired gruffly. "You remind me of my healer, who does not know her place in my household or when to hold her wavering tongue. She sets my nerves on edge with this seeing business. And just what is it you are in search of?"

Dristan continued to listen whilst Ian made several unidentifiable noises. He smiled in satisfaction when 'twas Ian's turn to injure some limb that now came into contact with an unseen immovable object. He heard what he assumed was a trunk lid being lifted. Moments later, sparks began to light the room when Ian took flint in hand. Afore long, a torch was ignited, blinding those nearby.

Dristan blinked, allowing his eyes to become adjusted to the bright orange flames. What he thought to be a room was little more than a small round area with a flat stone floor. He could still smell the wet dirt he had become accustomed to since entering this hidden tunnel and observed the wooden beams helping to stabilize the fortification. The ceiling was coated with soot, adding to the dusky aroma of earth, and there were traces of burnt torches on the walls, well used over the years.

Wall sconces were empty of torches that normally would have lit this modest area. 'Twas a clear indication that others had gone ahead of them. A lone wooden bench worn with age sat along one wall with a trunk opened to its right. A bit of fabric escaping the case caught his eyes.

Dristan strode the short distance and pulled out a dress whilst he caressed the material, knowing Amiria had once worn the garment. How like his wife to don a peasant's garb and still make the coarse wool seem eternally lovely whilst it graced her body. Gads, he must be going soft. Next, he would be spouting words of love and composing lays that would envy any bard who came to his hall. Eternally lovely, indeed!

Still, he carefully took the time to neatly fold the dress, placing it back in the wooden trunk. Visions of his wood nymph floated in his memory. His pensiveness must have shown on his face, for when he looked up and saw Ian with his own contemplative expression, he knew his thoughts were being mirrored in the younger man.

"A most beautiful and unusual woman is your wife," Ian pronounced.

"Aye, she is at that."

"She needs more time in the lists."

Dristan gave a slight groan. "I will see to it."

"See that you do. She is not one to just sit calmly with a bit of stitchery to keep her busy."

"I said I would see to it, Ian," Dristan said roughly. "Let us be about taking back that which is mine."

Ian nodded and crossed the room to light the way. He stopped abruptly at the next flight of stairs. Kneeling down, he reached out to examine something found on the rough stones. He drew back his fingers and held them out to Dristan.

"Blood," Ian reasoned. "But whose?"

"There is only one way to find out. Let us be about it, aye?"

The group of men began to make their way up the uneven stairs, and Dristan marveled at the ingenuity of Amiria's ancestors. The tunnel had not been maintained in some time and was in need of reinforcement afore it caved in around them. If 'twas to be of further use to his own family, then some of the walls would need to be shored up. The uneven steps explained much for his abused toes, no matter the thickness of his boots. Still...if one could find the entrance, then so could another, and 'twould be just another route to lay siege to the castle's keep again.

Rounding another bend, the walls became tighter, but at least now they had a dim glow to light their way. Their progress increased quickly, and they at last achieved their destination. To Dristan's eyes, the wall afore them seemed but yet another barrier to his final goal of finding his wife. He watched Ian as the man hastily looked over his shoulder and grinned. Reaching out his hand into a small crevice in the rocks, Dristan heard a soft click as, amazingly, Ian pushed the rocks or doorway slightly open and looked carefully into the passageway of the family's floor. Even King Henry's knights were impressed from the concealment of the doorway.

"All clear," Ian assessed and swung the portal fully open.

"Keep watch men," Dristan ordered, rounding the corner leading towards the turret stairs. They were brought to an abrupt halt by a startled gasp echoing off the walls.

"My Lord!" Patrick cried. Running down the corridor, he hurled himself around Dristan's legs and held on tightly.

The boy's sobs became louder as he clung to Dristan. Clasping the boy to him in a rare display of public affection, he whispered tender words to soothe the troubled youth.

Patrick continued to spill the sorry tale of the fall of the castles defenses in a rambling of childlike frustration to make his meaning clear. Even now, Amiria would be making her way from the depths of the freezing cold prison she had found herself in. Dristan could almost see for himself the stubborn look in her eyes and tilt of her head as she searched out Hugh to enact her revenge against him. *Merde*...if he thought it once, he'd thought it a dozen times. She would be the death of him.

"You have done well this day Patrick, but I must ask for you to be brave for just a little longer," Dristan praised the boy with a comforting hand upon his shoulder. "Can you do that for me, my lad?"

"Aye, mi-milord," he squeaked.

"Then we must find you a safe place to hide 'til this is over."

Patrick cried out again. "How could I forget? I am so stupid! 'Tis Sabina, my lord. She is gravely injured and I was on my way to find Lynet so she might aid her!"

"Then hurry Patrick to your sister's chamber so I may see her."

Dristan followed Patrick as he raced along the passageway and opened the door with a mighty push. He rushed across the floor and gingerly sat on the edge of the bed.

"Sabina," Dristan whispered and saw she yet breathed.

"Our answer to the ownership of the blood, but how did she get injured? Ian asked broodingly. "I would have thought her to be with Sir Hugh in the Great Hall, enjoying the comforts of being lady of the keep."

"I have the dreadful feeling Hugh is the cause for the lady's loss of blood." Dristan began as he took her hand in his. She moaned in agony. Her hands were raw and he could only wonder how she came to be in her chamber. "I will kill that pestilent son of a whore for this offense, as well as all the others that have been marked against him in my eyes," Dristan growled, watching as Sabina's eyes began to flutter open.

"My Lord," she sobbed, tears pouring down her cheeks.

Dristan leaned down closer. "Rest easy, Sabina. All is well and we will see to your needs."

"But, my lord, I must beg your pardon for I—"

"Hush," he demanded. "You may say all you wish when you are feeling yourself again. If your constitution is anything like that of your stubborn sister, 'twill be in no time at all."

"I must needs unburden my soul, my liege," she began again, gasping for breath, "for I do not think I will live to see the morning's light. I do not relish spending my afterlife in purgatory without my confession...although 'tis no more than I deserve."

Dristan gave a short snort. "You may make known all you wish to Father Donovan once you have healed, Sabina. He will be more than willing to save your soul from eternal damnation. As long as Amiria and Berwyck's inhabitants are safe, you shall be forgiven for your part in this mess we are now in."

Sabina reached up in an attempt to caress his cheek, but her hand fell limply against her breast. "You are benevolent, as much as you are handsome," she said, wheezing. "Amiria has done well, having you as her hus—"

Dristan watched Sabina's eye's roll back and her head fell against her pillow. He frowned in thought of another innocent lass falling victim to the lecherous Sir Hugh.

Turning to Patrick, he reached down into his boot and pulled forth a dagger. Kneeling down afore his page, he fingered the blade as he had done numerous times since his youth.

"My sire gave me this when I was young and the blade has served me well," he began.

Patrick interrupted him. "My Lord Dristan, there is something of import I must as yet tell you. 'Tis about Aid—"

Dristan cut off the boy's words. "I vow to find your sister and see her safe, Patrick. Take this dagger, 'tis yours now. Bolt the door, and guard your sister well," Dristan ordered, handing the boy the knife. He watched but a moment's hesitation 'til Patrick held the blade as if he had been given the greatest treasure he had ever held.

Without further words, Dristan and Ian left, and with the closing of the oak portal, they heard to their satisfaction the bolt sliding into place.

"Find Lynet, Ian, and keep her safe. Bring her to Sabina when 'tis possible. I go to see to the more rebellious sister, whom I am sure is up to her pretty neck in trouble," Dristan predicted. "Once Amiria is safe, I shall then see to Hugh!"

They clasped each other's shoulders in a sign of solidarity in their missions and reached for their swords. Their blades in hand, they made their way silently down the turret's stairwell followed closely by the king's knights, who were ready for action. If Hugh were to see the fury blazing in the Devil's Dragons eyes, he would have willing fled from Berwyck's gates of his own accord. At least then his head would have still been firmly in place.

FORTY-TWO

*L*IFE WAS GOOD. Hugh regarded the table in front of him, laden with food and drink, and was pleased. All had gone according to plan, with the exception of that little spit fire he had thrown into the pit. He reached up and felt the tender gashes left on his cheek, smiling despite the pain it caused. Perchance it had been worth it, knowing that red headed wench would be beneath him soon. All she needed was a lesson in humility, and from his own all too familiar experience in the castle's pit, she, too, would learn such a valuable message and never defy him again.

He fingered the sword lying in front of him on the table and watched the amethyst jewel wink at him from the fire light. His expression was smug as he leaned back in his chair, surveying the Great Hall. Those tapestries depicting the MacLaren Clan would be one of the first things to go he decided. He reached for the chalice in front of him and admired the red ruby set firmly within the silver metal. Twirling the stem between his fingers, he chuckled that all he had desired had finally come to pass.

"Laugh if you must, but I will not rest 'til I know Dristan of Blackmore is not breathing fire down upon my neck!" Gilbert spoke wearily and subconsciously rubbed the back of his head.

Hugh's smile faded to be supplanted by a grim look thrown at his cousin. "The keep is mine," he hissed, taking a deep taste of his wine afore slamming the cup down hard upon the table. The sound echoed off the walls and hung in the air like an omen to their impending fate.

"Aye, Hugh. The keep is yours...at least for now," Gilbert answered grimly.

A movement caught Hugh's attention and he watched as a young woman scurried between the shadows cast upon the room and the light from the torches hanging upon the walls. She turned briefly, feeling his stare, and he heard Gilbert catch his breath. He gave an appreciative glance at the honeyed colored hair escaping the plaid wrapped around her head even though he preferred her sister. All too quickly, the girl ducked her head and escaped rapidly out the hall's door, holding her precious bundle.

Hugh scrutinized his cousin, who continued staring upon the closed door with a look bordering between lust and awe. His brow raised in question when Gilbert at last brought his attention back to the conversation they had been having.

Gilbert wiped his hand across his eyes as if to clear his vision. "Who was that?" he asked with anticipation.

Hugh slapped Gilbert upon his back. "Now, that is more like the cousin I know, lusting after a ready wench!"

"She did not appear a mere servant, Hugh, despite her clothing depicting such."

"She's the youngest daughter of the keep. Fancies herself the castle's healer since that witch Kenna conveniently disappeared," Hugh replied, taking another sip of his wine. "Tried to hide herself from me in a pair of breeches, just like her damn sister, but she didn't fool me. I threatened to rip her boyish garments from her little body in front of my men if she didn't change into a gown as was fitting."

"She looked like an angel," Gilbert said as he, too, took a drink of ale and wiped his mouth with his tunic sleeve. "I would not mind having a bit of fun with her."

"Have at her then, just do not get too rough," Hugh ordered. "I still have use for her to tend the wounded."

Gilbert rose to leave, but afore doing so, he quickly gazed about the room only housing a dozen men, lazily drinking their fill. "You should bring more men in to guard you, Hugh," he said, taking one last gulp of his ale.

"There are more than enough here to see to the safeguarding of my back." Hugh's confidence he was well protected was high as he nonchalantly gave a wave of his hand, dismissing his cousin.

Gilbert shook his head at the arrogance of his cousin. "A whole garrison of knights will not be enough, should the Devil's Dragon penetrate the castle walls."

Hugh again waved him off, knowing the impossibility of that occurrence, and watched in amusement as Gilbert quickened his pace to find Lynet. He had secured the castle, and his men were stationed upon the battlements, keeping watch on the country-side for any signs of an approaching army. He was positive Dristan was unaware of the tunnel that had provided him such an uncomplicated entry, but at his first opportunity, he would see to closing it up. No sense in taking any chances.

He stood and lazily stretched his arms above his head, think-ing he would fetch Amiria so she could service his needs. All he needed to do was dump a few buckets of water on her to take away the stench of the pit. Grabbing his chalice, he hastily gulped down the remaining wine, not caring that what he drank was not ale and was meant to be savored and sipped at his leisure. He had just placed the goblet back upon the table, when he turned to watch in horrified alarm as a knight, wearing familiar armor, came crashing down the keep's stairs.

Hugh blinked, not understanding how Amiria had come from above with several unknown men ready to battle. But, nay! There she was coming with the prisoners from the cellars below. Was this the work of Satan? For how else could she be in two places at the same time? The wench would not escape him this time.

The sound of steel resounding off steel, as his men came to their senses and attacked, replaced the only moments earlier quiet and pleasant atmosphere of the room. Apparently, escaping was not what the prisoners from below had on their minds. They meant to take the keep. *Where the devil had they found swords?* He fumed.

Hugh threw himself into the fray of men, who fought with a vengeance to regain what was rightfully theirs. He barely missed being hit in the head as Cook came barreling out of his kitchen swinging a cast iron pot towards him. Even the peasants were revolting.

Hugh raised his sword, using its hilt to knock senseless the man afore him. He turned to take on another opponent but stood there in shocked silence. There before his eyes was the one man he had least expected to espy, and from the look on his face, he was a man determined to take back what had been stolen from him. Instead, Hugh would send the so called dragon back to the Devil!

Amiria hovered along the wall in the kitchen, keeping her promise to Riorden to remain safe. But her hand twitched on the hilt of her sword, a sign of her wanting to enter the fray of fighting. She would not gaze in the direction of her captain for she knew her promise to him was about to be broken. 'Twas only a matter of time afore her resolve to remain steadfast in her promise to keep her word would finally crack. Apparently, even granite could crumble given the right circumstance and force.

Her eyes scanned the knights who were taking on Hugh's men. She frowned in confusion, since none of them were familiar to her, with the exception of those who had made their escape alongside her. Those numbers were indeed few.

The sight of unforgettable armor caught her immediate attention as the torch light hit the silver metal frame so similar to her own. She did a double take at the warrior who was fighting most bravely with his back towards her. Try as she might, she had no way to determine how he had come by her brother's armor, for she would have assumed he would have been buried with it. The scoundrel would have a lot to answer for when the fighting was at an end, for she would ensure her brother's stolen property was returned to her family posthaste.

She continued to watch this knight in particular with a high amount of interest. In truth, she could not take her eyes from him, since all his mannerisms were beginning to appear achingly well-known to her heart. Finishing off his foe, he turned to take on another only to stare in her direction. He lifted the visor of his helm. Violet eyes met violet eyes from across the room. With a quick satisfied smirk, he let the plate fall back down over his face and threw himself back into the skirmish.

To say that she was stunned would be an understatement as her heart hammered wildly within her breast. *He lived*, her heart screamed! *Praise be to God, Aiden was alive!* With mayhem running rampant all around her, 'twas into this commotion that her senses began to once more reel as Dristan and Ian came running down the turret stairs. It appeared Dristan had brought reinforcements, as well, since a score of men poured from the stairwell to join in the fight occurring in the Great Hall.

Amiria observed Ian's look of relief when he espied her and watched him quickly flee the keep, slamming the door behind him. Her husband's glare from across the room and the fire of his steely gaze caught her attention next, especially since she felt as if she had been scorched by its heat. If words had been spoken between them, she would have remained in the alcove of the kitchen, safe and out of harm's way. But safe was not in her nature if she felt she could be of some use, so she ignored Dristan's look and brought forth her sword. Her promise was at an end.

With her actions, Dristan's battle cry rang out and several of Hugh's men gave a moment's pause to digest the fact that the true lord of the keep had returned, using the same entry they themselves had managed. Their moment of hesitation was their undoing, however, as one after the other was felled by quick thrusts of swords from their enemies.

Blood began to pour from the dead and wounded, seeping into the rushes and collecting in small pools upon the stone floor beneath. Footing became treacherous, at best, and still, the king's knights pressed onward in the name of His Majesty alongside Dristan's remaining guards. Their numbers were few, and yet with each stroke of their weapons so, too, were Hugh's men. The drink that had filled their bellies made them clumsy and some began to surrender in defeat.

Amiria continued to fight her way through the turmoil around her, concentrating on reaching her destination. She wanted her damn sword and, after catching a glimpse of it upon the high table, no one would stand in her way to reach her prize. 'Twas a testimony to the arrogance of Hugh to be feasting, instead of keeping a steady eye on what he had falsely claimed, however briefly that had been. She continued to parry her thrusts, using her borrowed sword as an extension of her arm and was half way to her objective, when she came face to face with Hugh.

A smug look washed quickly across his face. As their two swords met with neither planning to yield, he surprised Amiria by reaching out and grabbing the back of her neck. Pulling her quickly towards him, he smashed his lips to hers in a wet hungry kiss. He pushed her away and she faltered in her step. She heard her name as 'twas yelled harshly by her husband, who was fighting his way to her side. Her brother was too preoccupied fighting off two of their enemies to be of much help. She wiped her mouth in disgust.

"When this is over," Hugh sneered, "I intend to take you right here on the floor amongst your fallen comrades."

"Ha! I think not," Amiria retorted with a smirk, knowing Dristan would give his last breath to save her err that hideous event ever occurred.

"Let us end this then."

"I believe my Lord Dristan plans on doing just that, along with my brother," she smiled knowingly. "I hope you had not planned to live yet another day," she taunted with a laugh, "or that you cared to keep your head. It will be a fine example of a fool resting on a pike outside my gate!"

Fury burnt brightly in Hugh's eyes as if he knew she believed him inadequate to retain the keep as his own. He brought up his sword in a mock salute. Amiria insulted him further by spitting at his boots. "Kill them," he screamed, caring not that his numbers of support were diminishing rapidly. "Kill them all!

Amiria continued her attack by hacking away at Sir Hugh's blade with a satisfied smile on her face. Aye, she had come a long way in her training, as she performed several of the moves that her husband had taught her. From the corner of her eye, she saw Dristan. From the look on his face, it appeared as if he was unsure if he should reprimand her for not staying put or to praise her efforts with her swordplay. Yet still he continued his advancement in her direction.

'Twas not 'til Hugh threw a punch, causing Amiria to go flying to the floor in a heap that she became aware of how determined her husband was to reach her side and come to her rescue. Dristan made fast work of the man in front of him, who fell to his knees and begged for mercy. Dristan gave a quick nod of his head, and Cameron came, dragging the man to the far wall to be held with the others who had already surrendered. The day was lost for Hugh, who appeared to come to the same realization as he stared into the blazing eyes of Dristan.

Amiria held her breath as the two men fought alone. Their blades sang as they met, and still they battled on. Dristan threw the first punch, causing Hugh to stagger backwards.

"That is for my wife," Dristan bellowed righteously, and he began to nick away at Hugh, piece by piece, with a satisfied gleam in his eyes.

Amiria watched in satisfaction as blood began to pour from Hugh's wounds whilst he attempted to inflict the same on his opponent. He missed his mark, time and time again. For all of his attempts, he was only awarded more slices to his own flesh. Panic reached his eyes along with his need to flee, even as he lost his footing and landed on the wet bloodied floor.

Dristan must have thought he was to surrender, for he turned his back on him and hurried to Amiria's side. She was attempting to rise from the floor, although she still felt dizzy from the blow she received. Since the opportunity presented itself whilst Dristan was helping his wife, Hugh quickly leapt to his feet and ran towards the stairway leading up to the tunnel, apparently to flee Berwyck the same way he had entered, and with his head still firmly attached to his neck.

Amiria scanned the hall to notice her brother slipping out the keep's door. She turned her attention to the man afore her and gazed into Dristan's worried eyes. She leaned lovingly into the palm of his hand that he had placed upon her bruised check and gently kissed the inside of his wrist. His eyebrow rose in such an intimate gesture, and not caring who was witnessing his care of his wife, he leaned down and pressed his lips upon her own trembling ones. She tried to smile, but winced in pain from her attempt.

"Dristan!" someone yelled and with sword in hand he rapidly rose to see the last traces of Hugh's booted feet whilst he hastily made the first bend of the stairwell. He made to follow but got no more than a few steps. A scream rent the air, followed by Hugh's limp body rolling back down the way he had come. Dristan went to Hugh and turned the man over with his boot. Two dirks protruded from Hugh's body, one of which he did not recognize and was neatly inserted up to the hilt in the man's chest. The other he could not fail to notice. 'Twas a very familiar dagger protruding from Hugh's stomach. Hugh opened his eyes, gasping for air, and grimaced.

"That stupid wench killed me along with that brat of a boy!" Hugh gurgled. Giving up his last breath, he saw no more.

All turned their attention to the turret and saw Sabina, who barely managed to carefully make her way down the stairs with her arm draped along Patrick's young shoulders.

"Is he dead?" she whispered.

"Aye, I should think so, my lady," Dristan declared approvingly.

Sabina nodded, giving her brother a comforting hug and what sounded like reassuring words for his help in ridding this world of that vermin. Two of Sabina's ladies came out of hiding to assist her as they began the long winding climb back to her chamber. Amiria prayed her sister could rest in peace with no burdens troubling her mind.

Dristan rushed back to Amiria's side and she welcomed the support to help her rise. He held her at arm's length, ensuring her safety afore he crushed her in a fierce embrace. Her arms wrapped around him and she sensed a force beyond mere mortals right itself in the world surrounding them.

"You gave me such a fright," he said in a husky whisper, and she shivered from his touch.

"Me? Surely you jest, my lord."

"Do not ever do such a foolish act again, Amiria, or I shall lock you in our chamber and never let you out!"

She pulled away from him slightly and caressed his cheek. "And will you lock yourself in there with me, as well, my Lord Dristan?" she said suggestively, taking a step closer.

His chuckle rumbled in his chest. "You can count on it, my lady."

"Then it may well be worth it," Amiria laughed and grabbed her sword to see who else she might take on next. Her arm was gently taken once again and she looked up into her husband's stormy grey eyes.

Dristan took her sword and put it in her scabbard slung low on her hips. "Such a saucy wife I have married!" he declared, with a warning in his eyes for her to desist. "Killian! Come see you to my lady that she takes her ease 'til I ensure the rest of the keep is once more secure."

Amiria rolled her eyes, annoyed again she would be pushed aside in such a womanly nature. "Dristan, I—"

"Do not question me, Amiria, in this, I beseech you," he said harshly, and she knew he saw the wounded look that fell upon her face. He took her chin and tipped it up to receive his kiss. Over and over, did he indulge in the tasting of her, 'til she felt her world spinning. With one more look at her, 'twas clear he would leave her as breathless as he himself was feeling. Reaching out, he lovingly caressed her hair and offered her a bit of praise. "You did well, *cherie*, but I would ask you give me no further cause this day to worry over you, at least just this once. Tomorrow, we can begin again with your training."

Amiria smiled in delight, knowing he did not expect her to remain confined forever in the hall. "As you wish, Dristan."

He looked at her suspiciously but saw no reason for further alarm. At his motion, Killian came and led her to the hearth to warm herself by its glowing fire. Satisfied she would stay put this time, Dristan took another look upon her afore he called to Riorden and several of his men to follow him as he left the keep to search out his garrison to secure his land once more.

FORTY-THREE

IAN INSPECTED THE INNER BAILEY with a practiced eye and thought, *Dristan will be pleased when he's finished with his business inside the keep's walls.* The portcullis was already being raised, admitting the remainder of the king's army. Hugh's men began to flee in every direction imaginable with the sole purpose of keeping one's hide from being captured. All knew 'twould not be pleasant to answer to King Henry or, even worse, Dristan of Berwyck. Better to die in battle than swinging from a rope.

Through the chaos currently ringing out in the courtyard, a faint cry of alarm caught Ian's attention, and he swiftly took note of the direction of the sound. He glimpsed hair the color of the sun as a young woman was unwillingly dragged into Kenna's hut. Such an occurrence was out of place with those trying to flee with their lives. 'Twas obvious from the displeasure of the lass's continued screams that aid was in order. Since he had been tasked to find Lynet, he knew from the color of the hair he briefly witnessed that the girl was deep in trouble. Ian quickened his stride, hoping perchance under all the shyness Lynet usually showed the world, there housed a bit of her rebellious sister's qualities. 'Twould keep her safe 'til he reached her side.

Sword in hand, he neared the dwelling. Reaching for the door, Ian was startled to hear a loud bang followed by loud curses. Pushing open the door, he proudly gazed upon Lynet wielding a heavy skillet. From the look of things, she had defended herself by waylaying her assailant in the head. The man looked dazed, but still drew his sword forward with a look of disbelief showing on his face. To be knocked senseless by a mere slip of a girl could not be good for one's ego.

The look Lynet cast Ian from across the room clearly showed she was never so happy to see anyone in her life. A silent understanding passed between them, and she wisely backed herself into a corner away from the two men who were about to come to blows. A draft of cold air raced across the room from the open door. It drew a horrified gasp from Lynet, causing Ian's attention to return to her. Anger consumed him, seeing the remnants of her gown exposing her breast. The skillet slipped through her hands, rattling on the floor as she hastily gathered the torn fabric together. Ian's temper rose as he leveled his eyes on the man who had taken such liberties with the lass.

"You were a fool to think you could touch someone as innocent as Lady Lynet and still live to tell the tale," Ian swore, advancing on the angry man afore him.

"A few more minutes and she would have been mine," Gilbert declared with a smirk of satisfaction.

Ian's gaze ran over the man's features and knew he had come across his afore. "You look familiar to me, or am I mistaken?" Ian queried. "I would at least like to know the name of the man whom I will aid in meeting his master in hell!"

"Aye, you know of me, not that it shall matter. I am Gilbert, cousin of Sir Hugh."

"I am sure you will meet your cousin again for I doubt Lord Dristan will allow the man to see another sunrise."

Gilbert spat in the dirt. "My cousin is a fool, and I more so that I followed his idiotic plans." He licked his lips whilst his gaze drifted up and down Lynet, who raised her head in defiance. She grabbed the skillet once more. "Mayhap 'twas worth it."

"Go ahead and just you try coming near me again!" she cried out, shaking the pan towards him. "I'll gladly give you another lump on the other side of your head so you have a matching pair!"

Ian chuckled. "It appears the lady is not interested."

"Harrumph! I could have changed her mind."

Ian's brows drew together in a frown. "And now you dare insult her in my presence?" he growled and advanced, bringing his sword forward."

Gilbert met Ian half way across the room, and their swords rang out in the air. "Better to die at a pretty girl's feet than what the Devil's Dragon would have in store for me!"

"So be it," Ian shouted.

The two men, who were of the same size, danced around the furniture, each testing the other's worth. But Ian had the advantage from having trained with Dristan. His claymore sang out with each stroke that he wielded. 'Twas clear Gilbert was nowhere near his match, nor his equal. From one look in his eyes, he knew it, as well!

Starting to tire, Gilbert was shocked when his sword went flying from his hand. He stumbled a bit and once he regained his footing, he reached inside his boot for a dagger. With a mighty yell, he charged at Ian and the two went flying through the wall with bits of wood splintering around them. Those in the courtyard began to cheer in Ian's favor as 'twas evident Dristan once more held Berwyck as his own.

"Finish him," Dristan called out, certain Ian would see the deed done.

A confident smile crossed Ian's features. He put away his sword and took dagger in hand.

Lynet poked her head out of the new opening of the hut then ran to Dristan when he called to her. He protectively held her in his arms.

"Do not worry, *ma petite* sister," Dristan said, loud enough for all to hear, giving the girl a slight hug. "Ian will avenge your honor."

"Of course he will," Lynet said in confidence.

Some held their breath as the two men circled one another 'til they came together with muscle and sinew bulging in an effort to survive. Ian managed to finally knock Gilbert from his feet and when he rose, anger blazed ferociously in his eyes. He swiped his knife at Ian; once, twice, thrice, and still Ian easily remained untouched, causing Gilbert to grow more reckless in his attempt to kill the man afore him.

Ian had had enough of Gilbert's games and advanced on his adversary with a calculating gleam as he assessed the man for his many weaknesses. His dagger sliced through the air with precision and speed 'til the blade crossed against Gilbert's throat. His eyes momentarily showed a look of surprise afore he fell to the ground dead.

Wiping his blade and returning it to his boot, Ian turned in the direction of the cheering crowd. He watched as Lynet disengaged herself from Dristan and ran to him. Flinging herself easily into his arms, he caught the girl and held her close.

"You came for me!" she said in a breathless whisper. "I knew you would."

Ian cleared his throat, overcome with emotions, knowing Lynet was safe. "I will always be here for you when you have need of me," Ian said carefully and placed a chaste kiss upon her forehead.

"Well done, Ian!" Riorden shouted. "May our Lord Dristan have peace upon his land!"

A deafening cheer rose up from the villagers who had come to the castle for protection. They were joined with the garrison knights calling out good health to the lord and lady of Berwyck.

Ian felt Lynet's arm go around his waist and gave in to seeing the adoration in her thankful eyes. He pulled her closer and saw a beautiful smile alight on her face, and he gladly returned it with one of his own. She deserved a moment of happiness. Not thinking of the consequences of his actions, Ian leaned down and tenderly touched his lips to hers.

FORTY-FOUR

THERE WAS A CAUSE FOR CELEBRATION as Hugh's men were led from the bailey by the king's men. One knight among the many Dristan did not recognize caught his attention, and he bellowed out for the man to halt. He watched as the younger man took a deep breath afore raising his head. Their gazes met and Dristan strode forward to confront the man who was obviously Amiria's twin brother.

"I feel we have met afore," Dristan stated with a smirk upon his face. From the expression on Aiden's visage, he apparently did not find anything amusing.

"I do not know what you are talking about, nor do I see a reason for your mirth." Aiden's teeth were clenched whilst his hand fingered the hilt of his sword.

'Twas so reminiscent of his own unconscious actions that Dristan's laughter echoed in the air. He slapped the younger man on the back and, although the effort would have caused many a man to stumble from the force of it, Aiden held his stance, much to the pleasure of Dristan. He would look forward to training with his wife's brother.

"Do not take such offense. There is much we must have speech about, but I must needs ensure that all is secure with the holding," Dristan declared, watching Aiden's gaze follow the king's men as they left the baily.

"I would like to accompany them back to London to ensure none escape and make my plea afore King Henry." It appeared he wanted to say more but clamped his mouth tightly shut.

Dristan observed the man and could understand Aiden's resentment of finding his home occupied by an enemy. "Your sister and siblings will wish to see you afore you go," he stated, attempting to reason with the man.

Aiden only shrugged, "I have been gone for several months. A few more will make no difference 'til I return."

"As you will, then."

Aiden turned to leave but halted his stride to level his gaze upon Dristan over his shoulder. "Take care of my family or you will answer to me!"

"They are now my family, as well, Aiden. You have my word I shall keep them safe."

Aiden nodded his head and took off in the direction of the barbican gate. Looking around the baily, Dristan realized that Berwyck and all its inhabitants were once more under his protection.

Dristan motioned for his knights and those closest to the castle's family to return inside the keep, knowing the garrison would take charge of returning his domain back to order. He smiled knowing who awaited him inside, and without further haste, he quickly took the stairs two at a time to return to her side. He looked forward to their reunion for he had a cheeky wife to tame, if only a little. He gave a shout of laughter. Mayhap, if he thought long and hard about it, 'twas, in truth, the Devil's Dragon who had at last been tamed!

Hushed tones filled the lord and lady's bedchamber as their shadows were cast upon the walls. They knelt side by side with their two heads touched one to the other. Amiria's hand grazed over Dristan's naked shoulders marveling at the strength she felt beneath her fingertips. She could perform this simple loving act a hundred times more and still she would never tire of touching his wondrous body.

She raised her head, reached for a cloth and dipped it again in the warm water. Dabbing at one of his wounds, she set the cloth aside and smoothed some ointment over the cut. 'Twas not deep, but still gave her cause for concern. She would spend the morrow in the chapel thanking God above that Dristan had returned to her for the most part unharmed. From this point forward, whenever he was to travel, she would spend time on her knees and pray to St. Christopher to always keep him safe.

"Do they hurt much?" she questioned softly with another gentle caress. She marveled at the feel of his warm skin upon her hands.

"Nay, my love. Do not fret so. I barely notice anything but your tantalizing touch," Dristan replied, leaning over and nuzzling her neck. He began to nibble his way upwards 'til his mouth touched hers and a contented sigh escaped her.

His words finally registered in Amiria's mind and she sat back on her heels to stare into his eyes. "What did you call me?"

Dristan gave her a lopsided and devilish grin. He then had the nerve to begin laughing from what she assumed was her own look of amazement him from his words. He caressed her hair afore leaning in for another stolen kiss. "I called you my love," he said in her ear with a seductive promise.

She wrapped her arms around his neck and played with the silkiness of his hair. "You love me?" she asked hesitantly.

"Was there any doubt, my sweet wife?" he asked with a look of teasing. He put his hand over his heart, as if wounded. "I thought my love making would tell you 'twas so, but mayhap I must show you again."

He lifted her up in his arms carrying her to their bed as she squealed in delight. His gaze roamed over her body once he laid her down upon the coverlet, and she attempted not to blush in embarrassment. Coming to lie next to her, he rested upon his elbow watching her most intently, and Amiria's heart fluttered in her chest in excitement. Taking a lock of her hair, he twirled the tresses between his fingers. It seemingly came to life at his touch and curled around his fingers as if claiming him for its own.

"What is it, *ma cherie?*" he asked, when she only continued to gaze upon him with a strange smile.

Amiria took her hand, placing it around his neck and brought him closer. "I love you too, Dristan," she said shyly. "If this is but a dream, I pray I never awake."

"Ah, my dearest Amiria...if we are slumbering, than glad I am we have found each other not only as we sleep but in our waking hours, as well."

They smiled at one another and shared another kiss. Their breaths became as one just as surely as their souls would be bound together throughout all time. Amiria thought on her words to him some time ago, and her eyes twinkled with joy with thoughts of their life together in the years to come.

"And will you love me for as long as your heart may see me, husband?" she inquired hopefully.

Dristan took her chin and tipped her head up slightly and nodded. "Not only will I love you for all our years together, my love, but I shall do so for all of eternity," he honestly declared.

Satisfied at his declaration, she smiled again. "Then love me now, my dragon," she breathed breathlessly. "I so adore it when you make me burn."

"As my lady commands," he said and lowered his head to seal their fate. He showered her with his love far into the early morning hours 'til they both at last were sated and met their slumber.

She never doubted he loved her ever again.

Epilogue

THE GREAT HALL WAS FILLED with those who had come to celebrate the wedding of the castle's healer and Sir Geoffrey. The banquet table was bursting with food to satisfy hungry appetites. Ale, mead, and wine flowed freely, much to the joy of those who partook of the bounty always found at Berwyck. The lord and lady of the keep had opened their doors to both the garrison knights and the villagers to share in the prosperity of their land. Life was good for those under Lord Dristan's care.

Amiria sat at the high table and watched the revelers enjoying themselves. She ate little, with the exception of a bit of bread and cheese to help calm her stomach. She had a chalice of watered down wine within her reach, but even that only added to the queasiness she sometimes felt.

Placing her hand on the slight mound rising from her stomach, she smiled blissfully. The babe was strong and Dristan was more than pleased to know they would soon have a bairn to care for. When she told him she was pregnant, she had been thankful Killian had been there to catch her husband when he fainted dead away landing in a heap upon the floor. A laugh escaped her at the remembrance of her knight rising from the stones wondering what had felled him. She sometimes thought he was still embarrassed at the memory and only hoped he would survive the child's birth.

Amiria surveyed the hall with a practiced eye and noticed everyone seemed to be enjoying the day. Kenna looked divinely happy. A circulate of brightly colored flowers with flowing ribbons adorned her head. Her gown of a light pale green was outshone only by the green of her eyes. She laughed gaily as whatever words Geoffrey whispered in her ear. 'Twas clear Kenna had also found a love match and a knight that would do anything to please his lady. Amiria was happy for her, especially with the knowledge they would continue to make their home here among Berwyck's walls.

Her young brother danced and tapped his feet in rhythm to the lively tunes the minstrels were playing. Patrick flourished under Dristan's care and took his responsibilities as page most serious. 'Twas a joy to see him so carefree and she had the feeling, as he grew to manhood, that he would end up breaking a few hearts of the fairer gender. Amiria supposed that in a few years, Dristan would find a foster home for him to squire at. She had no doubt he would see that Patrick had only the best of lords to serve.

Searching the hall she espied Lynet, who sat forlornly at one of the few windows located on the ground floor. Amiria shook her head sadly for she knew her sister continued her vigil as she awaited Ian's return. She could tell from the heavy sighs of her sister that she was most likely shedding a tear or two whilst her heart continued to cry out for him.

Amiria and Ian had another bittersweet departure when he once again decided 'twas time to leave Berwyck and yet he had not left alone. Taegan and Turquine decided they were in need of an adventure, since the castle walls had seemed too domesticated of late for their taste. Thomas of her guard had left, as well, if only, he said, to continue guarding Ian's back. Dristan had released them from their oath of fealty and was thankful the remainder of their guards would stay loyal to him and Berwyck.

Another was sadly missing from her family besides her twin brother, who she would have a few harsh words with when he returned. Amiria herself had nursed her sister back to good health and yet she had been more than surprised when Sabina asked to be taken to Habersham Abbey in order to devote her life to God. Both Dristan and Amiria had tried to dissuade her from such a drastically different life she would lead. Yet one look at Sabina's face told them all they needed to know. During her recovery, Sabina had changed and had begged for Amiria's forgiveness. She gladly gave it, and Dristan himself had escorted her to the abbey, leaving a worthy dowry for the good sisters.

Shaking her head to stop her musing, she heard the minstrels begin yet another lively tune. Perchance just one dance would bring her out of her sudden melancholy mood. Since Dristan was holding court near the hearth with a bevy of people vying for his attention, she stood to join the revelers. As if she called him herself, Riorden came bowing low to her and offered his arm escorting her to the middle of the floor.

Amiria laughed in pleasure as the music reached her ears. The skirt of her dress twirled around her legs as her feet fairly flew to the beat of the lutes. Riorden spun her around and around 'til she was passed from knight to knight. Her bubbly laughter filled the air and she became dizzy, but even more so when she found herself lifted high above the floor. She stared down to find herself with her husband's hands carefully wrapped around her waist. She placed her own hands upon his broad shoulders 'til he slowly lowered her down the length of his body. She gazed upon him with mischief in her violet eyes.

Dristan held her against him and she enjoyed the feel of her husband's embrace. "What do you?" he asked in an annoyed tone. "You should be resting lest you disturb my son."

Amiria placed her hands upon his chest that he covered with his own. "You do realize it could be a daughter."

He looked at her and chuckled. "'Twould be just like you to defy me by denying me an heir."

She looked at him perturbed at his words. "You would not be pleased with a daughter, my lord?"

"I but tease you, Amiria. Do not go looking for your sword to take out your anger on me in the lists," he jested, "at least not today."

"For your teasing of me, I shall give you a daughter just to put you in your place," she declared, crossing her arms and tapping her foot to show her annoyance.

Her stance only seemed to amuse him more. "I have no doubt of it, my lady." He leaned down, bestowing upon her another kiss to soothe the hurt of his words. "Am I forgiven?"

She looked him up and down and then could no longer contain her mirth. "I suppose, if only you would kiss me again."

As Dristan's lips gently touched her own, a hush came over the hall causing even the minstrel's to cease their music. Amiria broke from their kiss to see what all the fuss was about. Everyone had halted their merriment and was looking in the direction of the keep's door. She poked her head from around Dristan's body since he blocked her view. She could only stand there in surprise 'til overwhelming happiness consumed her.

"Well 'tis about bloody time," She swore out loud, not caring that others may have heard her words.

"What is the matter Amiria? Does the babe pain you?"

Without another word, she ran from Dristan's side and all but launched herself into her twin's arms. She began with a heated reprimand 'til her emotions got the better of her with the realization her brother had at last returned. She burst into uncontrollable tears whilst Dristan advanced on them. Out of pure instinct, her husband reached for the sword at his side only to come up empty handed knowing she had made him leave his blade in their chamber.

"Amiria," Dristan shouted. "Cease your caterwauling woman err you hurt yourself or the babe."

"I canna help it," she cried. All could have heard her from London to Edinburgh if only her words would have been coherent enough to be understood instead of the meaningless babbling of a crying woman. It must be the babe to make her such an emotional mess. She turned into Dristan's arms whilst she continued to drench his tunic with her tears of joy.

A gasp came from those gathered in the hall as Amiria's replica pushed back his mail helm to reveal hair the color of her own. There was no mistaking her twin, as they were identical with the exception that Aiden was taller and built with a solid muscular frame.

"I came as soon as I could manage to escape court, especially after learning of my sister's marriage. I had thought I would need to avenge my sister's honor if she had been forced into such an arrangement," Aiden said with bitterness and narrowed eyes. Clearly he was none too pleased to see his sister in the arms of the foe that had seized his home. "It appears, however, that may be unnecessary as I have heard Amiria is most content with her choice of husband. Is this so, my lord? Is she content?"

"You would have to ask her yourself," Dristan said smartly and Amiria gazed up into her husband's face. He awaited her answer but she only managed to shrug her shoulders and sniff at her tears that continued to fall down her cheeks. She felt him reach up and wipe the moisture from her face.

"What causes my sister to cry and why is it everyone seems to be sharing some jest that I am not privy too?" Aiden said, reaching for the hilt of his sword.

Amiria held up her hand to halt her brother and laughed. "'Tis a long story I am afraid and one that may require some time by the fire for its telling. Where were you afore you unexpectedly made an appearance to help with our cause to secure our home from those miscreants?" she asked coolly as they began making their way to the hearth for their comfort.

With a mug of cool ale in his hand, Aiden began to tell the tale of how he had indeed fallen beside their father. As their sire lay dying upon the bloodied ground, he begged two of his guardsmen to protect his son and take him to one of the outer hamlets to heal. The two knights had done so, leaving him with a couple who had been more than happy to aid their laird. He told how in truth he did not remember much of his recovery, for he had been burning with fever. When the fever finally broke, he had months of mending in order for him to just get to the point where he could travel.

He looked around at the garrison knights who stood in awe, staring at a man they felt had returned from the dead. "Since I do not see Richard or Maxwell, I assume they now stand guarding our father once more," he said sadly. "I owe them my life. If not for them, I would not be sitting with you now."

"We are most grateful for your return, Sir Aiden," Dristan said honestly. "I know your sister and family have grieved most deeply over your passing. Glad I am that you have been restored to them."

"Well you certainly took your time returning home from your visit to court, you oaf," Amiria growled, raising her fist to her brother.

"Ach! I have barely walked in the door and already you begin your harping at me," Aiden muttered but threw her a knowing smirk. "Admit it, sister. You missed me."

"Nay, I will not add to your conceited head to spout such words to you. If you had but waited 'til we had speech afore taking off without so much as a by your leave, I could have told you all you needed to hear." Amiria stood next to Dristan's chair 'til she was pulled down into his lap. She put her arm around his shoulder and gave his cheek a quick kiss.

"I suppose I must needs get used to that," Aiden retorted at their display of affection. His look told her he was feeling put out to see his sister being held so by a man he had not approved of.

"Seeing as he is the father of my child and will make you an uncle in several months' time, I think 'twill be for the best, brother."

He guffawed. "It may take some getting used to," he returned gruffly and turned to pull Patrick and Lynet both into a fierce embrace. Amiria watched her brother from above their heads and she gave him a silent look that spoke volumes between the twins. She watched as he smiled at her, and she could do nothing other than return it with one of her own.

Amiria's happiness radiated upon her face and reflected in her sparkling eyes. Her family was around her, she had her husband's child growing within her, and had tamed England's most formidable dragon, who loved her with all his heart. Aiden's question to Dristan afore he told his story hung in the air as she realized she had never answered him. Perchance words out loud were truly not necessary.

Aye, she was indeed most content...

AUTHOR'S NOTE

As an author, I try to be as accurate as humanly possible when depicting my scenes and plots for my stories. Since *If My Heart Could See You* takes place in the middle ages, it's impossible to be completely authentic to the time period.

From a history standpoint, I would like to clarify several aspects of my story. *If My Heart Could See You*, is a work of fiction. When deciding on a location for my castle, I wanted to find a town close to the England/Scotland border. I found Berwick-upon-Tweed and was pleasantly surprised to find that at one point in time there actually was a castle sitting on a cliff. For whatever reason, I changed the spelling of the name and created my own variation of what "my" castle would look like in order to fit my storyline. Little remains of Berwick Castle today and a train station now sits approximately where the Great Hall (demolished in 1847) would have been located.

Berwick's strategic location was, in fact, the reason the land was being fought over for centuries by two countries through siege, raids, or takeovers. Between 1173 and 1174, William I of Scotland attempted to take over northern England. The land was ceded to Henry II of England after his defeat. It would later be sold back to William I by Richard I of England to fund his crusade.

William I was imprisoned after attacking the south of England. He was only released after he agreed to the *Treaty of Falaise* in December 1174 where he publicly gave homage to Henry II, along with surrendering five key Scottish castles to Henry's men. For the purposes of the later portion of my story, I eluded to this as having William I being introduced as Henry II's "guest."

The MacLaren's residing within Berwyck castle is entirely fictitious on my part. Although they are an actual Highland clan today, their origins are uncertain. My research eluded that by tradition the MacLaren's were descended from a man called *Lorn* who was the son of *Erc* who landed in Argyll in 503 A.D. A more likely origin of the clan is that they are of Celtic stock and take their name from a 13th century abbot called Laurance of Achtow. It's also believed the clan were followers of the ancient Earl of Strathearn and were cadets of that ancient house where they fought at the Battle of Standard under King David I of Scotland in 1138. During the Wars of Scottish Independence, the Clan MacLaren fought for King Robert the Bruce at the Battle of Bannockburn in 1314.

Dear Reader:

I would like to take this opportunity to thank you for reading my debut novel, ***If My Heart Could See You***. In a sea of never ending lists of books, somehow you came across mine whether that was by social media threads, endless scrolling on the internet, or word of mouth. It's my fondest hope that you enjoyed reading Dristan and Amiria's journey to finding love as much as I did writing it.

The next story I plan to publish is my time travel. It wasn't what I originally intended to write but those pesky characters inside my head have a way of telling me their story is next and the direction I should take. ***For All of Ever*** will continue the story of Dristan's captain, Riorden de Deveraux and a woman named Katherine Wakefield, a very twenty-first century lady who he first espies as a ghost. It was a lot of fun to write and I hope to have it published soon.

Every author is grateful to a multitude of people who make her work possible and this would explain my lengthy acknowledgment at the beginning of this novel. But no writer becomes an author without the support of her readers and I once again thank you for reading my work. If you enjoyed it, nothing would make me happier than for you to write a nice review.

Until the next time, you can find out more about me on my website at www.sherryewing.com. If you'd like to keep in touch, join my member page and jump into a forum discussion, or send me an email on my contact page.

With Warm Regards,
Sherry Ewing

OTHER BOOKS BY
SHERRY EWING

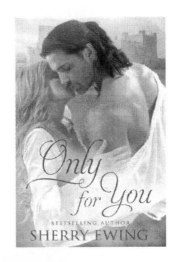

Available in paperback and eBook
at online retailers

ABOUT THE AUTHOR

Sherry Ewing is a bestselling author who writes historical &
time travel romances to awaken the soul one heart at a time. She
picked up her first historical romance when she was a teenager
and has been hooked ever since. Always wanting to write a novel but busy raising her children, she finally took the plunge in
2008 and wrote her first Regency. She is a member of Romance
Writers of America, The Beau Monde & the Bluestocking
Belles. Sherry is currently working on her next novel and when
not writing, she can be found in the San Francisco area at her
day job as an Information Technology Specialist. You can learn
more about Sherry and her published work at
www.SherryEwing.com.

Made in the USA
Lexington, KY
11 October 2015